THE TOWN BELOW

ROGER LEMELIN

THE

TOWN BELOW

TRANSLATED BY SAMUEL PUTNAM

INTRODUCTION - GLEN SHORTLIFFE

GENERAL EDITOR - MALCOLM ROSS

NEW CANADIAN LIBRARY NO 26

MCCLELLAND AND STEWART LIMITED

The following dedication appeared in
the original edition:

To My Mother and Father

PRINTED AND BOUND BY
HAZELL WATSON AND VINEY LTD
AYLESBURY, BUCKS, ENGLAND

INTRODUCTION

To such eminent practitioners of the art as Zola and Henry James, the father of the modern novel was Balzac; and Balzac defined the novelist as the recording secretary of human society. If we accept this bit of paternal wisdom, we must place Roger Lemelin among the important novelists of the great tradition. *The Town Below*, first published in 1944 as *Au Pied de la pente douce*, records the author's observations from within a society endowed by accident of history with qualities that are unique in North America. It is obvious that the eye of the satirist will seek the defects of those qualities. It is evident too that when a perceptive observer catches the image of a society in the throes of a major transformation he is likely to produce an exciting, not to say a "revolutionary" novel.

Here surely lies the explanation of Lemelin's initial impact, which triggered a literary explosion of almost unprecedented force in French Canada. Rarely has the first novel of an unknown writer been damned with such vehemence or defended with such vigour. "A marvel of collective psychological analysis," said one critic; "an attack upon our parochial way of life," wrote another. "Deliverance at last from a world of fake peasantry," cried one; "sheer agnosticism," thundered another. While the battle raged, the book itself was translated and adapted for radio, its author laureated with the *Prix David*, the *Prix de la Langue Française*, and no less than two Guggenheim awards. In 1944 a Canadian novel might hope to sell two thousand copies. *Au Pied de la pente douce* sold twenty-five thousand in the first year in the Province of Quebec alone.

It is now apparent that the literary storm which broke over the head of Lemelin was destined to clear the air for a whole generation of new writers, who work in an atmosphere largely of his creation. Within a year, it is true, powerful assistance was forthcoming from Gabrielle Roy, whose *Tin Flute* sealed the fate of traditional pastoral regionalism. Yet *The Town Below* remains the primary work of innovation, for Lemelin's was the first total commitment to the present in a society that had cannibalized its past to the point of cultural starvation. At this distance from those first anguished cries of outrage, we are no longer tempted to hurl the epithet of agnostic. But neither are we inclined to dispute the judgement which saw in the novel an assault upon the parochial life of French Canada.

v

Maurice Beaulieu has talked of the "sterility of the parochial cell." It is the essential realism of *The Town Below* that it puts the eye of the reader to a microscope which makes visible the barren pettiness inherent in this self-imposed spiritual *apartheid*. It is not with impunity that a people isolates itself within a tribal cocoon while the real world swirls past outside. The cost, as Lemelin's pitiless portrait shows, is paid in moral toughness, intellectual rigidity, spiritual fantasy. If it be true that man, as an existent being, needs to be reinvented with each succeeding generation, then survival implies an eternity of adaptation. Within the parochial cell of St Sauveur, *la survivance* is something else : here is none of the warm flexibility of living tissue, but the brittle defensive shell of the crustacean inhabiting an environment it feels as hostile and seeks vainly to exclude. Pressed within these unyielding walls the mind of man can not encompass reality, and reality shrinks to the limits of the tribal hallucination. Traditionally this was rooted in the soil of Old Quebec—that good earth which no writer before Lemelin had dared wholly to abandon; which continues, indeed, to offer at least a symbolic refuge as recently as Gabrielle Roy's *Alexandre Chênevert*. In Lemelin there remains not the slightest reminiscence of the *mythe agricole*. If there is thought of escape from "this filthy suburb," it is, in the words of Denis Boucher, "to the magnificent clouds above." In the town below, where no grass grows green, the bucolic life of the rural parish has become less a fading memory than a total irrelevancy.

Here, then, is the true "revolutionary" quality of Lemelin's novel : he has ventilated the roots that nourish the tribal dream. It makes little difference that he may have done so unwittingly (critics have referred to his "unconscious naturalism"), being himself city-born and an autodidact owing more to French than to native Canadian models. The fact remains that by immersing his proletarianized *habitants* in the harsh social realities of the town below, he has seized the drama of infernal transfiguration wherein the dream is warped into a tragicomic nightmare of self-delusion. Thus there is no contradiction between the "realism" of Lemelin, which provides the stimulus, and the fantasy of his characters, which is the response. The Latruche sisters, sublimating their thwarted instincts in a promotional campaign for the canonization of a pitiful adolescent; Sophie Pritontin, coveting sainthood for an obese and reluctant offspring forced into the hair-shirt of the ascetic; Tit-Blanc Colin, trapped by an alcoholic pledge into "blowing up" the religious "trust" with an outsize firecracker—all this may indeed look like caricature to the reader who, by habit of mind, persists in isolating the individual character. But in the context of the clash between fact and fancy, such responses are not unreal. They are fantastic, which is significantly different.

There is a danger here, of course—the same that threatens an artist like Erskine Caldwell, with whose work that of Lemelin presents so many analogies. The danger is that the slightest nudge may suffice to push an essentially tragic characterization out of the realm of social satire into the domain of mere quaintness for the amusement of the comfortable and the superior. Caldwell's Jeeter Lester suffered this metamorphosis at the hands of the Broadway stage, and it may be that some of Lemelin's creatures have not escaped a similar fate in his subsequent television series. But in *The Town Below* this threat never materializes, and the reason lies in the freshness, the directness, the copiousness of the author's powers of observation. This goes to the centre of Lemelin's art, which is a function of his immediate perception of visual reality—another quality of the autodidact, perhaps, for the induced assumptions that veil the world from others are in Lemelin delightfully inoperative. He sees what he sees, naïvely and without preconception; he reports it vividly and without reticence, from Barloute's toes "curling over the knots in the floor" to the back of Lise's neck —"how white it was!" It is noteworthy that auditory experience is almost immediately transmuted into the visual image: Lise's voice rises "crystal-clear, like a spring bubbling up in the sunlight"; the choir "deciphers the Gregorian music as numismatists do the inscriptions on old coins," their mouths forming "O" on the high notes, "U" on the low notes. The impression is strong that Lemelin sees the world more intensely than he hears it or feels it.

This predominance of visual experience sets the boundaries and defines the nature of Lemelin's social satire. The eye, however keen, scans only the surface, however broad. Though individual emotion, particularly that of youth, is intermittently captured, the psychological reflections in *The Town Below* do not generally surpass such echoes of La Rochefoucauld as the thought that "there are certain egoists whose need of approbation finds its first expression in the temptation to give all." But this is merely to state that Lemelin is in no sense the poor man's Proust. He is perhaps something more important. Consider his "social biology"—as Balzac would have called it, not without some measure of delighted approbation. Like a skilled bird-watcher in the field, his clear eyes their own best binoculars,

Lemelin separates his species, describes their habitat, charts their plumage, catalogues their habits. The Mulots are recognizable by their gaudy colours, the Soyeux by their missals ("the more zealous carried two"); the Mulots prefer the nine o'clock mass ("levity and religious worldliness"), the Soyeux the ten o'clock service ("pious formalism as dependable as clockwork").

Reliance upon the eye gives something more. It makes Lemelin, like his own Denis Boucher, an onlooker rather than a participant, thus affording full scope to a sense of the ludicrous that has provided some of the most delightful humour known to Canadian writing. The Liberal Party caucus at Bédarovitch's second-hand shop is unforgettable. So are the exhortations against the imminent threat to the parish of the scourge of Moscow, delivered by the good Father Folbèche ("In the seminary he had occasionally been at the head of his class in rhetoric").

But ironic detachment is not emotional indifference. Ultimately it is from love that the satirist speaks, even at his most savagely sardonic. So Lemelin loves; not, it is true, with the tender blindness of affection, but with the stern clairvoyance of concern. He is drawn to the brawling movement of his own Human-Comedy-in-miniature by the same invisible cords that bind the Denis Boucher of the story. His subsequent works, which offer no new terrain of observation, testify to the strength of that attachment. And so the overwhelming desire to "break out" goes far beyond the promptings of self-centred irresponsibility : like Boucher again, he is moved by a mystic urge to bring a new reality to the dream deformed. The very nature of his realism drives Lemelin to reject that "instinct toward deformation" which reflects "an inferiority complex, an unconscious admiration for the phlegmatic character and certain other qualities of the Anglo-Saxon, as we in our weakness and timidity let our own values lie stagnant as if we were ashamed of them."

So the walls of the parochial cell are rent asunder, not alone for what may be let in, but for what may be let out upon the world. Here lies the universality of Lemelin, and the reason that, with The Town Below, French-Canadian literature, without leaving its own milieu, finally overflowed the confines of its geographical frontiers. Thus the art of Lemelin is in the exploitation of the local to illustrate the universal. Such is his panoramic grasp of the life and movement he portrays that, like Caldwell's Georgia or Farrell's Chicago, Lemelin's St Sauveur is a window opening upon the whole world of man's habitation. Let it not be thought that this man is without nationality; but his nationality enlightens, it does not obscure, his view of truth. In this, Roger Lemelin joins that company of writers of all countries of whom Longfellow said: "Their roots are in their native soil; but their branches wave in the un-patriotic air that speaks the same language to all men, and their leaves shine with the illimitable light that pervades all lands."

GLEN SHORTLIFFE

Queen's University
Kingston, Ontario
March 1961

TRANSLATOR'S NOTE

THE scene of this novel is St Joseph's parish in the suburbs of St Sauveur, in Quebec's picturesque Lower Town, at the foot of the long, winding Pente Douce, or "Gentle Slope," that connects the Lower with the Upper Town. In this parish there are two social classes: the Mulots (feminine: Mulotes) or workers, literally "lazy good-for-nothings"; and the Soyeux (feminine: Soyeuses) or middle-class residents—the literal meaning of the word is "silky" or "silken." In addition, there are the Gonzagues, or bigots, who, though belonging to the Soyeux, constitute something very like a class in themselves. (They derive their name from the St Gonzaga Society.) These terms, being in reality untranslatable, have been retained in the English version.

There are also political alignments that play a prominent part in the story and that cut across class boundaries, the two chief parties being the reds and the blues, or, respectively, the Liberals and the Conservatives. The terms red and blue date from a time when the Canadian clergy took an active part in politics and would thunder from the pulpit: "Heaven is blue, hell is red, you will know for which side to vote." The Liberals, it may be remarked, still adhere to the tradition of the early-century premier, Sir Wilfred Laurier. As for the separatists, or ardent French-Canadian nationalists, they form a movement rather than a party and will be heard talking of "the Race" (meaning the French Canadians), the necessity of a "strong nation," of rebuilding the youth, etc. This nationalist spirit is reflected in such an organization as the St John the Baptist Society with its parochial sections or branches.

On the other hand, the "communists" that are referred to in this book are not to be taken seriously. They are the product of the overheated imagination of the bigoted and ambitious Monsieur Pritontin or afford convenient sermon material for a Father Folbèche, that is about all. There are, of course, real Communists in Canada but they do not appear in this story.

There are certain other allusions in the book that perhaps call for a word of explanation. Some of these are of a historical character. Anyone who has visited Quebec will be familiar with the name Lévis, that of the famous marshal, François Duc de Lévis, who surrendered Canada to the British in the eighteenth century. This will explain the appellation Lévis Guard, applied to the guard of honour at St Joseph's, the function of which is to usher in church and parade on state occasions. There is also Henri Bourassa, most famous of French-Canadian nationalist leaders, who is mentioned in passing, and there is the seventeenth-century Jean Talon, greatest of the French governors. If one adds the name of Father Antoine François-Xavier Labelle, late-nineteenth-century priest and statesman noted for his colonizing activities, the list of historical personages will be complete so far as the reader of the present story is concerned.

Among contemporary figures may be noted Bolduc, famous for her rendition of Canadian folk songs, and Henri Deglane, champion wrestler of the early 1930's. Pamphile Lemay, Joseph Boucher's literary idol, was a romantic nineteenth-century French-Canadian poet who imitated Lamartine.

A word should perhaps be said regarding certain nicknames that depend wholly upon sound-connotation for their effect. "Barloute," for example, is commonly applied to all women of Feda's sort; little, active, boastful men are known as "Tit-Blanc" (the "Tit-" being an abbreviation for *petit*); while individuals who are physically strong and inclined to be braggarts are called "Pitou." None of these names has any special origin.

In connection with the wrestling match, it may be observed that Canadian wrestling is more or less a free-for-all, marked by a use of the fists and feet that is not permitted in the United States. As a result, it is rather a bloody affair.

While these preliminary explanations may be helpful, the reader will soon enough become so absorbed in the strange new world into which he is plunged from the opening pages of this fascinating tale that he will feel no need of guideposts.

Throughout this translation I have had the advantage of the author's kind and helpful advice on all doubtful points. The task has been a difficult one, owing not alone to the peculiarities of Canadian French and the abundance of local argot but also to the frequent psychological subtleties of the narrative. At the same time it has been an experience so rewarding that I can think of only one other with which to compare it; that of translating Jean Cocteau's *Les Enfants Terribles*, some eighteen years ago. Both books hold all the pathos of adolescence; both are poetic, dramatic, and alive. Each in its own way (for they are of course very different after all) is heartbreakingly beautiful, yet has about it the ineffaceable glow of morning and of youth.

SAMUEL PUTNAM

PART ONE

The Cry

CHAPTER

I

THE shrill sound of the police whistle gave everyone a start. St Joseph housewives interrupted their washing, small lads quit their play, and idlers in the restaurants lifted mole-like faces toward the sun. What was it? The cops again? Who was their victim this time? One of the gang? All the Mulots were keen on the scent; they must rescue one of their number from the clutches of the law. They were prepared for such emergencies as this, prepared to put up an organized defence. Courtyard gates were purposely left open for refuge, and the urchins with slingshots in their mouths filled their pockets with pebbles. The big lads, meanwhile, their hands thrust into their trousers, sauntered off in the direction of the Pente Douce, as the Soyeux, cowering in their kitchens, expressed their horror of such hoodlums, who were a disgrace to the parish.

All eyes turned instinctively toward the "Cape," for this was the shortest path by which a perilous descent could be made from the Upper Town, where most of the depredations occurred. At the top of the Cape, in front of the Dominican monastery, several priests stood waving their arms as the culprits, half leaping, half rolling, scrambled down the almost vertical embankment, scratching and tearing themselves on the shrubbery, which quickly sprang back into place behind them with a shower of pretty autumn leaves. From the balconies the fugitives looked very small indeed: like lice fleeing through the hair of some tawny giant. Then came a glimpse of their mudspattered white shirts, tight over their enormous chests.

"Stop them! Stop them!" the monks were shouting. "Our apples! Our apples!"

Father Folbèche, the parish priest, who was engaged in watering his garden, found consolation for the shame he felt by reflecting that they at least had left him his flowers. The whistle sounded once more and a long black car drew up at the foot of the Pente Douce to await the delinquents.

"It's the cops, fellows!" cried Denis Boucher, who was bounding along in front of the others. They hesitated furtively. Should they turn back? It was not to be thought of. And there ahead of them, in triangular formation, were three gendarmes from the police car, waiting to pounce upon them. The Mulots, large and small, had already surrounded the officers and were walking up and down, obstructing their path, asking them for matches, doing everything they could to hamper them. But when they heard Boucher's excited cry they realized the culprits were the members of his hated, overbearing gang, and from that moment they ceased to be accomplices and became enemies, lining up to form a barricade to make it easier to capture the young upstarts who waged their own special kind of warfare, who put on so many airs over their book learning, who pretended to have no use for girls, and who, in short, were neither Mulots nor Soyeux.

It was the fugitives who launched the attack, the police bracing themselves to meet it. In three jumps Denis was upon the first officer, who made an attempt to seize him. The gendarme, however, had not reckoned with the strength of this sinewy youth of eighteen. With a sudden squirm Boucher bowled him over and continued on his headlong flight, bearing down upon the other two, a few yards farther on, who with the automobile constituted a sort of rampart. As they saw him coming they spread out a little that they might have a better chance of grabbing him; but just as he was within arm's reach he quickly ducked and slipped through their hands like an eel. The automobile still barred his way and he did not have time to run around the end of it. In a couple of leaps he was over the hood, coming down on the pavement of the rue Franklin on the other side. Apples spilled from his shirt and the little Mulots fought with one another for possession of them. All of which happened so rapidly that the policeman who had been knocked down had not yet been able to pick himself up.

"Hurrah!" shouted the urchins enthusiastically. They were punished for this by knee thrusts in the small of their backs; for the older lads were jealous of the fascination that Boucher exercised over the younger ones. His mocking laugh could be heard in the distance; he was proud of this successful manœuvre. In the meantime, the Langevin twins and Jean Colin had likewise managed to slip past the flurried gendarmes, whose turn it was to hesitate now. Not knowing what to do but obeying a natural impulse under the circumstances, they gave up the chase after Boucher and set out in pursuit of the other three, their handsome blue uniforms crackling while their white bell-shaped helmets danced above their foreheads, which were bathed in sweat from the unaccustomed exertion, and took on the hilarious appearance of carnival masks.

Denis had continued down the rue Montmagny. Germaine Colin offered him a refuge in her house, but he ran jauntily on past her. The two Langevins and Jean Colin, with the police close on their heels, whirled at the corner of the rue Chateauguay and dashed down that street. They had not gone far when, after pausing for a few seconds, they suddenly turned to the left. Paying no attention to the dogs that yelped in summer and in winter ran in the dog-sled derby, they briskly clambered over a fence, made their way over the roofs of four sheds, dropped down into a yard, and then climbed some more fences. Unexpectedly, they found themselves in the garden belonging to the churchwarden Zépherin Lévesque, which was the envy of the parish. It was separated from the adjoining property by a veritable palisade. Anxiously, they ran over to the gate, but it was locked. As they huddled in the entryway they heard women's voices.

"My Lise back from the convent! It's too good to be true, my dear. What a charming life we are going to arrange for ourselves. With your education you are sure to be made president of the Daughters of Mary. I must say I've had my fill of that Eugénie Clichoteux who is always the centre of everything, at entertainments and in church."

The pleasant but sulky voice of a young girl, a voice modulated by long recital of lessons, broke in upon this flow of words.

"I love you a great deal, Mama, but I cannot understand your ambitions. I'm afraid it's going to be dreadfully boring here. The boys fighting and screaming, the women wrangling from their balconies—it seems to me that was not the way I imagined my life in the outside world would be. My girl friends—"

"Conceited young thing!" Robert Langevin, ordinarily timid enough, was indignant.

The youths in their anxiety listened distractedly to this strange talk. Their hearts were thumping, the sweat glistening on their foreheads. They pictured to themselves a prudish young miss in glasses, with her braids under her chin, a rickety neck, and a small head that came up to a point and only needed an old lady's bonnet to fit her out for attending a wake in some wealthy home.

"You are a woman now, my daughter, and you must learn to care for such things." Madame Lévesque spoke in an offhand manner, inflating her voice as she uttered the most sonorous words in her vocabulary. She had been saving them up for ten years for this brilliant offspring of hers who had been graduated from a fashionable convent school. "Your girl friends, my daughter," she went on, "must be left to lead their own lives. If you only realized how different things are from your dreams."

"But really, Mama, this place—?"

"You'll come to love it, you'll see. You will be queen here! Take your father's case. When I first knew him he had his little aristocratic tastes. But he was a businessman. And with a few dollars he is the leading citizen here, while at St Dominique—"

"Darling Papa! I love him. Does he absolutely insist on my singing tonight?"

"Indeed he does! Monsieur le Député will be there, and Eugénie will be eaten up with jealousy. What a triumph for you. Don't refuse, Lise."

"Let's do something!" said Colin, who was worried at not being able to find a hiding place.

"Break down the door!" suggested Jacques Langevin.

They hurled themselves against the solid wooden panel, but only succeeded in making a lot of noise. The sweat on their foreheads was cold, for the police were already in the garden next door.

"That must be the milkman, who wants to get into the yard," said Madame Lévesque. "Go open the gate for him, will you, Lise?"

As the girl came out of the house she was still immersed in thinking of her new life, of the roseate dreams that she had cherished for so long and that now were clouded over with a dark uncertainty. It was, accordingly, with something of a shock that she encountered the defiant group on the other side of the gate. She was surprised at finding herself face to face with the Langevin twins, each of whom was short and ruddy with a mop of red hair. She let her eyes roam over Jean, a strapping youth with blue eyes, a nut-brown complexion, and a burnished forehead fringed with unruly curls. The habits of the convent were strong within her, and at the sight of strangers of the opposite sex she had for a moment the illusory impression of chaste precincts being violated. Blushing deeply, she dropped her gaze, too frightened for words.

"The police are after us," Robert explained. He was flustered by Lise's beauty.

She glanced up at them timidly. Jean Colin appeared to be paralysed by her presence. All he could see was that mouth of hers; the future hung on what she was about to say. When she spoke, it was as if in a dream.

"Ah! So the police are after you?" She thought of the nobility of old France, of those atrocious sans-culottes who had pursued the holy priests and the good bourgeois, so pale and haggard-looking. As a result of her reading she had some while since come to conceive of life as a possible repetition of all those chivalrous events with which the romances were so filled.

"Quick!" she murmured mysteriously, as she opened the gate leading into the rue Colomb. She put them into the garage, and they were no sooner hidden than the breathless, impatient voices of their pursuers were heard.

"You haven't seen any young hoodlums down this way, have you, Mademoiselle?"

The marauders held their breath, Jean Colin being unaware that his right hand was resting in a puddle of oil upon the work-bench.

In reply the girl mechanically stammered out a sentence or two that she had nott had time to master. "Why, yes, I have! They ran out through the gate there. I was afraid, so I locked it!"

"Damn it!" bellowed one of the gendarmes. "We've let them get away again!"

"They're going," whispered Jean. Nervously he ran his oil-stained hand over his damp brow; it left dark streaks behind it. There was a silence, and then the door opened part way.

"They have gone," panted Lise. She was pale but enthusiastic.

The twins came out, lowering their heads as if to hide them. Jean was the last to appear. Lise had to smile as she caught sight of his grimy forehead, and he blushed, delighted to see that he was not wholly displeasing to her.

She wore a simple, green-dotted white dress, slightly open at the neck, which seemed to set off her youthfulness and enhance the charm of a convent-bred modesty that was at once hesitant and eager in the presence of unlooked-for discoveries. The airy brightness of her new gown was in unforgettable and joyous contrast to her black schoolgirl uniform, solemn as a cemetery, as unrelieved and unexciting as a desert; and if she so frequently drooped her long lashes, as if to imitate Lamartine's heroines or Louis Veuillot's young ladies, it was rather to cast a stolen glance at the folds of her dress or the crescent-shaped fastening of her bodice. Like a youth from a poor family who is sporting a new necktie, she was conscious of her graceful, supple throat. In the convent she had kept it as jealously hidden as one would a love letter, but now she was both pleased and astonished to find it thus freely exposed to the sun. In the presence of Jean, Lise was no longer laughing. Her lips, unskilled at feigning indifference, appeared to be pouting. Was it because she had furnished shelter to outlaws, or was she thinking merely of the brown curl with which she caressed her chin?

"How nice you look!" Jean's smile was an embarrassed one. When she did not answer, he went on in a timid voice, his head held awkwardly to one side. "We're not really thieves, you know." At this point a lump ran down the leg of his trousers and a big apple, barely ripe, rolled over his toes and across the courtyard pavement. He dared not pick it up for fear of seeming too concerned.

"Just see what fine ones they are! It's the season. If the police would only leave us alone. Will you have some?" Thrusting a nervous hand into the opening of his white shirt on which the mud had formed little splotches and arabesques, he selected the choicest specimen and looked about for some place to wipe it but found none. "Go ahead and eat it."

The Langevin brothers, a bewildered look on their faces, had come back, and they now made the same offer with trembling hands. Smiling, she took the fruit, all that she could hold of it. "Is that the reason why the police were after you?"

At once the same words leaped from all three mouths: "And they never catch us!" They said nothing of Boucher. Lise's astonishment caused them to puff out their chests.

How charming was this ragamuffin bravado! The spontaneous homage of the three marauders reminded her of Maid Marian and Robin Hood's men. The hesitant breeze of her thoughts was lost in a vague, romantic reverie that had to do with things past even as her gaze rested unseeingly on the objects about her. For her, the present served merely as an echo of the past, and since the tendency of schoolgirl dreams is toward the ideal and the unreal, Lise found herself tossing in time and space like a bit of driftwood that is always on the point of settling somewhere but never does. The light-skimming, wavering glance with which she regarded the lads in front of her reflected this inner vagueness; and then, suddenly, a startled look came into her eyes as she stared at Jean's leg. Bending over, he perceived the hole in his trousers through which his knee was visible.

"They are my everyday ones," he stammered. He would have liked very much to show her his fine brown suit with the stripes.

The girl was becoming conscious of her surroundings once more: the clothesline strung with underwear, handkerchiefs, diapers, towels—nearly white, all of them, and flapping in the wind like the multitudinous symbols of people without a flag. Upon the neighbouring shed a tomcat was stoically sampling the unsavoury remains of a rat as Bédarovitch the ragman went down the rue Colomb crying in his hoarse, singsong voice: "Ra-a-a-ags— Ra-a-a-ags—" Abruptly confronted with this disturbing reality, Lise dropped her armful of fruit.

"You mustn't throw it away!" said Jean, as he bounded forward to recover the apple he had given her. "It's the best of the lot."

"Aren't you coming back, Lise?" Madame Lévesque's heavy voice was audible a short distance away.

Frightened at this, her daughter now pushed the marauders out, whispering to Jean, who was the last to leave: "Whatever you do, don't tell anybody."

He gave her an understanding smile. "My name," he said, with a strange tightening of the throat, "is Jean Colin. I'll bring you some plums tomorrow." He came near stumbling over the threshold as he backed out.

Lise's face was red; for the Abbé Charton was standing there, watching the youths in amazement as they emerged from the garden. Coming up to the convent miss, the amiably smiling priest studied her closely.

"I've brought you my arrangement of the *Parce Domine* for three voices. Here it is."

Glancing back, the lads laughingly whispered to one another that the Abbé Charton was making up to the family because Zépherin Lévesque had just bought an automobile. Jean Colin smiled up at the telephone poles. So the pretty stranger was going to sing that evening!

Denis Boucher kept an eye on the Mulots by way of making sure that they did not turn him in. It gave him satisfaction to see the small lads deflating the tires of the police car as the older ones dispersed. "They're afraid!" he muttered to himself. He laughed at the sight of the gendarmes coming back empty-handed from the chase. His friends were safe. Ah! how proud he was of being the pet aversion of those Mulots! How he loved to see them tremble like rats in front of his eyes! And the same went for the Soyeux who made so much of their wealth and intellectual pretensions. Intellectuals! He had it in him to flatten them like the leaves of those books they were always talking about. As for the women! He would never love any of them but would drag them after him like logs all his life long. Only they would not be the girls of St Sauveur, for they had known him when he was small and his mother used to beat him for starting fires or throwing stones at passers-by. The conquest of the world would begin at the frontiers of this "Sewer Town" (so called because of the water from the Upper Town with which it was flooded in the rainy season), of which he called himself the king. His reflections were interrupted by the Abbé Bongrain.

"Was the harvest a good one?" the priest called to him jovially. He was bringing wood to Méo Nolin, who had injured his fingers and who received donations from the St Vincent de Paul Society. The Abbé Bongrain took a sort of stern pleasure in manual labour and was not in the least mindful of the twigs and bits of bark that clung to his cassock. Boucher gave him a friendly look.

"It was all right," he said, "but there was a little rumpus. Here, catch it!"

The priest so beloved by the Mulots (he was like an almoner to them) caught the apple which Denis tossed him and, mopping the sweat from his forehead, took a hearty bite.

With a nervous laugh, the young man leaped the fence, landing in the middle of his brother Gaston's poultry yard. The frightened hens found refuge by huddling against the weird-looking bosoms of the roosters which now began scolding because the intruder's feet were a threat to the chickens pecking the rich soil.

A hoarse, anxious cry rang out: "Careful, Denis — Crazy — My chickens!"

Gaston came running up as fast as he could, his hips swaying with his uneven gait. He had a man's face on a child's body, a body that looked as if someone had started to demolish it with a sledge hammer. His brow was lined with wrinkles, and he seemed to be forever engaged in solving some problem. There was a crease at the corners of his mouth that conveyed an impression of disillusionment and, at the same time, of naïveté. It gave him the abnormal appearance of those who have suffered before they have lived. Rickety and useless, his long arms swung by the side of his slanting body like tropical creepers. Three years the elder, he looked up to Denis as a sort of god, for Denis was big and strong and had often fought until he was bloody to avenge some mocking insult that had been offered to the invalid. When Gaston spoke of his brother, he always said "Denis" in a piping voice in which all too much pride was revealed.

Misfortune for him had been a kind of vocation. Having

suffered an attack of pleurisy accompanied by a pus infection at the age of four, he had later had a severe case of measles which, as his mother put it, "had gone to his ears." Becoming deaf, he had afterwards developed a falsetto voice. Later still, in the days when a thoracoplasty was regarded as a daring operation, he had undergone a rib-section. He had recovered, but from year to year they noticed that he bent over more and more, for an alarming spinal curvature had set in. His right shoulder, lacking ribs to support it, had sagged to such an extent that, the heart being imprisoned in too narrow a space, a cardiac affection had resulted. Today, the invalid found himself a prey to the slightest emotion; and here he was now, confronting his big brother and breathing hard.

Denis surveyed him thoughtfully for a moment, then offered him a couple of apples.

Gaston shook his head: "Don't want them, not ripe." Then he changed his mind and took them. "Still stealing? The police will get you."

"The cops? To the devil with them, old man." And Denis ran his hand through Gaston's hair, rumpling it until it stood up in rigid tufts around the oversized head. The sick lad grumbled and bit his brother's wrists.

Denis now proceeded to clear the yard of the brats who infested it, whose hands, stretched out toward his shirt front, were threatening to undress him. Laughing as he did so, he suddenly stopped short: his mother was talking to that gendarme again! Motionless, a mist in front of his eyes, the young man wet his lips. He remembered the feeling of despair that had come over him when they told him that this guardian of deserted streets had been his mother's lover for the last four years. What had become of that beautiful legend about the love that existed between his parents, who, he had believed, cared for no one but each other? Aware of her son's presence, Flora Boucher turned pale and took a step or two backward from the wall over which she had been leaning.

"That's my lad, Noré. Do you think he's big enough to get on the force?"

Denis stared at them without saying a word and began juggling his apples. By way of ridding himself of his embarrassment, Noré started speaking of Gaston's hens, which the boy was in the habit of raffling off at ten cents a ticket when they had reached their full growth, and Flora took advantage of the situation to sell him three chances. A look of avarice distorted the invalid's queer face as he snatched the silver coins. They would go to swell his savings toward the purchase of an automobile. Madame Boucher, who would set out with the raffle tickets as soon as one of the hens weighed eight pounds, was fast becoming a serious competitor of the Latruche sisters, who went about selling photographs of the young parish saint, a recent discovery.

"At least," they would remark insinuatingly, "we are working for the Lord."

As Flora was pointing out the site of the confectionery shop which they were about to open for her ailing son, Gaston painfully mounted the stairs that led to the place where he kept his savings, beneath the image of the Sacred Heart. Halfway up, he paused and put out his hand to the hollow of his hip to get his breath. Then he began counting on his fingers: "That makes five times my fingers in dollars, with three dimes. Father says I'll need ten times my fingers. That takes time." He sighed, and his sagging shoulders appeared to sink down to his hips. Meanwhile, the gendarme had managed to slip away without being too obvious about it. As he went off whistling, Flora, her eyes flaming, seized Denis by the arm and shook him impatiently as she had done when he was small.

"Leave me alone, will you?" he said. "Don't be playing that farce about whipping me, to hide your embarrassment. That doesn't go."

Flora's eyes were bloodshot. "Thief! Thief!" she screamed at him. "What shame! We have you educated at a private school so that you can become a clerk in an office, and you're a bigger rowdy than the worst of the Mulots."

"I notice you always use my apples for your jelly." He spilled his booty on the table as the young ones came running up. Then he drew himself sharply erect.

"Yes," he said aggressively, "that humiliates you in view of your relations with the police. But you are the real thief, for you have stolen Father's confidence." He pointed to Noré, who was going down the street.

Mother and son now faced each other threateningly. Theirs was a violent, unrestrained anger, one that revealed the true character of each of them.

If one had not noted a certain bagginess under the eyes, Flora Boucher might have passed for a young woman inclined to stoutness. Her shoulders were square-set and her movements forceful and abrupt, but she was pretty and it was natural for her to laugh when she was not involved in a dispute of some sort. She displayed a certain affectation which rendered her

the more picturesque, considering her illiterate work-
ackground. Since her father had been one of those
work who never work, while her mother with ten
to support had been compelled to go from one house-
another among the "foreigners" of the Upper Town, she
upon herself as a woman who had attained a certain
, a certain social position. She was no longer, or rather she
strove not to be any longer, a Mulote. She had arrived; she now
belonged to that class of workers who, at St Sauveur, may envisage the possibility of becoming churchwardens and enjoying
their day of triumph. A hope that was all the better founded in
her case in view of the fact that Joseph Boucher, her husband,
was a calm, silent man—and therefore endowed with an air of
dignity—whose parents had been middle-class people who had
come down in the world.

It was originally intended that he should marry a notary's
daughter who had a dowry of eight hundred dollars. (Flora
always spoke of this young woman with a contemptuous curl
of her lips.) But Joseph Boucher, alas, had been born with a
roving disposition and had left school to go and live in the west.
Having come back to Quebec stranded, some years later, he had
met Flora in the St Sauveur quarter while searching for a dog
which had been stolen from his aunt, a lady of means. (In
speaking to the neighbouring women, Madame Boucher would
frequently mention inheritances that were soon to be expected
from her husband's side of the family.) Despite his unstable
temperament and because he was so sentimental and passionate,
Denis' father had quickly fallen in love with Flora's brown
eyes, her coquettish ways, and her lively and exotic mannerisms; and she did indeed possess a keen intelligence and a heart
of gold. When Joseph first met her, she was just recovering
from the pain she had experienced in dismissing a certain
jealous and exacting suitor—the same Noré, now a St Joseph
gendarme. She had shed many tears over it, even though the
years that they had gone about together had been stormy ones.

And so Joseph, an expert in psychological sedatives, had at
once begun flooding her with his free-verse compositions. How
splendid! A poet all her own who could cause her to forget her
sorrow! But Flora's father, a practical-minded drunkard, was
unable to see a possible drinking companion in his daughter's
"young man." Of an evening, he would spy upon Joseph from
behind his newspaper, stealing a glance at the pictures now and
then, since he could not read. This young fellow was for him an
antipathetic enigma, an unsociable individual with long, slender

hands and a pale face. By way of getting him out of the house at an early hour, he would hover around the grandfather clock, winding it energetically and coughing all the while. Then he would take off his slippers, hold them side by side in his hand, and wait.

"That lad, my girl, is too easygoing," he would say. "He's too sweet on you. If he doesn't work, he has no business wanting to marry you. I'll have to give him his walking papers."

Inasmuch as his prospective father-in-law was near to being a colossus, Joseph was led to reflect that perhaps it would be better for him to look for a job. He would hang about the corridors of the Parliament Buildings and, just as Flora's sisters were returning from work, would come out with a bustling air and a newspaper under his arm. Then came the war. He did the heroic thing and enlisted, and this act of gallantry on his part resulted in his being married, in view of the allotment his wife would receive. As soon as the Armistice was signed, he had gone to work on the construction gang in the grain elevators along the wharf and after that had become permanently employed. His family circle today, comprising ten children, was apparently complete, and Madame Boucher with great magnanimity would distribute heaps of baby clothes to young married couples. As the tots came, Joseph had taken on a crabbed mien. There was nothing of the *vers-libriste* about him any longer; he rather resembled a tree that with the coming of autumn had shed its flowers, fruit, and leaves. The mother, on the other hand, seemed to blossom out, and for each new angle that became visible on her husband's body it was as if a new curve made its appearance on hers.

As she was screaming to her son that she was a respectable woman, voices were heard calling Denis from the yard.

"That's right," shouted Flora, "go on to your Mulots. Ignorant lot! That Jean Colin who was born two months after his parents were married. Everybody knows what La Barloute, his mother, is."

She began peeling the apples that had been left on the table as Colin and the Langevins gathered around Denis, and Gaston came out to join them. Denis, astonished to see them so agitated, gazed at each of them in turn. Jean, especially, was unable to stand still.

"It's almost unbelievable," he said. "Just imagine—" He broke off as he saw Madame Boucher, who had come to the doorway to listen. "Come over to the shed."

They had crossed the street, for the Colins lived directly opposite the Bouchers. Gaston followed them as best he could, putting into each breath he took all the energy that a feeble person expends in trying to keep up with the others; he was breathing harder and more painfully all the time. The "shed" was a tumble-down coachhouse that was rotting from the ground up—how it remained standing was a miracle.

"Let's sit in the victoria," suggested Robert Langevin, the lazy one.

The victoria stood in the centre of the shed, as black and memory-laden as a coffin on wheels. Jean's grandfather Colin, old man Pitou, had been a coachman for the tourist trade and it was the family's title to fame to have an ancestor who had driven American millionaires about.

"Let's help ourselves from the buffet," said Jean, lifting up the carriage seat. There were the stolen apples. He watched his leader out of the corner of his eye, enjoying Denis' curiosity. Finally he could contain himself no longer. "It was a girl who hid us," he said. "And a pretty one!" he added in an enthusiastic tone of voice.

Denis frowned. "Who was she?"

"Père Lévesque's girl. You know, the educated one, who was away at the convent."

"Who is that?" asked Germaine Colin, who had just come in with a bundle under her arm. Denis gave her a look.

"Mind your own business, you," Jean rebuked her. At sight of Denis, Germaine decided to stay.

"Sit down here," whispered Robert.

"I just finished scrubbing one of those ceilings," she said. "But look at the two bucks I got for it."

"Don't be telling us your troubles," said big Jacques Langevin. "Listen."

Gaston slipped a thin arm into the front of his shirt and handed Germaine an apple. "Eat it."

Jean began his recital with that slight degree of exaggeration that expansive souls display in relating their first exploits. The Langevins interrupted him frequently, for they wished their leader to know that they too had been present. Denis was silent. His right eye was almost shut as if in mockery while the other held a reflective look.

Gaston, who did not understand all that was being said, kept his gaze fastened on Germaine's chin, her hair, her bosom, and the holes in her stockings which afforded him a glimpse of the chapped flesh of her knees. Her face was beautiful, and her lids appeared to be drowsing above her eyes, which were young and full of life. They were like any other pair of eyes, except that they were neither blue nor grey nor black but a little of each. Her hair was faded-looking, and there were a few tarnished curls on the back of her neck, the remains of a permanent. At the corners of her thin lips a faint crease held a hint of derision : the narrow bed of a puny pride sapped by poverty. Germaine at eighteen was already old, having lost amid the mops she plied on other people's floors that naïve trust in happiness which is natural in the young. A glint of sunlight through a crevice in the roof played upon her face but was poorly reflected there owing to the dried perspiration and the grime which her features had absorbed. Beneath her rumpled, tight-fitting dress her bosom was suggestively outlined, and at sight of it Gaston's big childlike eyes beneath his man's forehead became so animated that one would have said the look in them was inspired by lust.

Jean was spreading his arms in declamatory fashion : "That's just what she said to me : 'Don't tell anybody !' And maybe you think she didn't know how to talk."

"She talked to us, too," put in the Langevins. Denis kept silent.

"She'll make a swell girl friend for you, a young lady," remarked Germaine.

At this insinuation, Denis sprang up, showing his large, strong teeth; there was a gleam in his brown eyes and his face was savagely contorted.

"I was waiting for you to say that. There you are, parish love affairs again. That's the way love gets you. Are you like all the others, then?" He turned to Jean : "And you, Colin, in love already, you who were bragging you could overcome it? Don't you realize that it means the end of your freedom? Haven't you noticed how the love of our parents has turned into kitchen wrangling?"

Jean blushed but said nothing. He was thinking of Lise and how she had asked him not to tell. The Langevins were protesting, their little eyes sparkling from among their freckles.

"You have to get married some time or other. And besides, love is not always the fault of the girls !"

"Shut up, you idiots ! Their charms are like glue. But I'm here to protect you, my lads." Denis was particularly concerned with maintaining his domination over Jean, whose silence led him to believe that he was still in command. "I had faith in you," he continued, "in a gang that would be independent of girls."

"Those are fine words, I must say," was Germaine's admiring comment, "but Jean is old enough."

"That's no concern of yours!" Jean snapped, turning upon his sister. "This is a man's affair."

The dispute was interrupted by the arrival of Tit-Blanc Colin and Chaton, the worm vendor, who was Jean's formidable rival in that business. Jean's father was drunk and had his arm around his companion's neck. Chaton made for the worm box and lifted the lid.

"They're rather fat and sluggish," he said, crushing a clod of earth with the gesture of a connoisseur. "You don't have such an awfully large stock. For a lot of creepy worms like these I can offer you a couple of dollars."

Jean looked him over contemptuously. "They are not for sale. And what's more, I can show you a thing or two, Chaton."

Tit-Blanc solemnly raised his arm. "It's no use, Chaton, old pal," he said. "Those worms bring in too good money. They are bread and butter." Slyly the drunkard made the rounds of the group, and then, suddenly, he snatched from Germaine's hand the two-dollar bill she was twisting between her fingers.

He flourished it triumphantly as Germaine gave an anguished cry: "Father! That's for my dress! My dress!" She burst into sobs.

With a sanctimonious smile on his lips, Tit-Blanc was about to put the money in his pocket when there came a hoarse growl. The drunkard's arm being within reach of Gaston's mouth, the invalid had sunk his sharp teeth into it. As his victim screamed, Gaston seized the banknote and, pantingly, handed it back to Germaine. He stood there at her side, the wraith of a man, trembling all over and scarcely knowing what he did; for this impulse to which he had yielded represented for him a week's store of energy. "Don't cry, Jamaine, don't cry." And he ran his emaciated hand through the girl's hair, lavishing upon her his invalid's caresses, as feeble and faltering as his body. He was awkward at expressing his sympathy, for he had never forgiven himself his own sufferings.

Tit-Blanc, meanwhile, was sucking his bleeding wrist. Catching hold of Gaston's collar, he jerked the lad violently toward him. "Damned hunchback! You're going to pay for this!" But he had no sooner made a move in Gaston's direction than Denis was upon him hammering him with both fists.

The elder Colin was a strong, stockily built man, and the two of them now rolled over on the floor as Grandfather Pitou, who had come up to see what the noise was about, shouted: "Give it

29

to him, Tit-Blanc! Let him have it in the belly—in the belly!"

Féda Colin, her hair standing up, dashed out of the kitchen, crying: "He's drunk again! He's spent all his pay once more!"

Bent over the fighting pair, Gaston anxiously followed the course of the struggle, indicating with wraithlike gestures what his brother should do to overcome his adversary.

"You bastard, I'll kill you!" Tic-Blanc roared. Suddenly Denis got a firm hold under the older man's head and began pounding his nose, and then Jean leaped on his friend's back.

The fight was becoming a free-for-all when the door to the entryway opened and a grave voice rose above the din: "Is that the way you love one another?"

Abashed by the presence of the Abbé Charton, the participants in the fray fell apart. The priest, who rarely took sides in the rows of his parishioners, strode forward majestically, his eyes full of solemn dignity, his mouth quivering with sorrow.

"He struck Jamaine, he did," said Gaston, pointing a finger at Tit-Blanc.

The Abbé laid a chubby hand on the drunkard's hairy arm, and the elder Colin with religious unction suffered him to do so. The atmosphere was a ceremonious one, as at high mass. As for the lads, they were tired and were trying to find an excuse to leave. In the victoria, Charton and old man Pitou had begun a checker game.

Having examined Tit-Blanc's wound, the Abbé Charton produced from the depths of his capacious pocket a box of adhesive tape, which formed a part of the worthy vicar's ministerial equipment. Every morning, after mass and the reading of his breviary, he would stroll through the streets in search of minor injuries. He sought them out with a tranquil devotion, and the Mulots were good patients; he never missed one of their brawls, and his mouth would water at the sight of deep gashes. He felt that he was gradually becoming a physician of the poor in a cassock, a sort of Curé of Ars—but with an added distinction, that went without saying.

Each evening, at the hour when every good Christian was engaged in meditation, Oscar Charton would indulge his heart in dreams of heroism, yielding to grandiose reflections that had to do with the courage he displayed—a man of his station in life —in fulfilling the duties of his ministry. It was at such times that he felt himself lulled by a symphony of charitable thoughts to the languid accompaniment of aristocratic sighs. Between himself and reality he interposed these sentimental barricades behind which he entrenched himself in a beribboned virtue. This man, so self-satisfied, brooded upon his tastes and did not like to discuss them; any objection raised would have wearied him, and so he cherished them in silence. He was, then, in turn a solitary intellectual, an unknown musician, and a voluntary hermit among men and saints. He loved the countryside and by way of procuring rides cultivated the friendship of those among the Soyeux who had automobiles. The drama of his life occurred when he mounted the pulpit; for the Abbé Charton had a deep and solemn voice and Monsieur le Curé always assigned to him those sermons that called for a bit of pathos.

When the good priest who was also a poet felt the first murmurous titillations of an intellectual ecstasy coming on, he would flee to the silence of his room and devote himself avidly to science, literature, and music. In a fever of inspiration, he would rumple his hair, undo his collar, cast a befuddled eye over the volumes in his library, run a hand over his dusty phonograph records, snatch up his pen and bite it spasmodically, and pace the floor impatiently with a hammering tread. But all this would suddenly cease as the grating voice of the Abbé Trinchu cut short his poetic fit.

"Not so much noise, Charton!" the other priest would call from the floor below.

His arms would fall to his side, and it was then that he would go out into the street, armed with his adhesive tape. Thus his life was spent, between the parish house and the public thoroughfare, between the convulsions of a sterile beauty and the injured children of fecund mothers.

The Abbé Charton, who was studying the Langevins and wondering what they could have been doing at Lise's house a short while ago, now became aware of Gaston's presence and told him to stay. The invalid, however, was anxious to leave. The priest for some time had been bothering him about taking the measure of his deformity; for the Abbé had in mind inventing a brace that would enable him to walk upright, and the poor fellow did not wish to show the holes in his back. His brother provided a distraction.

"Come along, Gaston," said Denis, who did not care to be bandaged. He darted Tit-Blanc a contemptuous look: "Mulot! You have milk in your veins."

Once outside, Gaston was jubilant: "You gave the swine a thrashing, eh?" Then he made a face: "Ugh! That's some father Jamaine has!"

Denis shrugged his shoulders. He was gazing absent-mindedly at the sheet-iron plaques that stood out from the houses like ears that had come loose. There were inscriptions in black on white or vice versa, all of them the same but displaying every mistake in spelling which the French language permitted: *"vers de paiche," "vairs de pêches," "verres de peiche,"* etc., all of them signifying angleworms. To a schoolmaster's eyes Jean was an educated lad, for the spelling on his sign was correct. He sold them at twenty-five cents a hundred, and although he was a city dweller he would wait for a rain with as much anxiety as any farmer. But what competition he had! It came from the small Mulots exploited by Chaton, who was bent upon monopolizing the business—the Abbé Bongrain did not hesitate to call him the "worm magnate," which flattered his self-esteem. Chaton bought the little animals at five cents a hundred and sold them at a profit of ten cents. But he was a no-good and a natural-born ignoramus, whereas Jean knew how to fatten them up. How red they were, those that he had, and how cleverly they could slip through the fingers of the clumsy fisherman!

There was a small group of vendors who were in the habit of gathering the worms of an evening in the Parc des Braves, after a rain; and the lovers upon the benches, between kisses, would rail at these imbeciles, whom they at first mistook for members of the morals squad.

Denis disdained this vulgar traffic, but he was none the less keenly aware of the constant lack of small change in his pocket. An anxiety clutched his heart: "Shall I have money one day without becoming like them?" He listened to his mother singing in a loud voice "La Légende des Flots Bleus" and then went back to his reverie. At bottom he was glad that his friends did not have his powers of resistance where women were concerned. He thought of the entertainment that evening, what it would be like. Who was this Lise? He began laying his plans to get hold of fifteen cents.

"Father!" exclaimed Gaston. Joseph Boucher was making signs to his son, good-naturedly tapping the extended pockets of his coat. As the men came home from work the Jewish peddlers were to be seen decamping from the houses with their merchandise, for it was only with the womenfolk that they bargained effectively. Denis was gazing toward the Upper Town, picturing to himself a gang so powerful that he would have to exert all his strength to remain the leader. But Jean would follow him, he could depend on that.

CHAPTER

II

When the elder Boucher had finished emptying his pockets of the grain he had brought back from the elevators, he came into the house and washed himself thoroughly, taking pains not to leave any of the dust behind his ears. Denis kept hanging around him. What was the use of asking his father for money? He would only start making a speech about how they had worked their fingers to the bone to put him through school. The youth clenched his fists, and when he spoke it was in a sharp tone of voice, for it humiliated him to be intimidated like this.

"I'd like to go to the entertainment tonight."

"That's your business."

"I need fifteen cents. I'll give it back to you."

"No loans. We give you twenty-five cents for Sunday, that's enough! Look at your brother; he knows how to get it. Stay at home with him and amuse him."

Gaston protested, but still he had a vision of Denis reading him the illustrated stories in the newspaper. Flora Boucher did not like Denis to go to these affairs, for she sat in the reserved seats next to the churchwardens and people looked at her when her son created a disturbance. She now put in a word, her hands upon her hips.

"Joseph," she began, "do you know what he did this afternoon?"

Taking the offensive, Denis came back at her: "It's all on account of Noré," he said. And he went on to mimic his mother, whom he had overheard reminding the gendarme of their past: "Ah! those were the days! Do you remember when we went cherry picking?"

Flora turned pale, but disconcerted as she was, she did not fail to note the arrival of the Abbé Charton, who appeared as a kind of Providence. "Monsieur l'Abbé!"

"Dear Madame Boucher! And how are you?"

"Thanks to the good Lord, my family and I are all well. Did you find the canvas for my son's brace?"

Joseph Boucher went out to give the hens some grain, and Denis had a sudden idea. To go to the cupboard and take three empty milk jars and stuff them in his shirt was the work of a moment. Then whistling nonchalantly, he made for the door. The Abbé Charton, a charming smile on his lips, greeted him cordially, for Denis possessed a fine bass voice and was a possible recruit for the choir at high mass. When the young man saw that he was no longer being noticed, he ran out and hastened to Bédarovitch's place.

The junk dealer was occupied with unharnessing his decrepit horse, which he called his "old nag." The poor beast was so skinny that one had the impression that the shafts served him as a pair of crutches. The cart, perched upon its limping wheels, was of a pale yellow hue, as if someone had endeavoured unsuccessfully to give it a coating of gilt. It was overflowing with bits of copper wire, old rags, bottles, and old bedsprings. It was, in short, a catchall for objects worth nothing to anyone save to the Jews of the ghetto. The only thing was, could one definitely assert that Bédarovitch was a Jew? There were all sorts of arguments pro and con. For example, his sunburned skin afforded no clue, for his was not the olive-brown complexion of the Oriental. Moreover, Jean-Baptiste did not have a long beard to twist in his right hand in the manner of his pseudo-ancestors. Semitic or not, he had one characteristic mannerism : while he was talking to you he would clack his false teeth with every sentence. This was not a whim on his part, as he tried to make it appear, but was due to the fact that his plate was not one made to order; the explanation was simple enough : he had found it in the dust-bin of Monsieur Folbèche, the parish priest. People did not know what he was talking about when he remarked mysteriously : "You may take my word for it, what you hear is not out of the Curé's mouth." And he would clack his plate once more.

Bédarovitch was said to be of French-Canadian descent. It was whispered among the parishioners that his grandfather, a certain Bédard, was a real Frenchman whose reasoning had run somewhat like this : "All the Jews succeed in business here. I will make myself a Jew." He had accordingly set up shop in Quebec, being at pains to add to his name the profitable termination; and proudly decorated with this "vitch" that so many Jews sought to hide, he had prospered. Jean-Baptiste, who clung to traditions like a career patriot, had kept up his grandsire's deception, and his shop had become a true museum of rags, old bottles, and broken-down beds. Old clothes, copper wire, watches that no longer ran—he took all that the quarter had to offer; his cart was the gulf into which all cast their odds and ends in return for a few pennies. Having exhausted their unemployment compensation, the women would frequently sell him an old corset or an out-of-date hat to get the price for the movies or a bingo party. And who could say whether, with those Mulots, he was not to a certain extent a receiver of stolen goods?

"Still the same price for three empties, Père Baptiste?" Denis inquired.

"Wait inside at the counter. Ah, greetings, Tit-Blanc! Greetings, Bison Langevin! How goes it?" said Baptiste to the pair that had just arrived. He returned to the shop with a set of bedsprings over his shoulders, forming a sort of collar about his neck. The door was low and one would not have thought there could be so many things behind it. Upon an ancient chest of drawers that had shed its paint and now served as a counter stood an apothecary's scale in forlorn state. One wondered if it was for sale, too.

It was a roomy enough place in the back. On one side of the partition could be seen a heterogeneous heap of old iron. From the other side came voices to which the odour of tobacco smoke seemed to cling. Pictures hung from the walls. There in effigy were Wilfred Laurier, Ernest Lapointe, Mackenzie King, and at the far end was a photograph of Cardinal Villeneuve, next to the image of the Sacred Heart. The heart of the statue was heated by electricity while its toes were warmed by a well-trimmed lamp. The image was painted red, for Providence is on the side of the Liberals. Big sheet-iron letters which one of the members had patiently cut out of empty canisters swayed opposite the entrance, announcing: LAPOINTE LIBERAL ASSOCIATION.

Like the big organizations, this suburban club had its president, its vice-president, its sergeant-at-arms, its little banquets and celebrations. And all this was conducted by the master hand of Gus Perrault. It was fine to hear the members address him as "Monsieur le Président." A city-hall functionary, he was king among the workers, who were more obsessed by the myth of steady employment than they were concerned with political principles. He held a diminutive court at which all lent him an attentive ear and readily fell into the proper fawning attitudes. For Gus Perrault, who loved to make speeches, found every occasion a suitable one for "mounting the rostrum." By way of getting off to a better start, he would first emit a formidable "Ha." Like certain poets, he had his own little tricks in summoning inspiration. A prudent man, he spoke in a loud voice, almost shouting, for otherwise he could hear himself thinking, and that disturbed him; and so, he bellowed and chewed over his sentences. The deputies, aware of his prestige among the workers, handled him with gloves, and from time to time they gave jobs to members of his club. The fortunate one who was chosen then had the right to address Monsieur le Président as "Gus," and later, by way of celebrating the event, they had in some fiddlers and the guest of honour paid the expenses.

This little association lived by the mirage of a cavernous bureaucracy. The workers, glad to see their party take power at last, had come to believe in nothing but the wonderful jobs which the government could provide. Their ambition, as artisans or day labourers, had narrowed to following in the footprints of their deputy. The only thing they could think about was a permanent job, and they saw but one means of attaining that end : to become some kind of rivet, bolt, or wheel in the party organization. It was commonly said that the quarter was ridden with poverty and hunger, but the truth is that it was suffering from a more dangerous affliction : the poison of machine politics. The inhabitants of St Sauveur were divided into three classes : the separatists, the blues, and the reds. When one of the parties came to power, the vanquished inevitably fell into want and the result was unemployment, feverish looks, a succession of brawls, and the prolonging of enmities. If a blue was elected to city hall or the Legislative Assembly, a red lost the place that was coveted by every Conservative.

This ebb and flow, this clean sweep, this joyful coming in and gloomy going out took place regularly every five years. The separatist or independent workers, always discontented, were forever trying, one after the other, the two political colours. For ten traffic policemen who sped around happily to the rhythmic chug of their motorcycles there were ten ex-policemen who watched them go by with hate-filling glances. The same rancour existed among the street sweepers and the elevator "conductors."

It was in little clubs such as this that the decadent mysticism of the bureaucratic spirit found a shrine.

Tit-Blanc and his friend were greeted with jovial exclamations.

"Monsieur le Président," said Bison Langevin, father of the twins, "I'd like a word with you."

Tit-Blanc clapped Denis on the shoulder. The young man looked him over. "You're brave, aren't you, seeing you've got your gang here? That doesn't worry me." Tit-Blanc spat on the floor at Denis' feet by way of showing his contempt. If he were only a Mulot six feet tall !

"Here's your fifteen cents," said Bédarovitch, "and the next time wash them out."

Denis was about to leave when from the corner where the young Liberals were engaged in a discussion he heard Lise's name. They were laying bets, each wagering that he would be the first to kiss her. It was all Denis could do to keep from egging them on as he thought of how annoyed Jean would be. And then, suddenly, he felt like breaking their jaws. He went on back, his hands in his pockets, lightly kicking their chairs as he passed. No one spoke, for they could tell that he was looking for an argument. But he was satisfied and strolled over to lean against the frame of the door.

Seated on long, low benches close up against the wall, the men were enveloped in smokehouse atmosphere from the fumes of their pipes, and through this fog their eyes gleamed like marbles. Over to one side, near the Sacred Heart, sat Gus Perrault, his black horn-rimmed glasses on his nose, his hair carefully smoothed down, a cigar in his hand. He was listening to Bison Langevin, who was whispering his request and his hopes. He would wrinkle his forehead at moments and at other times would contrive to interject a word or two—"I'm looking after that affair of yours"—between a couple of "Monsieur le Président" preambles on the part of his interlocutor. Broko Lallemand, father of ten children and out of work, was shouting the loudest of any of them. If he had no work, it was because they suspected him of being a blue.

"Pipe down, you fellows! We can't hear what we're saying," Paul Ménard, the wood vendor, called out. He was closing a little deal with Tit-Blanc.

The air was laden with chicanery. Méo Nolin, jealous of the lads who had learned their trade at the technical school, was seeking to pick a quarrel with Bison Langevin. He wished to place his sons in the Parliament Buildings and as a red believed that he was in line for it, but he did not propose to have them taken on as do-nothings, loud talkers who pretended to be plumbers, like Bison, for example. But these bursts of anger died down almost at once. The Mulots were plotting against Denis and were having fun with their "bully," the club's strong man, who was afraid of him. Voices rose and fell, and Tit-Blanc, who believed that he was whispering, was the loudest of any of them.

Denis studied them all, searched their faces, and wondered why it was he felt such a distance between these men and himself. Yet he had hit upon no theory, had formulated no new order of things! Did he at least have convictions? A vague anxiety gripped him, but this environment prevented it from attaining any depth. Did he know where he was going? It tired him to discuss the subject, and far from being drawn to this or that opinion over which the others argued, he was rather inclined to burst them all like bubbles and show up their ridiculous aspects. Did this feeling of superiority come from the fact that he was an educated young man who had studied stenography? A tinkling of the door bell interrupted his reflections.

"Our good Abbé Bongrain! Why, if it isn't Monsieur Pritontin!" exclaimed Bédarovitch. "We don't see very much of you."

There was a silence. The Mulots smiled sarcastically, for this man who had just entered was the most despicable of the Soyeux. The choleric Adolphe Pomerleau, tormented by political worries and a fanatic on the subject of social systems (he went about selling pamphlets for little-known movements), now gave a sigh and, indicating his uncle, Anselme Pritontin, addressed the other members of the group.

"Don't be too hard on him, gentlemen. He has his troubles. He had counted on being appointed churchwarden this year. As if anybody had a better right to the place! A regular churchgoer who never misses mass."

"He's a good citizen but not rich enough for them," said Père Didace Jefferson, who never failed to get in his anticlerical digs, ever since Monsieur le Curé had seemingly gone over to the conservatives.

"The family even made a novena," Adolphe went on. "I am telling you that my aunt wept when she learned he had lost out."

"I can just see him carrying the canopy," put in Denis.

Out at the counter a lively discussion was going on. "Five dollars, Monsieur Pritontin. These chandeliers are not worth even that. No! It's no use; I can't give you a cent more."

"Be fair, Monsieur Bédarovitch. Just look, they're all bronze and each one holds seven candles."

"They're far from being pure bronze—from some impoverished church, you know."

"Take five, Monsieur Pritontin; it's a good price," counselled the Abbé Bongrain in his gruff, good-natured voice.

"But that will not cover half the expense of an altar for my oldest boy. He has a true passion for playing mass. You can tell that the priesthood is in his blood. Now, if the money were to be spent for sinful purposes, such as I could mention—"

"Good evening, my lads," the priest called out as his tall figure appeared on the other side of the partition. The Mulots took off their caps and greeted him cordially, and Gus Perrault left Bison and came over to join him. Pritontin, meanwhile, was casting a wary eye over the room. Piety fairly dripped from this Soyeux, seeming to melt his human personality and replace it with a cloud of dignity. It was distasteful to him to see the Abbé Bongrain slapping the Mulots on the back. He was thinking what his own attitude would be if he were a priest.

The abbé would smile at one of the group, make some bantering remark to another. It was plain to be seen that this strong individual, imperturbable as a Pharaoh of old, was a friend to all of them. He was not a handsome man. His stiff straight hair resembled a horse's mane and could only be close cropped. His features were large and looked as if they had been well kneaded by his big, awkward hands. The eyes alone stood out. Exceedingly mild and filled with blue-grey glints, they were like azure beads that had been inadvertently dropped upon this mass of crude flesh. At first sight, he gave the impression of being a sturdy, square-shouldered, good-hearted child who had nothing to do with the sins of grownups. In the confessional he had a gesture for conferring absolution that could be compared only to a vigorous stroke with an axe, arrested halfway. He loved the workers and his priestly soul conveyed the illusion of a benignant deity who was laying his hands upon you. Hypocrites were frank with him, for he had a look that made them shudder. It was through him that the Mulots formed a conception of their God.

"Everything all right, Denis my lad? And when is Gaston going to open his confectionery shop?" Tit-Blanc pricked up his ears at this.

"Next week, I think."

After whispering to Denis that he too had a fondness for picking apples, the priest went over to Broko Lallemand, who voiced his usual complaint of having no job.

"Gus, can't you do something for him?"

"The deputy has his name on the list," replied the president, with an evasive gesture.

"The black list," said Méo Nolin, who knew all the communist catchwords.

"It's too bad, but that's politics for you," observed Père Didace, a hereditary Liberal.

"With such a government the proletarian will never find work," declared Adolphe Pomerleau, the leatherworker, who was growing a moustache like Hitler's.

"It's the trusts that are devouring us!" cried Bison Langevin.

Adolphe Pomerleau arose majestically and surveyed his audience. He was a small, thin man but he worked his jaws energetically. Running his hand carelessly along the brim of his hat, he began : "It's the capitalists who have pocketed all the money. And where has all that brought us? To economic liberalism!" He stopped here, staring straight in front of him at the horizon of ideas. Then he lowered his head and sat down, resigned to the explosion which he knew his words would produce.

"*Merde!*" shouted Langevin. "You don't know what you're talking about." He at once darted Gus Perrault an apologetic glance, for he had caught the latter's frown.

"Keep still!" the Abbé Bongrain sternly commanded. "You elect governments, so put up with them. A social system is something more complicated than you think." The abbé was at heart a great admirer of Laurier.

Tit-Blanc, who was still drunk, now became aggressive. "You can defend the trusts," he said to the priest; "you're part of them."

This created a chill in the room. The men glanced at one another, knowing that they were about to witness an extermination. The Abbé Bongrain clenched his fists behind his back, but he was quite calm as he bent his gaze on Tit-Blanc.

"Yes," he said, "a trust that twice has saved your job for you. We are members of a trust, but you came to wake us up in the night last year, when your wife was in childbirth."

Pritontin, on the other hand, was thrown into a small convulsion by the insult which had been offered to the Church. He came forward, pale and trembling. It was an outrage, a thing like that. Imperceptible hiccups rose from the bottom of his throat, as if his anger had been cut to shreds by the sorrow that he felt.

"Drunkard that you are! If that isn't a terrible thing, I ask you. And they wonder why religion is on the decline!" He looked to the Abbé Bongrain for support, hoping it would be reported to Monsieur le Curé that he, Anselme Pritontin, the one whom they had passed over, had defended the Church's cause.

"Shut your mouth, you pillar of the Church," said Méo Nolin, who liked to hold forth on justice and equality. "Monsieur l'Abbé can take care of himself. And anyway, you're a Soyeux; you're not one of us."

The priest knew how to deal with such stupidity—a gesture

would suffice; he knew how to speak the word of truth to the poor, while remaining charitable toward this fellow Tit-Blanc. But of a sudden all the energy and ardour that was in him died down and he appeared to be smiling at his own weakness, at the weakness of humankind. He was thinking of the rows down there in the mines at Thetford, when he was earning the money to pay for his schooling. He had also shared the pleasures of his fellow workers, but he had found them vain and had sought and attained beauty as he conceived it. Today as yesterday, his life was made up of the "incomprehensible" that had come to take on a soul. At the seminary they had looked upon him as a social climber in a cassock, this big lad from the mines who in his fits of anger would let drop a "damn" for the simple reason that he had been used to hearing it down under the earth. Was it his fault if such expressions clung to him like twigs even as he mounted heavenward?

He looked the group over, eager to transmit to them all the goodness of the world as seen through his own eyes; he longed to prove to them that they were really big, however small they might feel themselves to be.

Realizing that it was his turn to speak, Père Didace, the club's oldest member, arose. He cleared his throat, batted his lashes, and assumed the tone of voice that he used at banquets.

"Gentlemen," he said, "this is no time for speechmaking. But there is one thing I can tell you : my father was a Liberal, and I have been one for forty years, that is to say, ever since I reached the age of reason."

"It was about time, old Didace," said Gus Perrault ironically, "for you're all of sixty now." Gus was jealous.

"I was born a Catholic, and I'm proud of it. And the Liberal party in its politics is proud to stand side by side with the Church and its principles. Laurier—"

"That's worth a good cigar." Once more Gus interrupted him, for he could scarcely conceal his annoyance at not being the only one to make pompous speeches.

Anselme Pritontin by this time had recovered from his breathless indignation. "Are you going to prevent me from entering my protest against the sacrilegious expression that was used here?" he demanded to know. "The Church is a trust! When it has given us everything, religious education, piety, faith, hope, charity, traditions—"

"And chandeliers," added Tit-Blanc.

This was more than Pritontin's heart could bear. "If you rail against the Church," he burst out, "that's because you are married to a whore. Everybody knows what your Barloute is."

"Sue him; I'm a witness," urged Chaton, for he went in for lawsuits.

"You damned hypocrite!" And with a bellow Tit-Blanc threw himself upon Pritontin.

"In the belly, Tit-Blanc, in the belly, the belly!" cried Denis, getting worked up.

Pritontin was on the verge of fainting. "Monsieur l'Abbé! Save me!"

The priest leaped forward and separated the pair with a grip of steel: "Look here, Monsieur Pritontin, calm yourself, calm yourself; you're too good a citizen to be discussing politics."

Pritontin was ready to weep from anger and impotence. "Ah, no," he said, "this is not going to be the end of it." And he made for the door.

Bédarovitch, whose interest it was to keep on good terms with the priest of the parish, hung on to Pritontin's arm. "I hope you are not offended, Monsieur Anselme. He's an impudent fellow, Tit-Blanc, and he's drunk."

"I trust you will not take what a drunkard says seriously, my dear Monsieur Pritontin," said Gus Perrault, who wished to maintain friendly relations between the Church and the Lapointe Liberal Association. "The Church and the Association." "Gus the President." How well that all sounded! A feeling of grandeur came over him in little waves.

"I am not going to permit my religion to be attacked like that. I have told you so." With this, Anselme Pritontin made a hasty exit; for the Abbé Bongrain was preparing to leave and the aspiring churchwarden wished to arrive at the parish house before the priest did. He accordingly trotted off as fast as he could. He was a man who attributed his own sentiments to all the world, and his latest ambition had so distorted his point of view that he had come to believe anything furthering his own cause belonged to him as of right. He revelled in advance in the grateful look on Monsieur le Curé's face.

Back at the club, the Abbé Bongrain was bidding them good night. "I'm leaving you, my lads; I have three baptisms." He gave Tit-Blanc a long look and went out.

There was silence for a moment, and then Méo Nolin's mocking laugh was heard. "You have nothing to say when *he* looks at you, have you?"

Tit-Blanc swaggered out to the middle of the room. He

tightened his belt. "Do you think it's going to stop there? It's time I was doing something about it."

The others smiled at this. "Are you going to apologize to Pritontin?" Gus wanted to know.

"Me, Tit-Blanc? Apologize? Never! Him and his Church— I'll blow them both up; I'll kill him," he roared, gesticulating wildly.

"What have you done, got yourself a bomb?" asked Méo Nolin sarcastically, taking his cue from Gus.

Tit-Blanc stopped short as if paralysed and regarded them with a fixed stare; then he suddenly burst out enthusiastically: "That's it! I have it! I'll put a bomb under Pritontin's seat at high mass."

"You're drunk, my boy. Why, you'd kill him."

"A big firecracker, rather."

"Don't be a fool, Tit-Blanc. We all know that your mother was reading the *History of the French Revolution* when you were born."

In the face of these objections Tit-Blanc did some thinking and assured himself that his indignation was real. He began gritting his teeth as he thought of Barloute. Him a cuckold? A solemn expression came over his drunkard's face. "I'll show you what nerve is, you Mulots."

"Yeh, but a big cracker like that makes a lot of noise," Méo Nolin reminded him.

"For ten cents I can get an extra big one."

"He wants a silent revolution," said Denis.

There were exclamations on all sides. The slumbering audacity of the Mulots appeared to awaken when confronted by the possibilities inherent in this exploit.

"They sell them for a penny, also. They're not very big but they make a sharp noise, enough to scare you," explained Chaton, who did not like people of quality to see him taking part in disturbances.

"That's all right," agreed Tit-Blanc, "but it must go off."

"How are you going to light it?" asked Bison Langevin. "You'll be up in the front of the church."

"Yes, and there I'll not be able to strike a match." He was hoping now he could get out of the affair, for it occurred to him that he had spoken somewhat hastily.

"Have someone pass you a lighted butt," suggested Denis.

"Now you're talking!" said Méo Nolin. The idea of frightening Pritontin and creating a small scandal was not displeasing to him. "Bidonnet, our sacristan, will be glad to do it. He doesn't care much for Father Folbèche, a question of wages, you know. What's more, the sisters have taken over the laundering of the surplices, and that means the loss of five dollars a week to him."

Tit-Blanc was beginning to fancy the idea again. Suddenly, he raised his head in a manner that seemed to increase his stature. He had made his decision.

"O.K., lads, tomorrow, at ten o'clock mass."

He went out with a firm stride. It was plain that no one took him seriously. Would he carry out this act of bravado? They doubted it very much, knowing him to be drunk. Denis watched him leave and he became angry. Tit-Blanc had aroused in him once more a thirst that would not be quenched. Yet another deception awaited his eager young heart. He ran home to supper now. That girl Lise must find him handsome, strong, not at all like the others. But untouchable so far as his heart was concerned.

His mother was looking for her milk jars.

CHAPTER

III

ANSELME PRITONTIN was walking rapidly, without noticing that from time to time he stubbed his foot against the upraised planks of the sidewalk. He was talking to himself, as if muttering a prayer, evoking in his mind the various expressions of the curé's face in an effort to find the one that seemed to give him the most satisfaction.

"He will be sorry, right enough! To have overlooked a man of my worth! No, it is not remorse that I expect of him. After all, he's not a sinner! It was simply forgetfulness on his part, he was so taken up with his prayers. Holy men do not understand anything about earthly things. He must have been influenced by Zépherin Lévesque, Commander of the Knights of Columbus. Monsieur le Curé will regret it, I'm sure. Oh! I'll forgive him. What will he say to me, anyhow? I'll help him out so that he won't feel embarrassed. He will be horrified when he hears about those communists. The only thing is, will he be so occupied with their seditious activities that he will forget the injustice done to me? I'll remind him of it with my well-known tact. He's a goodhearted man; he won't know how to apologize to me, but I'll make it easy for him, make it seem natural; I'll put him at his ease without his knowing it. After I've gone, he will think of how tactful I was and will be all the more grateful to me. The gratitude of a priest—what an honour for me!"

He fingered the big black beads of his weekday rosary in the depths of his pocket. "I'd like to see Zépherin Lévesque's face when he hears how I've uncovered this nest of sedition. I can just picture it! Why, this is a terrible thing!" He shuddered.

As he reached the parish-house gate, Anselme Pritontin realized that the indignation he had felt at the club a short while ago had disappeared. Here he was, thinking of that communist affair as coolly as if it had been a routine matter! He was alarmed at this. He longed for the sacred fire of inspiration, like a young journalist who wishes his article to show the marks of genius. Anselme stood there, turning about on first one foot and then another as he eagerly sought for the word, the attitude of mind that would put him in a rage. He called up the memory

45

of Tit-Blanc's head, raised it to a level with his gaze (and he was quite tall), looked it in the eyes, dishevelled the hair, and added the drunkard's puffy red face and the alcohol gurgling in his mouth. The hands of the ambitious Soyeux curled like claws about to descend upon Tit-Blanc's cheeks. He thought of the man's strumpet of a wife, that Barloute who in the days gone by had made a mockery of his youthful passion. But it was all in vain. The sacred fire would not come, and Anselme Pritontin was deeply grieved. He tried another method: thought of the obvious decline of the Faith; and this quickly brought him to the conclusion that he was more pious than these wicked ones. But where was his anger? Was he really angry?

There was a sudden gleam of light through the big window of the sacristy, and he caught sight of Bidonnet, who was lighting the tapers of the new candelabra. Pritontin gave a start.

"The jealous wretches! So, I defend religion because it provides me with old chandeliers, because I want to be a church-warden! They are liars, those low-life Mulots! To be a church-warden! To be a churchwarden! Because *they* have no chance of being one! As for me, it is not that I am interested merely in the honour of the thing; my wife, who is in delicate health, has her heart set upon it. That's natural enough, seeing that she has two brothers in holy orders. And then there are the children who must be worthily prepared for the great task. But what they say does not worry me. It will be a pleasure to show that —that fellow Lévesque the stuff that I'm made of."

He rang the bell, anxious, trembling all over for fear he would lose his mood of exaltation before someone came to open the door. He could hear footsteps.

Footsteps could also be heard in the rue Colomb. They fell at first with a regular beat, and then of a sudden the pace quickened, only to slacken once more like the panting spurts of a motor that is out of order. There was a smell of roast beef and fried potatoes in the air. Flies knocked against the gaslights with a buzzing sound, forming a kind of accompaniment to the rhythms of the street. Tit-Blanc was endeavouring to convince himself that he was not drunk.

"If I was drunk, I wouldn't be so brave." He looked down at his feet and was astonished to see how straight he was walking. "I can't back out now, they'd take me for a coward. After all I said I was going to do it, I can't go and tell them it was just to hear myself talk. I swear to God I don't want to do it. He never did anything to me. Nor the priests either. It's damned silly to do a thing like that in church. Let's get it straight. He has a lot of nerve, that swine, going around saying that my wife is a whore! Even if I am poor and take a drop now and then, I can pick a virgin as well as he can. It's true, I always went in for the ones with good figures."

This flattered him. He recalled his conquests of long ago. But another thought came to startle him: "That bastard can't have any proof, can he? Could he have tried to make her before I married her? You never can tell with those pious old hypocrites! Wait till tomorrow, I'll get him off his knees."

Tit-Blanc felt himself to be immense, all-powerful. It seemed to him that all he had to do was give those ramshackle dwellings a blow with his fist and they would come tumbling down like a house of cards. He could feel mounting from the depths of his bosom a thunderous symphony of courage, a vortex of flaming swords that hewed down all obstacles on the path of vengeance. He was conscious of a strange desire to hum, then drew in his lower jaw by way of containing this glorious flood of sensation. Taking the middle of the street, he had the impression that the houses with their lancelike chimneys were an imperial guard in his honour. Then a sharp pain darted through his jaw as he tried to close it. Ah! Denis Boucher's fist. "He'll pay for it, too; the whole family will pay."

This was a great day for him. He had not known that he possessed such will power, such strength and determination. He cast about for those who deserved his vengeance, but his mind was not one of those that can take in a number of problems at the same time. The figures of Pritontin and Denis appeared to him as a pair of Cyclops' eyes which he would have to gouge out before he could reign over the Mulots. He paused in front of the house to admire the way in which it stood at the corner of the street, and gave a smile of satisfaction. "I never thought of it before!"

He entered the house without closing the door, having thrown it open with too violent a gesture. "I am boss here! Jean, here is ten cents for you; go to the hardware store and get me a firecracker. And be quick about it, for I need it right away."

Surprised and annoyed, Jean left without making any reply, for he was too busy thinking of Lise. Féda Colin told her husband he was acting like a crazy man, that everybody was looking at him.

"I've had enough from you," he shouted back at her. "The things I put up with on account of your reputation, Barloute!"

Féda, whom the milkman addressed as "Madame," did not

like to be reminded of this nickname. "My name is Féda, Tit-Blanc, and if there is anything to be said against Barloute, it's your fault."

Tit-Blanc did not feel inclined to argue the point. "We'll settle that later. First, I'm going to see about our shop."

He began measuring the walls, figuring where they would put the counter. His family was disgusted with him, all except his father. Old man Pitou had taken part in the riot of 1917. He had a face like an old quarter-moon; it was almost entirely covered by a dark red splotch while the rest of it bore an inflamed look as from an excess of gaiety.

With a relapse into childhood, he applauded Tit-Blanc's announcement: "A shop! Be sure and lay in some chewing tobacco!"

"Madame Boucher is opening a shop for her Gaston, Féda remarked, with a shrug of her shoulders.

"Well, they're not going to have the laugh on us any longer; they're done with taking the bread out of our mouths. That Joseph Boucher is a hog. He's not satisfied with earning twenty-five dollars a week. Ah, little Mamaine! I'm going to buy you a pretty blue dress like the ones you see in the big grillrooms." And with an air of good-humoured complicity, he pointed a scolding finger at Germaine.

She was indignant. "I don't want anything from you," she replied. "Take it away from poor Gaston—never!"

"That's right," cooed Féda, "you're a girl after my own heart."

"Oh, I know you," said her husband. "You have no nerve; you'll be poor all your lives." He washed his hands of them contemptuously.

"It's not that, Tit-Blanc. The hunchback may put a spell on us. The Good Lord will punish us for it later!"

"You can't do anything these days without having the Lord on your heels. It wasn't that way in our time."

Féda was stupefied. Tit-Blanc was striding up and down the kitchen floor with uneven gait, for it was full of knobs and excrescences. Beer bottles stood guard near the sink. Jean returned and tossed the firecracker on the table. He still looked surprised.

"I'm the boss here!" cried Tit-Blanc as his eye fell on the cracker. He had to shout and assert his authority in order to stifle, to deaden the fear that was rising in him.

By way of calming him, Féda showed him a letter calling attention to the fact that a payment was overdue on the sofa they had bought. He tore it up, for at that moment his mind was on bigger things. She served him a supper of beans and bacon, but he merely drank his tea without tasting any of the food. Germaine was looking at herself in the mirror, arranging her hair like Claudette Colbert. Jean, who was shaving, was so nervous that he cut himself. He was thinking of Lise's smile and how he would soon be seeing it.

Old man Pitou was fidgeting. "When are you going to open your shop?"

Féda shook him. "Be quiet, Grandpa," she said. "I don't want to be late for the bingo game."

She was hurrying as fast as she could, for the chance of winning something always excited her.

Gaston Boucher was supporting his head like a globe in his right hand, his forehead pressed to the windowpane, between the curtains. He was watching Germaine and Féda as they left for the party at the parish house. Denis came out shortly afterward, having been detained by a recalcitrant lock of hair which would not stay in place. The invalid sighed and gazed sadly at the pile of illustrated stories he had taken from the drawer in the belief that Denis was going to read to him.

"Come along with the rest of us, Gaston," his mother begged of him; for she too was anxious to be there in time for the bingo game.

"I don't want to, Mama. I don't understand what they say; they talk too fast."

But he was thinking especially of the curious glances of the girls as he made his way to his seat. He went upstairs, to the hiding place where he kept his savings beneath the hollow image of the Sacred Heart. Slowly and thoughtfully he ran his hand over the banknotes and the silver coins, as one might smooth a fur in thinking of the winter to come. "In a car it won't show, sitting down." He thought of Germaine's smile, of the girls who with their beaux went up to the monument of an evening. He could imagine how the couples conversed, with tender murmurings. Those young fellows walked straight and were not short of breath.

The sick lad stared at the plaster Christ, fancying that it heard what he said. Faith surged up in him like a jet of flame. Was he to belie the impossible? Dropping to his knees, he took his rosary and began saying his beads in an exaggerated whisper. as he had seen old women do in church. His voice was hoarse with exaltation. "Don't be mean, dear God; I want a good body; I want to breathe easy. I want to be straight, I do." He stopped short in desperation and stared at a pencil drawing that he had made of his brother André. He had given him a harsh face with coarse features, rugged as a bit of jagged rock. And the strange part of it was that the portrait resembled André. His mother assured people that she would have sent it to the Beaux-Arts if Gaston had been willing; but then, Flora Boucher was not hard to please and, to hear her tell it, her children were exceptional beings.

Gaston gave an anxious glance through the window to make certain that his hens were in the chicken-house. Then, rummaging in a drawer, he took out Denis' last-year's suit. Slipping into the coat, he climbed upon a chair in front of a mirror to see how he would look if he were big like his brother. He found that the coat was too long and there were hollow places on the right side, under his sunken shoulder. That was on account of the hump. Realizing this, he made a wry face. The cuffs came down almost over his fingertips, but there was an air of distinction about that, he thought. He made an effort to straighten up and only succeeded in making his heart beat more rapidly. Gazing at his hair, straight as stubble, he wondered if some day it would be curly like Denis'. He had large and beautiful eyes, but it seemed to him that they were too big and the lashes too long for one as small as he; the effect was ugly.

Suddenly he turned pale. His hands and feet were becoming cold, and then a clammy flush came over him; his nails were blue.

He gave a raucous, choking cry : "Papa, Papa, hot, cold, hot, cold." He had not had time to take off the coat.

His father came running, throwing his pipe from him on the way. "My God, what's the matter with you now? What a life!"

Gaston was flapping his arms like a scarecrow, for the bird of death was hovering near. "I'm going to die, Papa, I'm going to die—I'm afraid."

"Come, Flora, come quick!"

Gaston was suffocating. Joseph chewed the hairs of his moustache, feeling faint and at a loss what to do. Putting on her hat and scolding the invalid at the same time, Flora hastened up the stairs. She acted as if this attack were no more than a child's whim. But while she made light of it, these chills and fevers that her son suffered were nevertheless beginning to alarm her. "Don't be playing thermometer, silly boy," she said. And pinching his cheek, she made him lie down. Joseph suggested calling a doctor.

"And throw a dollar out the window? I have my medicine book here. And anyway, you can see it's only a nervous spell. I had the same thing when Denis was born."

"But look, his hands are blue!"

"His veins are clogged; his blood doesn't circulate well. What he needs is a physic." She became angry. "Are you trying to find ways of keeping me from going to the bingo party? You're hateful, that's what you are; you're jealous. What do you want me to do, slave my life away? You know very well, if it was anything serious, I'd be the first one to send for the doctor."

Gaston was recovering now. Greatly disappointed, he took off the coat that was too big for him. Joseph thought that he had put it on to keep warm. With a sob, the hunchback turned his face to the wall. "I've had all I can stand, all I can stand!"

"Don't be getting ideas in your head, my child. Go to sleep, will you? Mama's going to win a dollar for you at bingo. Lucky boy, he's going to have a business of his own, and here he's crying!"

Gaston had his own vague thoughts concerning this state of infancy in which his parents kept him swaddled.

Denis stiffened his muscles and assured himself that his suit fitted him well. Catching sight of Jean and the two Langevins, he imagined they were talking about the way he was dressed. That was all they were good for: to concern themselves with such trifles. Impatient to realize his ambitions, Denis already, by way of showing his superiority, had clothed himself in the prestige of his future success. It was not that he saw any grandeur in being a stenographer and having gone to a private school! His vanity in this regard was a thing of the past. But his eagerness to live gloriously led him to glean from the future all the most likely sprouts and transplant them into his as yet untilled present; he would enjoy for a day their promising verdure and then on the morrow would despair at seeing them wither so quickly. In his imagination he upset all rules and achieved the impossible; he conquered the world and claimed his destiny like a god. As for his true successes, which were those of the ordinary youth, he found them disillusioning, and would lament the mediocrity of others, whom he held responsible for the fact that the flood of light he knew his own bosom contained was only manifested by the tiniest of gleams.

If other men were so small of stature, it was because they could not come to know what it was by which they lived. It was Denis who, at St Joseph, kept the shop of truth, and he would dispense his wares from time to time in return for a little admiration. As for women, they belonged to another world, and he was contemptuous of the weapons they wielded. He who demanded intelligence despised the only intellectual ones he knew among them. They crammed themselves with Delly and Bourget and would discuss a work like *Divorce* as one does theology after the sermon at nine o'clock mass. He found such discussions vain and empty. He would break in upon them by saying: "I know some books that are really fine!" And he would stalk away.

This kept him in a manner shut in upon himself, and he would assume a haughty air to cover his inability to put into words the things that he felt so deeply. Most of the girls, like the Mulots in general, read only the cheap popular fiction, the *romans-feuilletons*, and were interested solely in discovering the means of snaring a suitor—"and they were married not long afterward." He did not propose to let himself be hooked. They had become his enemies, a threat to his undefined goal. Convinced that marriage would be the prison house of his destiny, that high destiny that he envisaged, he looked upon a woman's face as an epitaph, displayed in the course of chance meetings with the sex. He preached freedom and, seeking to identify himself with the masterpieces that he read, ignored the fertile and spontaneous resources of his own being. It revolted him to see Jean so occupied with his toilet this evening. He felt a savage desire to go over and rumple his hair, muss him up, put knots in his necktie. He was in a cruel humour.

"Why, you have powder on your face! And that tie! Look, why don't we go for a walk? It's foolish to stay indoors on a night like this."

The suggestion did not appeal to Jean. He was near to telling Denis that this sudden fancy for a stroll came from a lack of money. But he preferred to go on speaking of his toilet, even though it made him blush. "I shaved myself this evening. My beard is so stiff. Do you soften yours up first?"

He kept moving his hands restlessly in his pockets, as if obsessed with the idea that someone was trying to prevent him from looking his best for once. He did feel, it is true, that it was rather daring for him, a worm-vendor, to dress up in such a manner on a weekday evening. But his yellow polka-dot tie was pretty, wasn't it? Lise would appreciate it later on. Would she notice the powder on his face? He blamed Denis for his uneasiness—Denis, who overwhelmed him with his air of authority, who gave him his dreams. The Langevins were remarking that they would like to see Lise again. Feigning astonishment, Denis toyed with the watch chain that hung from the pocket of Jean's coat.

"Ah!" he said, "I understand now. Symbol of slavery!" His tone was contemptuous. "Go on, you're a budding Pritontin. Ah! you heard about your father?"

"Leave my father out of it. He has nothing to do with it. You have to be well dressed when you sit in the reserved seats. It costs ten cents more—"

Jean had struck home and he knew it as he saw Denis turn pale. Reflecting that Lise was the cause of this meanness on his part, he hated her. Nevertheless, the happiness she had given him with her first smile was something that he preserved intact; it was something that Denis could neither divine nor lay hands on. The thing that humiliated him, rather, was his bashfulness, his undoubtedly ridiculous bearing ever since he had fallen in love.

Disgruntled because he lacked the necessary ten cents, Denis made up his mind that he would get himself a reserved seat. He said nothing, however, and Jean was relieved. Life was suddenly fair again, and it was with real animation that he threw back a stray ball from the Mulots who were playing in the street. Going over to lean against the embankment, Denis coldly eyed the girls who passed. They either smiled at him or treated him as a show-off. He was surprised to find himself flattered by such homage and resolved that he would yield only to their bodily charms, a weakness which he ascribed to those passions that a young man naturally felt. A man he assuredly was, for today he no longer blushed as he thought of a naked woman. Whereas, the year before—

Jean was playing with the coins in his pocket. He was somewhat concerned. Was it out of contempt that Denis kept silent? He went over to him.

"Will you come along? I'll pay the difference. You needn't be huffy about it. I've had a good week."

"All right, give it to me; I'll pay you back fifteen." He had a vision of a multitude of empty milk jars as a source of independence. He gave Jean a furious look. "Well, are you through patting that money of yours?"

"Look! There he goes!" cried the Langevins. Denis did not turn and Jean appeared to be more interested in Méo Nolin's daughter as Zépherin Lévesque went by at the wheel of his automobile, the newest in the parish. A man who was fond of show, he drove slowly, and the lads had a good opportunity to gaze at Lise, but she seemed unaware of their presence. Jean made excuses for her to himself. She would prefer to see him alone, he felt sure. He was fortifying himself against the sarcastic remarks that Denis would probably make. The latter now proposed a business arrangement, thinking thereby to kill the thought of love.

"She should be able to get her father to buy his worms from you. He's a great fisherman. That would mean one customer the less for Chaton." Denis' mind, however, was not on what he was saying, for the glimpse he had had of Lise's eyes had brought him a feeling of tender melancholy, of the sort that one experiences in the silence of open spaces, beneath a tranquil sky.

Jean was insulted. He had rather expected Denis to adopt a scoffing, unceremonious attitude toward Lise. But such a suggestion as this! He was astonished that he had never before been ashamed of the traffic in worms. He had never thought that a woman would be able to disgust him with it. Carried away by the new and ardent song in his heart, he had already broken with his past. Embarked in a strange boat, he had shoved off from the familiar bank that was the Jean Colin of yesterday: the Jean Colin who dreamed of exercising his muscles, of obtaining a monopoly of the trade in angleworms, and of achieving victories over the Mulots while Denis applauded.

The happiness of first love, a happiness he was only beginning to know, had come to disturb all this. It was senseless to speak to Lise of the great and lofty things of which he dreamed and at the same time to tell her, in the intervals of lovemaking, how he dealt in these curious little animals, so fat and shiny, that served as bait for fishes. Was he to explain to her how they slipped through your fingers, fled up your sleeve, and came out at your neck?

Was he in love with Lise? Since when? Was it, then, an accomplished fact, something that had already taken place inside himself? As he looked at Denis, he realized that his friend's rage, his gibes, had put the girl in his heart as no smile of hers could have done. Ah, to be able to rid himself of this Boucher, who was like a cover to his life, holding him down to earth when he wished to soar.

"Why, Monsieur Pritontin!" exclaimed Denis. "How comes it you're on foot? That's not in the least like a churchwarden. Just look at Monsieur Lévesque. He's somebody, he is!"

Anselme Pritontin pretended to be indifferent and ducked in time to miss the ball the Mulots threw at him. He smiled craftily, for his was a joy above all the automobiles in this world. He was dreaming of how surprised these wretches would be, tomorrow at high mass and next week, when they learned that he had purchased the Abbé Trinchu's big Buick. He would arrive before Zépherin and would park in front of the main entrance. He would take the priests out riding. . .

The young men now fell into step with their elders. The Langevins, who had never sat in the reserved seats, could not wait to beard the Gonzagues, those pious ones who constituted the élite among the Soyeux. They could be seen upon the stage, congratulating Lise upon the part she was to take in the program. Would she tell them of her adventure that afternoon? At the moment, she was preoccupied with her curls, her lace ruffles, and the impression she would make upon Monsieur le Curé.

People were walking briskly toward the parish hall, the women gesticulating excitedly as they spoke of their luck at the last bingo party. The dignified Soyeuses, with mincing steps, took the sidewalk across the way. The meeting never began until they were there, since they occupied the front rows. They would hesitate for some little while before entering, with a show of reluctance, for there was a law against bingo games. The Mulotes on the other hand, were delighted with the prospect of a wholesale raid by the police. They could picture themselves up at the city hall, chattering noisily and stabbing the gendarmes in the back with their hatpins. And the Abbé Bongrain would be there, too! What a picnic and what a babel of tongues! Although the game was forbidden all over town, St Joseph's parish hall continued to hold parties and the Mulots encouraged the Curé to defy the authorities. They expected that the law would swoop down upon them, but the police avoided this corner as they would the plague.

Bingo was especially popular with young married couples, concerned with furnishing their homes, and many of them had here laid in a supply of bedspreads, flatirons, pillows, and other accessories. The majority of the men who came merely smoked their pipes and discussed the church debt. For most of them it was an opportunity to look at other men's wives in a way that would not "start something." There were not so many of these skirt chasers, after all, but there were always some who waited at the rear of the hall for the evening to start so that they might pick out the group of women that appeared to offer the most diversion. There was Bidonnet, the sacristan, who possessed an Adam's apple so enormous that when he took out his handkerchief one wondered what it was he was going to wipe. A frank, good-natured chap, always ready to unburden himself, he went about picking up bits of gossip here and there with a sacerdotal ardour. The elderly Mulots, who cared neither for parish parties nor for bingo, had gone to discuss politics and play cards at Bédarovitch's place.

Many young women from other parishes were present this evening, for in addition to bingo there was a special attraction: the "Theater of the Air" company was putting on a performance of *La Buveuse de Larmes*, and those who felt sentimentally inclined and were anxious to glut their appetite for passionate melodrama had turned out in considerable numbers to witness a piece which less emotional temperaments might find a little ridiculous. Denis had said that he was not interested in girls, but he had taken up a position at the edge of the sidewalk so that they could see him to full advantage—his greatest advantage being that they did not matter to him. Occasionally one of them would give him a wink, whereupon he would turn to his friends and say : "Did you see that?"

Then they all went upstairs, for the parish hall was on the second floor, above the church. The edifice as a whole had the appearance of a warehouse to which a belfry had been added. The parish was a poor one, and they had not as yet been able to complete the building of this temple, which had nothing substantial about it except its foundations. At the door a group of urchins were waiting for a chance to slip in without paying. A little later, after the performance had started, they would be raining kicks upon the thin doors, which must have been made of special wood, since they had been withstanding this assault for some ten years now and still were capable of a vigorous resonance. These shameful carryings-on had given the St Joseph parishioners a reputation for being badly brought up. The Soyeux, horrified by it all, blamed the Mulots. Finally, as a last resort, they had stationed a gendarme at the door; but he was a symbolic gendarme and an art lover. Passionately fond of the drama, he always sympathized with the villains and became so interested that he forgot his duties. At that point, Pritontin would come trotting out, and in winter time the small lads would throw snowballs at him.

Denis and the others now entered the hall. The ceilings were dirty and cobwebs hung from the corners of the room.

"Be quiet, you !" Pritontin warned them. He knew them well, for ever since they were children they had been misbehaving in the parish hall.

They gave him a haughty stare. "An usher !" The vendor of

56

chandeliers opened his eyes at this. "Here are our tickets; look at them!"

"What's back of all this?" muttered Pritontin, suspiciously. "Gonzague!" he called, "find them some seats."

One of the Gonzagues came up, with a gesture of repugnance. There were a dozen of his kind there. They were known as "Gonzagues," or "the curé's pets," and it was looked upon as a natural thing that they should have for their pastor a pious attachment that amounted to a kind of adoration. For the most part they were solemn-faced, serious-minded young men who no longer attended the seminary. People never said of them "They've finished the seminary," but "They don't go to the seminary any more." Denis insisted that they were too flabby to withstand the system of education. And Monsieur le Curé, who paid certain bills-rendered to cover their scholastic expenses, had made it plain to them that they were wasting his money, since they did not have it in them to become priests like Monsieur Bongrain nor colonizers like the famous curé Monsieur Labelle. This passion for the seminary, however, was soon extinguished in the young Soyeux. It was certain rumours going the rounds concerning the probable canonization of a young St Joseph seminarist who had died under peculiar circumstances that had been responsible for the vogue.

The Gonzagues did not care for Boucher and his friends who, each in his own way, represented all that they had spoiled their lives by giving up. Denis and his kind were supremely clever at getting out of scrapes, whereas the spirit of submission, stigma of the schools, was spread all over the faces of these pious young men, like a rotten fruit.

When Jean indicated that they wished to be seated in the row behind the one reserved for the guests of honour where Lise sat, the usher glared at them but restrained himself. "Take those seats; they are just as good."

"Come on! We're sitting here," announced Denis.

They made a great deal of noise as they sat down and the scandalized Soyeux began whispering among themselves. Flora Boucher was proud and Barloute Colin could see in the situation possibilities of getting herself talked about. The Gonzagues, who had decided that Lise was one of them, had gathered at the rear of the room and were talking matters over, nervously, as if they had discovered a plot. Hearing the commotion, Lise, like the little girls of the quarter, yielded to her curiosity and looked back to see what was going on. She had been well reared; but her instruction in good manners had been purely theoretical,

57

and so she instinctively followed the fashion of St Sauveur before she had time to think what the manuals of etiquette had to say on the subject.

Then it was she caught sight of Denis. He did not take his seat at once but stood there arrogantly looking the crowd over. This, as Lise saw it, gave him an air of distinction; for she had acquired a false conception of what constituted greatness and expected it to be accompanied by a certain amount of disdain. From then on, she vainly sought an excuse for turning her head once more. Besides, there was that ribbon on her shoulder that would not stay in place and kept tickling her ear.

"Nervous?" her mother inquired fussily. Madame Lévesque was enjoying the jealousy of Eugénie Clichoteux, former queen of the young Soyeuses, for Lise—

Denis, who always became nervous when he felt a crowd behind him, was talking in a loud voice. "I don't like your being so familiar with her," he was saying.

"Sh-sh-sh! Not so loud!" Jean begged him. "She's not going to give us away. You can see for yourself she's not that kind."

"We're not so interesting when we have our faces washed, observed Robert, who was a sensible lad.

Lise had recognized them, but it was Denis with his haughty air who fascinated her. The others, now that they were neat and well combed, lacked that originality she had at first discovered in them. To her romantic mind, heroes who felt the need of improving their appearance when they knew someone was watching them lost much of their worth. Jean may have believed that his handsome brown suit, the close-shaven down on his face, and his yellow tie with the green dots gave him an advantage, but for her all this merely stifled the true character she had found in his oil-streaked face; it conferred upon him a mediocre appearance, that of a vagabond in Sunday clothes. He was envious because she looked at Denis, but thought that she was trying to steal a glance at him out of the corner of her eye as women have a way of doing.

Upon the stage, the image of the future church, painted upon the wrinkled curtain, appeared about to fall in ruins before that edifice had been erected. There were a number of peep-holes through which the actors' noses could be seen protruding beneath the ravelled threads. The Deputy now arrived, followed by Gus Perrault, and the audience rose and applauded as Monsieur le Curé smilingly seated them at his side. The worthy priest then let his gaze wander over the room and bit his lip with satisfaction as he noted that it was filled to overflowing.

In his eyes, it took on the aspect of a purse stuffed with money to the bursting point.

A few Soyeuses were still coming in. It was eight-thirty, and Jean-Paul Labrie, the stage manager, rapped three times with a hammer that belonged to his father, the carpenter. The sacristan's eldest son Jacques, being a privileged character, was in charge of the curtain. The noise died down with the lights and the *Buveuse de Larmes* made her appearance. In the first act, there were two dead and one wounded. Monsieur Pritontin, who was a great lover of dramatic art, deplored the fact that the blank cartridge, being too damp, had failed to go off. Those who prided themselves on being critics studied the moustaches to see how lifelike they were. Denis wished that he could have Messalina's red mane, to set fire to. He liked to give the impression of being a violent lad, violence to him being a semblance of power.

"I'd wring her neck!" he said, in a voice that all could hear.

Madame Langevin, a big woman who sympathized with the "innocent" ones in the play, agreed with him and went him one better: "I'd do worse than that to her, so I would! I'd scratch her eyes out!"

By the time the first act drew to a close, all the terrifying words that had been spoken, the shrieks of vengeance, the scenes of sublime and tender affection, and the cry of "wicked adultress!" had made as deep an impression upon the audience as a river upon a bed of clay. Handkerchiefs fluttered like distress signals, profound sighs came forth from tightened throats, eyes filled with tears, and hearts that life had hardened took their humid revenge.

"It's too bad!" whimpered Barloute, mingling remorse with her tears. She thanked God she had been spared any suicides in her family.

"It's a good thing we know it's not true," remarked Flora, reassuringly.

"Don't all cry at once or you'll drown that 'drinker of tears,'" was Denis' ironic comment.

"Such impudence!" cried Madame Langevin. She was indignant. "He can't appreciate it, it's too beautiful!"

The Deputy, who had a big belly, kept tapping it with his program as he surveyed Lise with a friendly gaze. "It would be very easy to find a place for her at Parliament House, Monsieur Lévesque."

"I have no doubt of that, with your influence. But I prefer to keep her at home."

"Oh," said the Deputy, "I don't have so much influence as people think. I like them to tell me that I do; but you can imagine what it is, with everyone expecting me to use it in his behalf. The influence is not equal to the affluence."

They both laughed loudly at this witticism. Pinasse Charcot, commander of the parish guard and an enemy of Zépherin Lévesque, the honorary commandant, was watching the latter's manœuvres with a spiteful look in his eye. He was a Conservative and was anxious for the next elections to come around so that he could give his Deputy the boot. Grondin, a tavern keeper and a timid Liberal, was endeavouring to find out if he would be able to obtain a licence for the coming year. The Deputy reassured him.

"I have slain my last two lovers!" screamed Messalina on the stage.

With this terrible announcement the act ended, and a wave of indignation rolled up toward the curtain as it fell. Monsieur le Curé made a wry mouth. To his mind the piece was not an illustration of the divine grace of mercy. The author of the adaptation was an elderly ham who, after having had his fling at acting, had gone in for the manufacture of explosives. He now came forward to speak in humble terms of all the sleepless nights which he had spent upon his task. He had been in Hollywood ten years ago, following a dramatic debauch at the popular theatre of St Sauveur where he had set four hundred and fifty good housewives to bawling, and he let it be inferred that he would be leaving for Paris the following week to receive his laurels from the French Academy. Denis pricked up his ears at this, for the mention of literature awakened an instinct within him. In his opinion, the fellow was a mediocre hack, and he shuddered at the thought of the honours that were coming to him.

Lise was nervously rolling a sheet of music in her hand. For her it was a great occasion. She had sung in the convent, but there had been no deputy to feast his eyes upon her and no lads like Denis Boucher to listen to her. She was vaguely yet distinctly conscious of the difference. The commandant Pinasse, a jolly fellow, was master of ceremonies. As Lise saw him going up on the stage, she had a clammy feeling.

"It gives me great pleasure to introduce to you the daughter of our churchwarden and honorary commandant. She is going to warble for us 'Les Figues—'" He bent over toward Lise: "What's the name of it?"

" 'Les Filles de Cadiz.' "

" 'Les Figues de Cadice,' ladies and gentlemen. And I may tell you that she is no Bolduc."

The speaker's stentorian voice filled Zépherin Lévesque with rage. He himself suffered from chronic laryngitis, which was a great handicap in competing with Pinasse for command of the guard. He made a grimace. How vulgar the fellow was! He could see a kind of vengeance in this inept announcement.

Eugénie Clichoteux, in the midst of other young Soyeuses, was chattering away. The group laughed discreetly at Pinasse's little jest.

Very pale despite the fact that her face was burning, Lise came near stumbling as she mounted the steps to the stage. Her mother, wishing to make herself conspicuous, held her back for a moment and adjusted a fold of her dress. Then all was silence. Jean was listening to his own heart as it beat an accompaniment; it seemed to him that it rivalled in tempo the fingers of the guest organist at high mass. As for the Langevin twins, they would have liked to take this girl upon their shoulders and bear her in triumph. Had she not provided them with a hiding place? Her voice was one made for telling falsehoods to gendarmes.

That voice now rose crystal-clear, like a spring bubbling up in the sunlight. It was in turn coquettish, light and playful, sad, and then of a sudden, violent, detaching itself from the piano like water playing over moss-covered stones. It would run off in trills, only to dissolve in a charming musical lament. Like the swallow's flight, it was now capricious, gently palpitating, and again would hover in the form of a sigh that seemed to be the echo of some magic song the angels sang. Denis' face was frozen with surprise. He had come forward and taken Lise's vacant chair. For him her beauty was lifted like a flag above this exhibition of the ridiculous. Jean noted the effect upon his friend and was proud that Denis was so interested; but when he saw him applauding frantically, he became uneasy, fearing he had already been dispossessed. It reminded him of the apples they stole that were just beginning to ripen.

"Whoopee!" Robert burst out, "what do you think of a girl like that hiding us from the cops?"

Jean's mouth was dry. What would Denis have to say? He would not say anything, for he was planning to steal her, Jean was sure of it.

Barloute Colin thought it was all very beautiful, quite "classic," for her Jean was in a reserved seat tonight and she must live up to him. Flora Boucher played the sophisticate.

61

"You can tell she's been well trained. Ah, the opera! Joseph used to take me often when I was a girl."

"She seems to me a little stuck-up," said Germaine Colin doubtfully. At family gatherings she sang the love songs she had heard on the radio, and the walls of her bedroom were covered with the photographs of popular singers. "If they don't call her back for an encore, we can start the bingo game. Oh, momsy, I didn't tell you, did I? That's Jean's girl friend." And she went on to relate the little adventure of that afternoon.

"Well," replied Barloute proudly, "I always did say Jean would never marry a girl without a stitch to her back. But one so high up in the world as that!"

"Denis surely couldn't have been there," said Flora, with a note of assurance in her voice. She too, as a young mother (she regarded herself as young), was proud of her son and of his appeal to women, so long as he did not make use of it. The thought of such a thing was sufficient to make her heart beat faster, as if he had in reality made a masculine conquest.

"How are your lad's hens coming along?" Bidonnet, with the usual expansive look on his face, wanted to know.

"They're laying very well. Did you hear that Gus Perrault won the last lottery?"

"It's always those that don't need it," complained Madame Langevin. Concerned with placing her sons in the Parliament Buildings, she was convinced that Flora had gone out of her way to flatter Perrault in order to prepare the ground for Denis, who was trained for office work.

"They tell me you're going to open Gaston's shop very soon?" inquired Barloute anxiously.

"Monday night we're buying the lumber for the partition. Our place is so conveniently located and I know everybody. We'll serve ice cream, soft drinks, and cigarettes—just light refreshments, you understand. He gave me such a fright again tonight. If I can only win!"

"Ladies and gentlemen, the bingo game is starting! Have your tickets ready, and please don't throw your beans on the floor!"

"Let's go on back," said Denis, who did not care for games of chance.

"We'd better stay here," Jean protested uncertainly. "We'll disturb people."

"You're becoming very polite all of a sudden," said Robert with a smile. "Don't worry, your seat's reserved."

Stationing themselves near the entrance, they began talking

of Tit-Blanc's scheme. Jean now understood why it was he had been sent to purchase a firecracker. He thought his father was doing a rash thing but excused him on the ground that Tit-Blanc was youthful in spirit. Moreover, his attention was somewhere else.

"Look," he said, "the Gonzagues are going over to sit in our seats!"

"Shall we throw them out?" asked Jacques, who wished to show Lise was a fighter he was.

"No," replied Denis, "let's watch them. I have an idea that you'll get further with her than they will."

Colin looked at his friend closely to see if he was joking. Denis had an ironic smile, but he was laughing at the Gonzagues. Jean felt himself a man, one who could have all the women in the world if he liked. The truth was, these pious young men, in their efforts to make an impression upon a girl as well educated as Lise and one who sang so well, were comical enough with their mincing little gestures and mannerisms. Simperingly they passed their cigarettes, exchanged their bingo tickets, and indulged in all sorts of affectations, accompanied by cluckings of the tongue that ended in small bursts of laughter. Nearly all of them were haberdashery clerks and extremely conscious of the clothes they wore. The tallest and palest of the lot was bending over Madame Lévesque's shoulder to inquire about the result of her last euchre party.

"Just look at that big lummox; he wants to have her!" Jean was indignant. He had a vision of himself giving the Gonzague a terrible thrashing, one that would take all the hide off him.

"Bingo, ladies and gentlemen. All tickets are sold."

With forefinger and thumb raised, the women waited eagerly for their numbers to be called as they darted keen, threatening glances at the figures that were not upon their tickets. Flora Boucher, Madame Langevin, Féda, Germaine, some of the other housewives, and the sacristan—all hovered over that first row of five digits like beasts ready to pounce upon their prey. Those who had heart trouble or were more excitable had a hand to their bosom. The only sound was that made by their rapid breathing and the snapping of the beans used in indicating their numbers.

"Thirty-six, thirty-six," called the announcer in his matter-of-fact voice.

It was an English circus that had brought bingo into fashion, at the last provincial fair. The womenfolk were always blaming the announcer for their bad luck and having him changed every week. The passion for gambling aroused the primitive in them, and toward the end of the game half-stifled exclamations were to be heard from some of them while others expressed themselves in animated and colourful language.

"Stir them up a bit, will you?" called out Chaton's wife, who could tell a dirty story better than anybody in the parish. "It's always the same numbers!"

"There are only seventy-five of them," was the announcer's tart reply.

"I don't seem to have any luck," remarked Madame Langevin, becoming discouraged.

"My numbers are 'all shot,'" said Germaine, resentfully.

"I had a good card three weeks ago," Féda informed them.

Flora said nothing.

The sacristan was depressed. "I haven't had a single number that came out. It's disgusting!"

"Quiet! You can't hear what he's calling."

"What luck!" Flora suddenly exclaimed. "*Mon Dieu*, I've got one! Seventy-two! O St Anthony and St Gaston, make it come out!"

"Did you get a good one, lady?" asked Bidonnet. "Is she a lucky woman! She always wins. But then, she follows my way of playing it."

"*Soixante-et-douze*, seventy-two!" sang out the announcer.

"Bingo! Bingo!" shouted Madame Boucher triumphantly.

There was a great hubbub, with Flora insisting that she would take a hall lamp. Above the exclamations of chagrin on the part of those who saw their chances vanishing, the announcer's voice was audible: "Spread them out! We're going to check."

"It *would* have to be her again!" said the jealous mother of the Langevin twins.

The Latruche sisters, who disliked Flora because her raffling of Gaston's hens offered them competition in the sale of tickets from house to house, now came up to examine her numbers and make sure that she really was the winner. Flora herself was all smiles. She felt so kind and charitable at that moment. Then Féda, who was near-sighted, chanced to look down at her own number. Her eyes and mouth grew round with surprise.

"Stop!" she cried. "I have it, too! I had it before she did. I never noticed."

"Bingo! Bingo!" screamed Germaine and Féda in concert.

"It's a little late, Madame," said the man who was doing the checking.

64

"What do you mean, a little late? Just because we're not educated like some other people, do you think you can make fun of us? That prize belongs to me!"

"It's no use, Madame Colin. It will do you no good to shout. The prize is mine and I'm going to keep it." And Flora aggressively pressed the lamp to her bosom and at the same time thought of Gaston, to whom she had promised a dollar.

"It's the first time I've won. Do you think I'm going to let you rob me of it? Never!"

"Will you take a necktie, Madame?"

"One worth thirty sous," said Germaine disdainfully; for she had a sense of values.

The Latruche spinsters encouraged Féda with a glance. She now recalled Tit-Blanc's insult and blew her nose, tearfully. "You'll pay for that, Boucher," she said.

"You can call me Madame. Yes, Madame. We didn't get married in a hurry, Barloute."

"I noticed you had them fast enough!" screamed Germaine.

Féda felt her fingers curling. "Policemen," she said, "don't come around talking to me for hours at a time."

Pinasse Charcot with his commandant's voice broke in upon them.

"Quiet! Second round."

The silence was unbroken. Asking Madame Langevin to watch her number for her, Flora hastened to Bédarovitch's place to sell him the lamp before he closed. He would, as usual, offer a dollar for the grand prize and later resell it to the parish committee at $1·25, the regular price being $1·50. On the other hand, a number of housewives who frequented bingo parties and kept their prizes as trophies had parlours that resembled a lamp manufacturer's warehouse. These lamps were never lighted but were displayed to visiting relatives from Montreal. The result was an epidemic of lamps consigned to perpetual darkness, amounting to a sort of strike against the light company.

The second act was about to begin, and the Gonzagues still occupied the seats they had usurped. The friends now came forward with Denis in the lead. He gave a resounding kick to the first chair in the row, and Lise, turning, caught sight of him and was at once thrilled and flustered. Pretending to be astonished, the Gonzagues hastily decamped. Then it was that Jean realized he was no longer a vendor of worms. His gestures were expressive of a new and delightful sense of power; he felt that he could sweep everything before him if he chose.

"Will you smoke, Denis?"

"No, thanks; I don't use tobacco."

The curtain went up. The *Buveuse de Larmes* was now to receive her punishment. Denis had a feeling of lassitude. Was he the jeering lad of a short while ago? How did the world really look to him, anyhow? He wished he were somewhere else, in some Eden where he knew no one and where there would be nothing to do but feel sorry for himself, or rather for his past. Nonchalantly, he contemplated the back of Lise's white neck—how white it was!—as revealed in gleams and flashes between her dark, wavy curls. He imagined her as being a stranger to her sex, a woman in body only. The two of them would flee this filthy suburb, would go soaring up to the magnificent clouds above, where there would be no question of rising any higher. And then, in turn, he felt a great desire to have her fall in love with Jean and to render Jean wholly his debtor in this regard.

There are certain egoists whose need of approbation finds its first expression in the temptation to give all. Men excuse themselves for their meanness on the ground that it begins, often, as an act of tenderness, an emotion that grips them and, for a moment, takes them far from all the pettiness of life. It was this impulse to give generously what he looked upon as better than himself that Denis was experiencing. He was not thinking of Jean. The latter's frank, submissive nature and instinctive goodheartedness along with a certain weakness of will had led Denis to adopt him as his friend. What he did not realize was that Jean was for him a sort of intellectual prop, strengthening the edifice of self-pride that he had built up. The Langevins were no more than spectators. He was indifferent to them. He did not even want their admiration any longer, did not care to astonish them. Of little worth in themselves, they served at best as listeners, and it was for this reason alone that he bestowed a little friendship upon them, holding them in reserve until his crowning success should be achieved.

"Are you coming?" he said, rising abruptly from his seat. "I've had enough of this stupidity!"

Jean was stunned. "Are you crazy? I'm staying till the end. You don't pay twenty-five cents for nothing!"

"I understand!" said Denis contemptuously. Colin had a feeling that he was not equal to his new-found love.

"You die, atrocious Messalina!" cried the avenger as he plunged his dagger. "You who have left a trail of broken hearts and ruined lives!"

The audience applauded enthusiastically, deliriously. Denis

noisily kicked over his chair and shook his fist at the crowd. "Imbeciles! Imbeciles, all of you!" he shouted.

"What insolence! Quiet! Sit down!"

"Denis, listen to me!" his mother begged him.

The Gonzagues who were tiptoeing about the side of the room now gathered in a little group and ceased talking, appearing to be very intent upon the play as they saw Denis coming toward them threateningly. Almost running, he went down the aisle that led to the entrance. The silence of the outdoors, in which he hoped to find a refuge, was calling to him, and in his eyes was the feverish flame that one associates with heroic fugitives. A fierce joy welled up in him as he ran on—for he was running now—without looking back at the rows of faces foundering in mediocrity on either side of him. He all but knocked over the Abbé Trinchu and a couple of fawning churchwardens who were hanging around the priest. The doors banged behind him and, out of breath, he found himself alone with the sleeping city. Clenching his fists, he took a long, deep breath. The ramshackle houses, spangled with light, appeared to stretch away into the infinite, all the way to the mountains. Only the plaintive sound of automobile horns moaning in the distance came to disturb the retreat of the worker who had no car.

"How happy I am!" he exclaimed, running his hand through his hair.

He dropped down, a satisfied smile on his lips. His youth! What strength lay in that! The mediocrity he had just blotted out by his flight, these shanties stretched out at his feet and less ugly than usual in the darkness—they were but an unpleasant memory, the life of every day in all its littleness. His restive, stubborn youth had suddenly given a thrust like a battering-ram. Laying low the stupidity of men, it had plunged forward into silence, had become aerial, the master of its superior fate. Was not this the moment for him to be going away across the damp fields, taking the trees for ghosts and being afraid of them as when he was a child? A shadow came drifting over his shoulder. Lise? Yes, he would take her along. He would embrace her madly. But he would make sport of her— How then? What kind of madness was this, anyway?

He rose, as if to shake himself free. Was it, then, a woman who was at the bottom of this splendid mood of exaltation? No, no, he was not going to flounder there as the others did! Nervously, he walked through the deserted streets, telling himself over and over that this vision was but the accidental result of his overheated imagination. But those dark red lips of hers defied all bravado on his part; they made their way into his virgin thoughts, overthrowing all his pride, all his rancour, transforming them into a strange, unwonted thirst.

Deeply distressed, he wandered about on the sidewalks. There was the school where he had finished in the eighth year. He had been unwilling to continue his studies, believing that he had nothing more to learn. What remained was superfluous, the property of a caste of clever idlers. The sight of the school building depressed him, as did everything but the image of Lise. He made an inventory of his intellectual equipment and found nothing but cause for hope, a brilliant promise. Entering the house, he turned on the radio. He was trying to bring himself to love symphonic music. Slowly, his thoughts went back to Lise, and he was engaged in making all sorts of decisions, concessions, and compromises by way of deceiving himself when his reverie was interrupted by his father's sharp-toned voice :

"Shut that off, I have to get up at six tomorrow morning!"

"Did Mama win?" said Gaston, who had not slept. He was standing in the middle of the stairway, holding up his drawers with his right hand. The waistband did not fit well over his misshapen hips.

Taking off his shirt in front of the mirror, Denis gave a contented sigh. He puffed out his torso. He would be a fine athlete three years from now.

CHAPTER

IV

Tɪᴛ-Bʟᴀɴᴄ Cᴏʟɪɴ rose early after a sleepless night. He saw
Gaston leaving for five o'clock mass so that he could take communion without being observed. The drunkard had awakened
with a start, in the middle of a nightmare marked by bursting
bombs, and had not been able to get back to sleep. Not that he
was tormented by any feeling of hatred or anger toward
Pritontin. Rather, he was troubled by a persistent small voice
that seemed to come from the depths of his being and that set
forth all sorts of reasons why he should be merciful and pardon
the pious Anselme. Those cutting words, "You are married to a
whore," now seemed to blur and shade off uncertainly into an
alcoholic mist. He could not bring himself to realize that this
insult had really been offered him, was unable to imbue his
mind with it as with a species of strychnine that would inspire
him, Tit-Blanc, to an act of courage and send him running to
the church to blow up all the Pritontins in the world in one
formidable attack. The curious thing was that he even felt near
to liking the old bigot. Our revolutionary might accordingly
have slept peacefully enough, lulled by this affectionate impulse,
if human nature—even when deadened by alcohol as in Tit-
Blanc's case—had only been insensible to the spur of pride and
the prickings of vanity. Forgive Pritontin? That would be an
ignoble thing to do, unworthy of a Tit-Blanc Colin.

And so he had tossed and turned in his bed. He would sink
down against Barloute's angular frame, would give a start and
fall back on the other side of the bed, would stretch himself
out flat on his belly, then turn over on his side in an effort to
find an illusion of rest. But it was all in vain. At the very
moment when his eyes were closing or a slight torpor laid hold
of him, the detonation of a firecracker would snap the bonds of
sleep and pierce him to the heart. Not being able to endure it
any longer, he had arisen about five o'clock. Down in the
kitchen, Grandfather Pitou was chewing his old Canadian
tobacco and letting the cat play with his toes.

"Why, what's come over you, Tit-Blanc?" he said, astonished

to see his son. "You're losing your grip! You're getting old. To let a little jag like that set you off— Why are you up so early?"

"I couldn't have been drunk to do what I did."

"What did you do, my son?"

"I'll show you—at ten o'clock mass." He had meant his voice as he said this to be a mild roar, but it seemed to him he could hardly hear it. He then began drawing the old man out, in an effort to get him to relate the bold exploits of the gangs of old, those brawls in which noses had been broken and faces slashed. As he tried to shave, he cut his chin; and seizing the mirror, he banged it furiously against the wall and settled it in place in order that the sight of blood might inspire him with a savage rage. He was not at all pleased with his appearance; in fact, he looked terrible, with his drawn, bloodshot eyes. It is hard to have courage in the morning, when you first get up. Féda, her eyelashes enmeshed in wax, her hair standing stiff and straight as usual, and clad in her nightgown, now darted out of the bedroom.

"Ah, you're up! It's a good thing, for the Bouchers are opening their confectionery."

"You're spiteful, you are! After all, they've done nothing to us." Tit-Blanc was tired of it all.

"What kind of man are you, anyway, will you tell me that?"

"Will you tell me what kind of woman *you* are?" A lump of anger rose in his throat as he thought of Pritontin's insult. It had a paralysing effect on him and drove him to despair. He was too easy-going. What a terrible creature Barloute was!

"I'm a woman who has a heart. Yesterday you were all for eating them alive. Of course everybody knows that Flora has more flesh on her than I have." And Barloute's toes curled over the knots in the floor.

"You wasn't bad-looking when you was young," old man Pitou corrected her.

"When I think that I had bingo before she did. She stole it from me!"

Tit-Blanc envied his wife her violent disposition. He leafed through the *Illustrated Story of a Nihilist* and could only commiserate with the hero who had so little comprehension of the role of pacifism.

Angry cries came from Jean's room. Germaine was scolding him for having taken her powder the evening before. Under pretext of having customers to see before he went to low mass, Jean managed to slip out. In passing, he gave Tit-Blanc an affectionate look. The Langevins would forget all about their plums when that cracker went off.

"Gosh, Father," he said, "there are times when I'm proud of you."

Tit-Blanc, who was brooding anxiously over a cup of cold coffee, raised his head. He realized that Jean knew, and this to him was more of a spur than all the pictures of Nihilist outrages.

How beautiful are the Sabbaths at St Joseph, when the sun itself appears to be withdrawing for meditation during those moments that mark the Elevation of the Sacred Host! From hour to hour, the big bell with its deep, sonorous voice proclaims: "This is my Body. This is my Blood."

At the Boucher home, birds were singing in the trees, and Gaston's cocks, their hunger satisfied, were strutting about and proudly displaying their crests. It was as if all creation was aware of the Seventh Day. What a rich world this was! Gaston had another dollar, Denis the prospect of seeing the parish upset, and the Colins were nursing their revenge. Pritontin, above all, was humming with joy. It was with hope and alacrity that he attended high mass. And Jean this morning felt that all the luck in the world was his. Hands in his pockets and whistling away the horseflies that came buzzing about his head, he climbed the Pente Douce, then turned to survey the quarter. At the street corners, bright-coloured dresses shimmered in the sunlight, and there arose from all sides a gentle, soul-satisfying languor. One had the impression that the scene had been dropped down there. There was an immobility and at the same time a lightness to it that communicated itself to one's spirit.

Jean conjured up a vision of Lise and sought to enjoy it with all the intensity of which he was capable. He began drawing wide circles about his life, thinking first of those faces that he detested. Then the circles shrank as he went down into the depths of his own being. He thought of how Denis had seemed to encourage him when he had looked at Lise. He eliminated his friend by an act of generosity: "When he goes to pay me back my ten cents, I'll tell him to keep it." There remained only Lise and himself, but this was a joy that he adroitly held back. He pitied those for whom this Sunday was the same as any other—those who during the week, at the factory, promised themselves that on this day they would get away from it all, would go seek adventure and do any number of foolish things, but who, when the day came, would hover around home or the church.

"Ah! If all Sundays were like this one!"

Jean resolved to pick out the bluest and the softest plums and take them to Lise without anyone's knowing anything about it; above all, he did not want Denis to know. For he had a feeling that he would obtain no favour from her except on condition that it remained a secret between them. In Denis he saw a bloodsucker for whom the least of his friend's dreams represented merely something more on which to feed. He relished by anticipation the idea of establishing with Lise friendly relations of which others would remain in ignorance. This was a happiness that he would bury deep within him, and only she would be able to divine it in his eyes.

"Boucher," he boyishly reassured himself, "is wasting his time if he comes around me looking for an affair with a woman, which he says is the only thing that would interest him so far as they are concerned."

He gave a forward leap, into the orchard.

At the church door, the men were watching the women as they entered, exchanging little pleasantries with them from time to time. They were standing in clusters on the street corners, all of them carefully brushed and combed and somewhat ill at ease in their neckties. The Mulots could be recognized by the gaudy colour of their clothes and the Soyeux by their missals—the more zealous of them carried two. Arriving after nine o'clock, Tit-Blanc Colin protectively surrounded himself with his gang. In order to sense his power he had need of beholding in others the radiation of his personality. For years the church square had been the crossroads of the younger generation. In Tit-Blanc's time there had been no church there and they had gone to mass at St Malo's. "Ah! those were the good old days!" the elders would remark. "The young fellows then were not afraid. They used to fight the gangs from the other suburbs with bottles, and blood would flow every Saturday. We would take a little drink, and then, 'Watch out!' the lads from above would be down upon us."

There had grown up among outsiders a kind of legend in which these valiant workers from St Sauveur took on the aspect of notorious bandits. If they saw a youth who was ill-clad and impudent, they would say, in a frightened tone of voice: "There's a lad from St Sauveur who's looking for trouble." The deputies had been at special pains to keep this reputation alive, their excuse for not lending their aid to a working-class colleague being that they did not wish to occasion bloody frays. Like the lumberjacks and trappers, the young of Sewer Town had their *"boulés,"* their *"bullies,"* of whom Denis' grandfather on his mother's side had been one of the most famous. They went in for *noms de guerre* such as Tit-Blanc, Pitou, Tit-Ci, Tit-Ça, etc., a custom which in the course of time had fallen into disuse because the youth of today prefer American names, like Johnny for Jean and Jack for Jacques.

Whence comes this instinct toward deformation? Are not our Tit-Pits and our Johnnies merely the reflection of an inferiority complex, of an unconscious feeling of admiration for the phlegmatic character and certain other qualities of the Anglo-Saxon, as we in our weakness and timidity let our own values lie stagnant as if we were ashamed of them?

Bidonnet was arguing. "If I bring it to you, I'll lose my job, I'm certain of that. You know that fellow Gendron who's always sucking around the curate and is willing to take my job for ten dollars?"

"Yes," agreed Tit-Blanc, "it's a big risk for you to run." Shaking his head sorrowfully, he approved all the objections that were raised, magnified all the obstacles. He gave a start when Langevin remarked that he was lucky to get out of it so easily. Fearing the scheme would be abandoned, Denis now intervened.

"Not so fast!" he said. "I'll do it, myself. I'll bring you a lighted cigarette. That's how good a friend I am of yours." He was enjoying Tit-Blanc's discomfiture. The others expressed their admiration, Méo Nolin regretting the fact that Denis was not a true Mulot.

"There goes your victim," said Père Langevin, pointing to Pritontin.

Tit-Blanc was disheartened by this offer of collaboration. He was in for it now. He barely saw Pritontin as that dignified individual descended the steps that led to the church, which was situated in the basement. Zépherin Lévesque, with his wife and Lise and the tavern keeper Grondin were getting out of their cars in front of the main entrance. For the first time in his life, Tit-Blanc was sorry that so little friendship existed between the Mulots and the Soyeux. He would almost have kissed Anselme.

As the gang entered the church, they were greeted by the *Asperges me*. The humidity of the place was stifling. The foundation had been laid fifteen years ago, and the plaster of the ceiling, put on in haste by an unscrupulous contractor, would suddenly come loose and fall in large chunks upon the heads of

73

the parishioners. This happened especially at retreats, or when the congregation was reciting supplicatory chants; and the Mulots, who were not lacking in wit, asserted that this stale variety of manna was all that their obstinate souls deserved.

Noré the gendarme had stationed himself on his little platform in the rear. Having noted that the Abbé Charton was to say mass, he expected that the service would last for two solid hours. Denis recognized him and made up his mind to keep an eye on his mother.

The pews, consisting of a few wooden planks painted an orange-yellow, were incrusted with arabesques, intertwined initials, and hearts joined by an arrow. Many of the pious ones, the artisans of prayer as they might be termed, made expert use of the crucifix attached to their rosaries by employing it as a sculptor's chisel. The churchwardens were installed with becoming dignity in a handsome pew of their own, upholstered in purple-coloured plush. They sat all the way up in front, near the image of St Joseph, at the foot of which there rested a crutch. It had been brought there by a Madame Blouin, who had been healed one Wednesday evening the year the church was founded. Dazzled by this revelation, Monsieur le Curé had promptly organized his famous St Joseph Wednesdays, an event that attracted the pious from other parishes who, being unable to repair to Brother André's sanctuary in Montreal, found here a satisfactory substitute. But this was not Montreal!

The parish had its own way of doing things and its Wednesdays were its own religious specialty. Pritontin, always ambitious, had bought the first pew immediately behind that of the churchwardens, and there he sat in state with his wife. Next came the pew occupied by Zépherin Lévesque, whose feud with Pritontin had begun on the day when Anselme had deprived him of a seat in the front row by making a bid that was beyond the means of a streetcar conductor. Pritontin was constantly on his knees during mass, sweating out his false piety between two huge missals which formed a sort of bodyguard as he said his beads. Madame Pritontin, who suffered from heart trouble, was waiting for the offertory, when she would light her taper near the saint's image.

Tit-Blanc, his legs giving way beneath him, sat down in Madame Lévesque's pew. She did not dare ask him to leave for fear that people would say she was narrow-minded. He was leaning slightly to one side, weighed down by that enormous firecracker which was like a mortal sin in the heart of a pious communicant. Putting his hand in his pocket, he turned it over feverishly, tortured by the temptation to break off the fuse. He was praying fervently that some fortuitous circumstance would prevent the sinister contrivance from exploding.

There was a great hubbub on the platform where the choristers were. Perched like totems upon that immense ambo, they deciphered the Gregorian music as numismatists do the inscriptions on old coins. Since the Abbé Charton was saying mass, Monsieur Pamparin, the ex-choirmaster, was taking his place as conductor. He was fond of profane music and hymns composed by others, whereas the priest was in the habit of using his own arrangements, and when the choristers rendered one of his works in counterpoint, the compositions bore a mimeographed signature at the top and bottom of each sheet. The abbé had purchased an ivory baton and after much insistence (for the worthy pastor knew nothing about music) had obtained from the curé a magnificent lectern with a loudspeaker.

He would mount the podium like a cloud made flesh and let his glance roam over the members of his choir, magnetizing them with a look as he had heard it said that Toscanini and Serge Jaroff did. The men (tenors and bassos) on one side of the "organ" and the children (sopranos and altos) on the other side, led by a lay brother from the school who was not entitled to use the lectern, would open their mouths in the form of an "o" for the high notes and a "u" for the low ones. They conveyed the illusion of being possessed by that electric atmosphere created by the Abbé Charton's out-flung arms. What dynamism! How magnificent he was as he stood there gesticulating, red-faced and breathless, darting his fingers like harpoons toward various groups in the choir. He was a whirlwind of gestures, a musical scarecrow, over against the poor little harmonium that wailed like a defenceless virgin under the brutal attack of those voices. The good brother had no right to make gestures when the abbé was on the podium. A humble lieutenant, he was in charge of the "mouth positions" as his superior shouted exasperatedly: "All together now! All together!"

The real Mulots, prudent fellows on guard against the collection plate, remained in the rear, near the door. They surrounded the dais and as the choir sang would nudge one another with their elbows. "That's something like!" they would exclaim admiringly. When the piece was finished, the abbé would screw up his mouth by way of indicating that he was not satisfied, for perfection was something that was never to be attained. Meanwhile, his gaze would seek out the organist's mirror, the only thing upon the platform on which he did bestow a smile.

But on this particular Sunday the Abbé Charton was officiating at the altar. He read the gospel, appearing to wrap it in the swaddling clothes of his fervent, deep-throated voice. Dutifully he turned the pages, but was careful to reserve his store of fire for the activity to which he had consecrated his life: sacred music. Just as the priestly musician was about to take his seat, his first tenor, Caruchin, fascinated by a deceptive G sharp, forgot himself and held the note a trifle too long, after the others had finished, with the effect of an auto horn. The abbé stopped short and gazed toward the rear, his mouth expressive of censure while his eyes held a look of desolation. That fellow Pomparin again; he did not know how to lead a choir. Ah! these laymen, they knew nothing of the music of the angels! Following the priest's example, all heads turned; for those who were in the habit of attending high mass were as avid for such little incidents as the Latruche spinsters were for scandalous tidbits. The Abbé Charton's despair was increased by the presence of two jealous hangers-on, a couple of choristers from the nine o'clock mass! That nine o'clock mass! It was the cross he had to bear, the height of mediocrity so far as melody was concerned, representing everything of which he disapproved. A peaceful man, he mustered all sorts of disagreeable epithets by way of describing certain soulful musicians:

"They drag out the notes and run tremolos. Why do they do that? It takes away the religious feeling, you know. I can tell you in confidence, they are a lot of malcontents. I refused to have them in my choir. The way it is, they have a chance to sing solos more often. I ask you, where is pride going to end? *Mon Dieu!*"

The truth of the matter was that the nine o'clock choristers were the more successful in the eyes of the Mulots. They rendered popular hymns and their voices were more natural, more pleasing to the ear; they put much the same feeling into what they sang as they did into their love songs. In short, there was a quarrel between the two choirs that was never settled, like that of the romantics and the classicists. The trump card of the former lay in the abundant opportunity for amusement and ironic guffaws that was afforded them by the musical blunders of their enemies, while the latter found consolation as they saw the nine o'clock soloists choking, growing red in the face, and turning their heads a little to one side, amid a burst of laughter, in the humid silence of this church that was built too low on the ground. The attendants at high mass were more tolerant, it may be; but then, they almost never had to listen to solos, which made it easier for them to be charitable. And if there was one now and then, the Abbé Charton, forestalling any desire to laugh on the part of the congregation, would take it upon himself to render it.

How voluptuously he then inflated that deep bass voice of his, how he threw it out! How he made the echoes ring, causing the thin coating of plaster that covered the ceiling to tremble perilously! The only piece of music that his elderly choristers were especially eager to do was the *Parce Domine*. He would surprise them by suddenly calling for its rendition, and they would give him a look of profound gratitude as he turned away, all but indifferent, as if the favour he had granted them was nothing at all. If any of the choir made a mistake, the listeners assumed that this was merely the choral arrangement. There was, of course, the Abbé Trinchu, who knew his music; but on such occasions he would do no more than curl his lips disdainfully, in a manner that said all there was to say. This ecclesiastic with the high-bred airs was awaiting his transfer to a more cultivated and more worldly flock, one capable of being inflamed like hens on the spit by his rampant nationalism. At St Joseph's, individuals and their opinions were judged by the mass they attended. Nine o'clock: levity and religious worldliness. Ten o'clock: a pious formalism as dependable as clockwork.

At the end of each aisle the members of the Lévis Guard acted as ushers. Their task consisted of seating the churchwardens and the Soyeuses, and after them those among the Mulotes who had on new dresses. Made up of old bachelors and married men weatherbeaten with domesticity, this guard with its threadbare uniforms and its tarnished gold braid represented a last vestige of the military spirit. The honorary commandants were the big grocers and men of means; for the organization was divided into two orders, the active officers and the honorary ones. Out of this situation rivalries sprang up, the competition between Pinasse Charcot and Zépherin Lévesque being the most famous of these feuds. The honorary officers wore the striped trousers and only turned out for special parades, in order to show off their uniforms, while the others were clad in flaring hipped knee-breeches and devoted themselves heart and soul to the task assigned them. As for the privates, they were but a dozen parasites. Less numerous than the officers, they were not concerned with promotions for the reason that, possessed of no rank, they looked the part better than did their superiors. As honorary commander-in-chief, Zépherin was constantly harassed by the attentions and military communiqués of those among the ushers who were desirous of winning his influence. They would come up and whisper to him futile bits of information in the very middle of the mass.

As a churchwarden, he listened with a condescending air to the sergeant who, saluting him sharply, went on to say: "One drumhead caved in, *mon commandant*; one broken cornet slide; two rats discovered gnawing the breeches in the wardrobe."

A corporal presented himself before Abbé Folbèche to conduct him to the pulpit, a rudimentary affair consisting of a platform, painted and varnished, that had served in the election campaigns of not so long ago. Monsieur le Curé began by gazing around over the heads of his flock. Standing near the door was the same group of Mulots as usual; they might either leave or fall asleep during the sermon. The pastor looked at them. "Come forward, come forward, there are plenty of seats up front." No one stirred. The curate did not insist but, with an air of resignation, glanced at the army of Soyeuses clustered around him. He went on to read the high mass notices, complaining of the fact that people were unmindful of their dead, or else inflicted upon them the forced humility of poor relations in that heaven where they might dwell in glory through the simple payment of a low mass for their souls.

"I wish to remind you once again," he said, "that those who are unable to pay for a seat at mass should procure my signature so that they may obtain their ticket of admission. There is nothing difficult about it; you have but to come and see me."

Pritontin settled back in the corner of his pew, more and more.

"I warn you that in the future those who do not present their tickets will have to leave. With all the money that is spent on tobacco, drinks, and other luxuries, there is no reason why you cannot spare ten cents for the Lord. In order to avoid embarrassment, parishioners should purchase their tickets in advance. We will accept no more money in church."

He then announced that they would take up the "sou-a-meal" collection (that is to say, for those who were employed, a sou for each meal they had had during the week; the idea had come from Zépherin Lévesque, who was responsible for the name). Also, the collection of the Holy Angels and the Cardinal's collection. There was a clatter of pennies in copper plates. From the portico farther back came another clatter, a muffled one produced by urchins who were "pasting" their large-sized pennies against the wall. The falling of these coins created an echo to the collection inside, the whole constituting a kind of carillon with rattling effects. Denis, still holding his cigarette, was endeavouring to form some idea of God that would bring Him near. This out of pride, or because he was too indolent to go to Him. It occurred to him that this sound of dropping pennies in front of the tabernacle, here in this little church where the Christ should have been able to find a silent refuge and forgetfulness, far from Calvary and Jerusalem, must be for Him an all too poignant reminder of the thirty pieces of silver that had been paid for His body.

The Mulots, finding their posture hard on the loins, had retired to a sort of alcove formed by the stairway and a corner of the portico. There they lolled behind the pale blue vat where parishioners came for their holy water, on Holy Saturday. The little Mulots would sell it at two cents the half-pint to those of the Soyeux who disdained to mingle with the horde of youngsters that fell upon the cask with cries of joy. As for the sacristan, he cursed his holy water which he had to carry by the bucketful. Poor man! His hardest day's work was on the eve of the Resurrection.

Tit-Blanc wished that he too were standing at the back of the church, for he had just caught sight of Denis playing carelessly with a match. Germaine, seated with her mother in one of the side rows, was surveying Lise's hat; it looked distinguished to her. What a fine sister-in-law she would make! Gazing at Denis, she for once had no feeling of inferiority. God only knows what people in church think about during a sermon by a curé whose chief concern it to make his voice resound like thunder! Germaine was glad that Denis had made light of Lise yesterday. She began composing in her mind an affected little conversation that was to take place when she met the young lady for the first time. She weighed every word, studying it under the magnifying glass of what little education she had. Flora Boucher was thinking how impudent Tit-Blanc was, and noted to her great surprise that it was Jean who was really Lise's beau.

"Denis didn't want her, I suppose. He's so independent!"

Barloute, whose mind was on the lamp she had failed to win, was glaring at Flora with a hatred that was close to tears; for she was in the habit of deploring her fate as she lamented her leanness and the infidelity of Tit-Blanc, who was always running after women of distinction like Madame Lévesque. She saw herself grown old and cast aside amid a heap of pop bottles, ice cream, and chocolate bars. For he was determined to open that confectionery shop!

"My dear parishioners," the curé was thundering, "your humble pastor has seen fit to relieve himself of a task that has interfered with the proper administration of parish affairs. I have appointed M. Anselme Pritontin 'Distributor of Tickets.' He will be in my office from seven to eight o'clock in the evening. In making this choice, I have been guided by his prudence and uprightness."

All eyes turned toward Anselme as he with beating heart assumed the humble pose, closely related to hypocrisy or false modesty, that is sometimes to be seen in those who are first in their class. He was afraid they would applaud him and was glad he was in church. The Mulots who belonged to the club exchanged uneasy glances, foreseeing a catastrophe.

"My dear brethren, I have made a reckoning this morning of the religious vocations among us. During the fifteen years of our existence as a parish, ninety-eight of our daughters have left for the convent, thirty-eight lads have entered the brothers, and ten have gone on to the seminary. This is as much as to say that the enlistment in the army of Christ is progressing satisfactorily."

This was an obsession with the good Father Folbèche. In seeking religious vocations, he worked his little parish like a mine. He would have liked to make of the cassock, the clerical neckband, and the convent robe a palisade against sin, a sacred rampart, a sort of no man's land around his parish where tonsures and hoods might be seen springing up like crosses in a cemetery. Each day, at school and in the street, he made his rounds, tracking down young lads until they should avow a disposition for holy orders.

"A lawyer, my son? Why, there are thousands of them, and it is not always a clean profession, you know. A notary? *Mon Dieu!* How long would it take you to work up a clientele? And there are more doctors than there are patients. But with God, there are never too many. Think it over well, my son, and I will go see your father. I will help with the expense of the course."

The Mulots would smile quietly at this, for they knew so many nice girls! What was more, their dream was to become shoemakers or something like that. When Denis was twelve years old, the good priest had made him certain propositions, but our stenographer of today had torn his vocation to shreds in the apple orchards. The pastor had created (it was his life's ambition) a class of children whom he believed to be destined for an ecclesiastical calling. This troop of apprentices in divinity, this sacred legion of the young in blue berets with red crosses, had been stuck into the convent among the other classes and was under the tutelage of a nun. Since Monsieur le Curé desired to have them suitably prepared for the seminary, he had chosen a sister who was acquainted with the rudiments of classical culture. She would have them sing hymns from three-thirty to four o'clock and then would set them to waxing the floor, embroidering flowers for the Blessed Virgin, and cleaning their fingernails. The children did not leave the convent until near five o'clock, for they would remain to discuss their personal problems with their teacher. The young misses from the neighbouring classrooms, out in the corridor, would raise themselves on their toes and contort their shrewd little faces into an ironic grimace, but these twelve-year-olds, dignified as nuns, would return their stare with a calm Carthusian gaze.

For the curé they were a favoured lot, his special pets, and he pampered them with gold crosses, rosaries, missals, and lives of saints. All of which did not fail to create a certain amount of jealousy among the four hundred pupils who attended the school and who were not coddled in this manner. They were loud in their insistence that an injustice was being done them. Such an oasis of juvenile ardour for the cassock—Pritontin had two sons in the group—was a source of great annoyance to the recruiter for the Jesuit brotherhood, who, astonished at the small number of vocations for the juniorate, began to suspect a snake in the grass somewhere. An investigation had been started and the good brother superior, son of a crafty-minded peasant, had not permitted himself to be outwitted by the curé's rather obvious smile of self-satisfaction. He had bountifully organized little outings for the so-called St Gonzaga class and had conducted the pastor's beloved lambs to the juniorate, where he had shown them over the place, enumerating the advantages and slipping in mild comparisons between the state of a brother and that of a priest. All means were fair for awakening a pedagogic vanity in these young ones; with a faint and timid smile one could inspire them with a dread of the breviary and impress upon them the disadvantages of parish-house life, where one is often short of money and runs the risk of being routed out of bed at any hour of the night.

With the brothers, it was quite different. As many holidays as their charges had, two-month vacations in summer, a little retreat to make all right with God, and there you were! They might nap for days at a stretch. And then, there was that famous trip to Rome! It was not every little abbé who could afford to pay for it out of his tithes. As a result of all this, there began to be desertions from the ranks of the young Gonzagues, a circumstance that seriously disturbed Father Folbèche, who felt that there were enough children in the other parishes for the brothers to draw upon.

It was not from any lack of urging, then, that a St Joseph youngster failed to become an ecclesiastic. Monsieur le Curé frequently read off the figures by way of stimulating others. And this Sunday when he said "ninety-eight of our daughters," more than one pious lady, her eyes fairly drinking him in, appeared to be on the point of crying out: "Why don't you go on and tell them that I have two?"

The priest now assumed a modest tone, but there was a note of triumph in his voice: "My dear brethren, thanks to the protection of St Joseph, we have succeeded in having the rue Bagot made a part of our parish from now on." He was silent and closed his eyes as he awaited the acclamation of the angels. "This gratifying decision on the part of our beloved cardinal puts an end to the little misunderstanding that has existed between our curacy and that of St Malo, which formerly included the street in question within its jurisdiction."

The expression on his face was that of the stout-hearted peasant who joyfully strides up and down the corridors of the Palais de Justice after he has won his case. Monsieur le Curé Thomas-Etienne Folbèche knew what it was all about, for he had been able to pay his way through the seminary as the result of a lawsuit which his father had won over a neighbouring farmer in connection with a boundary wall and the damage caused by an enraged bull. Thus, this settlement of parish bounds was in a sense due to a civil suit of like character. Father Folbèche, however, would have been very angry indeed if anyone had told him that the profane tendencies he had inherited had contributed to his success in increasing the church revenues.

"I am pleased to inform you that the new parish visitor who has been placed in charge of this street is Mademoiselle Lise Lévesque, the talented daughter of our leading churchwarden. The receipts from our entertainment and bingo game were one hundred and twenty-five dollars. That is very good, and I am gratified. Since Christmas there have been almost no deaths, but the births have been satisfactory. I must repeat that where music is desired at weddings, the young ladies must be Daughters of Mary. I have had steel boxes made for our parish visitors to which I alone shall have the key. It seems that not everybody is satisfied with the system of envelopes, although I myself have full confidence in my beloved daughters."

Everyone looked at the Latruche sisters. Laying his book down upon the edge of the lectern, the priest put out the little pulpit lamp, then rubbed his hands. A stern look came over his face. The Mulots, shifting their weight to the other leg, made a wry face and glanced at one another impatiently. It was not enough for the Abbé Charton to dawdle at the altar; the curé must preach a sermon of his own before the Abbé Trinchu began. They were not accustomed to sermons from him. In the early days of the parish, his enthusiasm aroused by reading the life of Father Labelle, he had cherished the ambition of becoming a husbandman in the fields of morality and spirituality. Inasmuch as his new parish constituted the former slum section of the quarter, he had been assured that a great apostolic task awaited him here. Convinced that he would find himself in the midst of a lot of hovels inhabited by drunkards and prostitutes, where sins clung like mortar to the very walls of the houses, he had marshalled all his young evangelic ardour for the attack. But he had quickly come to perceive that the residents were not as bad as he had been led to believe. His superiors had simply taken advantage of his passion for souls and his inexperience in order to stick him off in this hole where no money was to be had. Necessity, however, is the mother of invention with curés as with statesmen, and so he had gradually withdrawn into his shell and had come to concern himself chiefly with finances, leaving to his vicars the task of preparing sermons.

He would weed out the pockets of the worker, asserting that the dollar is a vicious growth which hides the soul from God. The Mulots complained that sin was costing them more and more, but Monsieur le Curé was the magician of lightweight pocketbooks and gathered an abundant harvest, being held up as an example for young curés to follow. His special ability lay in creating the proper atmosphere, and as a consequence the Mulots, who did not permit themselves to be stripped without grumbling, had come to look upon the church as an enormous poor box into which one had to drop one's pennies. Summer was the season of outings, and there was an unusually heavy attendance at five-thirty mass; but if his flock then appeared to let down a bit, the pastor would quickly bring them to reason ("back to the fold," as he put it) in the early days of the autumn, by means of a retreat energetically preached by one of those Torquemadas who bind you with mortal sins, overwhelm you with sudden death, and bring the wrath of Heaven down upon your head like slabs of rock, preparatory to hurling you down into that hell where you will hear the terrible clock of eternity ticking away : "FOREVER, NEVER !"

Frightened by this, the Mulots would storm the confessionals, and the curate would thereupon relax his hold and give them to understand that a fat collection would appease the good Lord's anger. It was commonly said that the speed with which the church debt was paid off was a true master stroke for a parish as poor as this one. His Eminence, indeed, was thinking of conferring the title of Monsignor upon this priest who was so adept at reconciling the love of God with the concerns of the business office. Father Folbèche was consequently aglow with the dream of sending his voice booming out in a magnificent stone church, one near to being a cathedral, that should stand proudly with its back to the Pente Douce side. He was lulled by the glorious prospect of a title, happy to think of having a splendid parish house with a flower garden and with one entire floor to be placed at the disposition of those distinguished members of the clergy who would be certain to visit him. And so it was that the good pastor had found happiness in the very place where some naïve apostle, without initiative and overcharitable, would have worked himself to death.

He kept a hold on his little flock by denouncing houses of ill fame and penances redeemed with money. Like the capable leader that he was, he chose his churchwardens as a sovereign does his ministers. They were men who loved honours well enough to yield to the slightest whim of the one who bestowed them, and that was Monsieur le Curé. An absolute master, he had wished to create for himself an individuality different from all others and had adopted certain mannerisms which the best of the parish organizers—those eager for appreciation as expressed by bowings and scrapings—looked upon as downright rudeness. Whatever the sums they turned in to him, he never said thank you. And if occasionally some bolder one, unable to bear it any longer, called his attention to the fact, he would roll his eyes upward and say : "It is not for me, but for the Lord. There will be your reward." And he would point to the beginnings of the church edifice, as he gazed out over the roof, intoxicated by the vision of his cathedral and its elegant belfry.

This, then, was something : a sermon by Monsieur le Curé !

"There you are !" said Méo Nolin. "I knew it was coming."

"Pritontin didn't lose any time. And he got what he wanted."

Father Folbèche, in a voice that sounded as though he were announcing the end of the world or the death of His Eminence the Cardinal, was speaking solemnly, a distressed look in his eyes. He did not lick his lower lip as he usually did.

"Certain things are happening in our parish that have terrified me and have led me this morning to seek the powerful protection of our great St Joseph. My dear parishioners, pray, pray! The shadow of Moscow's claw is over our heads, is threatening our faith, our church."

The good housewives huddled in their seats.

"How long shall we be able to hold out? That is the question that I ask myself as I behold the horizon laden with black clouds." A ray of sunlight fell upon his hands, his bosom, his neck, leaving his head in some remote sphere from which his voice emerged like the angel's trumpet in the Valley of Jehoshaphat. "Who would have believed it, dear brothers and sisters, we have *communists* in our parish!"

His voice died in a sort of heart-rending tremolo. The Latruche spinsters, who wore the incipient beards like a diploma, gave a despairing "Oh!" They were breathing so hard they almost put out the tapers three feet away. It was as though a leaden weight rested upon the hearts of all of them. The men who went to confession once a year pricked up their ears; they were curious and delighted. Was the church going to be blown up? At last the sermons were becoming interesting. The priest's voice went on, thundering as in the days of old, when the parish was first founded:

"Yes, my brethren, *communists!* God has decided to try us, for it is in the presence of danger that the depth of one's faith is revealed. In this parish, my brethren, not far from this place of worship, there is a house that is known to all of you where our good workers gather, gradually to lose their faith. It is there that certain filthy creatures, the natural emissaries of Moscow, of Lenin and Stalin, perniciously sow the terrible seed of communism. No longer ago than yesterday, in this parish where we have one who is near to being a young saint, calumnies were uttered against the cassock, a holy thing, and the church was called an association of robbers! Women, wives, mothers who permit your husbands and sons to go there, beat your bosoms and bow to the will of Almighty God!"

Flora clenched her fist as she reflected that Denis was in the habit of going to Bédarovitch's.

"Down on your knees, my brethren, down on your knees! Pray the Lord to forgive them and to spare us; for as you know, it is the good who pay for the sins of the wicked. Repeat after me, with your arms crossed: 'My God, we beg thee, remove from us the communist peril. My God, we beg thee, remove from us the communist peril!' And now, dear brethren, may the power of heaven and our children in holy orders and the convent intervene to form an enormous rampart, even as we breathe the incense from our altars, mingling with it our most ardent prayers."

In the seminary, he had occasionally been at the head of his class in rhetoric.

"You all know this place, and it is for you to be on your guard against it. Twice already I have had cause to complain of it. Only last week, when my lightning rods were stolen, do you know that the copper in them, which was the reason for the theft, was purchased by that infamous shop, and that same shop then resold it to Japanese ships anchored here, those same Japanese that put our missionaries to a martyr's death? I swear upon the holy gospel, inspired by a holy wrath, that the next time I will notify the archbishop, who will take such measures as are necessary."

"He doesn't mean a word of it," grumbled Madame Pritontin.

"He's a blue, I'm dead certain of that," whispered Père Jefferson, with an air of conviction, to those standing around him.

"And now, my dear brethren, let us as good Christians speak of those things that elevate the soul and comfort us in the Lord. Our parish is not fifteen years old, and yet it has already produced one who in the course of the next hundred years may possibly be canonized. A committee of ladies under the direction of the Demoiselles Latruche" (they dropped their eyes at this point) "is engaged in compiling a list of favours received through his intercession. With admirable zeal, they have had picture cards printed and have composed prayers to go on the back of them. The necessary publicity has been taken care of, and from all parts of Canada messages of gratitude are pouring in for prayers that have been answered. Let us hope that our young saint will soon grant us miracles of a striking sort that will put him in the first rank as a miracle worker. He will do so before ten years have gone by, I am certain of that. Let us hope, also, that he will remember that it was here in St Joseph's parish that he was born and will bestow his favours first of all upon the faithful of this congregation. Let us rejoice in the Lord that He has furnished a new saint for the vast cohort of Heaven."

And he appeared to be saying: "Let the other parishes do as much!"

Madame Pritontin gritted her teeth and there was a spiteful murmur to her prayers. Her own sons were worth as much as this made-to-order saint any time. But they were still living! However, it would all come to light some day.

The curé was rapping on the edge of the pulpit as he commanded: "Let us kneel and pray for the building of the church."

It was a prayer that he himself had composed, one evening when he felt inspired, out of the remembered odds and ends of a pompous, heavy-handed rhetoric. He wrapped St Joseph in a bundle of praise, held him prisoner in a net of words; and overcome by so imperious a faith, suffocated by such verbal splendour, there was nothing for the saint to do but to abandon his celestial state a year from now and set himself to the building of a stone church that should bear his name. But the masons, jealous of the carpenters, were inclined to doubt his competence.

"Do not forget, my beloved parishioners, that if we succeed in getting together fifteen thousand dollars during the coming year, the archbishop will permit us to borrow the remaining hundred and twenty thousand needed for the construction of this magnificent temple. I count upon the protection of our great patron, who knows the heart of true Christians. And now, a sermon by the Abbé Trinchu."

Denis at this moment was reflecting on what the curé had said regarding the parish saint who had died two years before at the age of nineteen. He recalled with some uneasiness that he had given this "pasty-face" a drubbing for calling him a hoodlum. In the courtyard of the young ascetic's home was a cherry tree to which Denis had paid a visit, and the "saint," catching him in the act, had not hesitated to chide the proud, ambitious lad some years his junior, whereupon Denis had bloodied the nose of this youth of sixteen who wore a hair shirt and had ecstatic visions and whose health was undermined by tuberculosis.

"Bah!" said Denis to himself, as he rolled his cigarette between his index finger and his thumb, "if he's really a saint, he'll forgive me. It may be the only exciting memory that he has of his life on earth."

The Abbé Trinchu's grating voice arose as he began what promised to be an eloquent sermon: "My dear brethren, I am going to speak to you on the subject of charity."

By way of completing our collective portrait of the vicars at St Joseph's it is indispensable to paint in the principal features of this cleric. He treated the parishioners with a haughty air, carried a cane, came in late of an evening, and exchanged greetings only with separatists. For three years now he had been a transient here, awaiting a curacy that would come up to his aspirations, and he accordingly deemed it preferable not to form any attachments that he would regret having to break off. As a result, he remained in an abnormal state of prolonged indifference, having barely so much as unpacked his bag. Attributing to himself a strong will power and individuality, he liked to decide for himself just how much he should do. For it is not to be imagined that such a man took seriously those whose sole concern was with the petty things of life—little sinners and their sins! His program consisted in ignoring them, in having as little to do with them as possible. Even when he confronted them from the pulpit, he soared over their heads, addressing himself to the inhabitants of the moon.

Ramsay Trinchu, who prided himself on being a distant relative of Armand Lavergne, believed that he possessed the gift of eloquence. His sermons would begin on a languid note, faintly contemptuous at times, but they always ended in imprecations and sweeping gestures inspired by an unreal and misty nationalism. He would picture the "Race" as being submissive to the government and to the English as umbrellas are to the storm. Anything served him as a pretext for these sallies, from a reading of the *Rerum Novarum* to a sermon on sin in missionary lands. The good reds and the good blues, meanwhile, confident in their own political parties, would fortify themselves against these seditious utterances by dropping off to sleep.

"Awake, you sleepers, to the voice of the fatherland!"

He was silent, waiting for the effect, majestic as a Huron chief far from his decimated tribe. He was dreaming of some parish up in the clouds, which he would govern after his own fashion. St Joseph's was disgusting in the extreme, with this Father Folbèche who had but one fatherland: his curacy, and but one parliament: his Church. Where he meant to go, blue, white, and red flags would flutter in the breeze from every clothesline and telephone pole and would even serve as sacerdotal vestments; the juke boxes, in place of blaring forth jazz, would burst out triumphantly in patriotic hymns; and the dying to whom he administered the last sacrament would utter words that would go down in history. He had composed his own program in the form of a volume bearing the title: *The French Canadian, Master and King*, and Christ and the Virgin were proclaimed leader and patroness of the new party, while all defenders of the "Race" had a right to a general holiday.

One family alone in the parish enjoyed the honour of

receiving the Abbé Trinchu upon intimate terms, and that was the household of Clichoteux, the banana merchant. The abbé spent long evenings in his shop, discussing such problems as co-operatives, advertising, display, and the wrapping of merchandise. It was even said that he had financed the business to the amount of five hundred dollars. The grocers, realizing that to have a year-round priest in the firm was an excellent advertisement in itself, had maliciously dubbed the abbé "the banana king," and the young Mulots just out of reform school had picked up the phrase. Hiding in courtyards of an evening, they would start shouting this ridiculous epithet the moment Ramsay Trinchu, aged thirty-eight, would appear, tapping the sidewalk with his cane. For two months now he had been the owner of a car, a big black 1929 Buick which he kept in the Clichoteux garage. He would take them out riding on Sundays : father, mother, son and daughter; and the last mentioned, a girl of twenty, was so plump and pretty that tongues were soon babbling about her and the good abbé.

But now, during the last two weeks, an extraordinary thing had happened : Ramsay Trinchu no longer visited the Clichoteux! It was said that Bérénice Clichoteux, the mother, had caught the ardent nationalist slipping a note to her daughter that was not at all patriotic in tone. Ah, no, that would not do! Bérénice, a mother who knew her duty, as inflexibly upright as a symbol of the moral law, had definitely told him that he was no longer welcome. As a result, the automobile had been for sale, and Pritontin had made up his mind to take it off the abbé's hands. Obviously this was no more than gossip, a spiteful version provided by the Latruche sisters. They were neighbours of the Clichoteux and enemies of the Abbé Trinchu, who had never once presented them with any medals or rosaries. How rude he was! At confession, when you were too circumstantial and were complacently bent upon relating your sins in detail, he had a way of dismissing you with a wave of the hand, as if he were chasing flies.

"You have no idea how impolite he can be," Peuplière Latruche would say whenever the haughty separatist's name was mentioned. She was the younger of the two old maids, the one who had written to Rome to find out if a Saint Peuplière had not been included in the roll of martyrs. She had been advised to make a thorough search, especially in the catacombs, where she dreamed of being taken for burial at the age of eighty after she had choked to death on a holy wafer. She had read her Fabiola.

Cécile, the other sister, was equally indignant. "You would think the good Lord was his prime minister!" She was the one who, wholly ignorant of music, had purchased a harmonium in order that she might come under her patron saint's jurisdiction.

This old maids' gossip had reached Ramsay Trinchu's ears; and so it is not to be wondered at if today, in speaking of charity, his tone was by no means a charitable one. The delay in his appointment to a curacy, the cutting insult of "banana king," the business of the letter, and the apathy of St Joseph parishioners on the subject of Race, all conspired to give his sermon a bitter leaven of rancour.

"Shameless slanderers, you who rend the noblest of souls like burdock leaves! God will demand an accounting of you and of the way you vote; he will stifle you beneath the shreds that your evil tongues have plucked." And he recalled the dream he had had the night before, of a swarm of pinkish, babbling tongues.

"If my firecracker could only go off now, it would hardly be noticed," sighed Tit-Blanc.

"Now is the time," said Denis to himself, his heart beating, "while he's shouting like that." Going out into the portico, where a dispute was in progress over the "pasting" game, he lighted the butt, being careful to keep it hidden in the hollow of his hand, with the lighted end under his sleeve. He then strode down the centre aisle, clacking his heels as he came. The Abbé Trinchu saw him and was proud, convinced that this was an effect of his own eloquence. The Gonzagues, jealous of Denis, thought that he was doing it just to show off. Féda watched him as he seated himself near her husband and alongside of Lise, who could not believe her eyes. "Those Bouchers always hog everything. Now he wants to steal Jean's girl. He's taking advantage of the fact that Jean's not here."

Germaine felt a clutch at her heart. So Denis was going after a girl! It was the first time he had done that, and it seemed very strange. Flora Boucher was proud: all it took was a little nerve to go up and sit in the Lévesque pew. And that son of hers did not get his charm from any stranger.

As he caught sight of Denis, Tit-Blanc felt the sweat standing out on him. He thought he had an intrepid air, but the firecracker was shaking between his fingers. If only the gang from the club had not been watching him from the rear! Denis waited until the others took their eyes off him. He nudged Tit-

Blanc. "Give me the cracker. The cigarette's burning my fingers."

Tit-Blanc hesitated, then passed it to him. Imperturbably, one hand up his other sleeve, Denis lit the sputtering fuse. "Get down on your knees as if you were praying and slip it under his behind." Tit-Blanc did so, as if hypnotized.

Lise also was hypnotized by this big lad who had a flame in his eyes and who said his rosary as if he were muttering threats. She had dreamed of him all night long, had been unable to forget the savage manner in which he had stalked out of the parish hall the evening before.

The tiny fuse was sputtering—Pritontin was leaning back in his seat, fancying himself in the Abbé Trinchu's big Buick. "It will make at least fifteen miles to the gallon. Sixty miles a week. That's not too expensive. With my new duties, it's indispensable."

"It is a cowardly thing! You strangle society when you assassinate the reputation of your priests," the Abbé Trinchu was declaiming.

Puff — Bang!

Pritontin bounded forward, terrified. The explosion had almost wrecked him. Madame Pritontin was trembling, her hands outstretched toward the altar.

"The communists! The communists!" was the cry from all sides.

"On your knees, everybody!" the Latruche sisters called out. Their charms may have been faded but they were young when it came to initiative.

Life was bitter for the Abbé Trinchu. His oratorical revenge had miscarried. The looked-for explosion had come from a simple little firecracker. Half-dead from excitement, Tit-Blanc left the pew, his head down between his shoulders. The startled congregation did not know whether to cry murder or miracle. Having been awakened with a start, the gendarme Noré, looking very pale, came running up.

"Nab them! Get the communists!" Flora said to him as he went by; for she wished to let it be known that she was acquainted with the police.

Denis felt a desire to flee as fast as he could. He had violated the silence of the holy place. The firecracker had no sooner gone off than a piercing, terror-stricken scream was heard. One of the numerous rats that inhabited the building, having decided to attend mass and being dumbfounded by this most unusual occurrence which had come to break the monotony of the house of worship, had scampered over Lise's feet. Her head was swaying. She had fainted. Madame Lévesque also was sinking down, over her daughter's body, but with her it was always "just about to." The bewildered congregation did not know whether to dash forward or remain seated.

"Murder! Murder!" Pritontin began screaming, having at last recovered his senses.

With sweeping gestures expressive of his contempt, the Abbé Trinchu made for the sacristy. "You asked for it; now put up with it!"

Noré, the gendarme, embarrassed at having to perform his official duties in church, was very much befuddled as he arrived on the scene of the explosion. What was he to make of those bits of trouser leg and that acrid odour? It was very slight evidence upon which to procure a conviction for an offence as grave as this one.

"It was the reds that did it," said Pinasse Charcot, who was a blue.

The thing had been so unexpected that the members of the guard, forgetful of their uniforms, could only stand and stare at the police officer. Zépherin Lévesque, so dismayed that he was unable to move, kept muttering to himself as if he were praying. Denis in the meantime had picked Lise up in his strong arms. The gendarme was about to lay a hand on the young man's shoulder when Flora shouted to him: "Leave my boy alone, Noré!" Plucking at the flap of the policeman's blouse, Pritontin in despair showed him the remains of his trousers. Denis took the centre aisle and, to show how strong he was, left by the door that was farthest away. The girl's dress had slipped up over her bent knees and her white and dimpled flesh was visible.

"Good heavens! Just look at that! He had his hand on her thigh!" The Latruche sisters were all but swooning.

"If only she doesn't die!" murmured Zépherin, who had come up to Denis. "Maybe she's dead already!"

"How brave my son is," Madame Boucher was saying, her heart filled with pride.

Father Folbèche was busy restraining the altar boys, who wished to come up to the communion table so that they could see better.

"If it had been me, would he have carried me out?" Germaine asked herself discontentedly.

The lads at the rear, anxious not to lose anything of this unforeseen spectacle, were staring with wide-open eyes. The male choristers left off studying their sheets of music to envy Denis

his luck, and the lay brother who was their leader, quite unnerved by it all, played with his baton to attract the children's
attention. The Gonzagues, thoroughly vexed, were inwardly
calling Denis a swine, but the word did not pass their lips. The
Daughters of Mary were envisioning an epidemic of fainting fits.
The rest of the mass passed off unnoticed by anyone.

CHAPTER

V

THOSE in love are little concerned with social upheavals. Jean, who had injured his knee in escaping from the orchard that morning, had made himself an improvised bandage and was nursing his leg by way of killing time. As he sat there inactively upon the steps in front of the house, it seemed to him that high mass would never end. He was worried over his plums. He had chosen them with care, but would Lise be able to appreciate their special flavour—the flavour of stolen fruit? His hands went back and forth between his knee and the bag, his fingers caressing the plums as if they had been living beings. And then he gave a start: Denis was running past with Lise in his arms!

He was taking her home. Was she dead? It could not be! What had happened anyhow? Hobbling along as fast as he could, he stopped short before that terrifying door that had closed upon Denis. Should he go on in? All his courage crumbled. How weak he was, how soft! He turned back in desperation and sat down on the edge of the sidewalk facing the house. Since Lise had fainted, he would not be jealous. All he had to do was wait until she recovered consciousness. She would then find his plums all the nicer, would appreciate them all the more. What did it matter if her head had lolled on Denis' shoulder, her hair falling over him? It was a caress that meant nothing. And Denis would come out soon, he felt sure of that; he would not stay beside a girl who would learn when she emerged from her faint that he had carried her in his arms.

Jean gave a sigh. It was petty of him to be always obtruding himself like that, to have no more imagination than to be forever making excuses for his own weaknesses. He was ashamed.

Then the street began to fill with people. The Soyeuses in groups were talking excitedly, and from their terrified exclamations he assumed that some extraordinary event must have occurred. The Daughters of Mary were exultant. They stationed themselves like sentries in front of the Lévesque home. The gang of Mulots next invaded the street, and Jean mingled with them. Tit-Blanc was marching along with grandiloquent gestures, his eyes shining.

"He got what he deserved. It could have been worse than that. He's lucky that I have a wife and children. You are my witnesses. I am not a communist! Did you ever see anybody as cowardly as that fellow Boucher? I didn't like it a bit, having to do everything myself. Why, I had to snatch the cigarette out of his hands. How are you, my lads? Hey, there! Didn't you go to high mass?" he called out triumphantly to those Mulots who had attended the nine o'clock service and who, accordingly, had not witnessed his exploit. He went on to explain to them his theory of courage: first of all, you had to have nerve.

In the sacristy, a weighty discussion was going on between the vicars, Monsieur le Curé, and the churchwardens. They were all anxious to make an exciting bit of news out of the catastrophe that had just occurred. All except Pritontin. He was beside himself, overwhelmed by his wife's indignation, for Madame Pritontin was deploring the loss of the thirty dollars his suit had cost.

"This is not going to be the end of it," he muttered in confusion.

But they treated him like dirt, as an object of pity. In the presence of these contemptuous churchwardens who commiserated him as if he had been a pauper, he realized the vanity of the title that had been bestowed upon him: "Distributor of Tickets." Hiding the torn seat of his trousers with his Panama hat, he bellowed threats that ended in murmurs of assent.

The sacristan, who had succeeded in chasing out all the curious young ones from the choir, remarked to him sympathetically: "So they took your behind for a dynamite hole, did they?"

"Is it possible? Is it possible?" the Latruche sisters were whining. They hovered around the curé like the hinds of the Old Testament. "How our saint is going to suffer!"

"He's not the one who's going to have to pay for these trousers," cried Sophie Pritontin in her shrill voice.

The spinsters were taken aback. What did she have against their saint? They stared at the Pritontins suspiciously.

"I've had enough of this," said Sophie, addressing the curé. "Let them go ahead and arrest Tit-Blanc Colin. Let them bring him to trial."

This suggestion was met with a murmur of dismay. The churchwardens, who did not want any real trouble on their hands, became less bellicose. Concerned with protecting the Mulots, the Abbé Bongrain protested. Monsieur le Curé gravely clapped his hands for silence.

"On the contrary," he said, "we must hush it up. Whatever happens, there must be no scandal. The communists would like nothing better. That's when they're dangerous, you know, when you provide them with a rostrum. Just think of the wrong we should be doing to our saint. What would they think at Rome? In spite of the fables you have read, they would never believe that so fine an ear could grow amid so many tares."

"There is something in what you say, Father," the old maids chimed in. They were interrupted by Sophie Pritontin, who was almost hysterical in her vehemence.

"Your saint!" she screamed. "Your saint! Don't talk to me about *him*! Are we all to suffer on his account? He put on his hair shirt over his tunic, that's what he did! And I can tell you something else: you don't know who the real saints are. They are pulling the wool over your eyes, Monsieur le Curé, with all this publicity. *Mon Dieu! Mon Dieu!*" And she began sobbing on Anselme's shoulder as he slipped his free arm about her.

Greatly upset, he begged her to be silent; for he was trembling for his title. His eyes sought those of Father Folbèche, by way of signifying his desire to fall at the curé's feet and apologize. The full meaning of Sophie's insult was just beginning to dawn upon the Latruche sisters; and from their little gasps and the manner in which their thin arms shook in their flowing sleeves, it was evident that their anger was near the boiling point. They would have fallen upon the Pritontins then and there if the be-fuddled churchwardens had not pushed them out the door.

Flora, who had just lighted a taper for her ailing son, stopped them. She did not notice how angry they were. Thrilled with pride, she felt too magnanimous to humiliate anyone by letting her joy be remarked. "That foolish boy of mine, he's so tender-hearted. Did you see what happened?" Assuming a modest look, she studied their faces. In a flash, Cécile and Peuplière had a vision of Lise's thigh and Denis' hand.

"You poor mother!" they exclaimed.

"Poor mother?" Suspecting them of being jealous, Flora felt indignant but, in view of her own happiness, decided to over-look this insult. After all, they were to be pitied for not being mothers themselves; and above all, they did not know what it meant to be the mother of a lad like Denis. But what were they getting at, anyway, with that "Poor mother"? Why did they drop their eyes like that? Never had they appeared so ethereal. Peuplière was inclined to be reticent.

"Do you know how he was carrying her?" she asked.

"Did you see where he had his hand?"

Anxiously, Flora gazed in turn at each of their pinched faces. She felt a twinge of suspicion around her heart. "Did he have it above her knees?"

"You poor mother!"

The old maids were enjoying their uneasiness. They were having their revenge. This would teach the imperious creature to compete with their saint by running lotteries for Gaston's hens. The only thing that prompted Cécile's imagination was her own nostalgic longings. She proceeded to add fuel to the flame.

"He's at her side right now," she said. "He's whispering sweet words in her ear. He won't let her go. He runs his hand over her hair—Oh! will there always be passion in this poor world of ours!"

Flora's jaws were set. "Passion? My son? Come with me!"

What a day for the spinsters! How superior they felt by reason of their saint! They followed Flora with alacrity, forgetting their anger toward the Pritontins.

The crowd had grown in front of the Lévesque home. Jean wanted to leave, but not before Denis did. Urged on by Germaine, his mother laid a hand on his shoulder and shook him. "Your place is at your girl's side. Are you going to let Boucher take her away from you?"

"My girl? Not really. Don't make me laugh."

"You dummy, go on!" said Germaine. "You've already let her faint in somebody else's arms. I must say, you don't seem to care much." Her tone was contemptuous. She was annoyed at being so robust herself.

"Come, let's find out," said Madame Chaton, who could not bear to stand there at the door any longer. Denis was on her mind. Was Lise still in his arms?

The Mulotes and Soyeuses trooped into the house, Barloute dragging Jean behind her. There were exclamations on all sides. "Has Mamzelle recovered yet? We were so worried. Poor child!"

Despite the fact that Lise insisted she was all right, Zépherin, searching frantically for the telephone book, started leafing through the dictionary instead, calling all the while for smelling salts. He was so taken up with what he was doing that he was not even aware of the intruders. Slumped in a rocking chair, Madame Lévesque was suffering an attack of asthma. And so, it was with the eyes of a strange lad looking down upon her that Lise had regained consciousness, a lad who clenched his fists as he murmured words of endearment.

"You're not like all the other girls," he was saying. "Swear to me it's true that a lot of things disgust you just as they do me." He was threatening her as he strove to reassure himself. "Don't lie to me, whatever you do. It's just because you're weak that you talk that way. I've already had a chance to see."

He gritted his teeth as he caught sight of the curiosity seekers thronging about him, showering questions upon the two of them and giving vent to expressions of solicitude and admiration. Tit-Blanc and his gang were rummaging in the corners of the room, looking at the photographs. Germaine was trying to pick out the chords of popular songs on the piano. The Daughters of Mary were inquiring of Denis if Lise had not been too heavy for him; they seemed concerned about the matter. What an effort it must have cost him! Jean wanted to slip out, but Féda held him back. She jostled Denis. "She's not your girl. Let my lad sit there. Come on, beat it, you robber!"

At this point, Zépherin excitedly hastened over to them. "Out, out, everybody, please! Let my daughter have some air." He was careful of the manner in which he put them out, for he meant to run for office at the next election. At sight of his friend, Denis rose from his chair. It pained Jean to see the astonished look on Lise's face. There was a great chattering among the women outside. Then Flora pushed the door open. She was flushed and made use of her elbows in clearing a path for herself and the Latruche sisters, who wore their bonnets as if they had been plumes and who were fairly clucking with importance.

"Where is he?" she cried. "I want to punish him!"

Denis turned pale as Peuplière pointed to him, exultantly. "There he is! You can see for yourself, he hasn't stirred an inch from her side." Cécile dropped down complacently into the chair that he had vacated.

"Home with you, I say! I'll take care of you and your passion!"

"But Mama!"

"Ah, your mother?" said Lise with a smile.

"Are you better now, my child?" Cécile asked. "Is the numbness out of your limbs? Here is a picture of our heavenly protégé that we've brought you." Lise was bewildered by this meaningless talk. "What weak knees you must have!"

The elderly spinster was being charitable, trying to relieve the embarrassment of the situation by these banal inquiries. How she was enjoying it! Her eyes sought out the girl's thigh where she had seen Denis put his hand, and she went on to imagine

Lise acting out the little comedy. Her saint would never have done a thing like that. She had sat down in some haste, not perceiving that her skirt was lifted slightly, affording a glimpse of her black lacework garter. In a mood of desperation as a result of his mother's words, after all that he had confessed to Lise concerning his own temperament, Denis bent over and snapped the elastic on Cécile's skinny knee.

"You wear silk ones now, do you?"

Lise burst out laughing as Cécile gave a little scream and dropped her skirt in great dismay. Denis fled with his mother in pursuit.

"How brazen!" cried Peuplière.

Cécile was anxiously probing her conscience, being uncertain as to just how grave a sin she had committed. Had she not been guilty of tempting Denis by exposing herself like that? Peuplière, meanwhile, was happy down in her heart, for after this affair of the garter her sister was less chaste and she, Peuplière, now enjoyed a priority with the saint. Nevertheless, she pretended to be highly incensed and shouted her indignation for all to hear. Taking advantage of the confusion, Jean handed Lise his present.

"I've picked the nicest there were. The yellow ones are the best. Taste them."

Lise was annoyed. She looked at the plums, then at Jean.

"Why!" he said. "You remember yesterday. I promised."

Seeing the communist's son talking to his daughter, Zépherin sprang forward. "Out with you! Vagabond."

Jean went out, dragging his injured leg after him. Perspiring and ashamed, he hunched his shoulders as Zépherin hurled the plums after him like so many little bombs.

The old maids then took Monsieur Lévesque to one side, to put him on his guard against his daughter's nascent love affair. They gave Jean a sympathetic look as he picked up his scattered plums from the street. They were thinking of fastening this hoodlum on Lise. She would pay for that burst of laughter and for the readiness with which she had fainted in the arms of an impure wretch like Denis.

Germaine grew impatient as she reflected on how long it took Denis to ask her if he might come over and sit in the parlour with her. That easy chair that she so carefully arranged and rearranged every day, seeking to place it in just the proper light—how long was it to remain empty? Ah, that Lise! And that brother of hers, who would not bestir himself but who melted like butter when he came near the girl.

The Colin household was in high spirits. Their shop was about to bring them fame and fortune. They were moving furniture to make room for the counter. Beside his box of worms, Jean gnashed his teeth and squirted the juicy pulp from his plums all over the little animals. "Vagabond!" He nourished his wrath in order not to feel his pain. How premature he had been in exclaiming over his happiness that morning!

"You may as well get used to the shame of it, old man. You're a born cad, and that's what they're going to call you. You'll never know what it is to be somebody. Go hunt up Boucher. He laughs about it, but he means to be somebody all the same. Why are you crying? Because you are so angry? Damn it all, anyway!"

But Jean was not disillusioned, since hope for him had never been a reality. He had in a manner of speaking forgotten this, even though Denis had been there to remind him. He had caught a glimpse of happiness at high tide; and now, the tide was visibly receding as it did upon the long beaches, from the flatness of the rue Colomb. Ah, had he but been a capable swimmer like Denis, at home in all waters, taking advantage of the tempest as of the calm! But happiness had fled. The beach shone bright and empty now. Lise was not meant for him. She knew nothing of the filth of factories, of the pay that they take away from you. Boucher was a student; his past had been different from that of a worker's son who never knew peace, whom life was always trying to drag down; he lived amid the magic of books, wonderful books that spoke to you only of the future. Denis had robbed him, everybody had robbed him. The good Lord Himself had robbed him by sticking him away in such a hole as this when he would have liked to be a great man, of the sort that Lise could love.

"Going to be a damp evening, John. Good for worm hunting." Hilarious with prosperity, Tit-Blanc shook him by the shoulders. Jean was worried because he no longer felt any interest in his business; he had no heart for it. It was in vain that he pictured to himself heaps of worms that would bring him in piles of money. It was a lamp that could no longer be lighted, for the flame of Lise's smile had consumed everything.

Tit-Blanc was laying his plans for the opening of the shop. This was the day of victory. "And some dessert at noon, Germaine. Go get a half-pint of syrup."

Old man Pitou was already at the table. He was beaming. The

good old days of Sewer Town were back again, and his Tit-Blanc, in whom he had lost faith for a time, was showing himself to be a worthy son. Brawls, fist fights, the Mulot's provocative tongue were in evidence once again. The younger generation was not so bad after all! As for Féda, she was almost proud of her nickname, Barloute, when her husband tickled her and called her by it after high mass was over. She was so happy that she actually seemed to put on flesh. And the shop! And the look on Boucher's face!

Germaine, however, was sad as she made her way to the grocer's. Denis had not appeared to notice her new dress when she opened her coat. What could she do to attract this lad who was so surly toward ordinary folk? How was she to keep girls of more refinement from stealing him? What was that cursed "ideal" of his that had led him suddenly to stop laughing and start using his fists? What kind of affectation was this? If Denis married her, she would be clever; she would banish from her speech one or two vulgar, ungrammatical expressions. She would ask him if they could not live in the Upper Town because of his working in an office. She would play her part so far as education was concerned; she would stop associating with the Mulots, would buy stacks of books, and of an afternoon would slip away to meet her girl friends at the popular-priced theatre. Then she saw once more that cruel yet unsullied spark in Denis' eye, and she sighed for the dream that was in her heart.

A big head protruded over the wall of the Boucher garden. "You're pretty, you are, Jamaine, Sunday! Pretty, oh! pretty, your dress!" Gaston had paused in the act of feeding corn to his chickens. His smile was an expression of everything that happiness could mean to him. Germaine felt a tug of remorse as she thought how, at home, they were planning to rob him of his shop. Putting her hand through the opening between the planks of the wooden partition, she caressed his blond hair, which he must have combed for her especial benefit, and which in the sunlight held reddish glints.

"You are nice-looking, too, Gaston." That hand on his hair! The hens became birds of paradise to him, and the trees were big brothers. Thoughtfully, Germaine left off caressing him and walked away. Why was not Denis as tender-hearted as that? Why did he believe himself to be a kind of sword and spend all his time defying the world and his own future?

In the distance, the clouds were spreading out like enormous splotches of oil upon the blue of the sky. Jean was wearily preparing his angleworm layout. And then, suddenly, he revolted. No! He would not admit that he had wrenched that knee of his for Lise's sake.

Peuplière and Cécile Latruche were waiting for the hour of ten, to go to bed. The kitchen served these gossip artists as a studio. The younger one was mending a cassock, while the other, standing in front of a blackboard, was jotting down names and figures in a row. The two fossils had lost their personality along with the last vestiges of their unsatisfied capacity for human pleasure. In thinking of them, it was no longer their countenances that one called to mind, but rather the memory of a hypocritical piety that had the disagreeable smell of mould, dissolving like an acid what was left of the physical attractions they might once have had. This renouncement on their part being too unconstrained, too superficial to be offered as a sacrifice to God, they had seized with avidity upon the young parish saint who had had the decency to die. They crammed him with invocations, compliments, swoonings, and litanies, but without any pity for the obscure flesh-and-blood lad who had fasted too much upon earth ever to be a gourmand in heaven. Enjoying a respectable life annuity left them by their father, who had dealt in oysters, the demoiselles Latruche had given themselves over wholly to a gossipy mysticism, being convinced of their superiority over sinners like Barloute and fertile mothers such as Flora.

Prior to the discovery of their little saint, these parasites, disappointed at being refused admission to the Daughters of Mary and the Ladies of the Holy Family, had felt themselves to be of little importance, without an object in life. In view of this, it is not so hard to understand their sudden and furious devotion to this dead youth, whom they in a manner of speaking had rehabilitated. These aging spinsters had a purpose now; and if their past was wholly taken up with their virginity, the Ark of the Covenant for them, their future was filled with the disembodied form of a heavenly stripling. This is not to say that old maids who attain sanctity may not cherish a carnal obsession for a young ascetic such as the one that St Joseph's parish had produced. For the demon of lust has many ways of stoking his fires.

"Total : one hundred and ten dollars," Cécile announced.

"The portraits included?"

"Everything. The photographs of Monsieur le Curé amount to one hundred and three dollars and four cents. Net profit:

twenty-three dollars and thirty cents. Those of our dear little one: fifteen dollars for the printing; net profit: eight dollars and thirty cents."

"That will go for the flowers on his grave."

"In the form of a heart. Don't forget to notify the workmen."

"Very well. Give me the list of Mulots who are to be brought to God."

"Chaton; Tit-Blanc Colin, he's a new one; and Denis also, the little lecher." Peuplière simpered and went on to deplore that unfortunate affair of the garter. Aware of her disadvantage, Cécile was inwardly fretting and laying plans for vengeance.

"Poor Madame Boucher, she is really so kind-hearted and that invalid son of hers is such a trial. But we may see in that a punishment from Heaven. She and her vulgar backyard raffles trying to compete with our sale of photographs! And then there is Bidonnet, who spends his time talking against our beloved curé. And a special mass for Pinasse Charcot, who is having such a time of it with those unmentionable diseases that he contracted. It seems that he picked them up on the other side, in 1914. Ah, those French women and their love songs!"

"And let us not forget the demoiselles Brindamour. They go out automobile riding with young men at night. They are not refined, and what's more, they are going to be married to some store managers who are worse than the English."

With a feeling of uneasiness, Cécile went over to the window, decorated with ferns, and drew in a breath of the night.

"The Clichoteux have gone to bed. Poor woman! It is hard, when one is somebody in the church, to have to shut one's door on a priest. I wonder what our good little saint thinks of all that?"

With a self-satisfied air, they took up a position in front of his portrait, three feet square, painted by their nephew, a Beaux-Arts student.

"Just look at those eyes!"

"And those curly locks!"

Their exclamations were simultaneous. The old maids' eyes met in an instinctive flash of jealousy. Their pinched mouths, their teeth ready to bite seemed to say: "Who was the first to love him?"

Peuplière smiled magnanimously. "One must be worthy of his love, Cécile. You will have to improve your conduct. Your legs uncovered like that when you sit down—" Her heart was singing. In her joy, she beheld an undulating swarm of lacework garters coiling around her rival, binding her fast ten steps lower on the stair to Heaven as the blessed young saint let fall waxen tears.

Cécile could stand it no longer. "That Boucher must be punished;" she cried. "He's not going to have Lise Lévesque. Firecrackers aren't going to help him. And then there is that Pritontin creature who insults our child."

The two sisters suddenly exchanged a fixed stare, for the same suspicion had dawned upon each of them, and it grew at once and assumed the form of a terrible threat: at that very moment Madame Pritontin was plotting, was swiftly scheming to overthrow their heavenly protégé. But how? The spinsters recalled with terror the look of hatred that had burned in her eyes that morning. How could they ever forget it? And there was that Boucher woman, also, and her devilish son.

Quite overcome, Cécile and Peuplière sat down upon the bed. An hour passed and the tension became unbearable. Unable to control themselves, they threw on their clothes in tempestuous haste, quivering with excitement and each trying to outdo the other in a noble cause. They must go forth and confront danger, braving the darkness and the snares set by lecherous Mulots; they must beard the enemy in his lair. It was ten o'clock at night.

Voices reached the ears of the Latruche sisters as they were about to knock at the door of the Pritontin home. They stopped and listened.

"Me shut up?" Sophie Pritontin was shouting. "Me keep still? I'm going to speak my mind. You have no backbone, that's the trouble with you. So you're not going to make him pay for that suit of clothes? Are you satisfied with being a 'Distributor of Tickets'? Is there anything so ridiculous about signing a complaint? A little scandal like that would take the wind out of that puffed-up saint of theirs. At the same time, you'd be hitting at Lévesque, who'd love to see you out of the way and who is the Latruches' patron. But no! All you think of is honours. You keep mumbling about ambition, but when it comes time to strike a blow, you lose your nerve. You'll never amount to anything, not even an inspector of tramways. And you talk about having a car! A Buick!"

There was a silence, possibly filled by the stammerings of a limp and deflated Pritontin. He was heartbroken over what had happened in church and no longer counted on anything less than a miracle. That firecracker had destroyed something more than his trousers.

Outside, the old maids were stamping about, putting first an ear and then an eye to the keyhole. It was with some perplexity that Peuplière arose from this posture. "Their two sons on their knees, saying their prayers!"

Sophie's voice held them once more: "I want you young ones to note what your mother has to put up with. Such injustice! Stay on your knees, whatever you do. They're not going to be able to say that you keep your saint's diary sitting down. That saint of theirs! What a trumped-up affair! The little hypocrite! He knew he was very ill and naturally he was in a hurry to have a talk with the curé. All the lies that he must have told him!"

The pair at the door looked at each other. They were on the verge of fainting. They trembled from terror, then from wrath as that awful voice went on:

"What is it you're hiding there, Henri? Your hair shirt? Pull it down over your hips and don't put it on over your tunic the way *their* saint did. How fat you are! Aren't you ever going to get thin? He was a consumptive, which was what gave him such a childlike air. You'll be the death of me yet."

Her tone was tremulous with disappointment. Ah, to be a mother and see your sons canonized while you were still alive! There came a fresh outburst, a shrill cry of defiance: "As for those old prudes, the Latruches, you saw how I handled them."

At this point, the spinsters furiously pushed open the door and stormed into the room. "Hah! We've caught you at it! Robbers!"

Sophie, who was angrily stitching her husband's trousers, could only stare at them, open-mouthed, her arm suspended in midair. There was no time now to conceal her masterpieces. The sanctuary had been violated; the hope of a heaven all her own was melting away with the wax of the candles. No more secret competition as she prepared and refined her young saints with all the attention that one devotes to a good cheese. Standing there majestically, their nostrils flaring, the Latruche sisters were examining with contempt the walls covered with religious banners and holy images. Disdainfully, Cécile went up to the chubbier of the two Pritontin youngsters, both of whom appeared to have had their fill of daily devotions. On their knees, at that!

"Do you think, my child," she asked, pinching his cheek maliciously, "that with all that fat you are ever going to be canonized?"

This sacrilegious gesture brought a reaction from Madame Pritontin at last. She almost jumped out of her chair.

"Watch what you are doing! Don't touch them! They are pure, dirty old things that you are! People have not forgotten how friendly you used to be with Barloute Colin. And we know all about the love you have for your saint!" Her voice grew honied now. "You might at least have left him to Mademoiselle Lévesque. They're nearer to being of the same age."

"Be quiet," Anselme begged her, "be quiet in front of the children." All this was the last straw for him.

Panting under an avalanche of epithets and routed by Sophie, brandishing her needle, the spinsters fell back to the door.

"Get out, filthy creatures!"

The sisters could not believe their eyes. What a figure those fat little aspirants to sainthood would cut beside their own young man! It was, of course, a crime; but it only went to show how they, Peuplière and Cécile, had become the objects of envy. There was, however, a graver danger that threatened them. Sophie's insinuation that Lise, by reason of her youth, rightfully should be the one to concern herself with the saint filled the good ladies with an anxiety that rapidly became consternation. This was no time to be sleeping. The disaster must be averted at once. Lise being a refined sensualist, all they would have to do would be to find an earthly outlet for her affections. If she was left fancy free, might she not fix her choice upon their angel? Cécile recalled the girl's laughter over that affair of the garter. They must find her a decent sweetheart. Boucher? He was already too much of a rake for a young lady so inclined to pleasure as she.

An understanding look flashed between them. "Jean Colin?" They could see him taking Lise with him to hunt for worms. "It would serve her right, the young hoity-toity!"

They smiled as they passed the Boucher home. Shadows were moving about in the kitchen, and Flora's voice reached them: "Joseph, you're his father, and I'm telling you, he was holding her like that."

Gaston, disgusted by the idea of buttocks, was growling: "Damned swine. Denis. Damned swine."

It was with a jaunty step that the Latruches entered the Lévesque living room. Buried under her husband's medal-laden uniform, Madame Lévesque gave them a sign of welcome. A big, sturdily built woman, she was in the habit of crossing her legs at the ankles. Her thick ears had the appearance of being pasted on her head; her grey hair was caught up in an enormous topknot; a pair of never absent spectacles rode the bridge of her stub nose, handsome gold-rimmed glasses of the kind that a churchwarden's wife ought to wear. In short, everything about her was in striking contrast to Lise's air of distinction, but Pierrette Lévesque was not in the least concerned with this and for the moment was tranquilly engaged in sewing stripes on her husband's honorary commandant's costume. Oh, those gaudy uniforms that have never known the field of battle! Blood and grapeshot atone for a host of follies.

"My dear ladies! Out so late?"

The spinsters sighed in a manner that indicated they had something important on their minds. There was a confidential look in their eyes.

"We have come to warn you. It is serious."

Zépherin turned pale. So they were plotting against him, were they? He must see what there was to this. Lise smiled from behind the book she was no longer reading.

"Are you better, my child? It is too bad it had to be Denis Boucher who carried you out. Those impious ones take advantage of everything."

The girl slammed her book shut. "I think he's a noble young man," she said with vehemence. "It is his brutal frankness that I like about him."

"But nevertheless, it is good advice that we are giving you." They glanced uneasily at Zépherin, who was annoyed that these old maids without education should be advising his daughter, a convent graduate. With some embarrassment, he changed the subject.

"Can you imagine," he said, "the face that Pinasse Charcot will make when he sees my new uniform?"

"Ah, that man!" exclaimed Madame Lévesque, whose favourite occupations were slander, needlework, and knitting. "He never takes a bath!"

"My dear lady, if you could see the cockroaches crawling around in his bread!"

A violent man whose uniform was always spotted with flour and whose stripes were tarnished, Pinasse Charcot had been a baker for the last couple of years and was a veteran who had seen service in '14. Possessed of initiative and anxious to show off his powerful voice, he had founded the guard in the early days of the parish. He was a lukewarm Christian, but Corpus Christi, the feasts of the Sacred Heart and St John the Baptist, and the anniversary of Lévis were for this old soldier the outstanding days of his life. It was, however, at All Souls that his happiness became complete, for on that day they went to the cemetery to fire a few cartridges in a salute to the dead. An army man who had been through the mill, he had it in for Zépherin, who was always parading his brilliant galloons, his fine silver sword, and his red-striped trousers. What the devil! He, Pinasse, had been in the war. He knew the authoritative ring of a general's voice, and he had made the acquaintance of the girls of Paris. Zépherin, who was ostentatiously condescending toward him, looked upon him as the only enemy he had by whose hatred he was flattered.

"You will see, Mesdemoiselles, how envious he will be." And the churchwarden, a tall man slightly inclined to obesity, put his hands in his pockets and gave a satisfied chuckle.

Peuplière now launched the attack, but for once was not supported by her sister, who was busy observing whether or not Lise was guilty of the same imprudence as she with regard to her legs.

"With those bad diseases that he has," Peuplière was saying, "Pinasse may well be envious. But the worst enemies are not always the most impure. Beware, Monsieur Lévesque."

The admonition struck terror in Zépherin's cowering heart. "What do you mean?" he asked.

"You know very well, don't you, that Pritontin has been slandering you behind your back? Do you think he's going to stop there? Just imagine, he's accusing you of trying to protect the communists! On account of our saint, we have urged Monsieur le Curé to avoid any sort of scandal; but Pritontin will take advantage of this personal insult that has been offered him, this just punishment that has been inflicted upon him, to defile your reputation, which has always been so clean a one. Colin is the instrument of God's will."

Zépherin was paler than ever now, for there were the coming county elections at which he expected to be a candidate. He became violent.

"I'm only sorry the firecracker didn't do more damage! I'm going to congratulate that fellow Colin. Protecting the communists! People like us!"

He stopped short, for a dark look had come over Lise's face. Peuplière gave her a malicious glance. "They are saying that young Jean Colin has a real crush on you, and they are whispering it about that you are not indifferent to him. Isn't that so, you sly little minx?"

Annoyed by the conversation, Lise arose stiffly and went upstairs to her room. She sighed as the door closed behind her. At last she was far away from the old maids and their exclamations, from her father and his astonished looks, from all this parochial pettiness. A copy of *Atala* lay open on her bed. How good it was to breathe in her happiness, to feel it palpitating in the silence. She put on her rose-coloured dressing gown, undid her hair and stretched it out as far as she could. What a delightful sensation of relief. With a tranquil pleasure in which her whole being seemed immersed, she caressed the objects around her. The window was open, and she plunged her face into the yellow moonlight as into a basin of tepid water. Refreshed by the rain, the whole world appeared to be exhaling a voluptuous joy. One of Gaston's cocks was crowing. Ah, Denis!

She did not notice Jean, hidden in a corner of the garden wall and looking up at her, his lantern extinguished, his worm pail empty. Taking up her ivory-inlaid hand mirror, she posed in countless ways to make sure that her eyelashes in the light of the moon created just the proper shadow upon her cheek.

She wondered if Denis could sing and play the guitar. For Lise herself was a pianist. How unhappy he must be with that mother of his who had stormed into the house so unceremoniously, using language that was almost obscene. Good heavens, what sort of people were these, who talked so freely of thighs and calves and buttocks? No! these Mulots, with the exception of Denis, would never be able to comprehend Lamartine and Chateaubriand. She thought of Jean and reproached herself for the few minutes of conversation she had had with him; it seemed to her an abuse of confidence in view of Denis' nobility of character.

As a dreamy young girl in a fashionable convent school, she had listened to whispered descriptions of wonderful male cousins, glimpsed at vacation time, and she had mastered Chopin's waltzes for the reason that the sister had told her he was the good and faithful friend of the great George Sand, author of the piece about the ploughman, in the manual of literature. How then was she to envisage the first good-looking youth who came her way if not as a roseate, lace-fringed, doll-like creature, bringing her daisies which she would pluck all her life long—a creature who bore the sublime, unheard-of name: "My love"? For she was seventeen, and love had come to her!

Arranging her lamp so that it might be the affable witness of her thoughts, she climbed into bed and then proceeded to call up in her mind, with all the details that she could remember, a picture of this black-eyed, strangely tempestuous lad who had no fear of rats and who—immediately after he had muttered with clenched fists: "So, it's true, you do care for beautiful things, that's wonderful!"—had snapped an old maid's garter.

And she was going to prove it to him! Taking her pencil, she began looking for melodious phrases in her *Atala*. Tomorrow, she would buy some stationery with blue and pink envelopes. She stayed up until twelve o'clock writing in her diary: "It is midnight of the first day of my life, the day that love, chaste thief, entered my young girl's heart."

CHAPTER

VI

A CONFUSED sound arose from the parish. It was Monday, and in the school the brothers could be heard scolding the children. These teachers, newcomers at St Joseph, found it hard to get used to the unruly spirit of the young Mulots, who strove to imitate their fathers before them. Of an evening, in speaking of cuffs received at school, the elders would tell how when they were young they had routed the brothers with their inkwells. In the midst of all this brutality the curé's angelic Gonzagues went on practising their hymns, emitting little floods of harmony as the rest of the parishioners occupied themselves with household chores. Some of the women appeared to be spreading their happiness out in the sun, along with the diapers on the clothes-line, while others shouted insults at one another. Upon the balconies, certain mothers were shaving the heads of little ones, who cried because they could not scratch themselves. The incident of the firecracker was being discussed everywhere, more or less, with a dash of irony for Pritontin. The Soyeuses were whispering about Lise and her fondness for Boucher's gang. The young women were hesitant at first about taking this girl who sang so well into their circle, but Lise had won the mamas by fainting so spectacularly in church. There were even those who chided their older sons for not having been quicker than Denis.

The bump of commerce was also swelling, at the Bouchers' and at the Colins'. Ever since the night before, Tit-Blanc had been racking his brains to find out what it was his shop lacked. Now that Monday had come, a workday at the factory, he felt an intruder in his own house. He found it disconcerting to be home during the week, but in such a situation, could they get along without somebody like him? The counter, shelves, credit with the supply houses: these were things that called for something more than Barloute's quick temper and spiteful disposition.

She had her nose at the window now. "There's the lumber they're bringing in to the Bouchers'. People will laugh at them."

Germaine in front of her mirror was practising the proper

poses for greeting customers, and old man Pitou wanted to know every other minute if there was going to be chewing tobacco in the shop.

Across the street, Flora, her hands upon her hips and full of confidence in the prosperity that was to come, had no fears. Flushed with pleasure, she was giving orders to the truck-drivers and supervising the unloading of the lumber. Putting her hands to her mouth trumpet-wise, she announced to the Mulots that the shop would soon be open for business.

"Then maybe you'll stop flooding us with raffle tickets," Féda shouted to her.

"I'll leave that to the Latruches," she called back. Flora smiled, for she liked Féda and forgave her for what she had been in her youth. She was proud of her ability at carpentry as she set about making the partitions for the shop. Gaston, who loved having money in his hands, paid the men from the supply company without making any mistake. Then, suddenly, there came the sound of hammer blows from the Colins'. Tit-Blanc and Pitou, with their shirts off, were demolishing a section of wall.

"Didn't he go to work this morning, the bum?" asked Flora pityingly.

Then Tit-Blanc called to Barloute: "Is the Champlain ice cream coming soon? It's the best brand. And a good seller!"

Flora gave a start. The planks that she was putting up along the wall came tumbling down as she ran out on to the sidewalk. Féda, elated by her rival's discomfiture, began taunting her: "Just look at her, will you? She's fit to burst! Hah! you've lorded it over us long enough with that telephone of yours! Hey! look at that, will you? There's the soft drink truck coming to our place. Right this way, gentlemen."

Flora felt the pavement giving way under her feet. Her jaws were locked, and she must have been agitated indeed not to be able to give vent to her feelings.

Madame Langevin, who was returning from an interview with the brother superior who had punished her small son, laid a hand on her neighbour's arm. "Doing some building here, Madame Boucher?" she asked. Flora made no reply; her eyes were fixed upon that terrible door which this evening would swing open to engulf the future of her Gaston. "They seem to be hammering all around," observed the mother of the twins as she noted the mocking look on Barloute's face.

"You don't know, then, that we're opening a confectionery shop? You must drop in and see it as soon as you can. If we shut off your light, Boucher, you can use your hall lamp. Robber!"

"Sh-h-h! She might sue us," said Tit-Blanc prudently. He had expended the audacity of a lifetime in yesterday's undertaking.

"Heartless creatures that you are!" screamed Flora now. "The good Lord will not permit it. Gaston, Gaston, put a curse on them! Heh! come on, gang! Let's strangle them!"

At this rallying cry, Flora's friends appeared upon the balconies, ready to do battle; but when they learned that Barloute was setting up in the business, also, they were secretly rather pleased, for with a profitable business Madame Boucher would be going over to the side of the Soyeuses.

"Jamaine, too, a shop?" Gaston wanted to know. He thought his mother must be joking. He was happy about it, however, being pleased by the friendly competition, as he conceived it, on the part of the one he loved. Flora was not upset for long but fell to work furiously, laying planks and putting the counter in place. They were not going to rob her like that! But it seemed as if her stubbornness availed her nothing, for everything conspired to delay her. Did she go to telephone her orders in? The line was busy. And the young ones were rummaging through the cupboard, undoing the boxes of candy and putting their hands in the fresh paint. She was interrupted every minute, had to hunt for nails, run splinters in her fingers. "Who took the hand-saw?"

Concerned with those things that brought an immediate profit, Gaston collected the eggs from the nest and came to inform his mother that she owed him for a dozen. Then, pantingly, he set out in chase of those hens that had broken their eggs, to give them a beating. The clock was striking six when Joseph Boucher came home from work and caught sight of Tit-Blanc Colin putting up the sign on the front of the house. Barloute was gesticulating from the steps, calling to passers-by: "Come and eat the biggest ice-cream cones that you have ever seen! Come, come!"

Armed with a soup spoon, Germaine was trying to find a way of filling the cones that would be at once quick and attractive. Accustomed to being surprised at nothing except Gaston's attacks, Joseph was dumbfounded. Forgetting to give his usual glance at the hens, he rushed into the house, his hips bruised by the grain with which his pockets were stuffed. The children came out to meet him, still joyful over heaps of dainties they had found. They could not be brought to realize that these were for sale, and they were waiting with distaste for the first customer to put in an appearance. Joseph sensed the drama that was taking place, through the odour of scorched potatoes. Denis was singing "I've given you my heart," and Flora was intent upon replacing the electric light bulb which the youngest child had broken while playing ball with it. She was through with her work and had not yet noticed the counter had the wrong side out. She was more worried over having broken three jars than by the fact that she had placed the cash drawer within reach of customers. Gaston was panting and grumbling as he looked everywhere for a pop bottle which Denis, busy with an accounting problem, was hiding between his knees.

"Don't forget the ice cream, Mama!"

Flora turned threateningly toward another of the brats who was into the chocolate candies, called "honeymoons," laid out on little plates. The flies were wandering aimlessly about in the showcase, which had not yet been dusted and over which a sign had been chalked, reading: GENERAL CONFECTIONERY.

"So, you're home at last, are you? Where have you been ever since you quit work? And the ice cream's not here yet!" She was shouting at Joseph, deceived by his seeming calm.

"Two confectionery shops, Papa!" cried Gaston triumphantly, in his shrill voice.

Joseph took off his hat and brushed it, for he was orderly in his habits. "What else do you expect of the monkeys in this Lower Town?" he asked.

"That's right, go on and insult me. You married a girl of St Sauveur, you've had thirteen children in St Sauveur, so you'd better not say anything against it. You're too proud to answer me, are you? You're like Denis, who's been bellowing love songs ever since he put his hands—you know where."

Joseph knocked out his pipe and began examining his wife's handiwork. He who possessed no trade of his own always found something to criticize in what others more capable than he had done. "Those boards there are not well joined." He tried the door. "It grates. And your partition is lopsided. You've bent the nails down into the wood. Oh, well! It's all leftovers, anyway. You've written 'Confectionery' on the inside. Go see how it looks from the other side."

"You can criticize, but I'd like to see you do as well. I've worked all day long and you're not satisfied. My God!" Her chin quivered; she was about to burst into tears.

Joseph felt a sudden resurgence of the wrath he had known in his nationalist days, back in the time of Bourassa.

"We'll smash it all," he said, arming himself with an axe. "We're not going to have any shop."

"Not going to have a shop? Why, I'll put them in the gutter if it's the last thing I do. I'll not have to trig myself out in little blue dresses, either, like that hussy across the way. You'll see how many friends your wife has."

She was thinking of innumerable smiles from innumerable customers who would fill her house to overflowing with pennies. What was more, she was tired of being a housewife, of making beds and caring for children. She wanted to serve at the counter and devote herself to strangers. No credit with her. Then her mood became one of tenderness.

"Think of Gaston, Joseph," she said. "Everybody loves him. People will think it a shame for them to start up in the same business. Tomorrow, we'll begin a novena for him to succeed and for those robbers to lose everything. And I'm warning you, you'd better have a talk with Denis, for he doesn't want to go to church with us to begin the novena. That's understandable after what he did."

The doorbell rang at last. With angry looks, the young ones came running to watch over their booty, though they knew it had to be sold. Flora turned pale, then adjusted her smile like a dress as best she could. Gaston felt his head becoming cold while his feet were burning up. Joseph gave a "Peuh!" And the first two customers came in, full of curiosity : Madame Langevin and Madame Charcot.

Flora pushed the invalid forward : "Go and wait on them, Gaston."

"We've come to start you off, Madame Boucher. What a nice place you have here. I'm glad to see you have a large stock of candy."

"You have to have, with that underhand trick they've just played on us over there."

"But don't you have the same kind of ice cream that they do? Champlain cream is so good!"

"Don't talk to me about that! I was so mad today I thought I would die. They telephoned before we did. They have the rights for this whole corner, you know. We can't handle it now."

"The other is so thick and creamy," remarked Madame Charcot regretfully.

"Yes," replied Flora, in a deprecating tone of voice, "but it melts in your mouth like ice. I'm certain that Green Mountain is a hundred times better. If you only knew how soft and sweet it is! And just look at the colour of it!"

Flora was playing up her wares like any shopkeeper bent upon making a sale. Gaston's eyes were on the ladies' purses, waiting anxiously for them to open. Standing in the doorway, Joseph, who was used to thinking in terms of dollars, grew impatient and discouraged as he gazed wearily at the candy that sold for a cent. A lot of profit in that! It was maddening to think how slowly the pennies would pile up.

"Why, yes, I think I *will* have one of your three-cent cones," Madame Langevin decided, after due deliberation. "And you, too, Malvina? You have three flavours, at least?"

"We're beginning with three, you know, but we'll lay in more." Delighted at selling her first cone, Flora in a business-like manner picked up the spoon from the dish of hot water in which she was letting it soak.

"Is that what you use, a teaspoon?" The mother of the twins was disappointed. "They tell me they serve with a soup spoon across the way."

"But they put only a little bit in it. I'm not afraid to fill it up!" Saying this, she plunged her small spoon energetically for each cone.

"It's the shells that make theirs look bigger."

"You'll notice that I spread it all around. I don't leave my cones empty in the middle. You don't do that, you know, unless you're out to rob people. We decent folks always think the robbers are going to succeed better than we do, just because they're more crooked, especially when it comes to business."

"Here is your money."

Gaston snatched it and tossed it into the cigar box. The box already held three black pennies, a precaution on Madame Boucher's part, by way of showing that they had made some sales. She had had great difficulty in borrowing them from Gaston.

"Over on that side," she went on, "I am going to put a bench along the wall, for the young people who will be sure to gather here. I have pickled eggs to sell, too. Do you think that affair in the church yesterday is going to go hard with Tit-Blanc Colin?"

"Don't worry about that. Monsieur Lévesque called on him this morning. And the old maids came around later. If you could only have seen how nicely they treated Barloute. They talked over old times and laughed and chatted with her. They even left a picture of the saint in her shop. They're great friends.

really. And you can see for yourself that doesn't leave Pritontin much of a chance. No one is willing to sign his complaint against the communists."

At that moment, Flora realized vaguely that justice in that world is not in the interest of the greatest number. "Do you think that's going to be the end of it?"

"You may count yourself lucky, for your son was mixed up in it. Did you know young Colin had been invited to call on Mademoiselle Lévesque? Between ourselves, that girl is better suited to your boy, for she's not a Soyeuse like the others."

Denis dropped his pen. Jean? What was he doing at Lise's house. He had said nothing about it. Was he making his own decisions? The young man had the feeling that he was losing something, something that he had possessed only since yesterday. And it was not the haunting idea that his mother with her insults had put in his head, nor the way in which his hands had burned ever since she had recalled his innocent gesture.

"Good Lord!" Flora was saying now. "You need have no fear about that. I am well acquainted with the police. As for that Lévesque girl and her passion, I've seen to that. She's mad about him, you know. But I'm keeping an eye on him."

"And right you are, for he's at the age," said Madame Langevin, who was pained by the fact that her twins never did anything to get themselves talked about.

With tightly shut lips, Denis began pacing the parlour floor. He was unnerved by what he had just heard. Was Lise about to overcome his gang?

The young ones were crying for candy, and Joseph was grumbling because the table had not been laid.

"Don't forget," Captain Charcot's wife was insisting. "You must come and try our bread. We'll make you a good price, seeing you have so large a family."

A number of days went by and Denis, with little to say to anyone, would set out from home alone, neglectful of his gang. Strolling in the parks, he would dart contemptuous glances at the lovers there and then would go on to imagine himself upon some plain, being pursued by Lise, her hair floating on the wind. He would turn upon her, rudely: "It's no use, Mademoiselle." He strove to keep adrift between forgetfulness and the hope of seeing her again. That was the way it always was: threatened with the loss of some bit of happiness that had come his way, out of pride he would refuse to fight for it and, doing nothing, would wait until he had lost it. Since he had never been sufficiently unhappy to wish to die, he believed that it was a sign of weakness and cowardice to seek a consolation of any sort.

One evening as he was finishing supper, someone called to him from the yard: "Denis!"

Flora opened the door. "So, it's you, Jean Colin. You can just go away. My boy does not associate with people like you."

Denis' big body loomed behind her. He made a sign to Jean and the Langevins that he would come out and join them. While his mother was berating his friends, Denis took a couple of chocolate bars from the shelf and left by the shop door. His companions were waiting for him at the corner. Were they going to upbraid him for keeping to himself the way he had been doing? Thinking of this and of Lise—his thoughts always came back to her—he felt less their leader than he had been in the past. Jean was apologetic.

"We don't see you any more. You're not sore, are you? So far as the shop is concerned, I had nothing to do with it, you know."

Denis gave him a scornful smile. "If you were really what I took you to be, you wouldn't even mention it. You don't hear me speaking of it. Those are petty things. The bickering of my parents, like their love affairs, doesn't interest me. Don't you hate to imitate them like that?"

Jean wondered if he was alluding to that evening with Lise which the Latruche sisters wanted to arrange. Robert Langevin, who had asked Germaine to let him be her beau, was angry.

"You weren't so independent with the girls last Sunday!" he said. Jean thought of Lise in Denis' arm and was conscious of that persistent pain in his knee. He must find relief.

"And by what right," he asked, "do you try to control our feelings?"

"The right that comes from being the most intelligent."

They had stopped, and Denis stood there threateningly. He studied their faces taut with anger. The twins with their freckles impressed him as being funny. His own face relaxed and he smiled bitterly as he looked into Jean's worried blue eyes. Jean thought his friend was making sport of him. Was Denis so sure then, of having Lise? The Latruches were leaving the Lévesque home. They waved at Jean in friendly fashion.

"It's coming along nicely," they called out to him. "She's beginning to say yes."

Jean whirled upon Denis aggressively. "All right, so what! I've beat your time. I'm going to be invited to her house to spend the evening."

Denis hated him for this. Was Jean going to tell her that he, too, was not like the others? "You're not going!"

"Do you think you can stop me, just because you're jealous?"

"Jealous? You poor little creature. I thought you were nobler than that. Are you satisfied to be indebted for Lise to those old maids? Leave it to me. I'll get her for you. I'll throw her into your arms. But no, that would not be happiness, that would not be heaven; it would be the kitchen of your father and your grandfather all over again."

He was enjoying their astonishment. Then he felt ashamed of his stratagem, for he was lying. Why did he do it? He was silent, listening. The air was vibrant with the melancholy notes of a Chopin prelude. Denis looked up at the open windows of the house and Jean stopped short. He was listening, also. It was Lise. The twins were growing impatient. They were beginning to be annoyed by Boucher's mania for magnifying and complicating things, clothing them in the mists of another world.

"It's classical music. Come on."

"No, it's Chopin. But let's be going, anyway." What he wished to do was meet and cope with beauty, to recognize and then leave it, by way of proving to himself that he could in the same manner rid himself of Lise's image.

At the corner, they dropped down in their usual place, on the grocer's steps. Bending over the sidewalk, Denis amused himself by chasing the ants which were making furrows in the rotting base of a telephone pole. The tacit understanding that had held the members of his gang together that summer was already broken. Something had vanished, by a process as imperceptible as the first tremors of the ice just before it breaks in the springtime. The Langevins, who were going to work, Jean, fancying himself in love—the idea of exploring their hearts and minds was repugnant to Denis from now on. He would have liked to take these sorry fools and hurl them like blocks back in the Mulot quarry.

"I'll not let go of you," he muttered. Leaping to his feet, he tightened his belt and laughed in their faces. They were disturbed, but they did not realize as yet that the parting of the ways had begun. Did he mean to let them go? He was strongly tempted to do so.

"Go ahead and show your teeth! Good-bye for today. You bore me."

Where was that music coming from? He turned the corner and went down the rue Châteauguay, after first having assured himself that his friends were not watching him. Reaching the

Lévesque house, he leaped the rear fence into the yard and came out by the front gate. Thrilled to find that the music still awaited him, he sought to steel himself against becoming sentimental. What slender, expert fingers that convent miss must have! There was a certain stiffness to the playing for a time, and then, unexpectedly, there would come a passage rendered with a tenderness of feeling that took him out of himself and stirred him to the depths. From the street came the querulous chirping of sparrows and from a neighbouring courtyard the sound of a saw. The children must have been at their homework, and as the evenings were cool now, housewives no longer sat in chairs on the sidewalks with their cousins and sisters-in-law. Denis stole up under the window. Amid the shadows of the living room he could make out Lise's hair, her arms, and finally her white fingers on the keyboard.

Those fingers seemed barely to skim the keys, sounding half-tones like grave forebodings, with that voluptuous pleasure which those who are happy feel when they frighten themselves with lugubrious thoughts by way of better sensing their present well-being.

Chopin's music waits, it suffers, it grows in stature, it is filled with love, for the reason that it is about to cease. It is a music that thrills, inspiring marvellous hopes and a boundless despair. It is the singing and the weeping of sick lungs that one hears in his piano compositions. Youths, dreamers, those who sigh, consumptives will love him always, for he has an immortal light to shed upon that portion of mankind that loves and weeps voluptuously. His themes are feverishly developed around one key: the truth. He has left this legacy to those for whom death is the problem of the day, by way of conveying a feeling of grandeur to those who are the object of pity on the part of the strong and self-satisfied who revel in their muscular well-being.

Parting from the Langevins, Jean Colin also came to listen to Lise's playing. Perhaps this music was for him. She was waiting for him. He made an inventory of his faults that he might eliminate them in order to be worthy of her love. How foolish he had been the other day, to give up hope! Hidden like this, he felt nearer to her in his heart, was conscious of an inward fervour. He was not like Denis, occupied with reasoning things out, trying to convince himself that this music was for him no more than a fleshly song, an emotional cry, representing the voluptuous impatience of a young girl who did not know nor seek to know herself.

Yet Denis as well as Jean was experiencing his first ardent

sense of manhood and, carried away by the tempest of sound, was for the first time renouncing the rights of reason. Denis Boucher beheld the years of his adolescence floating away on those limpid and soothing chords, Lise's feverish right hand bore him off, transported him, kept him from thinking, prevented his asking himself whether or not he was in love with this girl. His life changed direction at that moment, passing from left to right like Lise's hands upon the keyboard. He gripped the window ledge with his fingers, felt a mad desire to embrace that body with all the stormy passion of youth. A cloud passed over his eyes. He turned back to the street.

Jean, his mouth gaping, looked as if he were drunk with ecstasy; he was riding toward distant lands where he would be recognized only by his way of feeling and loving. That skein of delicious, fever-inspired song that the piano keys unwound and that wound itself about his heart distressed him more than would the touch of her hands. For whom was she playing if not for her prince charming, and who could that be if not himself, Jean Colin?

This evanescent melancholy, these starts and impulses, this langorous feeling, all that Lise's playing provoked in him—what was it if not her soul? He pictured it as transparent, with diaphanous fingers shedding love and nobility. Her body was there only to cover over and conceal that which he alone had divined. But alas! How distant her eyes were! Did she really take him for a hoodlum? Supposing that Denis was right, and could really arrange things with Lise as he had said? It was better to confide one's hopes to a lad one's own age than to old maids. For Jean was resigned in advance to going with the stream, which was too violent for him to resist. If nothing else there was that throbbing pain in his knee to draw him to her: the knee which he had twisted for her sake the Sunday before. She was finishing her Chopin prelude. The silence seemed to hum for a moment as it absorbed these strange notes to which it was not accustomed, here in this quarter where all one heard was jigs on the accordion and where gossiping housewives and small brats bawled and wrangled all day long.

The desire to communicate with an unreal paradise brought the two lads together once more. Their glances met. Denis would have liked to knock Colin down, but he restrained himself and instead produced from his pocket the two stolen chocolate bars.

"Take them. I'll owe you fifteen cents."

Jean did so mechanically. He was ashamed. Denis had certainly been tracking down his dreams. They went off together without saying a word. Recognizing Denis' voice, Lise ran to the window. She had a feeling that he would not return, for the very manner in which he held his head revealed a desire to run away.

GASTON'S big round eyes glanced furtively at the kitchen window and, having made sure that his mother was not watching
him, he crossed the street, his long arms jerking at his side.
Breathing hard, with compressed nostrils, he made his way over
to the Colins'. He was happy to find himself alone with Germaine, who was seated upon a bench reading a popular novel.

She smiled amiably. What could she do to make it up to him
for having robbed him of his confectionery shop? For her, he
was like an image that had been desecrated.

"Hello, Jamaine." Germaine's knees were uncovered and he
stared at them, wondering what it would be like to touch them.
It must be a wonderful sensation, judging from the way in
which his mother scolded Denis about things like that. With a
serious look on his face he walked up and down in front of the
candy shelf. He had a problem on his mind: "Mama doesn't
like for us to handle the same kind of candy."

Germaine gave him an absent-minded glance and went back
to her hero on page seventeen. Gaston wondered how the well-
built lads went about it when they wanted the girls to listen to
them. He jingled the money in his pocket, for he had insisted
that his mother let him hold the liquid assets of the shop. With
what he had saved up during the last three years through
lotteries and the sale of eggs, it made a nice little nest egg. He
was not thinking so much just now of buying a car; that was
something in the distant future, and Germaine—well, there
were too many other lads around. He felt he must make a
purchase. "Two cents' worth of that candy, there." And he paid
with a ten-dollar bill just to keep her near him as long as possible, so that he could touch her hands a time or two.

"You're rich! Lucky Gaston. Wait, I'll go see if Papa has any
change." She come back quickly and caught him studying the
photograph of the saint, in whom he had no confidence. The
candidate for canonization was too young; he was not all
wrinkles like Brother André.

"Change?" Barloute was shouting at Tit-Blanc in the kitchen.

"He drinks up all the profits. When I think of the money we could make—"

"And you have no sympathy for your father," old man Pitou reproached him. "You would have such a good sale on chewing tobacco."

"People don't chew any more the way they did in your day, Father."

Gaston took back the ten-dollar bill. He hesitated, his hand in his pocket. "Germaine, do you still want Denis' picture that you asked me for?"

She came close to him, almost touching him. The invalid was silent, breathing harder than ever. He was hypnotized by the nearness of this girl for whom he felt a great but vague tenderness that came and went in fitful gusts. He dreamed of taking her riding in his auto.

Her grandfather now came out in his house slippers. Lifting the cover of the ice-cream container, he stuck his big yellow fingers down into it, then drew them out and sucked them stolidly.

Seizing the invalid's arm, Germaine shook him. "Did you bring it, my little Gaston?" she asked impatiently. "How good of you! Give it to me!"

Happily, the sick boy passed it to her. She took it and buried it in her bosom.

"There!" she said, planting a kiss on each of his cheeks.

Flora, pencil in hand, was lamenting the small profit from the enterprise: "Two dollars and a half in three weeks. It's disgusting!" She had hoped that the young people would gather at her place, and she cudgelled her brains trying to compute the profits the Colins must be making with the "gang" that hung out in their shop. On the other hand, she had had as customers the Daughters of Mary and the older girls from the convent, but they were very noisy and spent frugally. They talked loudly of their little adventures, for Denis' benefit, and Flora did not dare ask them to leave. As for the better class of Mulots, and of Soyeux as well, they were not to be depended on. Despite the fact that everybody kept saying "We ought to help out the poor invalid," the Boucher shop had not been a success. Germaine's sex appeal had attracted more custom than Gaston's infirmity. Above all, neither the Mulotes nor the Soyeuses, her rivals, cared to contribute to Flora's enrichment. Those whose conscience hurt them would assert that the Champlain ice cream which the Colins sold was sweeter than hers.

Delighted with the unlooked-for prosperity, Tit-Blanc seldom went to work any more, finding it more profitable to spend his nights collecting the rake-off on poker games. He could visualize himself as the proprietor of a famous gambling house of the sort to be seen in American movies; but each time a stranger entered the shop, the players would make a mad rush for the kitchen door.

As she waited sometimes until midnight behind a deserted counter, Flora kept asking herself what idea the good Lord could have in mind that He was so bent upon seeing that she did not prosper. She laid the blame on Denis, who had not made the novena to pray for the failure of the restaurant across the street. And wasn't it terrible, this habit that Gaston had formed of going over to buy at the Colins'? But the main thing was not to upset him. What was more, she had to purchase two dozen eggs that his hens laid every day or he would sell them to her rivals.

"Gaston! Gaston!" Her sharp little eyes darted over the poultry yard, but she saw nothing of him. "I'll bet you that's where he is!" she muttered, with clenched fists, thinking of Germaine. She was a woman who made quick decisions. "Wait for me! I won't be long."

She flung open the door of the Colin shop as suddenly as Jean might have picked up a stone to seize the earthworms beneath it. What she saw caused her to put her hand to her heart. Germaine was kissing her Gaston! Her Gaston who, by reason of his infirmity, knew nothing of women. Her poor Gaston, whom she had thought to be so sexless and so angelic. There he was, leaning his big head tenderly on Germaine's shoulder. Flora gave a leap like a tigress. "You bitch!" Striking out, she laid the girl's cheek open with the wedding ring on her hand. Reminded by this of the old-time brawls of the quarter, Grandfather Pitou promptly picked up a handful of ice cream and flung it in Flora's face. The blood was running down Germaine's cheek, and Gaston, very pale, took out his handkerchief to dry it.

"Mama!" he cried, and began trembling all over, calling for air. His big, pointed teeth appeared to be snatching at the shreds of life, trying to hold onto them. "Hot, cold, hot, cold!" A violent shudder ran over his body as, with a hand to his bosom, he sought to stay the impetuous beating of his heart. Terrified, but glad that Gaston had called to her in his distress, Flora took him in her strong arms and carried him home. This prevented Barloute, who had just come in, from striking her with the poker that she carried in her hand. Not used to the telephone which had been recently installed, she asked Chaton to go for the doctor.

Gaston came out of the attack; but his eyes were evasive, instead of holding a happy look at the signs of returning life. Later on, when he had grown calm, he smiled. Closing his lips tightly, he studied his purple-coloured nails and listened to his breathing. "I'm tired of never getting what I want." And from his panting breast there came a prolonged sigh that was like the barking of a dog in the night.

As the doctor came in, he pulled the patient's ears playfully. "Fraidy-cat," he scolded him.

Shaking himself, Gaston gave him a hateful glance. Did they think, then, that he was an imbecile? After Germaine's kiss, he had discovered in his heart the *amour-propre* of an adult male who had had no childhood. Just because his body was not like those of other people, did that mean that his mind must be different also? Yes! he must be crazy. He would have liked to shout his fear, with a torrent of words as they did on the radio. It was true, he was mad with the pain of it all, for he had felt like weeping ever since Germaine had asked him for Denis' picture. Then that awful obsession against which he had struggled for so long laid hold of him again, more acutely than ever: the image of a despairing man who had slashed his throat with a razor! With trembling hands, he repelled the spectre.

"Those knives! Take those knives away! I want to kill my-self! I want to die!"

The physician, whose specialty was obstetrics (in his youth he had dreamed of being the head of a large hospital), did his best to calm Gaston but was careful to keep his distance in order to avoid being scratched. Flora gathered up the knives that were spread out on the table and hid them in the cupboard.

"Don't be alarmed," the doctor explained, "it's only his nerves."

A woman of the people with a vivid imagination, Flora understood, and even went beyond the reality of things. She gazed at the Colins' sign, visible amid the last leaves of autumn. "That filthy creature!" she moaned.

"Want to get up, I do, want to get up."

"But you never did before. Wait until tomorrow. Mama's going to take your shoes and socks off. My! Gaston, you're getting fat! Just look at those nice round calves."

The doctor came up and, attentively but prudently, touched

with his forefinger the marks which the shoes had left upon the flabby ankles.

"That's not very healthy fat, Madame. Watch him closely. His heart is not at all good. You will call me if you need me."

Flora followed him all the way outdoors, staring straight in front of her. She was trying to remember all the sick persons she had known who had got well in spite of what the doctor had said.

Denis was coming back from school in the rue St-Jean. He was walking rapidly and his mouth was twitching. How could Lise have done it? Had he not seen at a glance, that Sunday after mass, that she was thenceforth the slave of the strange lad who had muttered: "As for me, I like what I do not understand"? She had no right to receive the confidences of other men, even though he no longer paid any attention to her. Yet that was what she would be doing very soon. That very evening, Jean would be seated at her side, touching her arms to begin with, palming off as his own the obscure utterances he had heard from the lips of his leader. Denis made up his mind that he was not going to let this pain him. Had he not been congratulating himself over his indifference to the girl, for the last three weeks? And now, she was taking Colin as second choice.

She was weak. Yes, that was it; and her weakness made any plans of conquest he may have had seem too easy. He had been so busy slaying his nascent love for her, pridefully sullying it with the taint of passion, that he had not noticed that winter was coming on. What did the ambitions of other people matter to him, the quarrels between the Colins and his mother? He had at first succeeded in bringing himself to behold in Lise a young woman who was no longer merely a churchwarden's daughter in fluffy lace ruffles that one must not rumple; one who was something more than a pair of thighs that dazzled his eyes and caused his fingers to hesitate; something more, even, than that mirage of flesh that one pursued in dreams toward the oasis of illusion. How many hours had he spent in routing the obsession of their two faces cheek to cheek, lifted heavenward, the gentle pressure of their hands! And then he had grown more enterprising, and with a great inward effort had freed himself of these noble dreams. The stages of love's novitiate were completed at last, and feverishly, before remorse should come to him, he had gone to undress the young girl, who now, all a-tremble, lay alongside his heart, as naked as he. At certain moments he was ashamed of this image and would muffle it up to the very lips; and at other times, with flaming cheeks, he would ravage his own sense of modesty. Ah! the days had been calmer than his soul. They had accumulated as slowly as the season's gliding leaves, delayed in their fall by a nostalgic desire to mirror themselves in the sun and play with the wind.

Continuing to mutter to himself, Denis with his quick, nervous step hurried past the pedestrians who were strolling leisurely along. He must give Jean a beating before supper time, must blacken his eyes; for he had resolved to prevent his friend from spending the evening with Lise. Suddenly, he almost stopped. That girl who just went by, in a stylish grey suit and with a pretty blue hat that sat coyly over one ear—was that she? How tranquil he felt at seeing her like this, so alive and with hair that was even more pleasing to the eye than it would have been to the touch! Denis, who could conceive of voluptuous pleasure only as occurring in the summer, in a field of high grass surrounded by trees that stood as the sentinels of his passion, was now afraid that he would not be able to preserve the void between himself and her until the following spring. He feared putting his amorous dreams to flight; for if he came to know her better, to talk to her and spend long evenings with her, he risked losing these ecstasies that he had known in solitude. He slackened his pace. Yes, it would be better to wait until next spring. People would say that he had a girl. A mistress was preferable. But all this was not preventing Jean from seeing her tonight!

With quick steps he was at Lise's side, took her arm. "Mademoiselle."

"Monsieur Denis!"

Already he felt like retreating, had an impulse to flee without saying another word. He was stammering. Humiliated by this, he pointed to the posters on the columns of the Porte St-Jean. "Aren't you going to the concert this evening?"

She did not even look at the announcements; she was enjoying his presence. "Why haven't you been to see?"

He came near shouting at her that he had left his place to others, a place that was to be had so easily; but he restrained himself as he reflected that this was the sort of thing his mother would have said. Lise fancied that he was timid.

"I was expecting you, Denis. I thought that you would call to inquire about me."

To inquire about her! The words sounded strange to the ears of the young savage that he believed himself to be. Etiquette, fashion, snobbery—what did he have to do with that? How far it all was from his cult of the primitive!

"I don't like to be expected. It forces me to adopt an attitude." Suddenly ill at ease, she gazed at him, blank-faced, questioningly. He laughed to reassure her. "I say foolish things just to appear strange. You don't care for surprises, then?"

His eyes nonchalantly sought out the horizon, for he was convinced that she did not understand him. Why was he so bent upon showing her the finer side of his character? He must make an effort to keep her from thinking he was too complex. After all, would a girl who was willing to spend an evening with Jean be capable of divining his purpose: that of falling like a kind of mysterious star, bringing luck into the lives of others who give up all hope of understanding? Being now in the rue St-Jean, far from St Sauveur, he felt that she meant less to him in every way. Bah! he would leave her to his friend this evening. "I'm becoming good-hearted," he concluded. Was he good-hearted? It was disillusioning. In a sudden rage, he would have liked to kick the legs of the passers-by.

"Will you come with me to the concert this evening?" He revelled in her embarrassment and repeated his question as if assured of her answer in advance.

"Denis, why didn't you let me know yesterday?"

"Because I never know what I'm going to do. And tonight I want to have you at my side, listening to music. Accept at once; don't begin by refusing, like the others, out of politeness."

She was floundering. Denis could not be aware that Jean was coming to her house to play cards that evening, she was certain of it. If he knew, he would despise her. She was unable to make up her mind what to do. There was a beseeching look on her calm and beautiful face; she did not wish to refuse. To be at his side! The memory of Jean, of the old maids, everything else faded away.

"I haven't bought my ticket," she said.

He was waiting for that. He threw back his head and laughed long and loud. He looked as if he were gargling. People turned to stare. Lise blushed furiously, ashamed of the fact that she did not have a ticket. Denis was enjoying her dilemma: Jean and the sofa or the concert with him. Did she suppose for a minute that he was going to let her pay her own way? Had he ever told her that he would not spend his money on girls?

"Do you think I haven't a sou? Yes, I'm poor, but I'm the one that's paying. Why do you force me to make an admission like that? I don't want to be petty in money matters. I know you think I'm boasting; but the truth is, I hate myself when-ever I feel that I'm on the verge of being humble." He became sad as he thought of the vista of muddy streets where he had been born and where he had always floundered about.

"You are strange, Denis," she complained. "It is as if one had to hurt you in order to win your affection."

"Ah." Had she, then, guessed a little of his secret? His pose of mystery, he felt, had been punctured; it now appeared as shabby and crumpled as old bills from creditors that one throws away. It was an account that had been settled. Bored with his isolation, tired of being misunderstood, he felt a sudden desire to kiss her, there in the middle of the street, then wondered if it might not be better for him to escape in order to keep intact his ardour and his plans for the future. All he knew was that at that moment his greatest pleasure would have been to caress her hair, to read verses to her, or to sit with her and watch the lights of passing boats upon the river. They walked on, with Lise's shoulder from time to time brushing his own. By way of dissimulating his happiness, he sought out little pebbles in his path that he might kick with his feet.

"Do you like Lamartine, Denis?"

"Lamartine?" He stared at her in surprise. He was about to tell her that Lamartine had been his idol when he was fourteen years old, and that, after having devoured *Graziella*, he had dreamed of writing a Quebec story in the same vein. The hero would live in a house in the Upper Town overlooking the river, and the characters would converse in the flowery language to be found in the bedside books of Canada. How could he once have deified that soft and flabby Lamartine, he who today was so rude and impulsive, so brutally frank in his amorous relation-ships? Fearing to lose his hold upon her, he did not put his feeling of condescension into words.

"Lamartine has talent," was his comment.

He was coming to handle this girl with care; for there was a sort of *Paul et Virginie* languidness about her way of thinking and feeling that contrasted strongly with his own impulse to shy away from all sentimentality. Then he became absent-minded and finally uneasy as Lise went on telling him of her schoolgirl preferences. He was trying to remember where there were pantries filled with milk jars. There would never be enough to pay for this concert. Just to show how unperturbed he was despite his lack of money, he suggested that they take a taxi.

"Let's walk on to the Monument des Braves," she said. "I'd like that better."

Relieved at this, he plucked a maple leaf and began chewing on it. He pictured the faces of the Langevins and thought of the coarse jokes which the lads at the club would have made if they had been there to listen to him now. But Jean would feel differently about it! For Denis was carrying out his threat of preventing his friend from spending the evening with Lise. He, Denis, would have her; but it would be at a concert, and there women do not matter. Then his thoughts became less nebulous and he was outwardly more calm and natural. They spoke of literature, keeping up a dialogue that was astonishing in its Utopian simplicity.

"Look at those lovers, Denis." And she pointed to the couples on the Monument benches.

"That's not the way I want to make love."

With disgust he recalled the vulgar manœuvres of impatient swains whom he and his gang had spied upon from behind the thickets in the park.

Pretending that he had an urgent errand, he let Lise return to the parish alone in order that they might not be seen together. He also had to find the money somewhere. On the way home he caught sight of Germaine, angrily scolding Jean. Why did he have to be so selfish? Why should not the whole family get something out of it? She could go over this afternoon and teach Lise her recipe for making fudge. What a good time they would have together over the stove. Lise would slice the pieces, some of them in the form of a heart for Jean and herself.

"Just let me catch you suggesting that!" For Jean wished to appear to Lise as an unhewn block, without family, with no other tie than that of their future happiness. And here was Germaine, wanting to spoil everything with her fudge! A familiar laugh broke in upon his thoughts.

"Why don't you let her? You can eat fudge and hold hands at the same time."

"Oh, to hell with you! What do you think I am?"

Denis on the spur of the moment had the idea of borrowing a couple of dollars. Jean was so elated he would not refuse. It would make him feel superior. That was the way it was in novels: Jean would pay for their escapade. But a sudden rancour kept him from taking advantage of the situation. It was altogether too easy. For the first time, he felt a distaste for acting as fictional heroes do. Jean had no ironical remarks to make and even went on to talk about his worms. It was with an uneasy feeling that Denis left him. If he was indifferent to Lise, why was the thought of being indebted to Colin so repugnant to him?

CHAPTER

VIII

GASTON was going to die! Joseph, distracted by his son's condition, had purchased fifty young chickens and, in order that the lad might be able to see them from his bed, had placed them in a coop in the kitchen, directly under the hot-air register in his room above. As a result, the house was filled with a chirping and squealing that rose above the usual din. Wandering into the kitchen, Denis cast an eye over the deserted shop. Flora thought that he was noting the absence of customers so that he might taunt her with the failure of the project; but instead, he gave her a pitying glance, his mind on the cash-box.

"You needn't be sticking up your nose at our bad luck," she said. "If all you can do is make fun of us, you'd better just keep out."

He gave it up. Any kind of understanding between them was out of the question. He was no longer the infant she had nursed at her breast. "That's enough!" he cried. "The only suffering that moves me is that which I inflict upon myself."

The hour was late, and where was he to find the money? He climbed the stair. There was Gaston, stupefied by a decree of destiny. Why did he have to keep running his hands over his swollen legs with that perplexed look on his face? Ah, what a thing it was to be great of soul and the same time incapable of rising to an extraordinary situation! Denis felt that all he was good for was to fall on his knees before this wretched brother of his, this wraith of a being, who lay there nourishing a futile revolt.

"Show me your legs," said Gaston in a tone of command, for he wished to compare them with his own, which were smooth and shining.

Distressed by this whim, Denis gave the invalid a searching look. How big and impressive the sick boy seemed all of a sudden! It was from him that the silence appeared to emanate. With some embarrassment, the leader of the "gang" rolled up the leg of his trousers: "Have a look, if you like. They're black with hair." Gaston put out his fingers to touch them, but Denis

133

drew back, laughing awkwardly. "It's not for men to be feeling other men's legs. Play with those dollars you've saved up."

Gaston thought of them, one by one. When he had a big pile of dollars, he would buy an auto and go riding with Germaine. What would it matter then if his legs were round, like those of women? He glanced down through the register, and called to the children to leave his chickens alone.

"Those hens are going to make you a few dollars," said Denis. "You're lucky." He wandered from room to room. Where had Gaston hidden his money, anyway? Nervously, he pulled open drawers and turned the linen upside down. All he found was children's panties, broken bits of rosaries, heads of images, and mothballs. He did not know that Gaston now kept his fortune in the pocket of his yellow bathrobe.

"What are you doing there?" Gaston was worried about the drawers where he had arranged his newspaper clippings (illustrated Tarzan stories).

"I'm looking for happiness." And laughingly, in order to keep his brother from thinking, Denis began calling him playful names as he feverishly overturned images, shook down the pillows, lifted up the linoleum. Nothing there!

"What time is it, Mama?"

"Six o'clock."

His forehead was covered with sweat. Then he happened to think of the drawer that his father kept in Flora's bureau. He opened it, his nervous fingers grating on the yellowing linen collars. Aha! here was the famous cigar box! He removed the papers, which were arranged with meticulous care, and which, when spread out, gave off a musty odour. He unfolded one of them and read: "My darling Flora, my poor little dear, one day we will go far from this place that kills all the most delicate impulses of your soul." He ran his eye over the missive, re-read portions of it, and glanced down at the signature. His father the author of such sentiments as these? He shuddered. So, the old man, too, had been unwilling to accept things as they were. And he had been vanquished! Denis stiffened. They were not going to trap *him*.

In addition to the letters, there were verses:

> When I beheld you scrubbing those filthy steps,
> My heart, athirst for harmonies, did weep
> To see that rose mirrored in such a pool,
> Its brightness shattered, which I would ever keep.
> Your Joseph, *January 1915.*

Smiling, Denis copied the stanza. No more would his father overwhelm him with his authority as a man of experience.

"Poor Joseph," he murmured, "your son will do what you failed to do. I'm going to write, I am."

The thought that he would one day be a writer was sufficient to drive away all his worries. This assurance that he felt was paradise itself. His mind was at ease now; the money would come. He gazed out the window that overlooked the poultry yard and gave a start. Why had he not thought of it sooner? For a writer it was a highly plausible solution.

"Denis! Denis! The knives! I'm afraid!"

He did not stop to soothe his brother but dashed down the stairs and sent his mother up to look after Gaston. The young ones took advantage of this to steal some candy as Denis ran out to the hen-roost. He was the master now. Yet he felt the same physical revulsion that he had experienced when he raided an orchard for the first time. He must kill. What a new sensation that was! "Which one shall it be? And how do you go about it?" He pitied the hens for not being disturbed by his unaccustomed presence. How stupid they were, these imprisoned vagabonds! Gaston had given each one of them a nickname. This one was Guitte, that one was Piquette, that one over there was Papi—words that were easy for him to pronounce.

Denis pointed a coaxing forefinger at Bobotte, an obscure-looking hen that was to the poultry yard what a mediocre individual is to society. Should he cut off her head with the axe? There would be blood! It would be better to wring her neck. Cautiously he crept up to her, his hands outstretched in a protective gesture as he showered her with all sorts of flattering appellations. But the poor creature, astonished that this big fellow who had never paid any attention to her before should suddenly woo her so insistently, darted out of his reach. She was not to be had so easily as all that! He followed her all the way to the hen roost, bumping his head on the perches as he entered. This resistance to his will that he everywhere encountered stimulated his fighting spirit. He was happy when he became impatient, and Bobotte's terror was a lash to his cruelty. Finally, hemmed in a corner, he had her at his mercy. The hen's grey body was throbbing like an enormous heart. He opened his arms and watched to see if the heart would beat faster. Oh, hell! He had put his hands in some dung.

With this, he pounced upon Bobotte, paying no attention to her distress; and closing his fingers over her beak, he gave his hand a rotary movement, but the body of the frightened hen turned with it. He hesitated, for he himself was suffering. Were all the things that he felt so sure of overcoming destined to slip from his grasp as Bobotte did? Would they always gaze at him like that, with big, expressionless eyes, so kind and yet so implacable? He placed the hen between his knees. Ah! if he could only see red, if those eyes only had a supplicating look, he would have no pity then. But there was no supplication in them. He forced himself to think of Lise, the despair on her face if he failed her. With a quick motion of his wrist he broke the hen's neck.

It was over. Bobotte gave a few dying flops, and Denis placed her in an old pail, dried his hands against the wall, and picked the feathers from his clothing.

Bédarovitch, who was an intimate friend of the butcher, bought the hen for a dollar and twenty-five cents. Denis then went to the school kept by the brothers and filched a few milk jars from the pantry. By six-thirty he had a dollar eighty-five in his pocket. That would pay for the concert, a taxi both ways, and two bottles of pop with five cents for a tip. His evening was minutely planned. Ah! Colin!

It was a dreary party at the Lévesques. Without Lise, the card game was unbearably dull. The Latruche sisters spoke of young girls who had been lost through having gone out with young men unchaperoned. Peuplière was ruminating over her disappointment, but Zépherin, who did not like to pass judgement upon his daughter, secretly felt that Lise was to be congratulated on being in the Upper Town tonight, at a good concert. He was put out to think that the Latruches were there solely on her account, and threw down his cards noisily just to show his defiance of them. And this fellow Jean Colin, with the sad eyes and hands that were already calloused—why did he have to be so silent and so intent upon the game? He, Zépherin, did not need these Colins any longer, either, now that Pritontin's ambitions seemed to have melted away like wax. Jean, however, was doing his best to be amiable to his host. He must learn how to handle him, must get Monsieur Lévesque used to seeing him, in case the time really came when he would have an evening with Lise.

This was something that he had good reason to doubt. It was too easy that way. With a love such as his, one did not fall into happiness like a drop of water. It is the water of the desert that is the best, for the reason that it is found beneath the parched sands. He did not hold a grudge against Denis, but rather felt sorry for the spinsters in their disappointment. He would have liked to talk to them about their saint, tell them that he was in the habit of praying to the dead youth. For the less disappointed the Latruches were, the more reason he had not to feel unhappy. He watched their faces closely to see if he could make out the signs of a smile, that restrained smile that the self-satisfied wear. One by one, each of the objects that Lise must touch in the course of the day came under his gaze. Take that chair, how dainty it was! That unfinished sweater upon the buffet, left there by her adorable hands which at this moment were applauding some great musician. It was worth sacrificing himself to be rid of that overbearing Denis, who thought more of keeping his word and commanding the respect of his friends than he did of the friends themselves. In short, his was to be a superior kind of love, a love never before known to the heart of man. And then, all of a sudden, he felt the pain of it all.

At ten o'clock Jean left, followed by the spinsters. He was almost impolite in the abruptness of his leavetaking, for he was tortured, stifling; he could not wait to be alone at the corner of the street and breath in the air.

Monsieur Lévesque bade them all a perfunctory good-night: "My daughter would have been so glad to see you, but you know how it is; she's so fond of music!"

"Music will not keep the Daughters of Mary from wagging their tongues, Monsieur Lévesque," was the old maids' parting shot. Closing the door behind them, they jostled the young man on their way out. They were angry with him, but took refuge in thinking of their protégé, who was more manageable than Lise.

Denis did not help her out of the taxi but stood there with his hands in his pockets. He felt sorry for her because her dress was too long, and was glad that he had told the driver to stop in front of the Latruches. He could see the pair hovering like shadowy skeletons behind the curtains, and he watched them mockingly. Lise did not venture to ask him why the taxi had stopped here instead of going on to her house, but timidly sought to take his arm. He shook her hand off and laughed, for he knew the spinsters would think it was a lovers' quarrel, and it gave him great satisfaction to have them suppose that Lise was begging him to do something.

It was good to inhale the musty odour of kitchens once more! He had a familiar glance for each entryway, recognized each stoop. On the horizon were the Cape and the Upper Town. He preferred it like that—as horizon; for when he dipped into the Upper Town as he had done this evening, he was disillusioned. He had found his parish execrable that morning, but he was glad to be back in it now, and drew it closer about him like a favourite overcoat. Here one could live without silly pretence, without being a stuffed shirt. He came near to telling Lise that he hated her perfume because it reminded him of the evening they had just spent together. He hated that crowd of wasters who had spoiled for him the excuse he had accepted, the only one he would accept, for being with Lise. He had pictured the concert hall as a place where one sat beside people of distinction to drink at the well of beauty. Viewed from St Sauveur, an event of this sort held enchantment. He had felt nauseated as he heard those in the row behind him discussing the jealousy that existed between the conductor and his first violinist, as he listened to the tongue-clacking criticism of Debussy, as he observed all the simpering and smirking that went on in the orchestra seats and in the boxes.

Yes, it was good to be back in Sewer Town, that great dark hole where one accepted nothing without exaltation. Up there one encountered more skeptical small talk; there were more painted faces awkwardly lifted above low-cut evening gowns with an effect that represented an admixture of sadness and hilarity. There were more empty phrase-makers to deafen the silent music lover like him. And then it occurred to him that all these things—rouged faces and shirt fronts at the concert, calloused hands and rags in Sewer Town—were mere external trappings. Where, then, was he to find a place for his disdain, if he was to spare the real values of life? Was he destined to remain wholly alone by reason of his complex temperament, a temperament that would not adapt itself to any mode of life?

It was good to be conscious of his own height against the background of these houses, so low, it seemed to him, that they barely came up to his shoulder. For this evening he was tired of the finer things, and above all of the great things one read about in books. Suddenly he felt a desire, a thirst, to break something, to cry out, to free himself, to be the ruler of a chaos. No, from now on he would do what he could to make others happy. Gaston, all the coming winter, would be glad to find him so simple and understanding. Bobotte's eyes—they held an expression as empty as fate itself. Curse the luck! He owed the greatest disillusionment of his life to the death of a hen. Where had Jean fled to nurse his sorrow? Where could he find him that he might throw this girl into his arms? He quickened his step. The Mulots gathered around Bédarovitch's door eyed the couple with astonishment. "Yes, my lads; but it's the last time."

Lise was pleased by the fact that her girl friends from the convent had admired Denis at the concert. How should she go about asking him for his photograph? "Do you have your picture taken sometimes?"

"No! The picture that I have of myself is not the kind you care to give to others. I hate mirrors."

"I am happy, Denis; but you said a little while ago that you were suffering, and you gave me such a look. Tell me that you recognized yourself in my eyes, that you saw the truth there."

He gritted his teeth. What business had she bringing his manly worries down to the level of her schoolgirl emotions? It would be well to crush her with insults, to destroy this vaporous self-confidence of hers.

"No, I do not recognize myself in you, Lise. I was sad to think how you had been false to others in order to run after me. How should I see myself in your eyes when you do not even resist me?"

"But Denis, I thought you were one who—"

"I am one who does not like to be taken for granted." He shook her arm imperceptibly. "Be an obstacle in the parish. Don't be content to float downstream like a straw."

"Tell me, Denis. How can I go back upstream with you?"

"Begin by hating me, by laughing at me. Shatter everything that can affect me. Find new beauties besides those of Lamartine, which are the prettiness of paper flowers. I've had enough of books, of music, of nobility. Live for one hour at least, Lise. Look, there's Colin on the corner, waiting for me. He's going to ask me if you were sorry to miss playing cards with him. But tomorrow evening you will pick up where you left off; you will tell him everything that you dreamed of telling me. Good night."

His face pale, he left her at her door. She watched him as he joined Jean, who was pretending to be unaware of his presence. She had a vision of Denis seizing this stranger, placing him between them, felling him with a blow, and then striding away over his vanquished body. He would glory in making love after that. How complex he thought himself to be, and how simple he really was! She smiled. Tomorrow she would pacify him with a romantic subterfuge of the kind that he despised. How she did love the young savage!

Denis paid no attention to the Langevins, who were lying in wait for him at the door of Colins' shop. He gave Jean a shove.

"I told you I would. Now you can have her. Be here tomorrow night, at eight o'clock. Say something!"

Jean looked him in the eye. He did not feel humiliated. Rather, he pitied Denis for his pride. What if he were to tell him to his face that he had no more use for Lise, by way of turning his friend's rudeness to despair? Jean lived on hesitations, could feel the truth hovering inside him like a mist. This did not disturb him; he realized that it was by putting questions to himself that he went on living. Poor Denis! Yes, tomorrow he would go. "Shall I put on my brown suit?"

This made Denis self-conscious about being so well dressed. The Langevin twins, who through Gus Perrault had been placed in the Parliament Buildings, now shouted at him, Germaine, who was furious with him. egging them on: "The lad who didn't like girls! You're a fine gang leader, you are!"

His gang? These Langevins, Jean, and himself. Was that all, the four of them? That summer they had been kings together and he had believed that they were innumerable and even formidable. But now that love had come, all else had shrunk and he, the leader, had stooped to passion. He was downcast, for he knew that later he would remember the hours he had spent as a child.

"Come along, Jean, I'll help you get some worms."

Jean, believing that he was being delicate, did not remark that this was the first time Denis had made such an offer.

CHAPTER

IX

THE next day, Saturday, was a big day for Jean. It was *the* big day, and he could hardly wait for it. His joy was born with the winter; for autumn, swollen with melancholy, had at last swept over the month of October like a tidal wave.

Ended for Gaston was the spectacle of rusty leaves beating against his windowpane. Ended was the jostling of the winds impatiently awaiting the first snow to be borne away. Ended, likewise, were the invalid's nightmarish dreams, filled with dark thoughts that fluttered like bats over his heart, against the brightness of his love for Germaine. Motionless, he watched the falling of the snow, light as a crumbling smile. What a thick, white muffler for his thoughts!

Happily, Jean hurried to look up Denis. What difference did it make to him that the police had raided his home on the charge that his father was keeping a gambling house? There was a darting pain from his wrenched knee, which was not improving properly, but he did not notice it. No pain, no sorrow could match his joy today. He would greet life with a smile. How should he behave toward Lise? She would be surprised when she came to know him. At first she would find Denis more interesting; but later she would be overcome by his own boundless, silent love, along about ten o'clock at night, when they were playing organ music on the radio.

Denis was leaning against his brother's henhouse, catching the snowflakes on his outstretched tongue and his eyelashes; they had a lukewarm feel and taste. He turned to Jean.

"Is your father still in jail?"

"No, he paid the fine. We're closing the shop, you know. The landlord will raise our rent twenty dollars if we don't."

He said no more, but Denis could not help thinking how pleased Flora would be. She was quite capable of having tipped off the police. "It's just as well you're through with all that."

"Oh, that's my parents' business. It doesn't concern me any longer. I cut loose from everything yesterday. I'm beginning all over again. Did you see Chaton this morning? I sold him my worms. He gave me ten dollars. For eleven thousand of them.

I'm getting out of it—too much bickering. Do you believe me when I tell you I'm making a new start? It will be good for me, you know."

Denis looked at the lad's blue eyes, shining through the snow-flakes. Jean was beginning to get on his nerves with his stubborn determination to sacrifice everything for Lise's sake. Love for him was becoming a hallucination.

"I wanted to ask you to let me have some schoolbooks," he was stammering. "Do you think I might be able to make something out of them?" His tone was one of indecision; he was steeling himself against laughter.

Denis glanced toward the school building, then at his friend. He knew the pages in those books by heart, and he had an empty feeling inside himself. Did Jean think, then, that he would find a solution there?

"Whatever you do, don't talk that stuff to her this evening. Come with me."

They went into the shed and Denis overturned a pile of books with purple covers. They were volumes which he had stood up proudly to receive, when school prizes were given out, but today they made him a little heartsick. He could see the strained faces of the parents, their look of triumph or humiliation as they sat there stiffly in their Sunday best.

"Denis," his mother called. She was supporting Gaston, who was wearing big felt boots. "Put a bench there for him, along-side the hen roost." The sick boy was gasping for breath, but was bent upon satisfying a sudden whim: he must have a look at his full-grown hens.

"You shouldn't let him come out, Mama." Denis was frightened by the idea that his brother might go hunting for Bobotte. Gaston was struggling furiously, and they had to seat him on an empty cracker box. Flora waited anxiously for him to become himself once more and start looking for his fowls.

"You keep an eye on him," she said, "while I go to the butcher's."

Denis did his best to distract the invalid's attention, pointing out the repairs that were being made so that the hens would not freeze. He showed him the spider webs, then brought out his own skis, his bicycle. He was sorry for this brother of his who was going to die. It was a kind of game to go on and describe Heaven for him, that lovely place of eternal rest where one flitted about as lightly as the birds. And then there were all the springs and fountains that gushed up among the clouds; that was something to dream about. Denis himself was in a hurry to go there, so as to be able to view the world from on high. His gestures as he said all this were impressive and in his eyes was the pleasure of a little child. But Gaston was inclined to doubt this mode of dying in which one did not have to pass through the stage of being a corpse. He recalled his aunt who had died the year before, remembered how he had greeted his acquaintances at her funeral. He was such a liar, such a fool, this big lad in front of him. And Denis meanwhile was perspiring as he kept on describing the angels and the automobiles that were to be found in Heaven. Jean was thumbing a dust-covered grammar and wondering what his leader's object was in all this.

Flora made sure that Germaine was not on the sidewalk. She caught sight of the Abbé Charton leaving the Lévesques' and was on the verge of going up to him and telling him of her sorrow, of Gaston's approaching death. She did not do so, however, for the abbé, with a mink cap on his head, looked altogether too happy. The urchins, throwing snowballs, were lying in wait for the Soyeuses. Chaton, with Jean's wormbox upon a sled, was singing merrily, for the smelt season was on. Glory be to God, he no longer had any serious competitor.

At the butcher's, the housewives were holding forth in front of the stall. The police raid on the Colin shop provided the topic of conversation.

"The good Lord had a finger in it, eh?" said Flora.

Seeing her, Madame Langevin came up, waving some tickets. "Can I sell you some for my party?" she asked. "It's for my twins, at the Liberal Association, this evening. Yes, Madame Boucher, we've engaged the organist at the nine o'clock mass and his Canadian dance orchestra. So do come; they're all friends of your boy."

The Latruche sisters bore down upon them, followed by Lise. The spinsters bent over and sniffed the meat, hoping to find a mouldy smell. Their faces were eloquent when Lise's back was turned. Flora was making her excuses to Madame Langevin, explaining that Gaston was at the point of death. And she wept as she announced that she too was closing her shop.

Lise gazed at her with a deep and silent sympathy. She knew now why it was that Denis was not happy.

"Poor boy!" said the butcher. "He hasn't the health that your Denis has." Lise thought of those athletic shoulders.

"It is better sometimes for 'our sons' not to be so muscular." The spinsters were making grimaces and moving their lips behind Lise's back as she stood at the counter, money in hand.

Madame Chaton yielded her place in line to the young woman, to be rid of her the sooner.

"That is very kind of you, Madame," said Lise, who was flattered by the courtesy.

"What a little hypocrite!" whispered Peuplière to her sister.

"Do you have a fowl?" Lise inquired.

"Yes, indeed, I have a nice big one," replied the butcher, hastening back to the icebox.

"Yes," observed Madame Langevin approvingly, as he returned with the strangled hen, "it has been well fattened, and it isn't spoiled."

Flora had not recognized Bobotte. "It's small alongside those of my Gaston," she remarked. "There's no comparison."

"But then, you're in the business, too," put in Madame Chaton. She had never won in Flora's raffles.

When Lise had left, the Latruche sisters came back to their interrupted conversation like two electrons that have been separated for a moment. "You poor mother, we must warn you—"

Again! Flora was nervous. She watched their faces anxiously. She felt ashamed already. Peuplière was exultant.

"So you let your son go out in a taxi with that girl, until eleven o'clock at night? She had him by the arm, was trying to take him into the Clichoteux courtyard, but he refused. It is plain to be seen that he has a little of that morality left that you must have taught him."

Flora was choking. Where had he got the money? Denis was lost to her. Gone, also, was her superiority over the other Mulote mothers. Denis was now lined up with their sons, in the ranks of the "chippy chasers." Ah! those hussies!

"You old maids!" she cried. "Mind your own affairs, will you? I thought you would be busy getting your saint's picture out of that brothel at the Colins'. Fine friends *you* have—that Barloute!"

The sisters turned pale. Ever since the Pritontins had been frustrated in their ambition, the competition of their sons in the market of sainthood had impressed the Latruches as being nothing to worry about. But on the day following the incident of the firecracker, when the situation appeared perilous, they had put up the photograph of the saint in the Colin shop. They must get it down at once and make amends for this sacrilege.

Flora left abruptly, without doing her shopping. She must give Denis a beating; that was the only thing that would help Gaston a little. She did not notice the Latruche sisters coming along behind her; nor did she notice Tit-Blanc, who, at Bédarovitch's place, was loudly telling the gang of the rumpus he had created in his cell and the witty things he had said to the frightened police officers. She saw Denis engaged in counting the hens with Gaston. The invalid counted twenty-three, Denis twenty-four. He was in agony and grew constantly more exasperated as he sought to turn his brother's attention to something else.

"Look, there's Mama!"

"Yes, here I am. Were you out in a car with that Lévesque girl last night?" She picked up a board with which to strike him. He did not stir.

"Quick! and get it over with," he said.

Gaston was tugging at his mother, begging her to count his hens for him. He called them by name, anxiously checked them off: Piquette with the big feet; Momo with the crooked beak; Tititte with the long neck. Since he had been hovering around Germaine, Flora was in the habit of telling him that these were his girls. With trembling legs, he now got to his feet. His eyelids were so heavy, but he must not sleep. Big drops of sweat stood out on his forehead and his pale tongue protruded from his mouth. He was stubbornly calling the roll of hens.

"Go ahead, strike me!" Denis was saying.

Jean out of tactfulness walked away but watched them from a distance. Half leaning on her club, Flora was closely following Gaston's actions. He suddenly gave a hoarse cry that was smothered in his throat:

"Bobotte! Bobotte! Bobotte's gone!"

Desperately, he clung to the wire of the poultry yard fence. Bobotte gone—that big hen that was so nice, that never made any fuss, and that always let the other hens steal her grain. Flora was supporting him as she looked around for the fowl, while Denis pretended he had discovered it in a corner of the hen roost. His mother could picture him with Lise, after they had left the taxi, their two bodies close together in the darkness. It was clear to her now: that hen the butcher had sold the girl a short while ago!

"She's in the yard, look well, Bobotte, Mama. Go see, Denis."

Denis would have liked to run away. Flora's manner was cold. "Come here," she said. "You killed her, did you? You sold her to get the money to take that girl out in a taxi?" Gaston was growing weaker; she picked him up in her arms. She began cursing Denis and sobbing. "It is you who ought to die."

Joseph came home and hastened to Gaston's room. His wife took him to one side and told him what Denis had done. Putting his pipe in his pocket, the father came toward his son: "So it was you who killed her?"

Denis thought at first of denying it. Then he sprang up and hurled the book in which he had seemed immersed to a far corner of the room. "Yes, it was I who killed her. I wrung her neck like that—crick! In the future, you're going to give me more money to spend."

Joseph could only stare at him, his eyes popping out of his head; he did not seem to understand. With his fists up, he shoved Denis against the wall. When the lad resisted, the young ones struck him across the legs, shouting, "Thief! Thief!"

Joseph restrained himself. "You're going over to the Lévesques and get that hen," he said.

"Never!"

"Then I will go myself!" said Flora, and throwing her shawl over her, she started to leave, but Gaston began calling just then.

Denis took a deep breath. There was a choking in the invalid's throat, and his lips were thin and sharp as if to slice the air that was too dense for his lungs. His mother lifted the bedclothes and saw that his legs were swollen all the way to his hips. They were cold as ice. Joseph turned to Denis: "Go for the doctor, you!"

Denis went with alacrity. He was glad to be outdoors at last, in the cold air, with no memories to haunt him. When the physician came he announced that the end was near and advised them to send for the priest.

"I'm losing my best one. They are the ones the good Lord always takes," sobbed Flora; and she set about preparing the candles.

It was six o'clock and dark already as Denis ran to the parish house. Through kitchen windows he caught sight of rows of heads bent over plates. At the Colins', Jean was shaving and was singing off key to drown out Barloute, who was scolding him for having sold his business. Denis stopped and looked at him angrily. Was Jean so sure, then, that he was going to call on Lise this evening? Barloute began finding fault with Germaine, who had on a new dress and was unwilling to serve supper because she wished to keep it clean for the dance. The dandies of the parish, nervous as the time for the party drew near, were railing at their neglectful mothers who would not look for buttons for their shirts.

Denis returned with the Abbé Bongrain. The altar boy, who had been interrupted in the act of eating his supper, kept ringing his little bell frantically as he chewed a forgotten mouthful and dried his lips with his free hand. The abbé had banished any trace of a smile from his big, round face, and his broad shoulders seemed bent now upon the Lord's work. At the sound of the bell, the Soyeuses parted their curtains and the Mulotes opened their doors and came out. A few of them followed the priest, among them Madame Langevin and her friend Madame Chaton, who seldom missed a deathbed scene.

In the Bouchers' kitchen there was a great tumult among the chickens, frightened by the bell. Gaston revived a little and asked Flora why Joseph was crying. She smiled and, with the simpering manner of a young girl, patted her husband on the back as if he had been an infant. Then the dying lad's eyes fell on the priest. He hesitated to smile at him, for the Abbé Bongrain's face was grave. Flora explained this anomaly.

"It is because he has the good Lord with him. The good Lord must be annoyed with you because you haven't been to see Him, isn't that right?"

There was a shrewd expression on Gaston's face. What was all this pretence about? The good Lord was not annoyed with him. What kind of farce was this, anyway? Why this apparatus that the Abbé Bongrain was setting up, all those lighted candles? (In order not to frighten him, Flora had never spoken to him of Extreme Unction.) Everybody was kneeling except the youngest, who had hurt his legs. He insisted on playing with the bell, and the altar boy was pinching him. Flora sent the child downstairs. When the priest lifted up the covers to make the sign of the cross upon Gaston's swollen feet, an astonished look came over the boy's face. Did the good Lord, then, have special favours for His chosen ones? He gave his mother a questioning glance. Suddenly, his temper flaring, he leaned out over the register. Why were his chicks squealing like that? The youngest of the children was amusing himself by chasing them with a ruler. "Leave them alone!" cried Gaston.

The priest silenced him by making the sign of the cross on his mouth. Gaston then took communion. How sublime it was to feel the infant Jesus entering his body even as the last spurt of energy left it. All was calm and peaceful, and there was a silence in the room that seemed to absorb the sighs of human beings. When it was over, the Abbé Bongrain's big-hearted laugh rang out, his eyes bent low over the boy's face. Gaston was almost happy now; he could feel joy falling upon him. He thought of that Heaven of which Denis had told him, with springs and fountains among the clouds: how nice it would be to go leaping from star to star on Germaine's arm.

The priest noticed Joseph Boucher in the other room, his fists stretched upward toward the ceiling. "I'm changing my religion. It's not right."

Denis hurried the altar boy downstairs. The lad was curious, and might tell the others that he had seen him, Boucher, weeping. The abbé was exhorting Joseph to be fair.

"I've had all I can stand. I don't want to see the end. Just think, he will not be there any longer."

"You're thinking of yourself, not of him."

Flora clung to her husband. "He's right, Joseph. We'll meet him in Heaven. We'll all be together there. We'll be happy."

Distressed at this, the children wanted to know if their parents would take them along. Denis went out. He wanted to see Colin, have a heart-to-heart talk with him.

Jean was waiting at the corner. He was in his overcoat, which was puffed out indicating that he was wearing his new suit underneath. Denis came toward him, dragging his feet. Jean made a snowball and threw it at the sign that announced his angleworm business. And it was only seven o'clock, too! He noted that his friend had on his weekday clothes and was bareheaded and dishevelled. Denis' indifference toward Lise impressed him as being truly marvellous. But it was the normal thing for the leader to keep others waiting by way of lending an added zest to the adventure. Jean felt that must conceal his eagerness. He put on a pensive air.

"I'd like to take a walk in the rue St-Joseph," he said. "We still have time."

"Yes, plenty of time."

Jean was disturbed by the sarcastic tone of this reply. He became conciliatory. "Nine o'clock will be soon enough. You have to shave, of course—"

"Listen, Colin, Gaston's dying. I can't leave him."

Jean did not so much as sigh. He had been prepared for this disappointment; even as he waited, it had been mingled with his elation. But he had had enough of never succeeding! He did not notice how avidly Denis was watching him.

"A sickness like that takes a long time," he said. "He's not going to die this evening, I'm sure of that. I knew you would find an excuse."

Denis' fist shot out to his chin and Jean lay stretched in the snow, which was faintly stained with blood. Denis bent over him, his teeth clenched: "Say it once more! I hate that Lise of yours. I never want to see her again. Don't mention her name to me you fool." He was almost crying. That cursed Lise for whom he had slain Bobotte! It was all Jean's fault. Flora, greatly agitated, was calling to him from the gate.

"Little brother, I love you," he muttered to himself as he ran toward the house. "I love you, little brother. Dear old Gaston, you'll forgive me, I know you will."

After his death, however, there would be a new beginning. It was Gaston who would swallow up his love for Lise, taking the memory of it with him, along with such meanness as seeking to control the feelings of others, of petty individuals like Jean. He was happy to be alone with himself on a higher plane, with only himself to conquer.

Gaston was dying now. He coughed with an effort and his feeble lips were covered with a white froth which Flora dried. "His heart is very weak," said Flora in a low voice to Joseph, who sat there stunned. They could hear the accordion from the club where the Liberals were dancing. Gaston asked if Germaine had left for the dance.

"Yes, the hussy! She went with the twins."

There was a faint sign of displeasure around Gaston's mouth. He gazed at his mother resentfully. Denis spoke up quickly, still winded from having run so hard. "No, Gaston, I can see her now. She's walking up and down the balcony."

"Thief and liar. It's not so. Mama, why are you mad at Germaine? Tell her to come see me. Mama, I feel weak all over. I'm going to sleep. Warm my feet."

It was the end. The dying have no need of gestures to tell us they can hold out no longer. We feel it. Gaston became delirious. He was no longer waiting for death; it was death that was waiting, merely, until the twitchings of his body should cease. In what was almost a singing voice, he said: "Denis. Liar, thief!" He was ready. He straightened himself, tautly, as if desirous of putting himself on guard against life before taking his leave of it. It was as if he had forgotten something. Three times, very precisely, he uttered a "*toi*," pronounced so perfectly that one would have thought him a person of some education. Then he sank back into the bed like the yet warm corpse that he was. The chickens were quiet but the accordion kept on playing.

When they went to undress him, they found his dollar bills, all torn, in the pockets of his bathrobe. Denis was assigned to paste them together, and one of his brothers helped him, in order to keep an eye on him.

"That will pay for the church," his mother said.

The doctor, a great lover of fowl, took his fee in chickens. He carried them away with him.

The uncles and aunts came for the wake. They would say their rosaries for a while and then tell funny stories. Joseph, out in the shed near the hen roost, was smoking his pipe and sifting through his fingers the oats that he had brought home the day before.

Denis was exasperated as he left the house. The immense calm of evening lay like ice upon him, for there had been entirely too much clamour in his heart ever since that morning. He saw Lise, clad in a blue dress, beckoning to him from the half-opened door, and shook his fist at her: "You will never have me." He continued on the run and climbed the Pente Douce in order to wind himself, for he preferred to pant rather than weep. To preserve a light heart, free of pain, had been his motto. And here he was now, barely skimming the path, starting at the slightest sound, ready to see ghosts. He ran on, plunging into the night as if he were going to meet a happy Gaston, who would call him his big, crazy brother and playfully pull his hair. But his sorrow only deepened with the darkness, under the burden of regret. His footsteps on the wet asphalt were as the rhythmic beat of Gaston's dying sneers: "Liar, thief!" He put his arm over his eyes, at the risk of losing his way. Utterly exhausted and perspiring all over, he felt like lying down in the mud that he might catch cold, fall sick, and put the blame on Gaston.

It was late when he came home, and his mother hinted that, with no more heart than he had, she would not be at all surprised if he had gone to the movies. Flora was at her wits' end, for she did not have enough sandwiches for those attending the wake. Germaine came in and laid a bouquet on the coffin, but Flora threw it in the fire.

As the funeral procession went by, the Latruche sisters told the other ladies how their cousin, the undertaker, had drawn two gallons of thick red blood from the dead lad. "You wouldn't believe it, a little body like that."

Pritontin attended the service and everyone laughed at the care with which he sat down. When Denis saw Lise crying, he mentally accused her of acting a part. He recalled the Mulots whom he had thrashed for calling Gaston a hunchback. He bit the inside of his cheeks and relished the taste of blood. There was Colin with his injured chin, devouring Lise with his eyes. No! Nothing had changed since Gaston's death. One thing only:

"You are the oldest now."

PART TWO

The Echo

CHAPTER

I

THE winter had seemed long for the reason that the snow had lingered until well after the beginning of spring. The flowers had not kept pace with the sun; for by the time spring was free at last of the great white blanket of cold and was just beginning to smile, June was there to swallow it up and summer was at hand.

Denis might well have told himself that the snows had borne away the past. Lise, that pretty passion of a melancholy autumn —what subtle part had she come to play in the complex of his ambitions as a writer? This was a question that he did not put to himself, even in the course of those long solitary walks that he took upon his return from work. He walked with a buoyant tread in this parish which he had always defied to vanquish him, strode on amid the Mulots, some with a shovel and others with a pickaxe upon their shoulders as they came home from their jobs on the sewer main. He would not permit himself to feel superior because he worked in an office, but dreamed of a revolution whose leader he would be.

One evening in July found him in the highest of spirits as he clasped in his hand a copy of a magazine setting forth the conditions of a contest for young writers. His novel was already written. He had begun by constructing a fantastic plot, which later, after he had ballasted it with a considerable amount of realism, had degenerated into a trite little autobiographical sketch based upon his frustrated yearnings. The great difficulty lay in the fact that while his heart was making grandiloquent speeches bristling with cruelty and was already drunk with the toasts of an anticipated victory, his style was inclined to bog down in a succession of metaphors overburdened with the sublime. What he was looking for was a commonplace theme. Denis Boucher, bard of the unknown man! What a sensation a novel like that would create in Quebec!

He did not notice the approach of the sight-seeing streetcar with its load of tourists from Montreal and Three Rivers and a few Americans from across the border, all of them neatly arranged in rows like Easter eggs in a Holy Saturday display. The conductor was stamping frantically upon his gong to clear the rails of the young Mulots who hemmed in this gala tramway, a source of pennies to them. The newly married couples and the tourists from Three Rivers were the most generous of the lot. The pseudo-antiquarians carefully studied the sloping-roofed houses, convinced that they were back in the atmosphere of Jean Talon as they clucked delightedly over this debris of the past. (Those shacks had been recently put up out of the rubbish of old buildings.) There were also a number of humdrum citizens and their good wives, and they were as insatiable as any mining prospector in their quest of fresh marvels to be viewed; for they had about had their fill of St Anne and Brother André.

"They say it was here the saintly young man lived?"

A handful of pennies came flying in Denis' direction and the urchins scrambled for them between his legs. The opening sentence of his book, which was on his lips at that moment, was transformed into an oath. As he cuffed the young Mulots, he saw the tourists laughing at the sight.

"No one asked you for your pennies," he shouted at them. "Get out, you stinkers!" And picking up a rock, he threw it at the streetcar. The mothers, standing in their doorways, hooted at him for this: did he want to stop the strangers from coming to scatter their coins? For even as their children learned to repeat "I love you, my Jesus," they were taught to say in English "Give me five cents, please."

"That one's stuck up because of his new job in an office."

Denis saw Madame Chaton approaching and did not have time to avoid her. "Ah! I'm not going to let you get away from me. I'm going to sell you a ticket for Pinasse's wrestling match. Come on, now, with your office job you can afford to pay fifty cents, like nothing at all. Don't go back on your own people." And motioning to her women friends to indicate that she would be with them in a minute, she held out the ticket. Denis hesitated. He must not let it be known that all he earned was seven dollars a week. Madame Chaton was assuming a fighting pose. She was a small, thin, jaundiced-looking woman, but as ebullient as a precipitate of sulphuric acid. "You'll learn some new holds," she was saying. "The stranglehold, they tell me, will be worth seeing. They're going to have the Killer Kid, who wrestles at the Forum."

Madame Pinasse, whose husband, commandant of the Lévis Guard, was a candidate in the popularity contest, was "doing" the other side of the street, convincing her friends that they should not miss the show, which was worth a dozen bingo parties such as those given by Zépherin Lévesque, the candidate of the Soyeux. What was more, the police were about to start raiding bingo games. The shrewder housewives insisted on a ten-cent rebate on their ticket and wanted to know if Madame Chaton did not make a percentage on the sale. Her husband was earning enough money the way it was, with his worms and his new business of selling blocks of snow for those who had no refrigeration.

The Latruche sisters, who were out soliciting for the Soyeux candidate, suddenly came running up, all out of breath, to Madame Pritontin, who stood in the door of her home.

"Madame Pritontin, your husband and Pinasse are drunk and are having a quarrel with Monsieur Lévesque in the parish hall."

"Don't pay any attention to what they say, Madame Pritontin," the commandant's wife called out. "They are just provoked because your husband and my husband are friends."

In despair over the way her Anselme was turning out, Sophie Pritontin slammed the door. The growing success of the Latruches, with the saint becoming popular all over the country, and the amazing fondness of her own sons for the heroines of the illustrated stories in the newspapers were near to being the death of her. She did all she could, however, to fortify her soul and strengthen her faith by way of preserving in the home that atmosphere of saintliness to which her offspring seemed more and more impervious.

"Quarrelsome creatures!" exclaimed the old maids disdainfully. Since they had been going around selling religious tracts, they had come to feel quite erudite and only held discussions with the clergy. They now entered their shop, which had recently been opened. It was a former potato-chip stand that had made a lot of money by the sale of motion picture magazines, especially a certain issue for April, 1938, which showed Dorothy Lamour in a sarong. But with the spinsters in possession, it could no longer damage the morals of St Joseph's parish, for the showcase now held religious books, rosaries, and berets for Young Catholic Workers. A small book bound in pale blue gave the directions for the year, indicating how an elastic virginity might be preserved within the marriage bond without being defiled by numerous births.

The parishioners need not worry now about the length of God's beard and the tortuous path of the beatitudes; for salvation was there in the Latruche's showcase, displayed under the benevolent and optimistic eyes of the saint that was to be. Letters testifying to cures effected formed a wreath for a treatise by a talented lay brother: *Key to Chastity for Adolescents Dis-*

covered. Most of the letters on display came from the United States and British Columbia and dealt with cases of neuralgia, the ills of young mothers, jobs obtained, stomach trouble cured, and enlightenment received as to vocations to be followed. The young saint had made a promising beginning. Over the protests of the fathers of St Joseph's Oratory, Madame Pritontin, acting in their name, had made a little investigation of these asserted cures. Offended by this, the Latruches had accused her of spite-work, and had remarked that in twenty years' time, with a little experience, their saint would be able to cope with cancer. And anyway, were they not living in a land of miracles?

Meanwhile, there was an argument in progress on the scaffolding of the new church, and Denis, thinking to make some first-hand observations, went over to see what it was all about; for he felt the need of a little irony to offset the vibrant and dramatic grandiloquence that he sensed within himself. The place was filled with an infernal din from the masons' hammers and the clash of steel girders that were being unloaded from trucks. A dispute was always going on between the workers and the idlers. The unemployed of St Joseph, sitting on stone blocks, would give their opinion and deplore the fact that the structure was too long for its breadth. Others, boiling over with a desire for revenge, would obstinately continue their card game, and the foremen would tear their hair in a vain attempt to dislodge them.

"Where is Monsieur le Curé?"

The Abbé Folbèche had taken refuge in the sanctuary in order to escape the indignation of those Mulots whom he was unable to employ as masons for the reason that they did not know how to lay cellar walls. Fortunately, work on the sewer main was beginning, which would relieve the situation somewhat. He was at present calculating the obtuse angle which his seat would form with the nave and the tabernacle. He would be the pivot of the house of prayer. The Abbé Charton was striding up and down the rood-loft, speaking to the workmen in a loud tone of voice and lending an attentive ear to make sure that his voice carried well. This loft was to be the exclusive property of the choir at high mass and the new organ would accompany only the specially arranged choral numbers, even though it had been donated by the father of the organist at the nine o'clock mass, which was something of a complication.

The panting sacristan Bidonnet, walking on crutches and with one leg in a plaster cast, was endeavouring to put the Gonzagues off the premises; for they had arrogated to themselves the privilege of visiting the shrine before the official opening. He did not care for these future sacristans. Among them were quite a number of the most important shareholders of the "Grace Company" (founded by Father Folbèche, shares and bonds at $10, $100, and $1,000, redeemable at the "Bank of Sanctifying Grace"). These gentlemen strolled through the church as if they were its owners, while Bidonnet, hobbling along on his crutches which creaked as he walked, hastened after the Abbé to discuss with him certain grandiose plans that he had for decorating the edifice; for the man who was substituting for him, a hypocrite, was offering his services for less money.

M. Folbèche smiled when he learned of the dispute between Pinasse and Zépherin Lévesque in the parish hall below. "I'll be down right away." As he tranquilly descended the ladder which took the place of a stair, the Gonzagues held out their arms, begging him to be careful. What a brilliant idea, this popularity contest between the two men, the winner to be the one who raised the most money. It was, of course, a little warm yet for such an event, which usually took place in the autumn; but the sewer main had brought a wave of prosperity to the workers of St Joseph, and he must try for a master haul with his net. The autumn? Pooh! A season when there were no cellars to be dug or snow to be shovelled. It was as poverty-stricken a time as All Saints! Why, even these disputes between Zépherin and Pinasse were a good thing. Father Folbèche cast a disapproving eye at the Abbé Bongrain, helping to fasten the stones that were to be hoisted by the crane. A little farther on was the Abbé Trinchu who was beginning to look with more favour on his sojourn at St Joseph's, now that they were to have a new church. He was accompanying the architect on his rounds, holding forth upon the theme of Roman art as compared with Gothic.

Denis followed Father Folbèche into the parish hall, from which came the sound of a lively interchange of words. Pinasse's booming voice, backed up by Pritontin's delicate little oaths, was sufficient to drown out Zépherin's indignation. The brave commandant was insisting that Monsieur Lévesque see to it that the hall was left clean for the next day, for the bingo party that evening meant there would be a terrible mess of strewn markers and overturned chairs. Experts from Montreal were coming to set up the arena for the wrestling, and the place must be in order for them, with no trace of the orgy of the night before. That match would be epoch-making, since it would assuredly enable him to win the popularity contest which ended the same evening. Everything was to be done on a grand scale, and the Lévis guard, under Pinasse's command, was to go meet the wrestlers at the train. Zépherin was fuming about all this, but as they caught sight of Father Folbèche, both commanders fell silent and became almost amiable toward each other.

"Monsieur le Curé," said Zépherin, coming forward with a constrained manner. "They tell me the police may raid my bingo party. Do you think I have anything to fear?"

The good priest smiled majestically. "The Church," he replied, "has its own laws which the law does not infringe upon." Pinasse gave Pritontin a roguish wink: their report to the police authorities would bear fruit that evening. The active commandant burst into his bellowing laugh. "I'll be within the law with my wrestling match. That, at least, appeals to men."

Monsieur le Curé tugged at his ear in some perplexity. These matches in which the participants wore tights troubled him a little. Why did not the other parishes organize similar affairs? "Is it dangerous?" he asked. "They tell me they make each other suffer, pull each other's toes. Are you quite sure it is a suitable form of entertainment for the parish hall?"

"Why, of course!" exclaimed Pinasse. "Just think. Wrestlers from Montreal, from the Forum. It's very refined. And anyway, it's all fake stuff."

The abbé opened his eyes wide at this. He could picture formidable-appearing, supple bodies floating about the arena like muses or crouched beneath the padded arms of their opponents, giving blows that ended in caresses. He could distinctly hear the low murmur of the crowd as it watched this charming exhibition of acrobatics on the part of well-muscled gentlemen who groaned and smiled in the embrace of their comrades. One could almost go so far as to invite the nuns.

"What are you doing here?" The abbé gave Denis a stern look. What business had he taking notes, this lad who was so strange, so intelligent, and who had turned out so disappointingly, who disturbed him more than the plottings and schemings of all the Soyeux put together? He was one to be watched. Thrusting his notebook into his shirt front, Denis made for the door without any bravado. As soon as he was alone he felt sad and depressed, sad at not having been able to capture anything that was accurate, simple, and true. Life in full effervescence was all around him, and yet he was unable to lay hold of it, living as he did in a dreamland of trees, flowers, and rivers. Was this the same old feverish grandiloquence that Lise had inspired in him, but from which, he had thought, Gaston's death had freed him? Was this inspiration, this urge to write, utterly false, a mere matter of reminiscences?

He saw the children running toward the Lévesque home as if it were on fire. Mothers were leaning out of windows and girls ran out on the sidewalk. Down at Bédarovitch's, the gang was standing at the edge of the street.

"He's nice!"

"She's the lucky one!"

"Stuck up, that's what she is!"

"Boucher, look at Colin, helping her on."

"Let me take it a moment, to show you how."

"Good heavens! I'm going to fall!" Lise, swaying from side to side on her new bicycle, was terrified.

Jean, greatly embarrassed, held her up, assuring her that she would learn. Denis at first thought of going down another street, but a kind of rage held him there as he saw Lise smiling at Jean and leaning on his shoulder. Why should he feel that way about it since she no longer interested him? He had thought that all memory of the girl from the convent had been consumed last winter, in the fire of his desires and lustful dreams. In his unassuaged passion he had accused her of banality; yet in spite of all these Mulots, in spite of Jean holding her up on her bicycle there, he could not put her in the same class with the others, with Germaine and her girl friends. Her black hair, which made her face seem paler still, fell down over her shoulders and seemed to be drawing her head backward. The dreamy languor that her eyes had held the year before had given way to a mild warmth that spoke of a love that was beginning to stir. Her throat appeared younger, more slender. Denis felt inferior as he saw her becoming a woman before he had become a man. His desires arose again as they had the past year, when they were still noble and stopped far short of possession. So the old flame was not extinguished, then? Had this fellow Jean, representing a friendship he had overcome, been able to upset everything by an exchange of smiles with Lise?

Returning home, he looked over his own bicycle, and then suddenly felt like demolishing it. No, he was strong, he was a writer! Taking his anxiety for inspiration, he went over in his mind the metaphors he had collected that afternoon, summoned his rancours and his sense of greatness, and then sat down and wrote the first page. The story burned him in the telling, but his words were cold; they were an apology rather than a narrative. The smell of cooking meat filled the room as he attempted to describe the fragrant scent of a garden, his opening scene.

Jean, scarcely browned by the sun, stood his bicycle alongside the victoria. His happiness today led him to look down upon his troubles: the strange disease that was causing his knee to swell; his poverty; his dreary acceptance of Lise's indifference to his love. And then, all of a sudden, at the very moment when he felt that he was sinking, as Denis, now employed as a stenographer, went on to inaccessible heights—at that very moment, when love seemed out of the question, Lise had asked him to go bicycle riding with her the next day. He began polishing the nickel plate on his bike. The ecstatic smile on his lips, the disjointed words he murmured to himself showed how grateful he was to the God who had not forgotten him. He was wonderful, God was! To allow him to go out with Lise under circumstances where his limp would not be noticed! They would stop somewhere along the road, in a glade of silence, a silence rendered iridescent by the moonlight. He would press her hand so gently, so tenderly that she would understand at last how much he loved her. He recalled how angry Denis had been, here beside this victoria, when he, Jean, had told of his first meeting with Lise. No, his love must not be a little parish affair; he had suffered too much for that.

He lifted the seat of the victoria and took out the grammar which Denis had lent him. He must hide all these books, or Tit-Blanc, when he was drunk, would burn them as he praised the ignorance of his grandsires who had come through all the same. He had not looked at these schoolbooks since the day when he had come to feel that a moody factory lad like him must have something more to offer an educated and dreamy-minded young lady like Lise. With a feverish smile on his lips, he drank in the arid pages that seemed so interminable, but he did not understand what he read. A pair of eyes, a hand, a row of teeth would sparkle between the lines. Jean made a furtive gesture as if to hide his book as Tit-Blanc slammed the door.

"You're still studying, are you, you good-for-nothing? I saw you out with the Lévesque girl. She's the one that's making you proud. You're ashamed of us, ashamed of your worms."

"I'm not ashamed. I'm getting older, and I don't like walking over pebbles. My leg hurts me."

Out in the kitchen, Barloute was bemoaning her fate. She spoke of going to see the boss of the factory, to ask him to give Tit-Blanc more work. It was poverty for her, the humiliation of the families of the unemployed, while her women friends stepped out with new hats, went to the picture shows, and ate dessert, thanks to the money their husbands earned on the sewer main. She was storming about, bewailing the fact that she could not go to the bingo party. She accused Tit-Blanc of saving his pennies for the wrestling match. Old man Pitou, leaning upon his cane, his hair whiter than ever and his face even redder, now came in. He was angry. He had not had a chew of tobacco for three days.

"Why don't you sell that contraption?" And he gave the bicycle a shove. "We didn't have anything like that in our day."

Tit-Blanc was delighted with the idea. "You could get twenty dollars for it!"

Jean leaped to his feet. "Why don't you sell your victoria?" he cried. "I'm keeping my bicycle. I'd leave home first."

"Get the hell out if you want to! A lot of difference it makes to us. You're not bringing anything in."

"I spoke before I thought. I'll go back to selling worms. Here. I'll give you all I've got." He emptied his pockets of the money he had been saving for the outing with Lise. As he fled into the other room, it seemed to him that everything about him was limping, even his heart.

Barloute shrugged her shoulders. "It's about long enough that you've been pretending there's something wrong with your leg, so you won't have to work. Don't think you're going to school, you loafer."

Germaine, who was preparing to leave the house, now put in her word.

"You'd better watch out," she said, "or you won't have your Lise for very long. I saw Denis looking his bicycle over a little while ago. He was oiling it up."

CHAPTER

II

FLORA was glad to see that Denis, despite his nineteen years, was not tired of study. She was proud, too, that she had kept him chaste, free from any feminine contamination! (She felt a jealous need of preserving, in this son of hers who was so sound of body, the memory of the sickly Gaston who had clung to her.) There was contempt in her glance as she caught sight of Germaine all aflutter over a good-looking young man in a passing automobile. Clasping her hands behind her back, the girl threw out her bust and closed one eye while the other appeared to be laughing. Denis would be annoyed if he saw her offering herself like that to other men when all he had to do was to take her. Flora almost called to her that Robert Langevin would make a scene and that he would have good cause to do so, but she restrained herself. Pursing her lips to control her mounting anger, she went on washing her windows. After all, that Germaine was nothing but a hussy who had poisoned the soul of her Gaston in a confectionery shop that had been stolen from his parents.

The rusty signboards in front of the Colins' gave back minute reflections of the setting sun, cruel glints that laid bare the wound in her mother's heart. Out of the tears that marked the months of mourning, Gaston had emerged afresh, had been born again into her life and had taken up his place there, as new and as saddening a phenomenon as the first grey hairs. As she overheard Germaine telling her brother to keep an eye on Denis, Flora swung her washcloth more vigorously than ever, and the motions that she made compelled her to draw in her increasingly plump figure until it was almost slender. "It's the dregs of my womanhood collecting there," she had remarked one day as she was draining off her cherry wine. The windowpanes were so clean by now that the inside of the house was visible as a chiaroscuro unspotted by the slightest particle of dust. Flora smiled as she saw the reflection of her face along with that of the poplar leaves, forming a mixture of light and shade in which it was easy to recognize Gaston's features.

Germaine was approaching hesitantly. "Madame Boucher,"

she began, "please don't be angry. I was just thinking how strange it is not to see Gaston sunning himself at the corner of the street." Flora's arm stopped, then resumed with a dynamic rhythm. The muscles of her face were tightly drawn, especially around the temples. Germaine went on talking, but all the time she was trying to catch a glimpse of Denis behind the curtains. "He never went far away. It was plain to be seen that he wanted to stay near you."

Flora could contain herself no longer. "He was my best one," she replied.

Germaine rubbed her hands fervently as Flora stared at her in astonishment, almost with pleasure.

"I loved him like a little brother. He saved for me the best apples that Denis found."

"With such teeth as mine I couldn't eat those apples, but he always insisted on my taking a few bites."

Germaine helped Flora down from her stool.

"He was so fond of flowers, too," the girl went on. "Did you keep the little bouquet that I put on his coffin? I cut those roses out of tissue paper."

Flora dropped her cake of soap. She could see the flame that had consumed that bouquet after she had tossed it in the fire in a moment of rage. She must make up for it.

"Come," she said, "I'll show you the nice cards of sympathy that we received, nearly all of them the twenty-five-cent kind."

This was something that Germaine had never hoped for: to make her way into Denis' home as simply as this. She could see herself there as a daughter-in-law, helping with the dishes.

"I don't know, Madame Boucher. If Robert were to see me. You don't know how jealous he is of Denis."

Joseph, just coming home from work, was astonished to perceive the two women going into the house together. Then he resumed his tired attitude and went out to lean pensively against the fence that had surrounded his oldest son's poultry yard. For they did not wish to do away with anything that had belonged to the dead lad: the image, and the hollow behind it; his bathrobe; the bureau drawers overflowing with pictures of athletes cut from the newspapers and with all sorts of little old trinkets of interest only to children—they all served to evoke Gaston's memory. He had become the great exemplar, the sublime child, to whom saints of renown were compared, and who was held up as a model for vicious youngsters to follow. Certain of those on Flora's side of the family even prayed to him, but it was only the unmarried ones among Joseph's sisters who sought Gaston's intercession.

Having quieted the children, who were impatient for their supper, Madame Boucher proudly displayed the cards of condolence which she had received. Denis was nervously pacing up and down the living room, trying to think what he could do to lend more interest to those incidental characters in his novel toward whom he had no feeling of personal ill-will. He stopped short at sight of Jean's sister. He did not like to see her here, though this room meant very little to him. Flora had chicken and asparagus for supper, and she allowed Germaine to help her get the meal ready. Slamming the door, Denis the misunderstood retired into his lair once more, surrounded by lamps which his mother had won at bingo parties. He now sought to turn his domestic rancours into a grudge against those who were more fortunate than he; and despite the smell of chicken and the clatter of knives and forks, he fancied himself the brilliant, fiery, impatient, genius-inspired phrase-maker that he would like to be. Then something that Germaine was saying sent a chill over him.

"He's a businessman, all right. You can tell that by the worried look on his face."

"Yes, and just imagine! He's assistant head of the correspondence department."

"They tell me he has a typewriter and a telephone beside him."

"Not to speak of his future, he'll be handing me seven dollars this evening."

Denis' face grew red with annoyance. Everyone would know that he earned less than the scavengers or the day labourers on the sewer main. How the Langevins would laugh at him, now that they were working in the Parliament Buildings. And Jean would no longer be envious of him. Gone now was the fever of literary creation. How could he shut his mother up? He felt impotent, paralysed. He allowed his ill-humour to feed upon the wrong that had been done him.

"Seven dollars?" said Germaine. She was thinking that she earned more than that scrubbing floors.

Flora bridled at this: "We're saving our pennies so that we can build near the cemetery. This is no place for us to be living. Down there, we'll be nearer our oldest."

"With the job he has, Denis ought to be able to get himself a fine girl."

"A girl?" And Flora laughed as at something that was in-

164

credible. "He's only a child. You saw what happened with that Mademoiselle Lévesque. I broke that up."

"You think so?" said Germaine, putting on a crafty look. "Did you see him watching her a while ago when she was out bicycle riding?"

"What's this you're telling me?"

Breathlessly, Denis waited for an outburst of wrath from his mother. Could he ever rid himself of the hold which that woman, whom he looked upon as being so "parochial-minded," had upon him? Yes, she was his mother, and he was attached to her by bonds which death itself would not be able to sever.

Germaine was evasive in her reply. "What I mean is, he might fall in love with her again."

At this point, Denis burst into the kitchen. "Go on home, you!" he shouted. "And right away!" He bore down upon Germaine as she, with flaming cheeks and an appealing glance at Flora, made for the door. There was a moment's silence, and then his mother let herself go.

"Hand over your pay at once. So, you're starting up again with that Lévesque girl, are you? Better not let me catch you at it."

Denis snatched a napkin from one of the children who was making a nun's bonnet out of it.

"I've had enough of this!" he cried. "I don't want any more of your protection. Pay some attention to your young ones, instead. When I was young, I was the only one you thought of, and you brought me up on beatings. And now, in order to bar my path, you abandon the others. You're like the hen that neglects her puny chicks to wait for the strongest ones at the gate of the poultry yard."

Flora began moaning and Joseph knocked out his pipe.

"Joseph," she said, "he called me a *'poule.'* That's the name they give to chippies in those French magazines! Don't you ever think of Bobotte, of the brother that you killed? Yes, my son, I'm going to keep you from the girls. I'll die if necessary, but I'll see to it that you don't throw yourself away on that Lévesque creature, out in the Gomin Wood."

At the thought of her dead son, Flora wept. Joseph, who had accepted everything passively since Gaston's death, put out a slender hair-covered hand.

"Denis, there is a song that says: 'Don't ever make your mother cry.' I hope that you are going to let us grow old in peace. Remember, your brother is looking down upon us. It is he who makes it possible for us to live together calmly and love one another. He has pardoned you; try to be worthy of him."

Exasperated by his father's melodramatic tone, Denis broke in upon him. "Leave the dead in peace, will you? It's life that I want."

Disconcerted, Joseph could only stare at him as he sat down to his plate of soup. He was trembling.

"I am going to sell your bicycle tomorrow," he said. "I never did like for you to keep bad company. And I want peace, myself, from now on, do you understand? I want peace."

The poor man was talking to the ceiling. Denis' face was pale. Sell his bicycle? From his sudden feeling of alarm he realized that, in spite of his contemptuous attitude, he had been forming new plans down deep in his heart, at sight of Lise. His mother's chidings had not prompted these impulses but had merely awakened them. They wanted to sell his bicycle, did they? He ate but little, then went to the bureau drawer and came back. His father had gone out to smoke his pipe under the poplar tree near the neighbouring shed, where Gaston not so long ago had stood to watch the automobiles go by. Denis came up to him, whistling.

"Have you found any buyers for my bicycle?" he asked. "Before you decide one way or the other, I'd like to show you this. I found it on the floor beside your bureau." And he handed him the quatrain which he had discovered the year before as he was hunting for Gaston's savings. One look and Joseph crumpled the paper in his hand. His skin, ordinarily pallid, now became slightly yellowish. By way of wetting his throat, he had to put his pipe back in his mouth and chew on it.

"No, I haven't found any buyers."

"Then please don't find any, Papa." He started to walk away, took a few steps, and turned back. "I made a copy of those verses," he said. "I hope you don't mind. They will make such a nice souvenir of the kind of compositions you used to write."

Joseph knew that he was being blackmailed. After all, it was not so long ago that he had been the sentimental idiot whom Denis was now so surprised to discover. As for the son, he no longer had any illusions about his father, who had not always been the mature and dignified individual he had known in the past.

Jean was already at the corner, in case Lise should arrive sooner than he expected; he did not wish to keep her waiting. Denis' manner as he came up was a sarcastic one; for he felt certain that Colin now knew how small his salary was. There was no doubt of it: Jean was smiling, and his pretence of ignoring the matter was more provoking than if he had burst out laughing. Straddling his bicycle, Denis circled his friend.

"You're starting out early, aren't you?" he inquired nonchalantly.

Jean made a vague gesture, with a faraway look on his face. He wanted to bore Denis sufficiently to cause him to leave. How amiable, almost obsequious, this fellow Boucher had become all of a sudden. Feeling rich as he thought of Lise's smile, the worm vendor for once was superior to all the lads who had been to school. Denis, meanwhile, was amusing himself by widening the circles his bicycle made.

"You'd better leave!" said Jean, with a note of urgency in his voice. "There's the Abbé Trinchu. He's going to ask you to be secretary of his St John the Baptist Section."

Denis went away but came back as soon as the priest had passed. His tone was not as ironical as usual. "Are you going to Zépherin's bingo party this evening? I prefer the wrestling, myself. Look!"

Zépherin was helping Lise mount her bicycle and was giving her all sorts of advice. She was not listening to him, but was smiling at the young men. Colin made as if to join her when Denis' voice brought him up sharply: "She's expecting me, but I'm not going."

Jean controlled himself: "She's expecting *you*? Ah!"

Denis did not feel humiliated by the lie he had told. He was enjoying his friend's astonishment. "You won't have much trouble teaching her," he went on casually. "I told her not to pay so much attention to her front wheel. You rascal! You just like to have her lean on your shoulder, that's all."

There was a queer smile on Jean's lips. "I've had a good deal of experience with women," he said. "No soft words. I'm rude to them, and then all of a sudden I put on an absent-minded look. That makes them curious and they want to get to know you."

Denis was startled, a question written all over his face. Was Jean making sport of him? All those whimsical impulses in which he had indulged the year before, all his grand and futile gestures—were they becoming weapons of conquest for the other lad?

"To think," Jean remarked, "that it was on her account you gave me a beating last year. Oh, I don't hold it against you."

Denis made no reply, pretended that his mind was on some-thing else. "How much do you earn a week?" he inquired.

Jean thought he wished to change the subject. "Five, some-times six dollars," he replied. His eyes were on Lise. He was preparing the speech he would make when they went out to-gether the next day. "She's leaving, Denis. It's too bad you're not going along. You're famous when it comes to riding a bike. That's why I'd just as soon wait until tomorrow night. She'll be better then. We can take the St Louis Road and come out on the Plains of Abraham. How nice it will be to look down on the river with the boats all lighted up and the dark water all around. I've always dreamed of a view of the sea from up high, with her beside me."

"And you'll hold hands, I suppose? Will you kiss her at once?"

Denis was growing nervous. Jean assumed a knowing air, but the truth is, he had not the slightest intention of kissing Lise. To sit beside her and share the same emotion, under the stars, far from books and complicated talk; to sit there silently gazing into the impenetrable darkness, mistaking the worm vendors with their lanterns for the will-o'-the-wisp— But those were childish things that Denis must have thought of at the age of twelve.

"Let's climb the Pente Douce," Denis suggested.

On the way they passed Germaine and Robert Langevin, who were going up the path arm in arm. It was the custom of a Sunday, when one had nothing to do, to ascend the slope and then take a rest at the top and see how the quarter looked when seen from above. But lovers would take this path every evening, on their way to the Parc des Braves, that large green-clad plateau furnished with convenient benches that seemed closer to the sky than to the earth. The caresses they exchanged here were less ordinary than those in the parlour at home. It was here that the lads of St Sauveur would come when a poetic mood was on them. It was likewise the rendezvous of little brats who had learned how to say "Give me five cents, please"; for Americans from across the border, thrilled at the thought that the battle of Ste-Foye was fought on this spot and that the cadavers left by that hecatomb now rested beneath their feet—a story told with great gusto by their guides—were not sparing with their small change.

The two cyclists followed a meandering course in ascending the long grey incline known to grateful kindling-gatherers as the Pente Douce. Their wheels glinted in the light of the setting sun. Colin made a wry face at each turn of his pedals, then dismounted and walked alongside his bicycle, out of breath and limping. Denis watched him attentively as he came up.

"Have you adopted that limp?"

Jean, who was suffering, wiped the perspiration from his face. "It swells up," he said, "whenever I'm tired. I got it one time last year when, just to amuse myself, I went to steal some plums."

Jean was stammering. Could he help it? And was it, then, so noticeable as all that? He could think of any number of explanations and excuses, but a growing fear that was close to anguish had invaded every fibre of his being. Here was Denis suddenly concerned about an affliction which he himself had for months done his best to ignore. Jean's terror was all the greater because it had seized him at a moment when he was happier than he had ever been before. He felt his soul, his courage shrinking, to take refuge in that joint, forming there a nucleus of resistance against an unknown enemy, while his heart, defeated before the battle began and bringing up the rear, could do no more than contemplate the coming struggle. The past and future alike appeared sad to him at this moment : the futility of his plodding studies out in the shed; his amorous disappointments of the last year; his worm business, which he must begin again; Lise's sympathy tomorrow night as she would advise him to take care of himself. When was it all going to end so that he really could start all over once more and know a little peace?

Denis stubbornly continued to speak of Lise. "You say you have certain tricks to charm her?"

Jean dully surveyed the river of green that streamed down from the Laurentides upon the housetops of St Sauveur, all the way to where they stood. "Tricks?" he repeated. "I shall try to be silent without being sad." When the meaning of what he had just said dawned upon him, he was happy. Denis stared at him in astonishment.

"Don't try to be complex. If I were you, I'd brush against her quite often, without appearing to do it on purpose, just to make her feel how far I kept myself from her, the distance between our bodies. You can see what the effect of that would be. She's like all the others. For you, that would be the best means of offsetting her education. And if she says anything about me, tell her I am very hard to get."

Jean taken aback arose from the bench in the Parc des Braves where they had dropped down. "But that's not the way I love her!"

"That's the only way of bringing her around to you." Denis was drumming nervously on the back of the bench. "You annoy me with those dreams of yours. And anyway, you'd better be taking care of yourself instead of concocting love affairs."

Jean was sure that Denis was suffering, and he felt sorry for him for having to mask his disappointment with a show of meanness. He laughed and patted him gently on the shoulder. "Come, I'm going to talk about *you*. You've changed since last year."

Denis gave him a shove. "I've not changed! Lise is not going to have me, that's all; I got away. I'm interested in literature." His voice was exultant. "I'm going to write a great novel. We're going to have our revenge, old man."

"I don't want revenge; I want to be understood. Are you going to write about the shoe factory and the terrible din that is more than we can bear? Go ahead and put me in your novel, if you like; I won't mind."

Picking up a handful of pebbles, Denis let them slip through his fingers one by one. He had never thought of speaking of the din of factories, of men condemned to earn their bread by concerning themselves with the feet of other men. His conception was something quite different from that.

"No! I mean to portray—to shout for all to hear—the weakness of our youth and the sentimental, narrow culture that is crammed down their throats. By way of equipping us for life, they stuff us with romantic nonsense out of the last century. And all we are good for is to make a conquest of the first washerwoman that comes along. Do you understand something of my revolt against woman? She symbolizes our decadence, the manner in which we cling to an outworn sentimentality."

"All I know," Jean replied, "is that I am in love, and I have no education. You are just saying what everybody says over the radio."

Piqued by this, Denis concealed his anger with a sigh. "You don't understand. I've had enough of books; and yet, at the same time, I am anxious to find some new form of intellectual expression. Yes, we are in a bad way indeed, for the reason that the culture to which we all aspire is a false culture."

Throwing out his chest, he listened as if his words must surely have an echo. At that moment they heard the police whistle and both listened attentively, their eyes sparkling, to the sound that had thrilled them as mischievous adolescents For Denis now it was no longer a question of Lise, of novels, of a new cultural ideal to be formulated. The old life laid hold of him once more. Jean was delighted at the idea of returning the way they had come, for Lise could not be far away.

"It's down below," he said. "Come on, let's go."

Mounting their bicycles, they raced down the Pente Douce. At the door of the parish hall two police vans were drawn up and the gendarmes were spilling out. It was already night, and the red glow of the lanterns upon the scaffolding of the church cast weird gleams on the big crane, motionless as a sleeping ostrich. Pinasse and Pritontin were pointing out to the police the basement entrance to the hall. From within, the voice of the announcer of the bingo game could be heard through a microphone.

At first, there was a general panic among the women players at sight of the uniforms. Some of them made a rampart of their bodies by way of protecting the prizes already won. The Mulotes, who in the past had done the loudest boasting about how they would kick the gendarmes out, now hurled mild insults at the officers but did not stir from their places. The announcer, a baritone at the nine o'clock mass, was very much befuddled as he sat behind the number-drawing machine which had been constructed by Dieudonné the carpenter, who had an inborn talent for that sort of thing. By way of impressing the players and relieving their minds of any idea of trickery, this machine was equipped with red lights that glowed each time a number came up. The baritone, who loved to play the clown and make the ladies laugh, did not budge from his seat but continued to hum a song he had made up, something about a man who always did his duty. As the police officers put in an appearance, he turned so pale that anyone could see he was afraid of his life.

Zépherin, who had always respected the law, was also white with terror. This meant the end of his candidacy. Haunted by the thought of a police record and possible fingerprints, he clattered about from one wing to another on the stage until he found himself face to face with a big gendarme running toward him in an effort to dodge his own wife, who was shouting that she would attend to him if he put on airs with her. Monsieur le Curé, who did not believe in yielding ground where religion was involved, set about reading his breviary; it was the first time that meditation had been of concrete assistance to him. The bravest were two ladies whom one would have expected to swoon with fear, the demoiselles Latruche. Puffing out their chaste bosoms, they haughtily confronted the horde of legal vandals. The police, who so enjoyed their enforced task of breaking up houses of ill-fame, were ill at ease in the presence of these obstinate virgins and surrounded them as if they had been a couple of reefs. They proceeded to investigate the seals on the prize packages, excusing themselves as they did so, and took away the winnings from the fortunate ones. This was none too easy a task, for many of the ladies, having faithfully followed the series of forty-three unproductive bingo parties, had obtained their first reward that evening.

"Bunch of communists! Why don't you go away and let us have a good time?"

The embarrassed gendarmes were, in short, extremely timid in the performance of their duties. And the Abbé Bongrain laughed at it all as though he would split his sides. In his heart he was not displeased by the incident. The Liberal party, to which he belonged, knew what it was doing in forbidding these games of chance. And so it was with considerable merriment that the priest pointed out Zépherin as the churchwarden squeezed through the tiny dressing-room window the circumference of which was less than that of his belly.

As those in attendance silently filed toward the door, Pinasse on the outside was shaking hands with the police officers and congratulating them while Pritontin passed around the cigars. The Abbé Trinchu, once more on speaking terms with the Clichoteux family, now that Emilie had entered the Grey Nuns and the gossiping tongues had been silenced, was leaning against the big Buick which Pritontin still coveted and was engaged in laying down the law. "The nation is going to be strong. Wait and you shall see." Now that he was almoner of the St John the Baptist section in the parish, let the government and the English beware.

Obsequiously, Pritontin ran up to aid Zépherin, who lay groaning by the wall of the building near the dressing-room window. He had wrenched an ankle and was dripping wet, for his fall had landed him in the ditch surrounding the foundations of the new church. Jean officiously took him by the legs, for he had a kindly feeling toward all the fathers-in-law in the world; Pritontin took the shoulders; and with Denis walking on ahead and Zépherin writhing, the procession was off.

Lise thought she would die when she saw them bringing her father home like that.

"THERE they are, I hear them. Quick, take me over to the window, daughter."

Lying stretched out in an easy chair, Zépherin was making much of his twisted ankle, heavily swathed in bandages. Lise impatiently left off creasing her skirt with her fingers and did as her father had asked, but her mind and eyes were on Denis. She frequently had a glimpse of him, and his attitude was so indifferent as to inspire her with joy and hope, for she knew that he was going through a struggle. She watched him closely now and wondered if he was spying on Jean, with whom she had an appointment. Zépherin distracted her attention as he made a gesture that scattered the sheets of paper on his lap. Those sheets were covered with figures, for he had been calculating the results of the popularity contest. It was not the pain from his ankle that gave the churchwarden a start, but rather Pinasse's booming voice, which drowned out everything, even the rumble of the drums. What a voice it was, outdoing the bugles, vibrant with victory. Zépherin rested his feet upon the window ledge, his injured member in plain view. As he lay sprawled there, his big red face looked from a distance like an overripe pomegranate. It had an almost sadistic appearance.

"I'm done for! He's beaten me, I know it. That wrestling match will be a success. But anyhow, I got away from the police safe and sound. Ah, wife, if you could have seen them bearing down on me, their hands on their revolvers! I was trapped, not a chance to escape. But by tripping one of them up here and giving a leap there and then dashing right through the stage scenery—you know, those sets with the angels painted on them—I managed to outwit them. That heavenly charge won the day. With a bound I was through the dressing-room window and flying from stone to stone, until I met with this stupid accident which clipped my wings. But all that doesn't reimburse me for the prizes they seized, paid for out of my own pocket."

Zépherin was quite breathless with the excitement of it all, fairly oozing pride; for had he not succeeded in making his escape from a very real danger? He who up to then had lived on as a kind of punctuation mark in the lives of others found it hard to conceive of himself all of a sudden as an active verb, as subject and predicate of the sentence. Madame Lévesque, wide-eyed, begged him to go to the country for a while.

"Duty, wife, duty!"

The guard of honour, escorting the wrestlers from the station, was now approaching, and Zépherin had them bring him his uniform and medals and lay his sword across his legs as he extended his injured foot and waited, all a-quiver. For a long time the functions of the guard had been limited to an occasional salute for the dead; but Pinasse, hard-hearted as he was, could not resist paying tribute to one who had suffered so nobly for the cause: Monsieur Lévesque should have a military salute. No popularity contest nor jealousy between commanders should enter into the matter where human suffering was concerned.

"I'll let you have my crutches when I'm through with them," said Bidonnet. Delighted to find a companion in misery, the sacristan came hobbling in. He treated Zépherin almost as a brother, but the latter, desirous of creating an atmosphere of the sublime, put on a superior air and closed his eyes with that condescension which might be shown by those who have lost an arm or a leg toward those whose wounds are of less magnitude. What especially prompted him to do this was the fact that he had caught sight of Monsieur le Curé, who, accompanied by Gus Perrault, was coming to suggest that he bring action against the government by way of establishing the legal status of bingo. Gus knew plenty of lawyers; he had the law in his pocket. What was more, the party was in power. Monsieur le Curé would even go so far as to appoint Gus a churchwarden on condition that he marry the widow with whom he was "boarding." The manna of bingo would thereupon descend once more upon those worthy mothers who, when the cares of the family were over for the day, had only this pastime to which they might look forward.

From now on, they would give as prizes tickets with an index finger on them, pointing toward "Parish House"; and then on the third floor, which had never been used for such a purpose, the tickets could be exchanged for the real prizes. Let them try to stage a raid! How many complications there were, when it would have been so simple, by having resort to a little theology to publish a kind of edict for the province of Quebec declaring that the game of bingo, the moment it crossed the threshold of

174

a parish house, ceased to be a game of chance, to become, in God's hands, a ceremonious act of Providence. It was simply a game that permitted of the mass distribution of rewards to exemplary parishioners. (The only trouble was that the Latruche sisters never won.)

But Zépherin had had enough of the police and all the bingo parties in the world. Monsieur le Curé, as it happened, did not have time to go into the plan in detail, for he had to wait at the main entrance of the parish house to receive the salute of the guard along with the wrestlers from the Forum.

What a fine sight it was on a Saturday evening when the guard, covered with imaginary glory, returned from a parade. The little Mulots would leave the supper table and run to look for their instruments so that they might go out to meet the army of grownups who comprised the Lévis Guard, their military ideal. How glad they were, these city children, to turn their disorder into discipline for once and to do their shouting in orderly ranks, under the direction of a tattered commandant.

The guard now appeared at the corner of the street. With buttons polished, gold braid recently renovated, and medals pinned to puffed-out chests—the wrestlers marched alongside the honorary officers—the parade spirit exuded from every pore, every spur and plume. The drum-major, a tall, lean man, astonished the spectators by keeping his baton whirling like a propeller, without ever reversing the movement as do rustic drum-majors, who never made more than five twirls in one direction and five in the other. An enormous fur cap, a kind of hairy column, reposed upon his dolichocephalous head. Behind him came the "bugles," their cheeks puffed out with the effort they were making, their eyes like those of swimmers, while their distended lips reminded one of the stewed plums that the thrifty Soyeux put up each season. The sergeant-major of the "drums" was haughtily wielding his drumstick with the tips of his fingers as Bidonnet's youngsters (he had twelve of them altogether) along with a whole swarm of youthful spectators did their best to imitate their lucky elders who could dress up in such gaudy uniforms and play "war."

Among the buglers were certain artistic souls who fretted because some of the urchins were beating time with hammers on empty lard pails. The grownups today, masculine and feminine, had another interest in the show.

"Just look at that big, handsome, curly-headed fellow! He's not any the worse for all he has to take." Madame Chaton was screaming her admiration for the wrestler to hear. "I'm going to have him show me some holds." Chaton, worm-pail in hand, gave her a furious glance. By way of protest, he rolled up his sleeves and displayed his own biceps.

At sight of his rival's injured foot, Pinasse had a thrill of superiority. At every block he would halt the guard and bellow meaningless commands that appeared to be echoed by his big, scarlet nose.

Bédarovitch, all dressed up in a suit of clothes he had got in exchange for a watch that would not run, was bent upon photographing the wrestlers with his camera. He was berating the urchins who jostled him and prevented him from getting the proper focus. As a matter of fact, this parish was beginning to get on his nerves, and he was thinking of moving to another quarter; for his prosperity was a source of annoyance to the envious and gave others the idea of setting up in competition with him. The Mulots were keeping a close watch on their wives, who sought to control their wandering glances as they reflected on the numerous children their men had given them (a dozen or so each) and, in their own way, speculated as to what might be, or might have been. How powerfully built those wrestlers were! Even the Soyeuses in their kitchens strove to convince their middle-class husbands that these fellows were not so vulgar-appearing as one might have expected, and that, after all, one ought to lend every encouragement to the popularity contest, seeing that it was for the Church's benefit. From the sidewalk, Denis compared himself to the participants by way of making sure that he was their equal in size.

As for the representatives of the Forum, they were stunned by it all and wondered what kind of place this was and what they had let themselves in for. The admiration of this throng was more distracting than the booing of spectators at a match. As they twisted their sweaters under their armpits, it was all they could do to keep from letting go with a few half-nelsons then and there. The Abbé Bongrain, meanwhile, in military stride, was telling them of the brawls in which he had taken part, in the mines of Thetford, and was endeavouring to learn from them the best means of overcoming an opponent.

The Latruche sisters, who were about to adapt their show-case to a new specialty—they had decided to sell the trousseau which they had prepared back in their unregenerate days— were scarcely able to conceal their contempt. "Athletes!" they sniffed. "Athletes!"

The Abbé Charton, who was standing beside the spinsters, found excuses for the gladiators; he was thinking of all the adhesive tape he would have to put on that evening. The Abbé Trinchu, a solitary figure, was digging at the sidewalk with his cane. He was concerned with the example set by these wrestlers and the disastrous effect it would have upon the Morale of the Nation. Capitalistic exploiters of the beastly in man, that was what they were. Try crying "Fatherland!" to these energumens.

As the parade reached the Lévesque home, the setting sun appeared to tinge with regret the beautiful uniforms of the guard. Zépherin's eyes filled with tears and his heart beat fast as his beloved company drew near to salute him as one might a general who had lost a leg. At that moment he even forgave Pinasse his voice, which furrowed the atmosphere like a plough-share. What a sad and noble and glorious feeling it was! His hands were trembling. They were passing now! He sighed. They halted, hands to their temples. What was Pinasse's idea? But the buglers were not ready.

And then, suddenly: "Play March No. 4! Quick step! To the parish house."

Lise kissed her father and smiled, for Denis was watching her from the other side of the street. The Latruche sisters, who had perceived what was happening, now hastened to the scene. Ah! that Pinasse, who had refused to let them embroider their saint in violet-coloured thread upon the banners of the guard —how they detested him! At sight of the Abbé Bongrain marching proudly along in the midst of the guardsmen, they sought to get the Abbés Trinchu and Charton to join them in expressing their contempt, but the priests, restrained by professional ethics, declined to do so. A priest marching with that rabble! That Abbé Bongrain was a disgrace. If only, with a little influence, one could get them to "transfer" this poor relation in a cassock. Had he not said that their saint was not a saint, adding that it was at Rome that questions of beatification were decided and not in the kitchens of bigoted and fanatic Soyeuses? The Latruches smiled condescendingly at Madame Pritontin, who, dressed in black, looked very discomfited and desolate between her own two "saints." Ever since her husband had got drunk that time, she had chastely kept to herself, sleeping in the children's bedroom.

Eager to know everything that was going on, the two spinsters slipped from group to group like a bodkin penetrating a woollen slipper, correcting morals wherever they went. Going up to Bidonnet, who, huddled upon his crutches, was telling the womenfolk about his accident, they inquired if he had applied their protégé's image to the broken bone, but the sacristan was inclined to take a gloomy view of things, his birdlike head wobbling on his big neck as he went on with his story.

"You know," he was saying, "how fast I am. The trouble is, that little one was out of place between two big ones."

"That little what?" Madame Langevin wanted to know. She had just returned from Montreal and was anxious to tell them all about it.

"The little service for Broko's lad, who died of meningitis. Then there were a couple of *rentiers*, one before and one after. Ah! but they were something, those services! Fifty dollars each! At seven o'clock I had to get the church decorated for the rich folks. At eight I had to take everything down and get ready for the poor ones. Then, at nine, put the decorations up again. I was standing on my stool, removing the things from the first service as fast as I could, for Monsieur le Curé down below was calling to me to hurry, when I caught my foot in the gold-embroidered *Libera me* banner, and then it was that I fell."

The exclamations of the women were interrupted by Pinasse's thunderous order to halt; and his wife, unable to hold in any longer, dashed forward. "Hurry, my dear," she said. "Everything is ready."

"All right, old girl! Gentlemen, in honour of your strength and your renown, my wife has prepared a little something for you in the courtyard of the bakery."

This invitation was received with cheers, Madame Chaton's voice being audible above all others.

"A sandwich and a drink of pop! That's some banquet for you!" grumbled the gourmets of the bugle corps.

As the wrestlers wiped the perspiration from their faces, they had a vision of themselves taking to their heels and fleeing madly amid a hubbub of drums and clashing bugles; for in this parish it seemed impossible to go anywhere without such an accompaniment. But Pinasse kept winking his eye at them by way of encouraging them to resist the temptation.

"Gentlemen," he said, "Monsieur le Curé Folbèche is awaiting us in the parish house. Let us go and pay him our respects."

The guard disappeared around the corner, followed by those who expected to be present at the banquet. The fattest of the women were puffing heavily but they trailed along all the same, even though they felt sure they would not be able to get in. The urchins were more cheerful about the matter, for the scaling of fences was no new thing to them. Denis had to hold his mother back, because she had recognized the wrestlers from those newspaper pictures that Gaston had collected and she was now waving the photographs in the air, eager to show them to the athletes and tell them how much her son had admired their prowess.

The street was deserted, but one could hear from afar the crackling jests from Pinasse's place and the various toasts that were offered: to the visitors' biceps; to the victory of the commandant in the popularity contest; and to the erection of a magnificent new church. Alone in front of his own house, Jean was endeavouring to persuade one of Broko's sons to go out and sell worms for him on a commission basis.

What a beautiful evening it was! As he caught sight of Lise, Jean sent young Broko on his way. At last! The big moment, the moment filled with happiness, was awaiting him. He called to Denis, for he wished his friend to see them set out together. Denis, however, though he had never known Lise to look so lovely, was careful not to show it. He merely leaned indifferently against a telephone pole. She was pedalling uncertainly, her eyes on the front wheel of her bicycle. Denis would have liked to see her fall and it was all he could do to keep from shouting at her to look farther ahead. What did Jean mean by searching for little things that might delay their departure?

"If I were you, I'd hurry."

But Jean smiled, as much as to say he knew how to keep women waiting. Then he started toward Lise. Denis was in a melancholy mood, and it was hard for him to conceal it. "Don't forget the tricks I told you of," he said.

Returning home, he took up his notebook. Literature, the absolute— But nevertheless, he was soon out of the house again; he was anxious to see if Lise was enjoying her ride with Jean. Hadn't they started yet? Jean was engaged in raising the seat of her bicycle, since he dared not tell her that her crouching posture was unattractive. In order to arouse their curiosity and spoil their pleasure by his mocking presence, Denis began writing in his notebook. Madame Langevin, who was hurrying to be one of the first at the parish hall, paused long enough to grow eloquent over this literary hero.

"You never get tired of books, do you?" she asked.

"I'm taking notes." He smiled and winked as Lise, in embarrassment, gave him a questioning glance. Madame Langevin raised her hands.

179

"I guess you're not one to become a monk, with the good job you have," she remarked.

Her admiration was cut short by the sensational arrival of Madame Chaton. That lady was screaming, her eyes popping. "Monsieur Lévesque! Monsieur Lévesque!" she cried, "I'm on your side. Come here, I want to tell you all about it."

Between her gasps they managed to make out that, in spite of her devotion to Pinasse's cause, he had refused her admission to the banquet. Chaton, jovial as usual, now put in an appearance, twirling his pail on the end of his arm. He played innocent.

"You're not hungry, are you? I imagine Pinasse didn't want to discourage the wrestlers with the sight of you."

Zépherin listened with delight to the proposition that Madame Chaton had come to make to him: she would reveal the amount of money Pinasse had already taken in for the contest. The churchwarden's ankle grew limber at this, and fired by a fresh enthusiasm, he resumed his calculations. All this exuberant activity made Jean nervous.

"Are you ready, Lise?"

She hesitated; it was she now who was putting off their departure. "If your friend likes, he can come with us."

Jean at once summoned all the will power that he possessed in an effort to protect his plan for them to be alone, that they might sit in silence by the sea. Arranging his pedal, he assumed a knowing air. "He's through with such things as that. He's interested in literature."

Lise stood there, motionless, quivering. That marvellous Denis whom she had fashioned for herself the year before had suddenly become a reality. He had emerged from a prolonged mist, from a time when he had been cold and distant, to take on new life in her young girl's heart, inspiring there a violent love that went beyond the romantic dreams she once had known. This unaccustomed fever that shook her entire being, this vague desire to caress him, to rest her head upon his firm shoulder, the aching need to run her fingers through his wavy hair—all this had slumbered within her for too long. But the great sun of literature made everything clear.

"You envy him, don't you?" she said. "Come, let's go."

Jean sighed. Ah! if they could only get away from the parish. He had her now. He felt sorry for Denis.

"I prefer to live poetry. Denis wants to write it, for others. He's all wrapped up in himself and has certain tricks that he himself is not conscious of."

The two cyclists turned the corner of the street, and Jean gave Denis a glance that held a daring promise, the promise that he would tell Lise of his love for her. It would be very simple, after he had brought up the subject of Liszt's "Dream of Love." She would begin humming it, and then of a sudden he would start talking. He smiled ruefully as he felt a shooting pain in his knee. He knew very well that, as they followed this road near the footpaths that led to the cliffs, the most he would venture to do would be to offer her a Coca-Cola. He called attention to the setting sun, disappearing behind the long shed of the car-barn, for the reason that he did not wish her to see Germaine, Barloute, Tit-Blanc, and Pitou waving good-bye to them and wishing him luck.

"Jean Colin! Jean Colin!"

He stopped and shut his eyes. He had foreseen catastrophe. Zépherin, his face congested and dragging his injured foot behind him with the bandage undone, was calling to him from the sidewalk. Denis tossed his notebook under the balcony of his home and waited. Jean was tempted to flee, but Lise urged him to turn back.

"Quick!" Zépherin was stammering, "go to the parish hall. Here is fifty cents for you. I want you to count the number of persons at the wrestling match. Then come back and let me know, and as winner of the popularity contest, I will take you on a picnic tomorrow, to Lake Sergent. Come, don't put on that stupid look!"

Jean could have wished the earth absolutely deserted, that he might weep undisturbed. But here was Madame Chaton, also, telling him that he looked stupid. Zépherin was jubilant. As soon as he knew what Pinasse's total receipts were, all he would have to do in order to beat him would be to make up the difference out of his own pocket.

Lise was urging Jean: "Go on, I'll wait for you." He gazed at her silently, his manner all but ridiculous. She knew that it would be too late when he came back. Denis then came up and shook him.

"Be on your way," he said. "I promise you she'll wait. Give me your bicycle. I'll watch it for you."

CHAPTER
IV

DARKNESS filled the deserted streets. Darkness and the buzzing of mosquitoes. All was quiet, as if in expectation of the cheers from the spectators at the wrestling match. Denis escorted Lise to the entrance of the parish hall without saying anything. Dropping down upon a step, he let Jean's bicycle fall to the ground. Was he teasing her again? Smiling, she came over and sat down beside him. He, meanwhile, was fighting off the happiness that had taken possession of him, the feeling that the two of them might go onward and upward together, toward the same ideal. How charming she was, sitting there upon the step! He made sure that her dress was hiding her knees. She caught his glance and gave an embarrassed smile as she folded her hands.

"There's a spider on you there." As she, turning pale, rose to shake it off, he burst into a laugh and with a hand on her elbow made her sit down once more. "I have it!" and gently pinching the back of her neck, he threw the imaginary spider away. His manner now became that of a small boy; for she had not stirred but was waiting attentively to see what he would do. "It isn't true. I just wanted to touch you."

She turned to him delightedly. "You've changed!" she said.

He lowered his head, half-pleased by this remark. How restful she was after all his literary worries. He had a feverish impulse to have done with hesitations and yield to her without remorse. The flesh was singing and its lyricism was irresistible. Upon his lips was a hunger for new things, a taste like that of fruit. He clenched his fist.

"I have not changed. I'm growing older."

Playing with her curls, she dared not tell him that during the past winter poetry, in place of enchanting her, had troubled her deeply. This was the first time that she had felt the need of confiding, and why did it have to be in connection with the thing that she most desired to keep secret? It was none of this young man's business. Already she was blushing as she thought of the ideas that had passed through her mind. Denis did not have to know that he had played the part of the amorous shepherd. Would it not be insincere to speak of such things when the entire horizon of the future was bounded by a kiss—not one of those smacks such as are exchanged on New Year's Day, but a kiss that would lend a breath of the romantic to an otherwise prosaic lifetime? She must say something.

"They tell me that you have a good job."

He got to his feet restively. Jean, then, had told her that he, Denis, earned seven dollars a week. But Lise was not throwing it up to him. She was, rather, astonished by his rudeness. Was he beginning his manœuvrings of last summer all over again? It dawned on him that she did not know, but he kept his anger smouldering. This girl who had stretched out beside him on the steps was no longer a sentimental child. His heart was chilled by her interest in his job. He could see himself as a good match, of the kind that clever young women would go after. He picked up a handful of pebbles, gazed at the crane that stood beside the new church.

Upon the scaffolding the stone blocks piled one upon another had the appearance of dismantled battlements. From the basement door of the parish hall a dense cloud of tobacco smoke arose, and there was a huge puff every time the door opened. They now caught sight of Jean's anxious face. In his nervousness he was smoothing down his hair, for he was timid about reclaiming Lise, not knowing if he still had the right. Denis grew impatient. His anger toward Lise was as exigent as any pleasure, and he wanted her to feel the whole weight of it. And Jean was coming back to interrupt it, was he? No, he owed it to himself to tell her the truth, and she should have it.

"Stay there a while," he said to Jean, pointing to the door. "There come the guests of honour."

The Gonzagues, annoyed because their places as ushers had been taken by the bugle corps, arrived late, like the rich at a concert. Jean went back hastily and resumed his post of observation, making note of the new arrivals. Pinasse, red-faced with pleasure, slapped him on the back.

"Reporting it for the papers, are you?" he asked. "Go right ahead; don't be afraid."

The crowd was strangely tense and all eyes were fixed upon the temporary arena that had been set up, as the referee threw himself against the ropes to test their resistance. It stood in the centre of a hall littered with bingo markers which Pinasse disdainfully kicked aside. The guests of honour were seated upon the stage and included the beaming brothers from the school, the ex-deputy of the Conservative party, the high-mass organist, the Abbé Bongrain, and those Soyeux who were on the verge of becoming churchwardens. Around the arena were grouped the Mulots who were most likely to go over into the camp of the Soyeux. Then came the Daughters of Mary, the Ladies of the Holy Family, and the gang from Bédarovitch's place. The last mentioned remained standing, with hands in their pockets.

Tit-Blanc was chewing on a butt. All he could talk of was blowing up the place. The beer had given him a fixed idea.

Monsieur le Curé, somewhat perturbed, was striding up and down the hall. Ever since the bingo party he had been ill at ease, and tonight he stayed near the door. As he surveyed that platform, surrounded by ropes and lighted by a single lamp, on which men who were nearly naked would soon be intertwining their limbs, he reflected that all this was not in the least praiseworthy. He stiffened as he recalled his plans for social reform, in the early years of his pastorate. Was he permitting himself to become "Mulot-ized"? For a number of days he had been low in spirit. This bellicose atmosphere was revolting to a soul pacified by prayer and litanies. His apostolic aptitude for sermons and epistles to his parishioners was being impaired and the wings of inspiration beat sluggishly these days.

After the police raid and the wrestling match, the curé felt that he was going to have difficulty in explaining things in the letter that he wrote to his flock twice a year, in St Joseph's name. Vainly did he delve into the bag where he kept his most redundant metaphors. "Shore of eternity," "River of sanctified gold," "Fountain of pennies in the garden of Heaven," "Cathedral diamond-studded with the sweat-drops of the poor," "Imperial palace on the barren prairie"—the fire of persuasion was absent from the lines he wrote, even though he did his best to revive it with dollar signs and exclamation points. Chin in hand, he was still lost in thought as he saw the Latruche sisters coming up to him.

"Athletes!" they remarked with a sniff. "Athletes!" Their excuse for being there was that they were keeping an eye on the Daughters of Mary.

Jean was about to leave, but remembering Lise's smile of satisfaction when Denis had sent him away, he stopped. Bah! He was coming to the point where he was content with leftovers. As long as she feared that he would return, she would at least be thinking of him. Lise did not really know him, anyway; she was dazzled by Denis' brilliancy. Despite the pain he felt, Jean was seeing things with an unwonted clarity. He told himself that others would never be dazzled by his presence. He was the incarnation of the ordinary, humdrum type of individual of the kind one had always seen and known. Denis was the sort who attracted attention upon his arrival; Jean's absence was regretted after he had left. It was all he could do not to leave now. Let her wait for him. When the pleasure of being with Denis had worn off a little, she would notice that her other admirer was not there.

There was anxiety among the spectators inside the hall, as well, but it was of a different nature. The referee in white trousers, followed by the wrestlers in their bathrobes, had leaped to the platform, and a hush that was almost religious fell upon the crowd. The only sound to be heard was that made by the Abbé Charton, as he undid his envelopes of adhesive tape. The good priest was in a daze, for this was to be his big evening, an apotheosis of the art of bandaging. Having received the usual instructions from the referee, the adversaries retired to their respective corners, where they flapped their dressing-gowns about them and bent over the ropes by way of hardening their muscles. Madame Chaton, too nervous to remain seated, was stamping around in the rear alongside the gang from Bédarovitch's. What formidable-looking fellows those wrestlers were! She liked them all very much, especially the young one who made the sign of the cross. This gesture on the part of the athlete made a favourable impression upon the members of the clergy who were present. In the meantime, those who were used to attending such events were discussing the various world champions and were authoritatively voicing their opinions regarding the contestants. After all, you couldn't look for an Henri Deglane in a parish hall. But the Daughters of Mary, the Soyeux, and the brothers wore an expression of pained expectancy as they awaited the hecatomb and beheld those muscles, too frankly exposed to lead to any evil thoughts. What was going to happen—? Then the bell rang.

There was an impact of flesh against flesh and a cry of pain was heard. The wrestling fans and Madame Chaton were the only ones who did not close their eyes. The monks flexed their knees and gripped them with nervous hands, and the respectable folk crouched in their seats, petrified with horror. It was with an effort that the Abbé Charton overcame his fear and distaste—which he attributed to a lack of acquaintance with profane things—as he followed the evolutions of the athletes and waited eagerly for the first cut. Monsieur le Curé himself stole a look and was not impressed. Where were those graceful bodily movements that Pinasse had promised him? The Soyeux and their wives huddled against one another in dismay, and then, after a terrifying silence, eyes were opened once more. The first shouts came from Bédarovitch's Liberals while the rest of the spectators looked on curiously. Madame Chaton, wholly immersed in the struggle taking place on the platform, was grieved to see her favourite's head being squeezed and to hear him moaning with pain. Like steam blowing off a valve, an exclamation burst from her:

"What are you trying to do, kill him, you big swine?"

There was a roar of laughter at this. Madame Chaton became furious as the young athlete received a hard kick in the face and the blood spurted, but the Abbé Charton smiled, thinking of his court plaster. The Soyeuses, the Daughters of Mary, and the Ladies of the Holy Family all were sitting forward on the edge of their seats, in a fever of excitement. A desire for vengeance was being aroused in the audience. The likable young wrestler gave a spring and freed himself while the ladies ground their teeth to keep from fainting. Kill him! Kill him! The Mulots were impatient with all this shamming, but the Daughters of Mary were beginning to rise up in behalf of their favourite and lend him a timid encouragement. Others, in the presence of this powerful nude figure, could only stammer embarrassed insults and obscenity. The hairy bully now bared his gums in a deadly grin and once more planted both his feet in his opponent's face. For a second time the young fellow went rolling all the way to the edge of the arena, but just as the crowd was feeling sorry for him, it was suddenly electrified to see him rise up in a rage, stamp about, gnash his teeth, and run his hand through his hair. The atmosphere of the room was overheated, and Monsieur le Curé could stand it no longer.

"Stop it! Stop it!" he begged, in a wan voice.

But it was too late now. The Soyeuses had become used to this cruel sport.

"It's not fair!" they shouted, half rising and shaking their fists. "Choke him, Monsieur, choke him!" Madame Chaton started for the arena and tripped on the carpet. "Pull his hair out! Pull his hair out!"

The young man then made a fierce onslaught, so irresistible as to arouse a delirious enthusiasm among his supporters. Even Monsieur le Curé showed his approval by nodding his chin. After all, he liked to see justice done. It was a terrible struggle as they came to grips. The wretch at last was getting what he deserved. The monks were rubbing their thighs enthusiastically, since shouting was hardly respectable in their case. The brother in charge of the eighth-year pupils at the school, a puny little man, squared away his shoulders and clenched his fists as he imagined himself doing the same thing to a big braggart in his class who was always defying his authority. On all sides, people could be heard talking of the various holds: the toe hold, the stranglehold, the half-nelson, and the like.

Then the referee raised the hand of the curly-headed young man and announced that he had won the first fall. Covered with blood, the athlete retired to his corner, where the Abbé Charton awaited him. Madame Chaton was there, too, jostling the priest, bent upon shaking hands with the victor. The Mulotes lighted up the cigarettes which they had rolled at home; and even the Soyeuses, who in order to appear more refined refrained from smoking at bingo parties, yielded to the influence of their surroundings and asked their husbands to supply them. A dispute was going on between the Daughters of Mary and the Latruche sisters, who were insisting that the young ladies leave this immoral exhibition.

At this point, there was a cry of terror from all over the house. The victor, whom everyone liked so well and who had refused the good abbé's ministrations (blood being the chief attraction of the evening), had recovered himself just in time to repel a savage attack on the part of his reviled adversary. Fear was written all over the face of the treacherous one, and with a bound he was over the ropes and fleeing from the arena, pursued by his antagonist, who was boiling with a leonine rage. This was the signal for a general stampede. The Soyeux bitterly regretted having chosen the front-row seats, and a number of future churchwardens' wives were near to swooning. The athletes were making straight for Monsieur le Curé, who was busy trying to calm the young Mulots, the fighting instincts of the latter having been stirred by this atmosphere of battle. There was no question now of reading the breviary as he had done the evening before when the police had come. Pinasse with upraised hand was running backward in front of the wrestlers, imploring them to stop, while with the other hand he sought to reassure Father Folbèche.

"Pay no attention to them! It's a fake, you may take my word for it!"

Everything calmed down then. Monsieur le Curé wiped the perspiration from his face and heaved a deep sigh. Ah! if he had but known! What would the heads of other parishes say, who talked so much theology and envied him his financial returns?

And what about his title of Monsignor? His Eminence would be bound to hear of it. Filled with righteous indignation, he mounted the platform.

"At eleven o'clock, the doors of this hall will be closed. That is the holy hour above." For the parish hall was now in the basement where the temporary church had been and the church was on the first floor.

Jean was endeavouring to shake off the atmosphere of the place. It served Lise right to have had to wait for him all this time. What a good trick he had played on Denis—how annoyed he must be! He paced up and down the hall, practising a normal gait. The thing was to get back to his bicycle without attracting attention to his limp. He thought of hopping on one foot and pretending he had hurt himself; but wouldn't she believe that he was making fun of her father? It was dark enough outside, anyway, so that he could leave without being noticed.

What! Where were they? The bicycle lay alongside the curb. Desperately he looked everywhere for the couple. A suspicion laid hold of him, and he clambered up on the platform of the crane, nearly knocking down the watchman's red lantern as he did so. The stone blocks were dimly outlined in the darkness and the old belfry lay upon its side in the middle of the scaffolding. Crumbs of badly dried mortar streaked the silence with their fall, accompanied by the sound of scurrying rats in the waste heaps. Then the moon burst through the clouds, flooding with light the darkest recesses of the stone piles. Two shadows appeared, close together. They were kissing there! Jean felt a cold sweat on his forehead. As he climbed slowly down from his point of observation, he was too sad for a moment to be able to collect his thoughts. Then a terrible anger took possession of him, and arming himself with a handful of pebbles, he started running as best he could in the direction of the traitors.

"Damned scribbler!"

Having succeeded in persuading his friend to go back into the hall, Denis had turned to Lise with a sigh. His fear that Jean would put in an appearance led him to forget his grandiloquent wrath. With her big, gentle eyes this girl in front of him was asking for his friendship. Putting himself on guard against his own heart, he tried a sarcastic smile, for he wished to discover in Lise's eyes an amused awareness of his small salary. She, however, smiled sweetly back at him.

"How funny you are!" she said, folding her hands once more.

"I—funny?" He took her hand. "I've been an idiot." The last trace of hesitation was swept away on an inrushing tide of joy.

"You haven't visited the ruins yet?" he suggested.

With a charming gesture, she took his hand in hers. "We'll play hide and seek there, you and I."

Denis frowned, put out by this remark. He had no time for such subterfuge. He had never been so full of ideas and schemes. His plans seemed clear to him, and yet he did not know what it was he was about to do. He found an excuse for the adventure—for his own weakness—by having it begin on the ruins of the old church, which represented his past. He would make love to Lise upon the spiritual debris of this hated parish and his kiss would be as a cry of victory. He had to laugh at the sophistry, but it made him happier than any reasoned argument. He did not hear the angry cries from the audience in the parish hall, for everything inside him was singing with hope, and Lise was pressing his hand so ardently and followed him so gladly that he was deaf to all else on earth; there was nothing but their happiness anywhere.

"I'll show you our hiding place." He repeated it stubbornly. "I'll show you our hiding place."

Their agile bodies united by their vibrant hands, they climbed the rocky peak and then came down into the hollow of the glades. It was not so shameful a thing to be in love! Was he really any the less exigent in accepting so joyfully today what he so haughtily had repelled the year before? It occurred to him that he was very young. Was it to be expected that one of his disposition should be content with sitting dreamily beside a fallen bell-tower, upon stones which tomorrow would form the body of a cathedral? No, he was not a Jean Colin, to be satisfied with a pressure of the hand as he watched a pair of tired leaves falling from the summit of a cliff upon the mirroring river below. Nothing of that sort, Mademoiselle! There was Lise beside him, aglow with love, her loins nearly crushed by his arm about her. They stopped. It must be here that the sanctuary of the old church stood. God was on his side and the astonished angels must be ready to applaud. And the devil was not angry, because he, Boucher, knew how to make everyone happy. This evening, in his honour, all creation was plunged in voluptuousness. At a single glance his eyes took in all the heavens and all the stars.

"One would think we were in the past," said Lise, panting still.

Denis controlled his eyes, but his smile said: "Yes, but a past where something is about to happen."

Lise was suffering from the constraint that weighed like a rock upon them. They were silent. Surrounded by building material, they broke away from each other in embarrassment. She could see that Denis was full of things he wanted to say, but instead, he let his eyes speak for him.

"My skirt," she said, disconsolately, "is all covered with dust." For she had been leaning against a stone that served as pedestal to St Joseph's statue.

Did she wish to leave? Pale, Denis came over to examine her dress. "But that stone is clean." And he added: "How bright your eyes are!" Dissatisfied with himself for saying this, he made her sit down and then crouched at her feet. The Cape opposite them and the red lantern on the crane to their left served them as horizon. How stupid they were, not to be able to find anything to say to each other. Lise was restless, disturbed to find a lover at her feet at last. Smoothing his hair, she earnestly sought to recall the counsels of the convent that had to do with carnal desires, but her heart in its exaltation bore everything with it. Denis shook his head under her caress; it reminded him too much of the barber. And anyhow, this conquest was not to be effected so rapidly. He was more concerned with gratifying the vanity of the flesh than with any pure and tender self-abandonment to the emotions of his heart.

"Yes, there is a little dust on your skirt!" He left his hand there. She was happy to find him in a tenderer mood and was glad that the dust had furnished an excuse. But this tenderness was becoming oppressive, was enveloping her in a kind of torpor.

"Supposing Jean should come looking for me," she said.

He rose abruptly, for he did not know how to remove his hand in any other manner. He would not admit to himself that he was incapable of true passion, having exhausted its possibilities by his feverish imaginings as an adolescent. Platonic love, that was the thing. A great calm came over him as he accepted the fact that he was not to touch Lise's body any more. He felt very sad now. Her body did not interest him since her soul lived for Jean Colin. He walked up and down the little clearing, stepping from one stone to another, his lower jaw contracting with smothered indignation. He tried to whistle and gave it up; but the silence was too much.

"I should not have come!" His tone was beseeching. "I know now why it is I hate women. I was afraid of falling in love with someone who would be unwilling to forget everything and follow me, one who had been in love with other men before me. But don't think that I am suffering. I am grieved, that's all, and am trying to explain—" He lowered his voice and stopped, at once astonished and afflicted by his own words. Enough of romanticizing. He must get away from these ruins, flee this tenderness that forced him to struggle so violently in order not to yield up his heart.

With a kind of violence, Lise seized his wrist and put it to her eyes which were wet with tears. "You're jealous! You're jealous!"

He was more embarrassed by the tears than by the accusation, but he did not withdraw his hand as she pressed her face against it and stammered out her happiness. Lise shook her head and her hair fell down about them. Tears were now replaced by fevered lips, and this made him feel ashamed. Putting his hands under her arms, he raised her to a level with his head. He was proud of being able to lift so easily a body rendered heavier by emotion. Clumsily, he pressed his lips hard against hers. She had caught him unawares. He no longer struggled; happiness had taken him by surprise and it had won. But he was tormented by a desire to say something original.

"Lise," he cried, "I love you! I have nothing to explain. But the more I love you the more I am determined to overcome all that sort of thing." And giving a kick to the little stones that had formed the old church and that represented the spirit of the conquered parish, he went on: "Along with the church, I am going to rebuild upon my ruins, but in doing so I will stay all the closer to my ideal."

He was dazzled by his own words; for since he had been writing, his greatest concern had been with fine speeches of this sort. He felt that he had hit upon something, from the literary point of view, in the pleasing discovery of a sentimental affinity between his own character and the church edifice. Lise was beginning to be alarmed by the length of time the kiss lasted. For her the word church was an evocation of hell. Her tears were dried now, and as the moon once more appeared, she thought of an admirable reply to make to this philosophic lover of hers. Gone was the thought of sin.

"You are going to be a great writer!" she exclaimed.

He pushed her from him. She had been playing a part! At the very moment when he was about to caress her hair, to be simple and tender, she had discovered his ambitious ruse. She was distracted, clung to him tightly, while he sadly withdrew his bosom to avoid the pressure of her breasts.

"Denis, if you weren't a great man, I wouldn't love you."

Suddenly, he moaned in pain as the rock which had struck him on the arm fell to the ground. Jean was standing there threateningly upon the future pedestal of St Joseph's statue. Forgetting the ache in his elbow, Denis strove to master the feeling of littleness he experienced at that moment. How big, how great his frustrated friend appeared to be, erect upon that block of stone, sharply outlined against the darkness, his head seemingly supported by the moon. Jean broke the silence with a dry laugh, thereby asserting his right to be angry. He had hesitated about showing himself, preferring to squat behind a stone and watch them as they embraced. It was with a strenuous effort that he had forced himself to leave off listening to them. To go on doing so would have meant acceptance of a petty role for the rest of his life. The sacrifice was made, and he had aimed at Denis, his friend. His sorrow was too great for his anger to appear anything other than artificial. Now that he, the avenger, stood there surveying them from head to foot, their embarrassment drove him to despair. Did their guilty manner mean that they were in love with each other? Lise was worried about Denis' injured arm, but he pushed her aside and fumbled in his pockets with a preoccupied air.

"Are your bicycles still there?" he inquired solicitously.

Lise was overflowing with happiness. Love had come to her—how wonderful! She was sorry for Jean, sorry because he was unable to grasp the immensity of their passion, hers and Denis'.

"We're in love. And is it with a rock that you congratulate us?"

Denis stamped his foot to deaden her words. "Don't you believe her!" he said.

Expanding his muscles and drawing inspiration from the skill of the wrestlers in the parish hall, Jean calculated the distance between himself and his friend and gave a leap, but Denis stepped aside and he fell, remaining there huddled on the ground, his hands grasping his knee as he choked back the groans.

"Did you get an estimate on the number of people there?" Lise asked. "Denis is going with us to Lake Sergent tomorrow."

Colin arose, very pale. Yes, he had it all down on a piece of paper. He searched his pockets frantically, for he wished to show her that he had succeeded in one undertaking, at least. He was covered with sweat. Where was that sheet?

Denis was preparing to leave him alone with Lise. The picnic was the only thing that interested Boucher. He would see Lise in a bathing suit and would admire the play of the sun upon her body.

"You must find it," he urged Jean. "Have you any idea where you could have lost it?"

Jean was greatly distracted, but as his eye fell on the crane his face grew calm. "It was down there," he said.

They hastened to the spot and found the folded sheet of paper lying on the platform. Jean smiled at them in a superior way.

"I left it there a while ago. I was watching you."

CHAPTER

V

IN St Joseph's parish the good always win at bingo; the others do not, at least unless they cheat like Madame Chaton. That, at any rate, was the way Zépherin Lévesque felt about the matter.

On this particular Sabbath morning the sun was warm and bright, and each time that it broke through the clouds it served to illuminate the departure of picnickers, both among the Mulots and among the Soyeux. Zépherin, all trace of his sprained ankle gone, was looking very spruce, his pride at winning the popularity contest having been purged of all meanness by the sermon to which he had just listened, one that was even more pompous than usual; but it was none the less with the stride of a victor that he walked around his automobile, with his magnificent tan-coloured boots, which resembled those of traffic officers, lending an additional sprightliness to his step. His face shadowed by his sun helmet, and his hands on his hips, he watched Jean polishing the nickel plating on the wheels of his bicycle. This, in order not to have to confront Madame Chaton's importunate gaze. He was reminded of her by the sight of her husband at Pinasse's side.

In the driver's seat of a wagon laden with women and overflowing with small brats, Charcot was holding forth at great length, dwelling on all the exertions he had made and insinuating, most indelicately, that Monsieur le Curé had favoured Zépherin in the popularity contest. But then, when he was a schoolboy and stood at the foot of his class, he had always said that the brother who was his teacher was unfair. The worthy Mulotes, quite satisfied with the world at large, accordingly lent him a deaf ear as they kept time to the whining of an accordion and began singing in chorus, seeing to it meanwhile, that the young ones did not go rummaging in the lunch boxes which their mothers had prepared. Tit-Blanc and Chaton were among those who impatiently watched the keg of beer in the back of the wagon.

Barloute was teasing her daughter, who was nervously pretending that Robert Langevin was crowding her. Germaine with a jealous look in her eyes caught sight of Denis as Zépherin's car went by them. He was holding fishing rods and was being extremely attentive to Lise. How happy the Lévesque party was going to be at the lake! Theirs was not the usual Mulot picnic in a cart, in a hayfield five miles from town where the men, after the game of softball, would proceed to get drunk. Germaine could picture Denis and Lise on the beach, the voluptuous movements of their knees in the sand and in the little pools of clear water, the refined manner in which they would tease each other. How she hated that girl! Gone was the time when she might indulge in a beautiful hope. They considered her an "ordinary" young woman. Giving her a pinch, Langevin bellowed at her angrily, demanding to know if she preferred the "swells."

Zépherin waved a greeting to Bédarovitch, who to the vast disappointment of Pritontin had just purchased the Abbé Trinchu's Buick. Then the sky began to cloud over, and from the carts and the automobiles alike the merrymakers glanced up uneasily at the heavens.

Flora, seated beside Joseph on the balcony of their home, was prophesying rain to console the young ones. But picnickers and fishermen invariably believe that the clouds are inoffensive and that the sun will be shining where they are going. Finally the vehicle that was the fullest of all, drawn by Pinasse's horse, got under way. As it went past, the demoiselles Latruche deplored the shorts of which they were able to catch a glimpse through the siderails.

Denis gave a sigh of relief. His mother had not seen him taking a seat in the automobile. Pierrette Lévesque had finally got her breathing under control. She wore a flowered dress of oriental design which she managed to reconcile amiably enough with her dignity as a churchwarden's wife. Lise, worrying about whether she should or should not have brought along a book, was grieved to discover that she had forgotten her bath slippers, but she blushed with becoming modesty as she reflected that Denis would see her in a bathing suit. Had she not posed for an hour in front of the mirror in an effort to rid herself of the foolish sensation of nudity which caused her to huddle her shoulders as if to hide her body?

At last they were off. Denis was angry with himself for feeling so timid in the presence of this girl whom he had kissed so passionately the evening before. It ought to be easy for him to be natural. He shoved against Jean, convinced that the latter was the cause of his embarrassment, and began speaking of stenography. This was something which Lise admitted she knew very little about, but on the other hand she had spent much time in studying the poets. Denis was humiliated by this; for if he pretended to be familiar with the sources of their inspiration, he was actually ignorant of their works; he did not even have at his fingertips those anecdotes that give many Canadians the reputation of being persons of some cultivation. Jean in his corner kept still, overwhelmed by the fact that he could discuss neither stenography nor poetry.

Finally they left the town behind them and those youngsters who had clung to the rear bumpers of the automobiles dropped off. They were in the countryside, which tremulously waited for the sun that winked from behind bright-coloured clouds. Jean did not stir. He was glad no one noticed that Lise's curls were falling over his chest. He had reached that stage of resignation where the crumbs of happiness sufficed him. He was even astonished that Denis and Lise did not exchange caresses in front of him, like the lovers he had known. All hope was not lost. In September Lise would perhaps go with him to the provincial fair. He could imagine her being hurled up against him in those mechanical cars, alongside the big merry-go-round. She would blush and free herself, and he would give her a nice smile. He began calculating the cost of this adventure and was still engaged upon his romantic budget when he suddenly realized they had reached their destination.

The lake was calm, disturbed only by the furrows of chugging motorboats. The trees, the summer cottages round about, and the mountains beyond appeared to hold, locked in their embrace, all the sunlight of days filled with happiness.

Madame Lévesque installed herself upon the veranda of the cottage, buzzing like a horsefly. She first opened a copy of Paul Géraldy and then dozed off. She was reliving the scene at the church that morning when Monsieur le Curé had bestowed his congratulations. Denis, who with Jean's assistance had dutifully brought in the luggage, watched her anxiously as she slept. Rubbing his hands together and with a masterful look in his eye, he glanced at the neighbouring underbrush. Lise would pay dearly for the confession he had made to her. When would Zépherin be done rigging his fishing rod? Nervously Lise tried on her rubber cap. It was the first time she had gone bathing at the beach. Having assured himself that Zépherin was settled upon the big rock on the bank of the lake, Denis went up to Lise and pulled her hair teasingly. If only he could recover the enthusiasm he had felt last night, before he kissed her.

"Are you going to bathe in your dress?"

Lise blushed, ashamed of her modesty. She looked at Jean and said nothing. He went out, having made up his mind to go in alone and not annoy anyone. It seemed that they had been waiting for him to leave, for Denis at once smiled pleasantly, convinced that Lise was merely teasing him. He glanced at the lake.

"I give you five minutes," he said obstinately. "Go ahead and undress behind my back."

She burst out laughing at this. She was astonished at the idea of donning her bathing suit anywhere else than at home. Uncovering her shoulder, she lifted the strap. "I left my suit at home," she said.

Under pretence of believing her, he went over to her, but as he came near he stopped and ran his hand over his eyes. He no longer felt any desire to kiss that shoulder.

"Excuse me," he stammered, as he gazed at her scapula, "I was thinking of last night."

She clung to this memory in order that she might not have to think about undressing. Her lips were trembling.

"You were so cold to me in front of the others," she said, clasping her hands.

This awoke the rancour in him. He shook his head, as if obsessed by something. "You must have been warm wearing that suit under your clothes, in the car." There was a silence, and then suddenly he rescued the conversation which had become so painfully embarrassing. "Come, get ready. I'll wait for you outside." And taking his own suit from his pocket, he looked around for Jean.

"I have one!" cried Zépherin. "I have one!" On his feet and greatly excited, he was balancing a diminutive perch on the end of his line. Lise came running up and begged him to be careful, and it was then that Denis had caught sight of her, although she was unaware of it. He took in all the details, trying out upon her the descriptions he had penned of the heroine in his novel, in the chapter where they went in bathing. Gathering up some pebbles, he threw them at her feet. She was startled and with a little squeal dug her toes in the sand, whereupon he stopped, feeling a bit ridiculous.

"Let's go in!"

He dived, splashing Zépherin with water. Jean, whom everyone had forgotten, followed him at a distance, the two of them meeting farther out. Zépherin was very much disturbed and

Lise had turned pale, but the young men, delighted by the terrified cries from the Lévesques, were swimming sturdily some distance from the shore, their dripping brown bodies emerging every now and then to glisten in the sunlight. The echo gave back their merry shouts as the transparent water sparkled all the way down to the bottom of the lake.

Lise, whose swimming education, like her accomplishments in general, was of the most elementary sort, had sat down where the depth was no more than about six inches and was splashing her legs. Quickly making for the bank, Denis took the canoe and, pushing it in front of him, grazed her with it as she showered him with water and with her happy smile. He said nothing, however, but kept his eyes open. Despite the distortion due to the water, he recognized only too well those legs that had haunted him one whole winter long, following the incident of the firecracker. He swam back to Jean in the middle of the lake and they began playing with the canoe, upsetting it, righting it, and taking their places in it.

For Jean it was sport, for he was the better and more nimble swimmer of the two. He dared not look toward the bank to see the admiration and surprise in Lise's eyes. How was he to know that from afar she took him for Denis?

"Shall we teach Lise how to swim?" Denis suggested, out of breath.

Jean blushed as the water dripped from his face. "You're not serious about that, are you? How are you going to take hold of her to— If it wasn't for her father, I'd be right there!"

Denis interrupted him, stopping the canoe with a firm hand. "What do you mean, you'd be right there? I'll ask you to show some respect for her. She's not a tart."

Jean remembered the manner in which he had seen Denis kissing Lise.

"Boucher," he said, "you're a swine. I know you. All you want is to be different from other people. When I'm natural and say what I think, you pretend you're a whoremaster. But when I start bragging, you suddenly become very sensitive and pure. I imagine you're more yourself when you're alone with her. Go on and teach her how to swim."

Shocked by what Jean had said, Denis was thinking hard as he swam toward Lise. Changing his mind, he swiftly came back to Jean and, gripping the overturned canoe, they faced each other. Denis was the first to speak. He was in a rage.

"What right have you to give me orders? I want women, you love them, that's the difference; I take them without falling in love with them. Oh, pardon me, I didn't mean to make you jealous." But at the look Jean gave him, his cynical laugh died on his lips.

"Have you forgotten last night, then?" Jean was saying. "Walls, even when in ruins, have ears. Your misfortune is that you are false. Your sufferings are those that you inflict upon yourself, in order to be a great man. That is why they don't make you any better. As for me, I am satisfied with those that life forces me to endure. And life knows its business. So stop tormenting yourself by scraping surfaces, by trying on the sufferings that are meant for others. Listen, after what I heard last night I know very well what has happened to you. You realize that your little philosophy of contempt for women has crumbled. And you resent it, don't you? You're ridiculous, that's what you are. Own up, now, that it is humiliating to have to start all over again, with my knowing all about it. You needn't be afraid, I know how to keep out of the way."

"Shut up, will you, you ignorant cripple!"

In the silence that followed, only the splash of little waves against the canoe was audible. Jean turned pale as he saw the convulsive look on his friend's face. He was astounded at the long speech he had just made. Denis was right. He was but a failure whose perceptions were sharpened by envy. His cheek, where the water of the lake was barely dry, was now wet with a tear. He let go the canoe, as if he wished to sink.

"That is my sorrow. And it is not one that I made for myself. Forgive me for what I just said. You will understand, once you're cured of your youth."

He swam on hopelessly, with no objective. Oh, to be able to put down pain as he did this water under his arm, in order to advance and get somewhere! Denis in distress sought to overtake him, but in vain. He had to turn back, bringing the canoe with him to the bank. He then put on his clothes; for after those words his friend had spoken, he could not longer bear to display his muscles. Returning to Lise, he asked her to accompany him to the wood. She made no attempt to hide her pleasure but walked along at his side, dripping wet, her hair tickling his neck. The water and the sun upon her flesh tended to blur the modesty that had been there before. He looked her over.

"Go put your skirt on," he said. "Otherwise the thorns will scratch you."

She excused herself to do as he had suggested; but she was troubled and afraid. To what temptation was he a prey that he should be so disturbed at seeing her in a bathing suit? Denis, meanwhile, turned to the lake to look for Jean. When Lise came back it was with a little pail in her hand; for in spite of herself, in her mother's presence she had had to offer the traditional pretext of looking for blueberries. Adventure was near at hand, there in the wood. Denis' feverish expectations were about to assert themselves, and she could not but be thrilled as she thought of a sinuous resistance that would turn his passion aside, divert it to the corollas of wild flowers, cause it to die down with the music of the wind and the airy warbling of robin redbreasts.

Coming up behind him, she put her hands over his eyes. "Guess who?"

It was his cue to reply: "It's the new fairy"; but instead, he repulsed her: "No child's play!" As he saw the desolate look on her face, he tried to be gay. "Come now," he said, "that's silly." He was stubbornly bent upon following up the point. "Can you conceive of me playing ignorant? That would be stupid."

"Is everything ridiculous, then?"

This question brought him back to what Jean had said. On behalf of that ideal to which he had devoted so many hours of exaltation, he was ever on his guard against the ridiculous. But he was beginning to have his doubts. Was it not imagination on his part, this suffering in which he immersed himself? Was the thing of which he had been so proud destined to cause others to overwhelm him with their pity; were they to look upon it merely as a defect of youth? His senses were lying in wait for him, to make him accept as others did the downfall of all his hopes. Out of pride, he forced himself to take his eyes off Lise's dress, already dampened by her bathing suit. He thought of Jean's accusation. Denis Boucher ridiculous because of his conception of nobility! He needed some outlet for the catastrophe that had befallen him, something that would transform it into an immeasurable sorrow. But they were already in the wood. Lise glanced at him uneasily from time to time and went on picking flowers without bending over; she did not appear to be concerned at not finding any blueberries.

"It doesn't look as if you would get a pailful," he muttered; and then he sighed. He certainly was not at ease. Halting suddenly, he seized her arms. Lise shut her eyes, for she was used to it by now: the kiss was coming. But, gripping her firmly, he held her off from him for a moment. When she pressed her body against his he did not repulse her. "Denis, I've found you again at last!"

He was conscious of the need of avenging himself, of making others, and above all the one he loved, share the self-resentment that he felt and feared. "If I should die, would you forget me quickly?" With a distracted look on his face he was imagining himself lying in a coffin, placidly receiving the spontaneous admiration of women who came to admire the higher type of beauty which sorrow had conferred upon his countenance. He shook himself by way of getting rid of this feeling of disgust as he beheld the being that he really was. The next moment, Lise was astounded to see him take to his heels. What terrible secret did he have to conceal? He ran first to look for Jean, then decided against it and climbed a wind-swept rock. He must build his future upon an act of self-sacrifice. He must discover now that Jean was a splendid person, and then, later, must himself become so big that he would look back upon the Jean he knew today as once more a petty individual. The past took flight in front of his eyes, along with the blue swallows: his first youthful intransigence; the breakup of the gang; Gaston's death; his love for Lise; his jealousy of Jean and Jean's hopeless affliction— That, Denis thought to himself, was something that he must find the means of overcoming, in order that he might surpass his friend. There was always his writing. From now on, he would magnify those who limped. With this, he grew calm again.

Huddled upon the sand of a cove, Jean held his breath as if to retard his thinking. The sun was warm, but its warmth could not penetrate all the way to his heart. In a kind of a stupor, he rubbed his knee and thought of Boucher's insult. He even came to the conclusion that it had been justified. Ah! to find one supreme consolation without having to die in order to attain it! In vain he recalled the Christ child of his youth, imagined the infant Jesus as being on the summit of a mountain, slowly descending to him; but halfway down the mountainside was Lise, smiling and clad in a bathing suit. He had discovered her luminous flesh, and her image already had lost its dreamlike opaqueness; it was now shining and real, something that his senses could grasp, a nuance of innocent eyes prevailing over forms that to him were new. He curled his lips rebelliously. Had he not suffered enough from her indifference? Must he be repelled by her body as well, the body that he now, suddenly and irresistibly, found himself evoking? That must be the way

Denis loved her. Once again, Boucher was there first. Moved by a jealousy he had not felt before, he arose; but the shooting pain in his leg was too much for him. There was nothing to do but submit to being robbed. He was doomed to unhappiness. There was no hope for him.

Returning to the lakeside camp, he took the axe and began chopping wood, stubbornly silent all the while. Would they finally go back to town where the sun was weary of artificial things, where Lise would once more be distant from him, and where he would be branded by reason of his father's habits? He gazed at the mountains and the sky with avidity that he might remember them on Monday, at the factory, remember them otherwise than as in a dream. There was a sound of something frying. Zépherin was stirring butter in a pan, since on a picnic it is the men who do the cooking. Humming a tune, Lise rummaged in the cupboard and brought out knives and forks with an awkward air, but way of showing Denis that she knew nothing about such things. Zépherin called Jean and asked him to go for ice cubes so that the perch they had promised Father Folbèche would not spoil; and then he noticed for the first time how the young man limped, for it was only the Friday before that he had wrenched his own ankle. Madame Lévesque and Lise also manifested concern. Jean blushed. He felt humiliated by their pity.

"I twisted my knee on a tree root," was all he would say. Lise wanted to rub it, but he was brusque with her. "I'm pretty tough," he added, as he left the house.

They were surprised by his attitude. Denis went out and caught up with him.

"Give me the money. I'll go in your place. Listen, is it true what Robert Langevin told me, that you had that accident one day when you were after plums for her?"

"Yes," replied Jean, with a tightening of his jaws. There was such a lump in his throat that he could not speak. He was like a child who cannot keep from crying and is ashamed of it. Boucher slapped him on the back.

"Go on with your woodcutting. Don't ask me to explain. I don't like emotional scenes. Excuse me."

Jean watched him admiringly as he leaped the rocks and ran off nimbly toward the village. Lise was disappointed to see Denis go. The rude manner in which he had run away from her a short while before had left her worried. Strolling down to the edge of the beach, she clumsily began tossing pebbles into the lake, thinking of him as she did so. Some of the pebbles would bound out and sink where the water was deep. It all depended on the way you threw them. Sometimes the flattest ones, with the sharpest edge, would go down at once. Why did Denis speak of dying?

Unable to control herself, she went over to Jean. "May I ask you something in confidence?"

He shuddered. He no longer believed in happiness. It couldn't be anything important. "Go ahead."

"Does Denis have some serious disease that you can't see? You ought to know." Her voice was troubled.

What did she mean, anyway? Had it come to a question of venereal diseases with her and Denis? Jean assured her that his friend was in good health, but she thought he was being reticent.

"Are you sure," she went on, "that it isn't heart trouble. At his age you don't have cancer."

It was Jean's turn to be distressed. He gave her a questioning look. Was she, with her education, merely making sport of him for her own amusement? She and Denis must have planned it a while ago. He said nothing but hacked angrily at the log. Lise gave a cry of pain. A splinter had struck her in the leg. He at once sprang to her side, his manner imploring, almost idiotic.

"It's nothing," she said. "Tell me more about Denis."

"You want to know if he's sick? You saw how he leaped those mounds, didn't you? His knees went in and out, as limber as could be—" He broke off, embarrassed by the admiration he had shown for the other lad's joints. "Maybe his sickness is literary."

She suspected Jean of being jealous. Why was it Denis never spoke of his book? She became coy.

"He never talks to me about his novel. Perhaps he is studying me as a model for his heroine?"

"Perhaps. He wouldn't take me. I am too good a friend."

A doubt entered Lise's mind. Was Denis only playing at love that he might analyse her? But why, then, should he have asked her with tears in his eyes if she would be sorry if he died? She preferred to think that he had no desire to deceive her and that when he had achieved fame he would bring it to her all of a sudden, as a surprise. She went away singing, in the direction of the beach. Too happy to think of danger, she made up her mind that she would go out in the canoe alone, now that her father was not there to see her. Jean called to her to be careful, but paying no attention, she loosed the boat from its moorings and dreamily seated herself in it, a smile on her lips:

"He's written a novel. How fine he is, how sensitive!" She began paddling like one who is used to it; for she was not concerned with the motions that she made; all that she could see before her was an open book, filled with beautiful phrases and containing a wonderful story, while over all, like a cloud, floated Denis' mobile face, fierce as his own savage, forthright words.

Jean had stopped work and was watching her anxiously. He felt a little guilty when Zépherin came out on the veranda and asked where Lise was, but he was glad of the opportunity to show Monsieur Lévesque that he knew how to mind his own business. He pointed to the lake as if it meant nothing to him.

"Lise! Lise! Come back here!"

Choking with fright, Madame Lévesque came out of her doze.

"Don't be afraid," Lise shouted to them. "I'm coming back!"

But no matter how she plied her paddle, she could not succeed in turning the canoe. She thought of Denis, how calm and concentrated he was whenever he had to find a solution for any problem. She now found what seemed to her a very simple one: if the boat would not turn, she herself would do so. She stood up, but it was already too late; the canoe was rocking and in her nervousness she capsized it. Her cry was swallowed up by the wave that swept over her. Pale and haggard-looking, Zépherin ran down to the water's edge and stood there helplessly. Madame Lévesque had fallen to her knees upon the balcony, her hands clasped as she prayed to Heaven with little gurgles of distress. Jean had dropped his axe and was pulling off his sweater. He ran, dived, and swam as best he could the distance that separated him from the overturned canoe. To look at the father, one would have thought that he was simply waiting impassively for the end of the drama.

Jean, beside himself with anxiety, feared that he would not reach her in time. Finally, he dived down into the trough between two waves, seeking to discover Lise's body in the watery haze. Half suffocated, he came back up to the surface, then dived again, this time farther to the left. He was growing discouraged and sick at heart and had come up once more for a breath of air, when he caught sight of a shadow swaying like a seaweed in the greyish water. With a frantic effort he reached the girl's side, seized her by the hair, and with what strength was left him brought her to the light of day. Filling his lungs with air, he then started swimming painfully with one hand, holding Lise's head out of the water with the other.

Zépherin was alarmed, thinking Jean would hurt her, but the latter paid no attention, for his water-soaked clothes, heavy as lead, were dragging him toward the bottom. Then a great weakness came over him and he realized that it was no longer possible for him to keep from going down. His mouth filled with water, he was losing consciousness—he turned for one last look at Lise, to beg her forgiveness.

Denis came along whistling, plucking raspberries with his free hand. Lise must be waiting for him. He darted a glance in the direction of the camp and saw the Lévesques on the edge of the beach, the father in water up to his knees, standing as if petrified. He followed their gaze and was so dumbfounded at what he beheld that his package dropped to his feet. A cold sweat stood out on his forehead. He was not the man to hesitate. Jean was making no progress but was obviously exhausted and trying desperately to keep Lise afloat. Boucher in his turn took a running dive. It was out of the question for his friend to hold out. As a matter of fact, Jean was already sinking when, with a powerful breast stroke, Denis reached out and touched him with his fingertips. The last ounce of his strength gone, Jean let go of Lise. The other lad then took her by the hair and swam with her to the beach, where he stretched her out. Her father fell on his knees beside her and Denis did not dare push him back.

"You are not dead, little daughter, are you?" Zépherin cried. "You are not dead, are you?"

For the first time in her life Madame Lévesque, who often had come so near to it, really fainted. Jean, who had managed to get to shore, now came hobbling up. He was weeping, and begged Denis to begin artificial respiration.

"I know," said Denis sharply, his nostrils twitching. "You can go look for a woollen blanket." Taking Zépherin under the armpits, he lifted him to one side, and then the two young men fell to work. Seeing that he had already kissed her, it was Denis who took it upon himself to compress her lungs and raise her arms up and down. With a quick movement, he ripped open her bodice, while Jean, too timid to touch her abdomen, busied himself with her legs. Denis gave an impatient look. "It's not a sin today," he said.

Lise had been in the water too short a time to be suffocated. After a few minutes of rubbing, the colour came back to her cheeks and she opened her eyes, gazing about her with a wan bewildered air. Forgetting his wife, Zépherin threw his arms around his daughter. "My child!" he exclaimed, "you're alive! I knew it could never happen." The youths were embarrassed by the sobs in his voice and started to walk away, but he detained them. Denis contrived to push Jean forward.

"My brave young lads! Colin, I am going to use my influence to get you a good job. You two are like our own sons from now on."

Denis was busy wrapping Lise in the blanket. "Thanks, dear! Oh, my head! My head!" Denis bit his lips.

"Would you have been sorry if—?" she murmured, taking Denis' hand.

"Hush! We'll talk about that later."

Jean turned aside. It was as if she had forgotten everything. He came back to the question that was troubling him. Did they, then, this healthy pair, have discussions on the subject of death in the midst of their love scenes? That "dear" of Lise's had frozen his heart. Madame Lévesque staggered and fell against him.

Having been too shy to bring along any change of clothing, Jean wrung his trousers out near the veranda. His teeth were chattering. Denis, his jaws firmly set, was undressing beside him.

"Are you cold?" Denis asked. His tone was indifferent.

"I was probably too hot before I went in," Jean replied. As he continued to shiver, Denis took Zépherin's sports jacket and threw it over his friend's shoulders. They stood there looking at each other, and Denis dropped his gaze. Hesitantly, he ran his hand over his hair.

"Up until a little while ago," he said, "Lise belonged more to me than she did to you. You have to admit that she came to me without my wishing it. But now you've won her and we are even."

"You are just saying that because you want me to protest and remind you that you saved both of us." Jean smiled sadly as Denis surveyed him from his head down to his knees.

"That's nice of you," said Denis. "Now I shan't have to beg your pardon for the disgusting thing I said to you a while ago."

Such mishaps always take away the appetite and make one feel like packing up and going home. Everything was dumped pell-mell into the trunk compartment of the automobile. Zépherin with his perch beside him proceeded to step on the accelerator, for he wished to be back in time for Monsieur le Curé to announce what had happened at the service that evening. After one has come through a great danger, it is customary to pamper oneself a bit, as one does a convalescent; and so it was decided that Madame Lévesque, following all this commotion, should take on a maid. Lise suggested Jean's sister and

Denis did not dare object. Reclining upon the rear seat beside her mother, the girl spoke of how grateful she was to the young men. She called Colin "Jean," which caused him to curse the chills that prevented him from enjoying his happiness to the full. He could not wait to be home and in bed, under the warm covers, that he might have an opportunity to think it all over. He had asked them to let him stand on the running board to avoid wetting the beautiful cushions, but what he really desired was to hear Zépherin's protests. The nearer they came to the city the less demonstrative Lévesque became, but he at least promised them their photographs in the newspapers and a life-saving medal. In the meanwhile they joyfully went ahead with plans that would bring them all together on Lise's birthday; she would be eighteen on Tuesday.

Zépherin felt that it was good to breathe in the dust-laden atmosphere of St Joseph's parish once more, where there was no water in which to drown and where he experienced a sense of tranquillity, self-satisfaction, and standing in the community. His generosity reached a climax as he drew up in front of his home and offered Jean a dollar. As he did this, he cast a malicious glance at the lad from an office who was holding on to his daughter's hand. Jean was white in the face.

"Sir!" he said, and there was real distress in his voice. He looked to Lise for support. Zépherin was astonished and kept waving the bill as Jean turned and fled. "It won't be long until you get your medals," he called after him. "Send your sister over to see us tomorrow."

At the offer of a dollar to Jean, Denis had dropped Lise's hand, and he too now disappeared. That day, that glorious day had left him terribly unhappy. If it had not been for the generous impulse that had led him to go to the village in Jean's stead, all would have been his. As it was, he had to share her. She was Jean's now. Jean was suffering on her account, and she did not know it. He looked at the monks and wondered if he was not destined to enter a monastery. One hope alone remained: his novel might win a prize.

Jean hastened home and, still shaken by chills, undressed as fast as he could. From his room he called out to Germaine to tell her of the offer the Lévesques had made. She was highly indignant at first. Was it not enough that she had come home from the picnic angry and disappointed? And now her brother was suggesting that, while her rival was making up pretty phrases to ensnare her Denis, poor Germaine should be scrubbing the floors. This sudden access of pride, however, was speedily overcome by the habit she had formed of accepting without revolt her calling in life. Moreover, when she should have come to see how Lise lived from day to day, might she not be able to point out the girl's faults to Denis, all those things that tend to lessen a woman in the eyes of a man? In that way she would possibly be able to rid him of the obsession that Lise was a fairylike creature.

Germaine said nothing to Jean of all this but, changing the subject, expressed her surprise at finding him in bed. He then, despite the fact that he was not feeling well, went on to tell her excitedly of what had happened that afternoon. Thrilled by what she had heard, she promptly ran out to repeat it to all the Mulots, who were gathered in little groups on the sidewalks and in the street. Insults were flying back and forth between the groups; for when one was the wife of a Mulot and went picnicking in a cart, one was more likely than not to be jolted into the arms of someone other than one's husband. Then, too, after such an event as Pinasse's wrestling match, when the fighting spirit had been stimulated by delusions of grandeur, the odour of new-mown hay, and the biting froth of a good light beer, one was apt to be suspicious and oversensitive and inspiration was wont to find expression in the form of bodily exercise.

What usually happened on picnics was this. There would be much merriment at first, loud guffaws interspersed with the wails of the young ones to the double-bass accompaniment of lowing cows. And then, without warning, under pretext that his wife had been insulted by some neighbour who had carried things too far in his scuffling, the Mulot's wrath would burst forth. His jealousy would be all the more intense for the reason that he was far from home and in a voluptuous setting, amid grass and green trees, those trees beneath which the first cuckolded husbands sought out their faithless consorts. All this would arouse in his primitive and sensitive soul certain dark impulses, and he would give vent to such a fury as had not been seen since the stone age.

The news spread by Germaine evoked a passionate interest. There was something unreal about that near-drowning in the lake. Ah! those Soyeux, they needed the Mulots to save them! The stay-at-homes, who had never seen the river but once, when the Conservative party staged a famous excursion to Quebec Bridge, opened their eyes in amazement. Lake Sergent —that was a deadly ocean, a fresh-water hell, no place for a light canoe. Germaine, to whom lakes and canoes meant happiness, gave a graphic account of how that wonderful brother of hers had dragged Lise out by the hair. On the crest of a wave Lise suddenly disappeared, and the narrator, inspired by her own story, saw herself being drawn out by Denis. They were on the beach now. She could see herself dripping with water, half fainting, losing consciousness as he strove manfully to bring her back to life. How feverishly he worked to see her smile once more! As she told how artificial respiration had been administered, the gang from Bédarovitch's uttered a voracious "Mmm!" as poor children do when they dream of a regal dessert.

"Lake Sergent is rotten with eelpouts," the trout fishermen remarked, contemptuously.

Then the cracked bell of the church announced that vespers were over and the chattering Soyeux came out in compact groups, flourishing their missals and clasping their hands. The more learned among them were explaining how you work the arms and compress the lungs of a drowning person, while those who were most deeply moved by the event repaired to the door of the Lévesque home. It was never in vain that one devoted oneself to the Church. Monsieur le Curé had been informed by Zépherin of what had happened and, overjoyed at sight of the perch, had mounted the pulpit filled with an emotion which he proceeded to put into fitting and solemn words. He described the adventure in detail, winding himself up in a skein of brilliant rhetoric. He particularly praised the courage shown by Zépherin who, aided by Boucher and Colin, had saved his daughter from a frightful death. After all, did not the good enjoy the special protection of Providence?

Denis, who had remained standing on the corner, unexpectedly found himself surrounded by a small crowd of persons whose admiration was reflected in their glowing faces. The Latruche sisters—especially Cécile, who had not forgotten the incident of the garter and who harboured a bitter resentment—insinuated that he had taken advantage of the occasion to embrace the girl against her will. That was the trouble with artificial respiration. Moving the arms and legs was all right, but when it came to massaging the chest! By saving the life of others one might very well lose his own soul. The Daughters of Mary, however, did not feel that way about it; they were chirping with enthusiasm. How wonderful it must be to be rescued in such a manner: the waves tumbling over your thighs like a silvery waterfall, your mouth filling with water, your eyes shut, and then, strong arms that lift you out of harm's way! They bestowed upon Denis their prettiest smiles but did not dare congratulate him for fear of losing their beaux among the Gonzagues.

Denis resisted these compliments but did not protest that Jean deserved them more than he. It had not dawned upon him that this vague uneasiness which he was doing his best to elude was in reality that suffering of which Jean had spoken that is not to be repelled.

Only the sight of his mother seated on the step kept him from going into Lise's house. He would have liked to give her a long embrace, revel in the nearness of her skin, her light-filled eyes; he would live with her the passing hour, without care, without memory, without hope. He waited for Jean to come out, with the secret intention of getting him to confess that the saving of Lise had been purely instinctive on his part, a kind of reflex action, with no bravery involved. Barloute called out that her son was in bed and that it was very stupid of Jean to get himself wet for the sake of the Soyeux, who only laughed at him. Denis frowned thoughtfully, then gnashed his teeth. Ah! that solitude was a trick on Jean's part. He was about to win by thus shutting himself up and enjoying, alone and in silence, the homage that was being paid to him. What a pleasure it must be! How sweet to the taste! From now on Denis would go back over each day of his life since that day last year when he had first known love; he would feed on, devour, exhaust each one of them. It was like looking over old photographs from the days when one was poor, after one had become prosperous.

Speaking of photographs, he had a mental picture of himself: a splendid lad at first, and then steadily evolving, each morning that brought him closer to Lise, toward an irreparable decadence. Hastening home, he saw from his mother's calm eyes that she knew nothing of what had happened. She had no company any more, for she was always talking of Gaston and would hint to her visitors that they had all of them let him die without doing anything for him. Having made sure that he was alone, Denis took out his manuscript from a pile of laundry and fell to work feverishly, hurling his own despair in the face of his hero with words that he believed to be sublime. He did not know where his misfortune lay: in undertaking to describe a great sorrow he merely succeeded in being pompous.

The next day, Denis came home from work later than usual, his coat puffed out by a package that he sought to conceal. He had hesitantly stopped in front of Lise's house, when Germaine with premeditated suddenness opened the door.

"Not now," she said. "Let her rest. I've just given her some orange juice. She's waiting for Jean to get better." Her ill-suited irony fell from her as she gazed sentimentally at the bulge in his coat. It reminded her of the time when, all a-sweat, he had come back from a fruitful foray in the Dominicans' orchard. "Do you still steal apples?" she asked. "You oughtn't to stretch your shirt like that. You look so nice when it fits you the way it should." Her bright eyes were fastened on his coat with loving admiration. How good it would be to have him for herself, this lad who was so strong, so handsome with his full and sensuous lips that stood out blood-red against the brown of his skin.

He gave her an ill-natured glance and made a gesture as if to keep her from seeing his package.

"What are you telling me?" He put the question reluctantly. "You mean Jean isn't well?"

She shrugged her shoulders. "He has a terrible cold. It must be a bad one, seeing that he didn't go to work. Father was raising the devil with him."

Startled to hear this, Denis at once went to his friend's house and knocked, and old man Pitou opened the door. Barloute caught sight of him from the kitchen and muttered that it was no use for him to be playing the hypocrite. Lise was Jean's; it was only a matter of months and they would be married. And wasn't Germaine already one of the family? That young woman, who had followed Denis, now dusted off the easy chair and dropped down in it.

"Denis, come over and try it." Although he did not turn around, she knew all the contempt that was written on his face.

He lifted the drapes that divided the room in two, inspected the bedroom, and assumed a sorrow-stricken tone of voice: "There he lies on his deathbed. We could do without that."

Jean half opened his eyes. "It's you, is it?" he said in a clammy voice. He seemed barely able to speak. "If this day would only end! Tomorrow I shan't have to think about anything but my knee; I'll be rid of this hammering in my head. One minute I'm hot and the next minute cold, so that I don't know whether I'm shivering or boiling."

Jean's straightforward manner of speaking merely confirmed Denis in the belief that his friend was taking advantage of his indisposition in order to rise above and humiliate his rival. The sick lad had a violent fit of coughing, and Denis shook his head as if a revolting thought had come to him. How shameful it was for him to be so petty when Colin was suffering. He had a dim feeling that what caused him to envy Jean was the fact that the latter did not occupy a neutral position between happiness and sorrow as he himself did. He was embarrassed.

"Take some cough syrup. Be wise and look after that cold."

Jean tossed the bedclothes nervously. "Lise—" he began. "Is she better?"

Denis appeared to find it absurd that this subject had not come up before. "She was looking for you last night. She wanted to thank you once more. Everybody's talking about you. You're a hero."

He enjoyed without remorse the unconcealed pleasure that lighted up Jean's eyes. The lie he had told gave Denis the illusion of being less guilty toward his friend; he was making it up to him. To be sure, he had declined to accept the compliments which the Mulots had showered upon him, but he had not given Colin the credit that was his due. Beside himself with joy, Jean had half risen in the bed. He was now talking enthusiastically, like a small boy, suggesting schemes and laying plans with a childlike spontaneity.

"And don't tell her it's on her account that I'm sick. I'll warn Germaine."

Denis looked at him suspiciously. "That seems a little melodramatic to me."

"Well, you write novels, don't you?" He was as playful and talkative as a man who had just awakened from a long sleep and is feeling exceptionally good. "You know, it seems funny for me to be suffering for her sake without her knowing anything about it. It's as if I were saving up my claims to her love." He blushed in confusion. In a flash he was back on the ruins of the church, could see that kiss and hear Denis' agonized confession. But all that seemed far away now. He glanced questioningly at his friend's stern face. He was sorry for what he had said. "Excuse me—I didn't think."

"Go on. I have it coming to me."

Jean's exaltation stayed with him, and he was no longer astonished by it. How happy he was! Lise had been looking for him to thank him.

"I don't need to tell you," he rambled on, "that it's no pleasure for me to lie in bed and drink herb tea. And maybe you think my mother doesn't make me take it! I never would have believed she was like that. Just let me hear them call her Barloute again. Last night, she was right there every time I woke up and called for her. And each time, I thought it was morning. I dreamed of so many things. I was reading famous books, I fell into a big net, and then, all of a sudden, I was out of it and playing music. All day long I've felt as if I had some education." He laughed mischievously, then turned pale. "That's always on my mind, and I don't like it; I was a lot more contented when I felt that I was ignorant."

Denis was glad to let him believe that this was irony. Ah! they were all alike, these uncultivated ones who were always worrying about culture. This inferiority which he discovered in Jean made him feel more comfortable, freed him of an apprehension that was growing upon him as he saw the strange state of mind that had taken possession of his friend. Without pausing to reflect, he broke the cord around his package, and Jean was astonished and deeply moved to hear him saying any number of pleasant little things.

"That's just because you're feverish. Don't play ignorant, you rascal. Own up, you can't wait to go to Lise's birthday party. Look, I thought it would be nice to get her a little present." He removed the paper and there were two brand-new books. Denis waited for the enraptured expression on his friend's face, Jean's awed manner as he stared at the titles in bewilderment. Germaine brushed the drapes.

"Are they for her? And I didn't get her anything. How thoughtless of me!" Was he not to have a chance to be grateful to her for the tone of voice in which she would thank him, no opportunity to make known to her through some delicate gift the immensity of his love and resignation? In desperation he tried to think of what he might give her, but only absurd objects came to mind: a pair of slippers, a rocking chair, even frying pans. He shook his head impatiently. "Tell me, what would you advise me to buy for her?"

Denis abruptly wrapped up his books once more. "Your present," he burst out, "is your illness, your right to be silent and to go on piling up your claims to her love."

Jean was purple in the face. "I might have known it! You came here just to taunt me. Why did you have to go through the farce of showing me that present?"

"You want to know? It was so I could see how small a one it is alongside yours." He spoke in a low voice, watching his fingers as they played on the bed-board. He did not feel like confessing that he had come there in the first place because he was uneasy and that later, acting upon a silly impulse, he had not been able to resist the temptation to show the present he

213

had bought. It might have been a box of candy that was hidden there, but books!

Jean turned away, wrapped the covers about him. "Leave me alone, I want to sleep." After Denis had been so beastly, was he to be believed when he said that Lise had been wanting to thank him? Oh! the uncertainties of those who are sick regarding the happiness that is left them! Denis went out, discontented with himself. It was always that way when he wished to be forgiven, when his heart was pleading. His attitude always betrayed him and others accused him of perfidy.

DENIS was on his way home when a window opened and Lise's radiant face appeared. Her smile was appealing. He went over, swinging the package he carried in his hand with a nonchalant air. If there had been a reproach in her gaze, it disappeared.

"What have you there?" she asked.

"Some books."

"How nice! Lend them to me, will you?"

His own smile was an embarrassed one. "They are on the Index."

That made her all the more anxious to read them, but she was careful not to let him perceive it. "You didn't come to see me yesterday."

She was not worried, then, about Jean? To see her like this, leaning out of the window, so vivacious, so much a woman already, to observe the slight tremulousness of her eyes and the languorous abandonment of her black hair as it fell down on each side of her face—inspired his heart with a passion for complete possession; for Jean also had a right to this vision. In despair, he studied her closely.

"I was sure," he said, "that you had recovered, and I thought you needed sleep. You didn't know that Jean Colin had caught cold? He was sweating all over when he dived in to save you, and now he's very sick. He has chills."

Lise had turned pale, and this for Denis was a defeat.

"I'll go see him." She spoke impulsively. "I know he's suffering, poor chap."

"You'd better be careful," he warned her, without thinking what he was saying. "He'll be all right by tomorrow. And what's more, he's not a poor chap. He saved your life."

"But without you, Denis—"

He muttered some excuse. He did not care to reveal his own egotism by admitting that he hated finishing jobs begun by others.

Their conversation was interrupted by the arrival of the most venerable of the Gonzagues, who was carrying a large picture with great caution. Father Folbèche walked ahead and would tell him when it was necessary to lift his feet because of the upraised planks in the sidewalk. The priest barely spoke to Pritontin, seated dejectedly on his doorstep, his skinny torso lost in a shirt that was creased with wide suspenders, while his glance held the hopeless envy of one who realizes that he is a failure and will never get where he wants to be. Those unconcealed suspenders, that seedy look told all too plainly of his disgrace. Pinasse by defeating him in the popularity contest had dragged him irremediably down into the Mulot's lair. But nevertheless, Pritontin's heart still burned with a bitter regret as one of the objects he had most dearly coveted went by.

Zépherin Lévesque, his face shining, came to open the door for the curé. He pretended ignorance, feigned surprise at seeing the package, but Pierrette spoiled it all by her impatience. "Is it your portrait Monsieur le Curé?"

With a sigh the worthy priest confessed to the secret which he would have preferred to keep locked in his bosom a while longer. "Ah, yes, that is what it is. You have deserved it. It is the third one that I have presented to winners of the popularity contest. Just look at that frame. It's worth all of sixty dollars."

There was a murmur of gratitude as the Lévesques in great excitement began looking about for the best place to hang the picture; but on the wall above the piano and alongside the photograph of the young saint was an empty rectangular space which indicated that the arrival of the curé's present had been anticipated. The photograph of Monsieur le Curé—for it was a photograph, not a painting—was four feet square, and the subject, despite the fact that he wore a simple black cassock, had the imposing appearance of a bishop. Those attributes that made him ripe for such a title were clearly evident in this likeness. But Father Folbèche, disdainful of earthly honours, was content to leave all that to Providence and bide his time, putting his trust in an enlightened archiepiscopate.

Lise, to her father's annoyance, remained at the window watching Denis. Just because the Gonzague was spying upon them, the whimsical and lovesick girl ran her hand over the young man's hair. He blushed and shook it off. From the Boucher kitchen two women also were watching them, with eager faces.

"What did I tell you?" said Germaine, fatalistically. Flushed with anger, Flora tore off her apron and clenched her fists. Must she go after that precocious son of hers and bring him home by the ears? Germaine, afraid of spoiling everything, suggested that they ought not to be too hard on the lovers. Flora, meanwhile, was angrily pacing the kitchen. How could she have overlooked that picnic? Who could tell what shady things had happened there? She had a vision of Lise and Denis and the passionate games they must have played on the beach, with an intermingling of water, sand, and flesh. Then, under pretext of drying themselves, they would have gone into the wood in their bathing suits. She could hear their mad laughter as they killed mosquitoes on each other's body. Suddenly, they must have exchanged a look, without saying anything; then they kissed, and tra-la-la. The greater the detail with which she evoked these caresses the more indignant Flora became; for love to her was what she had been when she was twenty.

In spite of her desire to fan Flora's wrath against her son, Germaine as yet refused to believe that Denis and Lise had actually kissed. How many years had she herself waited?

"Jean," she went on, "was there. He's in love with the girl because she's got a little education. And we Colins don't allow ourselves to be trifled with like that."

"Don't talk to me about your brother. I know my son; he's the image of me. When he wants something, he takes it. He sent your brother raspberry-picking, that's what he did. You can thank God Jean was not drowned."

Germaine stopped rattling the dishes. "You can thank my brother for having saved both of them. At that minute he wasn't picking raspberries. I can just see him dragging that Lévesque hussy out by the hair and Denis following after them, all out of wind. He's wonderful in the water, Jean is."

"What airs she's putting on! You're not going to run down my son like that. Just because he was a little smitten with Lise for a day doesn't mean that he couldn't save the whole raft of you, even if you were out in the middle of the ocean. And all the contests that he's won—what do you have to say to that?"

She shrugged her shoulders. It was absurdly impossible that Denis had not saved Lise. Germaine did not protest any further, and Flora, with an eye on the lovers, once more began mumbling about keeping her son pure and all that. It was an old story. She had brought him up in the right path, inculcating in him a respect for celibacy; for she still had young ones to satisfy her maternal instinct and so there was no need as yet of having recourse to another generation. Up until yesterday she had been so proud to think that her Denis did not frequent the Gomin wood with the "chippies" of St Sauveur! She was thankful that he disdained to go make love of an evening at the Monument des Braves. They had sweated to give him an education and enable him to study stenography so that he might attain the heights, but all this only rendered him an easier prey for a convent-bred girl with a bewitching voice and a veneer of poetry and a heart that was a veritable serpents' nest of impurity and seduction.

Poetry! Joseph's poetry was the only kind that had ever appealed to her. He had won her that way, but his motives had been pure. Fortified with the experience of a woman who knows what it is to be courted with beautiful phrases and saved by her virtue as a model if fecund mother, Flora Boucher felt that she was proof against the elegant wiles of a Lise Lévesque with that sinuous mouth of hers and her languid way of talking. Clenching her fists again, she thought how much she would enjoy giving Lise a phenomenal beating. She could see the creature writhing under her sturdy arm, humiliated in front of Denis. Inspired by the idea of this possible exploit, this exhibition of maternal vigilance, she picked up the tablecloth with a nervous hand and, going out onto the balcony, shook it vigorously. She did not even see the dipping sparrows, chirping with joy and making a sort of rasping sound as they brushed against one another in a scramble for the crumbs.

Left alone in the kitchen, Germaine put the dishes in the cupboard with quick, angry gestures. She was angry that Flora Boucher should wish to keep her son to herself to satisfy her own desires. After all the effort she had expended in getting Flora to hate Lise, it made Germaine impatient to think that in return for her zealousness in this regard she could not expect the slightest favour, could not look forward to one little evening with Denis. Her only reward was to wash the dishes from which he ate. What upstarts! They acted as if the human race existed merely to keep them company? She was ashamed, both for herself and for her brother, ashamed that in her love she thus had to abandon all pride, and that, for the sake of keeping on good terms, she had to permit this woman who was so boastful of her own family to cheat Jean out of the credit due him for saving Lise's life.

Fretting and fuming, she picked up the soup tureen, which had to be placed on the third shelf of the cupboard. It was hard for her to reach so high and she had to stretch herself. Just as she was putting the dish where it belonged, she made a false move and her arm pulled away the oilcloth that lined the shelf. Climbing upon a chair, she hastily began setting things to rights when her eyes suddenly grew large. There in front of her was a two-dollar bill, unfolded. It was a magical sight, like a king among all the coupons that had been tucked away there. What she did then was mechanical, purely instinctive. The next thing she knew she was standing in the middle of the kitchen floor, her apron pocket puffed out by the banknote. Her face was crimson, her heart pounding. How heavily did money thus obtained weigh upon one! Everything led her to believe that they would suspect Denis, in view of his shamelessness. And then Lise would hear of it and despise him. She gave a sudden start. Despite all her wretchedness, she could not betray her conscience, her dream of seeing Denis happy by her side. With a stiffening of her body, she climbed upon the chair once more. The door slammed.

"You're not as tall as I am," said Flora. "You have a lot of trouble putting my soup tureen away." It pleased her that Germaine had to use a chair. The younger woman was perspiring, trying to regain her composure. Her hand which held the two-dollar bill slipped out of her pocket, empty, almost shaking. She wiped her forehead.

"Yes, it made me a little dizzy."

"That's on account of your time of life. But you'll get over it. Tell me, is Robert Langevin serious with you?"

Germaine made a vague motion of her hand, for she was thinking rather of her own problem at that moment. Then she seemed to remember where she was.

"Did you hear about Jean's being sick?" she asked. "He was very hot when he dived in to save that heartless girl, and now he has chills, first hot, then cold. And he spits."

"Hot then cold? I'll bet you his feet are swelling, too." For Flora saw Gaston's malady everywhere.

"No, he has a swollen knee."

"It generally begins with the feet." Flora seemed disappointed, then appeared to think of a solution. Running over to a pile of diapers, she drew out a big book.

"You understand," she said, with an air of mystery, "there are certain pictures in it that are only for us women; that's why I keep it hidden from my boys."

The book bore the title: *Vegetable Remedies and Biological Manual*, and was by one Dr Narodetzki of the Faculty of Medicine of Paris. It was to this compendium that Flora owed in good part the consideration that was shown her by the other women of the parish, and she had begun to set up as a dangerous competitor of the doctors among the Mulots. With her, symptoms were never slow in appearing. She planted them like needles in the credulous ears of the neurasthenic or those who were regularly pregnant. Anatomy meant visualizing a multitude of ovaries in travail. In doubtful cases and where the patient had not purchased some of Gaston's raffle tickets, she would hint at cancer. Her medical training was rounded out with a knowledge of affections of the heart, that is to say, where there was a swelling of the legs and the nails turned blue. With an adviser so inclined to discover fatal diseases, it is not surprising if the gullible, afflicted with a sprained ankle or a rumbling of the intestines, readily came to believe that they were suffering from heart trouble or had a cancerous growth.

"You say he spits?" she inquired, studiously turning the pages. For once, it was not a female disease with which she had to deal; it was one located somewhere else than in the belly. She did not notice how nervous Germaine was, the futile gestures that the young woman was making.

"I have it!" she cried. "It's pleurisy. Go show that to your brother and see if he recognizes his symptoms. But be sure to take good care of my book."

Germaine had given up hope of finding a way to put the stolen money back where she had found it. She took the volume mechanically. Denis came in just then with the youngest of the children in his arms. That way, the package that he had hidden under his coat went unperceived. His mother gave him a scornful look.

After supper, in order not to have to listen to his mother's rantings and insinuations, Denis went up to the attic and, working at top speed, finished the manuscript of his novel. He did little revising; in literature as in life he did not like to turn back, since it only meant a bitter disappointment. He must live like the whirlwind, without thinking of what he had left strewn behind him. He must get through this crisis somehow, for it had one advantage, at least: it was experience. When he had finished his book he raised his arms above his head, but the ceiling was too low and spoiled the gesture he had wished to make. He sighed. The enthusiasm that he felt came from the fact that he had just killed off his hero. Then came a feeling of shame at the thought that it was only by exploiting great sorrows that he could work himself up to the proper pitch. There must be more than that to the life of an artist. As he went to the post office and mailed his manuscript, he was a little dispirited to find that he was no longer greatly interested in a story which had meant so much to him. He fancied it would be that way with everything which gave him pleasure.

All that evening he wandered about the parish, his hands in his pockets. He gazed for a long time at the nearly completed church, and as his eyes went up to the new belfry, his thoughts turned to those European writers who were engaged in a search for God. What a difference! At St Joseph, one counted on God as on a rich uncle. This to Denis seemed grotesque, and he came to the conclusion that, without any doubt, he had been deceiving himself as to his own superiority.

He did not suffer too much, however, from this mental agony, for he was physically hungry. A restaurant was out of the question; he had barely had enough money to buy those volumes for Lise. He forbade himself to think of Jean that he might not lose his appetite; for he could still hear the sick boy's fits of coughing. All the lights were out as he came into the house, and he listened attentively to the quiet breathing of his brothers, who because of the heat were sleeping on top of the covers. After waiting a short while, he tiptoed over to the cupboard and opened the door very carefully for fear it would squeak. There were the blueberry tarts, round and appetizing, spread out in front of his eyes. He was the mysterious burglar, pilfering and slicing up his mother's desserts. With a family such as theirs, the portions had to be determined in advance. He took one of the tarts, smiled, and began munching it greedily, taking care to indent the crust with little semi-circular bites in order to give his mother the impression that they had been left there by one of the younger children.

These nibbled mouthfuls gave him a great deal of satisfaction, caused him to forget his moral scruples, which he was beginning to look upon as far-fetched. He took pains to leave a morsel upon the plate that his mother might see it. She would accuse the youngest child but would not beat him too hard. It was the critical moment. He must get the door shut without making any noise. He gave a start. His mother, who had been lying awake thinking about what Germaine had told her, had heard a noise.

"What are you doing there, Denis?"

"I'm getting myself a drink of water. What do you suppose?" His voice was almost calm. He turned on the faucet.

"Come on upstairs and lock the doors," his father called to him. For Joseph, son of a middle-class family that had had a little money, did not believe in the safety either of private dwellings or of banks.

Denis lay awake a long time before dropping off to sleep. One by one he was going over in his mind and enjoying the things he had done in giving Lise artificial respiration. As he recalled the scene between Jean and himself, he was ashamed of his own grandiloquence. Then with a vast boredom he envisaged the stacks of bills that he would have to add up the next day. His spirit rebelled at this and, filled with a mad hope, he let his desires go wandering. He would be recognized as a great novelist. Then the thought that had come to him in front of the church a while ago returned to trouble him. The great Europeans were looking for God. Kneeling in his bed, he repeated three Hail Mary's and another prayer: "My God, I give Thee my heart." He prayed for the intention of art in French Canada.

Tuesday came at last, and Lise was eighteen years old. The day was so lovely that it seemed to linger like a perfume over the shanties. The chimneys sent up their blue smoke as if exhaling peace and happiness. At six o'clock Denis left home with drops of water from his dampened hair still standing on his forehead. Wiping them off, he shouted back to his mother that he was not hungry. He was afraid that Jean had not yet recovered, and this left a bitter taste in his mouth, since it spoiled his pleasure to have to combat his friend in his absence. With his gift in his hand, he went into the Colins'. From the door he could hear the sound of coughing and realized that Jean was in bed.

"Aren't you ever going to get up?" he asked as he parted the drapes. "Hurry, you only have five minutes." With the impertinence that comes from good health, he sniffed the clammy atmosphere of a fever-patient's room. Rousing from his torpor, Jean raised himself on one elbow. Was it really Boucher? He had an anguished feeling at sight of this being from another world, with a new suit, those square shoulders, a smiling face, and a tongue that was as nimble as the wing of a bird in flight. He rubbed his own tongue against his teeth and found that it was coated.

"Go out while I dress."

He must overcome this heavy feeling and join Denis, and modesty served him as an excuse for concealing the effort that it cost him. Once he had his clothes on, that would hide his weakness as the scabbard does the broken sword. It would be easy enough to make his way to Lise's house despite the energy he had to expend in combing his hair. He let the water from the faucet run over his head; the coolness of it was intoxicating.

"You're wasting away like the Lady of the Camellias," remarked Denis, who was annoyed by the atmosphere of the place. He was surprised to see his mother's medical book upon the dresser and started leafing through it, unthinkingly seeking out the definitions of venereal diseases. His friend's pallor upset his plans. He was astonished at being asked to leave the room. Behind the curtain Jean was panting as he drew on his shirt.

"Do you think it will be worth my while going, that I will enjoy myself enough to forget the taste in my mouth? I feel funny, as if flies were buzzing all around me. I can't stand it."

"What do you mean?" asked Denis, suddenly on his guard. Was Jean planning to work on Lise's sympathy?

The sick lad sank back on the bed. "Oh, but I'm tired!" he said. "I'll explain tomorrow. Yes, tomorrow."

"Well, I advise you to watch your step. You don't get women by begging them, by showing them your weaknesses."

Jean creased his forehead. The word "strength" kept buzzing around his head like an enormous horsefly that he was unable to catch. Leaning on his elbow, he shut his eyes. "Hand me my new trousers—there on the chair."

With ill-humour Denis brought them through the curtain. "Your mother should have pressed them for you. Here are your shoes, too. You'd better brush them before you leave."

Jean was overwhelmed by having to face these tasks. His feet were blue as they touched the floor and the sharp pain in his knee made him groan a little. He examined the knee and found it red and swollen. Denis, hands in his pockets, was posing in front of the mirror. Jean paused in the act of drawing on his trousers. The house was swimming about him. Was he going to have to beg these inanimate objects to be still? At last he was erect. Never had he seemed so tall; his feet down below looked like abnormal excrescences. As he began to adjust his suspenders, he swayed, almost fell. Clinging to Denis, he shut his eyes from shame at having to depend on the other lad's muscles for support. Denis was worried, and helped him back to bed. He did not notice that the flush on Jean's face was not due to humiliation alone, but to fever as well.

"It's stupid to have to hold onto you like that." What a relief it was to be stretched out once again, to have finally made up his mind that he would not go out any more. A new life was beginning for him, one in which he would find it more natural to remain lying down than to stand up. There was a note of protest in his voice. "I'm feeling sick. You go on alone, and tell Lise that I'm unsociable."

"I don't think I'll do that. You won't come, then? That's final? Very well, I'll stay home, too."

"And blame me for it. Go on, please go."

Denis laughed sardonically. "That's not so bad. I should have foreseen it. She will think of you more when you're not there." The words had slipped out, like a blush to a timid cheek. Since it was impossible for him to satisfy the desires of his flesh, it was as if he were jealous of the sentimental victory that his rival would win through suffering.

Jean held back his tears at this cruel remark. This was no longer the wonderful Denis of last year, who had painted the future in marvellous hues. He must now pay for his leader's disillusionment, let himself be trampled, unprotestingly, just as, once upon a time, he had let himself be carried away. All the effervescence of youth left in his heart now abandoned him and there remained only his sick and fever-ridden body. Physical suffering could claim him for its own now, could knead his flesh at will. He felt like an old man, content with his memories. He sighed.

"And it's you who say that, the lad who used to find his happiness in making others happy. Is it really you?"

Denis grew pale, went over to his friend, ran his long hand through Jean's hair. "How foolish we are, we two. What is it that holds us down in spite of the impulse that we feel to rise? It is just as I told you : love."

"No, it is because there are two of us."

Denis did not care for discussions in which others explained things better than he. He drew up the covers.

"Very well," he said, "just to satisfy you, I'll go. And we'll talk about you."

Jean did not ask him not to tell Lise of the nature of his illness. As the drapes fell back in place, his legs curled up in the manner of beings that have had the life crushed out of them.

ONE does not have desires unless one hopes to satisfy a hunger of the spirit or of the flesh. Denis was too disillusioned with himself not to feel that his plans for victory had fallen through. The atmosphere about him was a heavy-laden one and the future held a deceptive sneer, promised only defeat. One role was left him: that of the charitable friend. He imagined himself carrying Jean's love in place of a present under his arm. He would throw it down at Lise's feet and leave without saying a word. What did it matter to him whether he was forgotten or wept for? When the first woman who came along should say to him "I love you," then it was that he would want Lise to regret him. In his dreams, Denis was a pessimist merely that he might feel more keenly the spur of desire, a desire that of a sudden would blind him with its light. Jean had said to him: "Boucher, you love to invent dramas from which you emerge the victor."

But Lise was charming in a white organdy dress as she came to open the door and held up her delightfully confident face to his masculine lips.

"Happy birthday!"

As she hung upon his neck, stammering her joy, he felt all his lassitude leaving him, giving place to unfeigned emotion that was delightfully fresh and unspoiled. Then he drew himself up, pretending to be bored, for Germaine, near the stove, her face very pale, was keeping a close eye on them. She opened the parlour door under pretext of letting in the cat, which Denis hated for the reason that Lise was so fond of it. With an air of annoyance, he presented her with the volumes he had bought.

"I'd like to be rich," he observed, "but it is a great deal to be eighteen. When you are old, you need fine presents to fill up the void."

"Are they for me? I'm not going to thank you for them because I love you and that's better." "*Je t'aime,*" she had said, using suddenly the familiar "thou." It took him by surprise. Flushed with pleasure, she started turning the leaves. *A Man and His Sin, The Caress of the Ideal.*

"The newspapers say they are good stories," he explained awkwardly.

She closed the books and gazed into his eyes. "And when are you going to finish your own novel? Tell me, Denis dear."

He frowned and made an evasive gesture. So Jean had revealed the secret. If he failed, would he be like a thousand other dreamers, a mere talker who never got anything published but went on piling up sterile manuscripts? She guessed at his discontentment and made a wry face. The next moment her eyes were bright.

"And Jean," she said, "is he well again? I've been praying for him."

He hesitated. Should he carry out Jean's instructions and tell her that his friend had refused simply because he was unsociable? That would be to play his hand. "He's very sick. I bring you his best wishes."

She paled at this. "After supper we'll go see him. And we'll take him half the roses that Mama gave me." She was sure the flowers would complete a cure begun by prayer.

Zépherin now came into the room. With a slight touch he straightened the frame of Monsieur le Curé's picture and stood there looking at it, after which he went on to speak of the bronze medals the lads were to receive and of their photographs which, thanks to his influence, would appear in the paper.

The supper was a monotonous affair. Without solitude the love of adolescents is burdensome. Denis took a couple of pears for his friend. Perhaps the juice would refresh his mouth? In front of the mirror, Lise was arranging her curls. It was impossible to make out what she did to them, but they were more charming than ever. It was like a fresh spring that suddenly bursts through the bed of an old one. The majority of women know their hair better than they do their heart and therein lies their strength. Denis watched her in silence as she brought the beauty of her face to life. His calm masculine strength was deeply perturbed by the sight; for he perceived that her love and beauty were for him and that she was cruelly unaware of the being who deserved them, namely, Jean.

If Lise could only find Colin in so wretched a state that she would have no other feeling for him than pity! He trembled at the thought of Jean's courage, of how he would play the part of the charming invalid. The others were all out in the kitchen now. Having made sure that they were alone, Denis went over to her. Her delicate hands were still busy with her hair, she watched him in the mirror and smiled. It would be a kiss on the shoulder. He braced his muscles, shut his eyes, ready for the torture, the shame of it. His trembling hands rested on her neck, ran down her arms, came near encircling her waist. He felt his wrists stiffen against her warm breasts, but he could not bring himself to go any further. Her face was crimson as she turned to him.

"Denis!" she cried in a faltering voice.

He was panting, as if he had been running for a long time. How she must hate him, despise him! What he wished to do was destroy himself in her estimation and then reconquer her all alone, rid of all weaklings. He had to resort to ignominy in order to suffer! Now they might go see Jean, confront his fever and his love. He did not pick up the comb she had dropped. How was it that this contact of which they had both dreamed as of a forbidden joy was merely repulsive to them? She held back a tear; for he made no excuse, did not attempt to attribute his action to awkwardness. She waited until he showed a sign of moving.

"Come," she said, gathering up the roses which her mother had given her, "we must think of Jean above all. This is no day for us to be unhappy."

"Yes, that is what matters." A tremendous desire to overwhelm his friend with happiness laid hold of him. He was too disgusted at that moment to wish any for himself; he would pass it along to the sick man. But as soon as Jean began to make use of it, he would pretend that he had only lent it to him.

Germaine Colin watched them go out with a troubled look on her face. The door had been ajar, she had seen what he had done, and it had pained her to the core of her being. That was the end of her hopes so far as he was concerned. So long as he had remained the unsociable person whom she had admired from the time he was a child, there was a possibility of his being had by any girl who would prove to him her love; but now he would be less detached. She hated Lise more than one hates a rival, for Lise was the redoubtable flesh that, innocently, had destroyed her god. She hurried to finish her work, for she was anxious to go and shout her contempt in Flora Boucher's face, to show Denis' mother, very calmly, that her son was like all the others. She would keep the two dollars, and so much the worse for him.

She ran to the Bouchers' and rapped on the window with fingers reddened by dishwater. Flora nearly tore the wicket out.

"He had supper at her house, he kissed her, he—" Germaine stopped, humiliated. It would be better to keep still, wait until Denis came around again, and demand an accounting of him.

"He what?" bellowed Flora.

"He gave her two books as a present."

Madame Boucher ran in to shake her husband, who was deep in the newspaper and international events. He would wag his head with satisfaction at having foreseen such and such a catastrophe, this or that conflict.

"Your son has just given that chippy a present. And he didn't even kiss his mother on New Year's Day. Try and find his presents for *me*!"

Joseph, whose mind was not on the subject, explained that Denis was only just beginning to earn a little money. Impatiently Flora went back to Germaine but was careful to conceal the uneasiness that she felt. Where had Denis, whose salary was so small, found the money for these mad extravagances? She gave Germaine a searching look.

"How did he act when he gave them to her?"

"It was the first time I ever saw him look really stupid. Books! What a funny present! I'd have been mad if it was me. But she never let on. They were only worth about two dollars." As she said this, she twisted the stolen bill in her pocket. Her sly manner aroused Flora's anxiety.

"What sort of books were they?"

"I only had a glimpse of them, you know. The first was a red one, *The Caress of the Vampire*, and the other, *A Man and His Sin*."

"Just what I thought! Filthy books! She's snared him. Joseph, get a move on and go after him!"

She was pacing the kitchen floor, giving free rein to her anger. Joseph did not stir. He was thinking of the scene his parents had made when he told them of his decision to marry a girl from St Sauveur. They had called him a degenerate, blinded by lust. Today, the same thing was being repeated, in reverse fashion, in the case of his son. Flora dropped her arms in despair.

"There's only one thing to do, Germaine. Go out with him. Talk about Gaston."

Germaine came near handing her the two dollars. She ran home to curl her hair.

Denis knocked at the Colins' door unceremoniously.

"Sweet Jesus!" exclaimed Barloute, as she saw who was with him. "Can it be you, Mam'zelle?" She was loud in her expression of surprise; for Tit-Blanc, in the kitchen, was cursing all picnics and his son's illness, which was costing him money, and she wished to warn him of the presence of guests.

"I don't want to see anybody!" Jean called, thinking it was the gang from the club.

Disconcerted by this, Lise stopped smiling and lifted the curtain to wish him good day.

"Lise!" He had risen to a sitting posture.

She came in. How his room was suddenly transformed! It seemed as if it was flooded with sun, the sunlight being preceded by the visitor and her pure white roses.

"How are you, Jean, my friend? You are not play-acting, are you? I think it's true that you are a little unsociable."

He made no attempt to deny it. The bliss that he knew at that moment had a paralysing effect. He put out a trembling hand that was startling in its pallor from three days' sickness. She held it a long time, ill at ease, not daring to ask why they did not send for the doctor. He freed his hand with some embarrassment and spread out the flowers one by one upon the bed.

"Flowers," she explained, "have always been the most precious thing in my life."

Denis was downcast as he thought of the books he had given her. The drapes parted and Barloute's angry face appeared. "You have no business here!" she said to Denis. "Get out!"

He drew the drapes back in place without answering her, and then, taking up an old newspaper, began killing flies with it to vent his fury. He had a mad impulse to get out, taking Lise with him. In the presence of the invalid he had no mercy. It was only when he thought of him from a distance that he grew sentimental. Jean now stopped counting the roses, as if he had verified their number. He remembered how his mother yesterday had found a couple of bedbugs in the mattress.

"You'll have to excuse the appearance of this room," he murmured. He gazed at the shabby furniture, his eyes coming to rest with a worried look on his rumpled trousers tossed over the end of the bed and the tumbled covers.

"Just think, I owe everything to you and you alone." If she insisted on speaking of how brave he had been, it was in order to overcome the growing distaste that was aroused in her by the sight of this miserable room. Jean, meanwhile, was making all sorts of futile, almost weird gestures by way of holding her attention and keeping her mind off her surroundings.

"You're so good! You're so good!" he kept repeating, mechanically. Tired and perspiring, he lay back without moving. Why did not Denis leave them alone? It would be good to weep, to confess his love as one would a sin, to offer up his life, even his very soul in return for those roses that were already shedding their petals upon the bedcovers.

As they remained thus tense and embarrassed, there was a swaying of the drapes; for on the other side Tit-Blanc and his wife were listening and old man Pitou with his trembling hands appeared to be shoving them to make room for himself. Angry whispers were heard. Denis looked at Lise. The shame he had felt a while ago had disappeared and he was now inflamed by a real passion. This emotional exchange of confidences between Lise and Jean had awakened his jealousy; it annoyed him to see how well Jean's pure-hearted love accorded with her childish enthusiasm. He could hardly resist the temptation to interrupt them by inquiring if Jean still sold fishworms. Before leaving, he slipped Jean the two pears from the Lévesque table, which made the sick lad think of plums.

Outside, he walked along at Lise's side without saying anything. The fresh air had a soothing effect. Darkness was already falling.

"Aren't you coming in?" He shook his head emphatically. "Denis! Spend the evening with me." He came close to her, drawing in his lips that she might not notice how distended they were. With his hands behind his back, he lightly brushed her mouth. She stepped back, disappointed, but her eyes thanked him for being so prudent. "Denis. I'll love you always!"

He had to have his victories. It was in vain that she held out her arms to him as he walked away in silence. She dried a tear. In spite of the beautiful day they had had, he would not stay with her. If he thought that by flight he could become a great man—!

In place of going home, Denis went to the Liberal Club, which he found to be in a state of great excitement. Stones had been thrown through the windows, and the members were organizing a gang to go fight the blues who had done it. He proffered his fists for the expedition, and they were amazed but delighted. He had need of a brawl, for the pleasures that he had permitted himself thus far were too paltry to satisfy his thirst for the absolute.

About ten o'clock, he came home with his hair all dishevelled and his face badly bruised. Joseph at the moment was engaged in the circumspect operation of winding the clock and Flora, as she combed out her frizzled hair, was scolding him for setting it twenty minutes fast—she could not bear having to wait for the radio serials. As Denis came in, they were silent. Only the young ones upstairs went on with their bedtime stories. To save his face, he picked up a copy of Bourget's *Cruel Enigma*, which was his mother's favourite reading, and started turning the pages. She guffawed, and her high-pitched laugh had a more metallic ring than usual.

"Better be careful with that," she said, "if you want to keep it clean so you can make a present of it."

He closed the book and began whistling. It was better to keep still and not get into any argument. But Germaine would pay for this. Flora's face reddened under the unspoken insult.

"You little idiot, you're starting young, spending your money on good-for-nothing creatures."

Joseph, who had never given any presents to young women, did not like the trend of the conversation, his wife having often enough reminded him of Noré's generosity when he had kept company with her. He now came forward, his shoulders stooped and in his bare feet, holding the clock in one hand like a lantern and his trousers in the other hand. There was a tired crease on his forehead.

"That's enough!" he said. "Give me the two dollars you put away for the ham."

Flora shook her hair out impatiently. Lifting the oilcloth on the third shelf, she felt about for a few moments. Her hands grew feverish, and with a bound she was on a chair, her eyes prying everywhere. "It's gone!" Pausing, she turned slowly toward Denis. It was all too obvious. He was beginning to understand and was preparing his defence.

"You're lucky to have so much money to be making presents to chippies."

"It was money that I saved up."

"You lie, spendthrift that you are. It's impossible." The truth was there, staring her in the face. Her voice held a note of victory. "What were you doing in the cupboard last night?"

Humiliated at having to flounder about in this fashion, he stammered something about her giving the young one an undeserved whipping, as it was he, Denis, who had been into the tarts. His mother laughed loudly.

"A fine story! It was the young one, all right, who ate the tart. The toothprints were tiny ones." She heaved an indignant sight. "Give me back my money, you thief!"

His father was bearing down upon him threateningly. Joseph had laid his clock down on the sewing machine. It was inevitable! The usual kitchen homily, the drama of Gaston, the theft of Bobotte—words! words! Letting go the back of his chair which he had been gripping convulsively, Denis stepped aside to avoid his father. "I didn't do it, I swear! Papa, you believe me, don't you?"

Nonplussed and emotionally stirred, Joseph nodded his head by way of assent. For the first time, the man in his son was speaking to him. Denis fled to his room as Flora's voice made the dishes rattle. She was overwhelming Joseph with her contempt, accusing him of weakness. Noré drank, yes, but he had some character, And he had worked up to be a gendarme!

As she looked in on Denis, who shut his eyes, she let fly a parting shot: "Tomorrow, I'm going to do my duty as a mother!"

There was little sleep for the older ones in the house that night.

Denis was very much worried as he left for the office the next morning. Sensitive souls are capable of creating sorrows out of trifles, and this is an aptitude that is not impaired by a life made up of one trial after another. The expressionless look on his mother's face, her calm manner as she served him his breakfast, told him nothing that boded any good. In this he was not wrong, for Flora was planning to do a terrible thing. By force of auto-suggestion with regard to her duty of keeping her son pure, she had reached the point where she would have looked upon herself as derelict if she failed to carry out her plan. There was no question of any further hesitation. Her jealousy of Lise had blinded her judgement to such an extent that her rage could no longer remain confined within the four walls of a kitchen.

At all costs, she must get him away from this stranger whose sin consisted in being loved by Denis, a Denis who never kissed his own mother. The vague odour of lust and spiritual defilement which she had sensed in the relations of the young couple had now, as a result of her son's supposed theft, become the next thing to fornication. It had not gone quite as far as that, however. Her son! Her reading of Bourget's *Cruel Enigma*, picked up on Bédarovitch's second-hand counter (he did a small business in books, also), no doubt had something to do with the resolution she had just formed. No, she, Flora Boucher, daughter of the strong-minded Alphonse, would not be like that French mother who did nothing but weep when she saw her son abandon her for a mistress.

Half an hour after Denis had left, her indignation masked by the fitting attitude of a mother who goes to demand the recognition of her rights, she stepped out into the street with an imposing air. To her great surprise, she saw the housewives of the neighbourhood prattling around the Colins' door. Madame Chaton called to her.

"What do you think, Flora, the Latruches are trying to get their saint to cure young Colin's knee, but it doesn't work; he's like St Anne, who prefers to heal the Americans."

Flora had to resist her desire to go in the house, open her book, and rout the demoiselles Latruche. One could hear the moans and oaths of the sick lad, who felt that he must be incurable, seeing that they were having recourse to the saints. Madame Pritontin now joined them. She was out of breath.

"The healer is on the way. She's more dependable than saints that have not been canonized."

"There's no need of a healer," Flora broke in; "I have my book." This, she felt, was a sufficient answer to Madame Pritontin, who was eaten up with jealousy over the sensation caused by the Latruches. If only the healer could humiliate them! Flora crossed the street, paying no attention to the children who wanted to know where she was going. Her nervous fist shook the door of the Lévesque home as she knocked. Her bosom stiffened, her heart was hammering with excitement, but each rap that she gave strengthened her conviction. Germaine came to open the door.

"Get her for me!" was all Flora said.

Stupefied, Germaine did not ask any questions but disappeared into the kitchen. A moment later, Lise came out. She seemed happy.

"Dear Madame Boucher," she said, "do come in and sit down. Why, how young you look today!"

Flora clenched her fists to keep her resolution firm. She had pictured Lise as a haughty being, on the defensive, and she was disconcerted. There was a moment's silence as she tried to think of all the grievances she had against the girl; there had been so many of them the night before. Lise's hypocrisy, that studied smile of one with a superior education. Treacherous, that was what she was! A mother's heart was not to be bought off by pretty words.

"Don't try to put anything over on me." The light seemed to go out of her bright eyes, then she raised her head and stuck it out a little. Lise, very pale, had taken a step backward. Flora raised her voice. "You needn't contradict me. My son gave you a couple of books as a present."

Pained beyond words, Lise nodded. The visitor was almost shouting now, for she was afraid of not being able to go on. "He stole the money to buy them." Flora sank down upon a chair, choking with sobs. She was more ashamed for herself than for her Denis. Her glance was an imploring one : she was begging Lise to protest that Denis was the most honest lad in the world.

"Stole—stole—I don't understand." Utterly bewildered, Lise was staring at the curé's picture. Everything about her appeared to be sinking out of sight : reality, happiness, the very meaning of words. The volumes upon the table next held her fascinated gaze. Never had she known such distress as this, such sorrow. Life, the awful truth of things, her lost happiness— This woman could not be telling a lie, being his mother. If she could only cry out, drown it all with the sound of her voice or with tears. Her bosom heaved with her rapid breathing, but no sound came. With a trembling hand she picked up the volumes and handed them to Flora. "How could you ! My God ! My God !"

Flora took them, scarcely knowing what she was doing. Words of consolation and apology were on the tip of her tongue in place of the insults she had so carefully prepared. She was assailed by an uncertainty of Denis' guilt such as she had not foreseen.

"Go !" said Lise in a faint voice, "please go !"

As Flora left the house, the sun's heat made her all the more conscious of her tears. Alone in the parlour, Lise ran her hand over the cushions, as if asking them to share her grief. A great despair too often finds nothing upon which to lean. Shaken by sobs, she huddled on the divan. A piercing scream would have been a deliverance; the silence was unbearable. For unlike cries of joy, moans were lost in the stillness. Only her abundant tears told of a happiness that had crumbled, taking with it each day's modest store of memories. Denis a thief ! Was the only being she had ever loved one in whom she could not believe? No, it was all a horrible nightmare. Denis would come and she would throw herself at his knees and beg him to deny it, to explain. But he would not say anything because of his mother. She started at sight of the mirror. The memory of what he had done the night before came over her like a burn. Was that the real Denis? His seeming rudeness, his inexplicable actions—was it all no more than a mask to hide his baseness?

Her sorrow was so real that it did not occur to her to put it down in her diary. She went up to her room like an automaton, and it was all Germaine could do to keep from telling her the truth, that they did not make many lads like Denis. But did anyone console her, Germaine, when she was suffering? And Lise would not have permitted any intrusion upon her pain.

The false solicitude of doctors is annoying in the extreme. This was true of Jean as he struggled impotently against that species of enemy, the amateur healer. His curses were audible from the street, and Barloute, ashamed of his behaviour, could be heard begging him to be quiet. His swollen knee was by now a matter of common knowledge throughout the parish. It was a question as to who would succeed in imposing his own favourite remedy. Nothing interested the Mulots like dislocated members, or fractures, that afforded them a chance to reminisce concerning the exploits of famous bonesetters and the lawsuits that were brought by the doctors, who could do nothing, against these empiric geniuses, suits that were invariably lost. The Soyeux, on the other hand, were more inclined to put their trust in miracles.

The Latruche sisters could not let pass this opportunity of establishing their position, for the lustre of their apostolate had been tarnished by certain stories which Pritontin was tell-telling, stories that reflected on the purity of their motives. And here at last was a swollen knee that was apparently incurable. They had accordingly hastened to the Colins with photographs of their saint that had been duly blessed. Beset from all sides, Barloute did not know what to do. She felt an embarrassed respect for these withered old virgins who had evolved into miracle-workers, and found it hard to resist them. For this reason, she urged her son to be satisfied with the help of Heaven, since Tit-Blanc had refused him that of a doctor.

Seeming not to hear Jean's protests, Cécile and Peuplière thereupon began bustling about with the zeal of midwives as they proceeded to heat the flannel cloth that would press the holy image against the affected joint. The kitchen was filled with benevolent acolytes, enthusiastic over the possibility of witnessing a miracle free of charge. What a marvellous opportunity for the spinsters to regain their lost prestige! For some time now, wicked tongues, inspired by the envious Madame Pritontin, had been insinuating that the "saint," who had lived in this parish, had been neglecting his old acquaintances and that thoroughly scornful of his own noble race, he preferred to treat the Anglo-Saxons. Just go take a look at the Latruches' showcase; it was overflowing with the votive offerings of the English. While Cécile and Peuplière inside the house held a heated discussion as to which of the two should place the image upon the sick lad's knee—perhaps it would be better to have recourse to a married woman?—the skeptical housewives out in the street, disgruntled because they had not been admitted to see the show, were openly predicting that the photograph would not prove efficacious. They were entirely too hardened to believe in any saint who had come from the belly of a Soyeuse. Long live the healers!

"There she is now! Good day, Madame Trousseau." And Madame Pritontin ran forward to greet the woman, whom she had invited. The healer strode forward majestically, escorted by Grandfather Pitou, who had gone to the streetcar stop to meet her. Highly respected by reason of her many amazing cures in the past, she haughtily shook hands with the women at the door, who asked her for her address in case there should be a fracture or a cancer in the family. It was with admiration and something akin to veneration that the Mulotes touched the dress of this being who, pretending to possess nothing more than supraterrestrial powers (not those of a saint), represented a form of the supernatural that was to be preferred to the other kind which was so hard on poor devils.

When one let one's gaze travel up Madame Trousseau's tall, dried-up frame, one had the impression of climbing a ladder. Her youthful attributes, to which she had clung too long, appeared to have been ossified. As a result she bristled with protuberances held in place by long, vertical slats, and one was especially conscious of her arms, her legs, her sprawling feet, her prominent ribs, her mouth. And when she assumed the air of a physician and made a prognosis, she drew up her extremely wide lips in a little pucker by way of underlining the importance of what she said. What an enemy for the Latruches to combat! The incantations and poultices that had won her a reputation inspired her with a dynamic self-confidence which would surely prove annihilating for the old maids, whose inferiority was evident from the fact that they had need of a good-looking and pious young man who had passed to the great beyond.

With Madame Chaton, Madame Langevin, and old man Pitou leading the way, the healer burst into the patient's room, where the spinsters, aided by Barloute and some impatient neighbour women, were endeavouring to persuade Jean to let them apply the saint's image to his knee. He was stubbornly refusing.

Looking everyone over, Madame Trousseau broke the embarrassed silence with her shrill, authoritative voice: "Where is that knee they're telling me about?"

It was the spinsters' turn to put on a haughty air. "The saint," they informed her, "has undertaken the cure. Is it any of your business?"

Madame Chaton puffed out her bosom. It was she who had the honour of introducing the eminent visitor. Madame Trousseau looked more like a human ladder than ever as she waited for apologies. "I may tell you," said Madame Chaton, "that this is Pulchérie Trousseau, the one who cured Madame Leitec's cancer."

"Yes, a backyard sorceress. You are sinning against the first commandment of God." Peuplière had come forward, trembling with anger.

The healer stared back at her. "So the old maids are jealous of my powers? Just watch me!" Before Jean could prevent it, she had thrown back the covers. Taking the knee in her bony hands, she examined it, appeared to be deciding what it was worth. "Fifteen dollars if I cure him, nothing if I don't."

Cécile Latruche, as always, was shocked by this. "And we do it for nothing."

The Trousseau ladder seemed to bend in the middle. Madame laughed hilariously. "It's the first time," she declared, "that I ever knew Heaven not to charge anything."

Despite his tears, Jean had to laugh along with the others present. White with rage, the demoiselles Latruche made their exit, flinging a hateful glance at the grief-stricken Barloute as they did so. Encouraged by her success, Madame Trousseau gave Tit-Blanc no time to consider her offer, for he did not feel that it was worth fifteen dollars to cure his son.

"If those women hadn't gone," the healer remarked, "I don't think my gift would have worked. By the way, did you ever see my birthmark? It's a strawberry." The enthusiastic spectators clasped their hands and old man Pitou clucked his tongue and spilled the tobacco from his pipe. Tit-Blanc said nothing; he was suspicious. Solemnly Madame Trousseau raised her skirt and took down her stocking in the manner of a travelling salesman displaying his wares. A none too clean and yellowish thigh appeared in all its unalluring nudity, marked by a sort of shrivelled brown excrescence which Pulchérie at the age of twenty had called her "strawberry." Grandfather Pitou put his nose down close to it and nodded his head approvingly. That had been a very pretty leg in its day. Madame Chaton changed the subject.

"They tell me," she observed, "that you are the seventh daughter of a seventh daughter?"

"Yes, Madame What's-Your-Name. When Monsieur le Curé learned of it, he granted me the right to heal those diseases that the good Lord wanted me to heal. You can imagine how the doctors like that. But don't say anything about my coming here. They're jealous, you know."

"The priests nowadays are not such good sports," put in Tit-Blanc, skeptically. "They don't do that."

"There are some," Madame Trousseau went on, "who will try to tell you that there are saints today as in the olden times, but it doesn't happen any more. Not with all the theatres and silk stockings!" She was rambling on, in an effort to get Tit-Blanc to forget his doubts and bring him to believe that he had given his consent. She began laying out her herbs and her book of magic as the others in the room looked on with awe. As the healer cautiously went over to Jean, old Pitou drew his stool close to the bed as if he were watching a cockfight. With his one good leg the angry, fever-ridden patient prepared to defend himself.

"My son, you must let me do it. It's for your own good."

"I want a doctor! Get out! Get out! Denis! Denis!" he was gasping and frothing at the mouth.

"Jean! Be a good boy, please do!" Barloute scolded him.

There was a knock at the door. "Another Jewish peddler!" exclaimed Tit-Blanc angrily. "Ah, it's you, Dr Boutet?"

"How are you, Tit-Blanc? Someone here not feeling so well? Is it your wife, you rascal, you?" Smiling broadly, the young doctor explained that the Latruche sisters were paying for the call. He barely had a glimpse of a tall creature who looked like a bit of scaffolding and who fled in panic at his approach, her hat down over her eyes. The spinsters' sarcastic laugh could be heard from outside.

"It's my boy, Doctor," said Tit-Blanc, reassured. "He has a swollen knee."

"Where is the patient? Let me have a look at him." And the jovial young physician went over to the bed.

"A doctor!" cried Jean. "Thank God."

The medical man was interested and asked to be left alone

238

with the lad. Old man Pitou went out grumbling. A doctor: that meant death and ruination.

The Mulots needed the supernatural more than they did science. There was one man in St Joseph's parish who knew that better than anyone else, and that was Monsieur le Curé.

"IT'S quite a large knee," said Jean.

He had eagerly thrown back the covers and lifted his leg, for he would soon be cured now. This man for whom he had waited so long conferred upon his illness a sort of Legion of Honour decoration, and the smile that flitted about the sick lad's mouth told of the patience with which he had borne a pain which this wonder-working visitor speedily would vanquish. The doctor was carefully feeling the joint.

"An accident?"

"A small one. I had a fall while stealing plums last year. It swelled up and stayed that way. I haven't limped with it too much, you know. Last winter I put bacon rind on it, but I got tired of it. They're stupid, those old grandmother's remedies."

The doctor shook his head thoughtfully. "That goes back farther than yesterday. How long have you been in bed?"

"Since last Saturday. But that's something else again. I caught cold in it. I was out with a woman, you know" (here he put on a knowing air), "down at the beach. I got too hot, and when I came home I had chills and started sweating and coughing. Since then, I don't feel well except in bed. Last night I felt a lot better, but I'm still kind of drowsy." He laughed. "The main thing is my knee. It began to burn and turned red and then blue. I like a lot of colour."

He well might make light of something which this marvellous man would cause to vanish with a mere definition. Dr Boutet closed the patient's mouth with a thermometer and once more ran a skilled hand over the affected joint, which was bluish in hue and smooth to the touch. "What I was afraid of," he muttered. "There's an abscess there."

Jean watched him, barely able to conceal his impatience for a conclusion to be reached, as it would happen in a book. "I never saw many of those," he said, chewing on the thermometer. The doctor made him be still, waited a moment more, and took the thermometer out. The reading was 102! Jean was disconcerted. "I was angry a while ago and got myself heated up. Wait a moment and it will go back to normal."

The physician was not listening to him. "Do you have plenty of nerve?" he asked, looking him in the eye.

Jean puffed out his chest. "You don't ask that of the lads of St Sauveur."

As he went to open his medicine case, the doctor caught sight of Lise's flowers on the bureau (formerly a buffet) and bent over to smell them. He was surprised to encounter such luxury at the Colins'.

"The women don't desert you for a little thing like this," said Jean, with a show of unconcern. The young medical man wondered if she was a pretty girl. Would she come, perhaps, while he was there? Taking out a syringe, he adjusted a needle. The patient watched him anxiously.

With sinister mien, Dr Boutet came toward him. "You're lucky we don't have to lance it every day."

"Isn't there anything else you can do? That's expensive and we're not rich." Jean's tone was that of one who hopes the dentist is not in.

"It won't cost you anything. We'll call it a sample and let it go at that. Yours is the first case of the sort that I've met with."

Jean was beginning to have his doubts now; but if he had lost confidence in medical science, there was a compensation in knowing that he was suffering from an exclusive malady. This gave him a superior feeling, for pride may lodge in the microbe as well as in the vitamin. Having made his preparations and drawn on his rubber gloves, Dr Boutet inserted the needle into the abscess, very gently, without any shock. The skin was not very resistant and the incision was made quite easily. The syringe began to fill with a bright yellow liquid streaked with blood. Jean gazed in stupefaction at his knee, now deflated like a punctured balloon. The cure was a matter for another day, for he was suffering a pain which it seemed to him would never end.

The more pus came out of his knee the more he felt an inexplicable anguish creeping over him. His eyes came to rest in turn upon the physician's wrinkled forehead, the electric light globe, the violet-hued lampshade, his shoes with their twisted laces lying on the floor, Madame Boucher's big book on the dresser. All these objects suddenly took on a different aspect; they were quiet and subdued, as if in expectation of a catastrophe. They stared him in the face and he, terrified, did his best to master his fear. And then, with regard both to the pain in his heart and the pain in his body, everything suddenly became very clear, and no matter which way he turned his head he found neither hopes nor regrets but only a great clear-seeing lassitude, born of his anguish. Anything that he chose might happen—anything but death. That was something that went on forever, being eternally renewed, like a real sorrow. It is a weariness of joy, of pleasure, that suggests this exit which one never accepts.

He thought of the verses Denis had composed in order to compare them with those of his father:

> A naked vagabond beside the road,
> I sit and watch my happiness go by,
> Laughing at laughter and at those who cry,
> Without regret and with no hope for goad.

The doctor hermetically sealed the test tube and took off his gloves. "Any tuberculosis in your family?" He was certainly curious, wasn't he?

"Nobody in our family spits."

"Is Tit-Blanc your real father?"

"What makes you think he isn't?"

"Do you go out with the girls often? It's sexual relations I'm talking about, you young rascal." He knew the reputation of the lads of St Sauveur. Jean studied him suspiciously. Was the doctor making fun of him? Did he, Colin, look like a fellow of that sort? He gave a bantering laugh, for he did not wish to appear chaste in the presence of that man who had seen many things in hospitals.

"Oh, I have my little weaknesses, but not very often."

The doctor was still thoughtful as he prepared to leave. Going out into the kitchen, he had a talk with Barloute, punctuated with prolonged exclamations on her part, after which he returned to bid the patient good-bye. "I'll be seeing you as soon as I have the result of the analysis. Your mother will wrap your knee in a cloth soaked in alcohol."

He had already lifted the drapes. Jean would have liked to detain him. He did not as yet know the name of this disease which had to be passed upon in the laboratory. And then, too, why had the physician lost his jocular manner?

"Is it serious, Doctor?"

The man who was to have worked wonders hesitated as he thought of the ignorance of the Mulots. "It's a case of arthritis. But we'll get all that on the report."

Tit-Blanc escorted him to the door, then tiptoed back into the room as if the visit of this Aesculapius had put the seal of importance upon his son's affliction. Jean stuck out his leg triumphantly. "I have an abscess. Look." They would not accuse him of putting it on any more. He had a good reason for staying in bed. Tit-Blanc nodded his head and touched the knee with a stubby forefinger. This lad of his certainly caught some funny diseases.

Standing in the half-open street door, Féda was telling her women friends how they were going to analyse her son. Meanwhile, she sent for a half-pint of kerosene at the grocer's as alcohol cost too much. "My husband would rather make it beer." She was very much upset by what Dr Boutet had told her. Something was hovering over Jean. Going back into the bedroom, she began looking for bits of cloth to make bandages.

"Mother Trousseau shouldn't have run away like that. They want to experiment on you."

"It doesn't cost anything, Mama. He's so nice, and conscientious too. Papa, he even spoke of you. He wanted to know if you were my real father."

Tit-Blanc gave Barloute a furious glance and she left the room. He started pacing the floor. They had got mixed up with the doctors now and they would have to see it through. It drove him to despair as he computed the money he would lose on account of his son.

As for Jean himself, all he could do was think of Lise and wait for the doctor's second visit. With nothing else to occupy them, his eyes fell on Madame Boucher's oracle. Before looking up the definition of arthritis, he amused himself by reading all the details of childbirth and expended his sympathy on the unfortunate paralytics—how he pitied them! Coming at last to that gem among diseases which takes on aspects of beauty in the course of its cure, he spread open the book and assumed a comfortable posture. He expected to encounter big words and was surprised to find that he recognized at first reading the symptoms of his own trouble: pain in the knee. Calmly he read the lines, feeling sure that he would arrive at a conclusion that would bring him some consolation; but his eyes grew large as he came to the sentence: "Arthritis may be of tubercular origin." He thought it over for a moment, then feverishly read it again.

In a flash, he could see the doctor's anxious forehead, could hear him asking: "Is Tit-Blanc your real father?" he felt an anguish that seemed to grip him in the abdomen, his head was burning up, his mouth was thick. Why had the physician's manner been so grave? The lad now understood the uneasy sensation that had come over him while the abscess was being lanced. Reading the lines again and again, he began trembling. Did arthritis mean that an amputation was necessary or that he would be crippled for years and would perhaps end as a chronic invalid? He was conscious of a cold sweat that extended to the roots of his hair. Lise! Gone for him was all physical beauty. It was terrible to learn of such a fate while all the others went on living, wholly unconcerned, full of plans for the future. It appeared impossible that he should have stumbled upon the truth, the awful truth, in so ridiculous a manner that had in it so little of the spectacular. It had been by mere chance. It was like reading his own obituary in the newspaper, next to the comic strip. Tit-Blanc was growing impatient.

"Still have your nose in a book, eh? Are you doing it on purpose so you can lie there half dead? You'd better stop reading stories and playing sick; you'd better get well and get back to your job, for there are plenty of others after it."

These words for Jean were like insults that fall on the ears of a dying man. He was trembling. What was he to do? Release the fear inside him by screaming? Barloute would tell him to be still, for she was listening to the protagonists of her radio serial. He threw back the covers, made a quick movement in an effort to raise his knee. The pain was as if his leg were being sawed in two. It confirmed his apprehensions. The book had not lied. There was nothing for it but to go on to the goal that fate had set him : a failure to the day of his death.

Sinking back on the bed, he gave a deep sigh as he wiped away the perspiration. It had always been in suffering, never in happiness, that he had found the truth. Having regained his composure, he gazed down into the depths, too imbued with a feeling of his own littleness to experience any sense of dizziness. Must he, then, skip his youth and begin living again at thirty-five, a worn-out being? And he had scarcely been able to wait until he was twenty! He made up his mind that he would not struggle, would not combat the inevitable. What energy he had should be employed in bringing himself to accept his fate intelligently.

With a haggard face, he followed in his mind the swaying footsteps of that drunkard, his father. He glanced at his own shoes on the floor. A dead man's shoes, that was what they were, yet they did not dare throw them into the fire. What were they waiting for, those shoes? What was his father waiting for? Why could they not tactfully retire and leave him to his grief? They did not understand that everything about him was crumbling, that his youth had come to an end. An invalid.

A cripple. He had thought that was the lot of a few unfortunate strangers whom he had met by chance, from time to time, going along on crutches, to whom he had turned an indifferent face while according them his deep and silent sympathy. But he, Jean! He now would be the unfortunate whom others would pity out of the corner of their eyes. He had a feeling of revulsion as he heard the exclamations—he could hear them already—of the flirtatious young women : "What a shame! And he's good-looking, too." He could see himself during those first years struggling against the pious insistence of those who went in for pilgrimages and who would try to get him to visit all the shrines in the province. He would come to be a stubborn old man, and people would shake their heads and say that he had been punished for his lack of faith.

With a nervous movement of his hand he strove to drive away these obsessions that hovered about him like huge insects. Colin the cripple, Colin who went on crutches, that was who he would be from now on. And what of his love for Lise? His infirmity would be a formidable excuse for self-flagellation in this regard. For all hope had gone with physical comeliness. Even his trade of worm vendor would be beyond his capabilities. And to think that only last week he had shown himself so much better a swimmer than Denis. On that day he had dreamed of becoming an athlete, of devoting all his energies toward physical perfection, since he had failed to make the best of his school years. It was all over now. He was muttering to himself, there was a taste of tears in his mouth, and his eyes glowed with desperation and with a challenge : "I'd like to see you in my place, Denis my friend. Just try to raise an ideal on these ruins!"

He grew calm once more, ashamed of the jealousy that had taken possession of him. Instead of envying the fate of others, it was better to find the elements of greatness in one's own destiny. What a task! Resignation is not something that is suited to the first hours of a great sorrow. What one does at first is to struggle with all the strength at his command against the inevitable; it is only later, when he is prostrate with weariness, that he will tell himself—if he is wise—that there is nothing to do but accept his lot. For the present, Jean was in the stage of revolt. His gaze roamed impatiently around the shabby room, over the rose-coloured wallpaper with its dying flowers that still could never droop, the yellow ceiling, the filthy curtains that hung limply over the window ledge, his low bed with the same coverings always, his father conscientiously filling his pipe.

There was the crucifix. He had not noticed it since he became ill. God only knows what impulse toward faith had led him to fix his attention on those two bits of spruce wood with spider webs clinging to them at the corners. What an idea, that of getting the crucified Christ to cure him! He would not be so mean of spirit as to undertake it. To surprise the Christ by a loving acceptance of Him was more befitting to his pride. Nor would he have recourse to those heavenly subordinates and obtain from a saint a cure that would later bring an unpleasant feeling of compulsion toward Christ Himself. For he did not care to mortgage his entire life with a false virtue and ridiculous obligations. A man saved by a miracle is no longer the free man that God created.

Jean was astonished by these weird reflections but realized that they meant for him a rebirth of hope. It was with a kind of avidity that he once more fell to studying Madame Boucher's oracle. "This disease is caused by a lymphatic condition and scrofula." A cross reference. Under the word "scrofula" he learned that this meant a complete weakening of the organism, laying it open to all sorts of infections. The writer went on to describe the impaired constitution that resulted. His own, Jean felt, was deplorably weak. There was a mist in front of his eyes; he could scarcely see the page. "In the case of the scrofulous, the slightest fall—upon the knee, for example—may lead to arthritis." There was no need for the doctor to come back. It was stupid not to have known that he was but a bit of driftwood ready to be swallowed up in a sea of microbes.

He went on with his reading. His understanding sharpened by illness, he found that he was able to recognize as friends scientific terms that he had never mastered; they were perfectly clear to him now, in his pain. "The origin of scrofula is often to be found in the parents, in consanguineous marriages, syphilis, and alcoholism; and in the case of the patient himself, faulty diet and overwork at too early an age may be contributing factors." At last the veil had been torn aside completely. In his grief and wrath he began looking about for those to blame. He understood now why it was they called his mother Barloute. "Alcoholism, overwork at too early an age." The temptation to hate was strong within him; for everything that he knew of beauty, health, and love had forsaken him. With big eyes and a deeply furrowed brow, he gazed at his father. The guilty one. It occurred to Jean that he might have been the son of another man and another woman, healthy beings who would have bequeathed him sinewy and nimble legs and knees as flexible as reeds. He would then have spent the whole of his youth devouring knowledge as one does a dessert; and today, handsome, agile, diploma in hand, he would have been able to enter upon his man's life with a cry of victory on his lips, and in his joy Lise would have been there for him to pluck like a flower. But "scrofulous"! He shook himself to free the bedclothes from his feverish body.

As Tit-Blanc stared back at his son, he had the impression that everything about the lad was gesticulating, everything except those eyes of his.

"You needn't eat me alive," he said. "There's nothing I can do about it. It's not my fault. You'll be up and around yet, out playing games. Have you thought of all the money I'm losing? Ten dollars! And the worms that you had begun to collect again are all dead and dried."

By way of keeping his sorrow intact, Jean did not cry out. It was better not to say anything, not to indulge in any violent recriminations as an outlet for his despair. Down deep inside him there would be left, afterwards, only the stale dregs of a chronic, humdrum sorrow. Burying himself beneath the covers, he wet the mattress with his scalding tears, and rubbed his cheeks spasmodically from time to time.

Tit-Blanc noticed the book which had been left lying open. With an anxious frown, spelling the words out with difficulty, he began hunting for the sentences which had so disturbed his son.

It is from those who suffer that our best consolations come. Lise could bear it no longer. Her room was stifling her. She must know. Hastening to Jean's house, she knocked on the door. He would tell her the truth, would help her, through his faith as a friend, in rebuilding a greater Denis.

"I have come for news of your son, Madame."

Féda felt a thrill of pride. It was like the movies. ". . . your son, Madame . . ." And the doctor had been there. What a day! Her son's illness was conferring distinction upon the family. "The doctor is making an analysis, but I'm the one who puts on the bandages."

The house was saturated with the odour of kerosene. Lise was not taken aback by this, for she was impervious to astonishment. Jean's sickness no longer affected her sensibilities. Barloute showed her into the bedroom and nodded her head vigorously at Tit-Blanc to indicate that he should leave.

The girl remained standing in the middle of the floor, undecided. "Jean!"

He slowly emerged from under the covers and then, in embarrassment, straightened himself out. The least he could do was to look like a man lying down. He stammered, brushed back his hair, dried his eyelids. "My eyes are red," he explained. "The light tires them."

Unable to restrain her tears, she knelt beside the bed, her pleading face outstretched to him. "Jean, I am in such trouble. I need you."

He was petrified with hope. He would never have had the strength to take her in his arms, nor could his lips have lulled her little-girl's grief with wheedling words. For it must be some passing sorrow, nothing to compare with his own deep woe. But the miracle was that she had come to confide in him. He gazed at her, too stupefied for words, saw her bite her trembling lips, was aware of a little white hand upon the doubtful whiteness of the sheets. He did not seize that hand, did not cover it with his tears and kisses. Was it possible that she loved him just a little? It is our human frailty that endows our hopes with an element of madness. He did not dare interrupt her sobbing, for he dreaded hearing her confess that she knew all about his coming invalidism.

"I—I don't count," he said, "so long as you are happy. Tell me—"

"You are my best friend, aren't you? There was one day when you were willing to die for me."

He nodded his head as hard as he could, for his throat was too parched to emit any sound, despite the cries of love that tingled in his blood. Awkwardly, he put out his hand, then took it back in confusion. She would notice how feverish it was. It was a rough hand, like his heart. It was better for her to remain in ignorance of both. But she had seized his wrist.

"It is you who can tell me if Denis' character, his nobleness is beyond question. I must know. Do not spare me."

"I don't want to go on living, I don't want to go on living." His mind repeated the words coldly, like a mathematical formula. It was as if the violent blow just dealt him had driven him mad. Indignation blinded him for an instant. Denis, Denis, always Denis, the terrible leitmotiv that had heralded the reappearance of misfortune at decisive moments of his life. Denis' "nobleness." A fine thing! He did his best to recall the acts of treachery of which his friend had been guilty, but in vain. For Lise, weeping there, he could only remember the admirable things.

"Ah! Denis?" he murmured, after he had buried his disap-

248

pointment with a sigh. His voice was tired, for grief had embedded itself in his all too susceptible soul. "Denis?" he repeated. "His waywardness is all put on; he's acting a part."

"I was sure of it. Oh, Jean, what a darling you are." Almost playfully, she went on to tell him of Madame Boucher's call. What an unfortunate mistake. But she was wholly forgiven. Jean meanwhile was thinking distractedly of the theft of the hen, the missing milk jars. In order to keep Lise happy, to keep her from perceiving the conflict within him, he did not mention his doubts, since it seemed that sorrow was the only thing that could bring the two of them together, and that was something he did not want.

"I'll wager you have your troubles, too. You needn't tell me you don't, for my eyes, I am sure, do not deceive me. Tell me, has the doctor been here?"

He was frightened. Did she mean to go into all the details about microbes and all the rest and lay bare his shame with her sympathy? That was the disadvantage of being a mediocrity: one had to suffer in order to interest other people. He pointed to the objects in the room and sank his fist into his pillow. Astonished at this, with that delicate gesture that only women know she put the rebellious curl on his forehead back in place.

"I love you very much, you know that, Jean dear."

He rested his burning temple against her wrist. The door opened just then and Tit-Blanc came in. He could restrain himself no longer but must take advantage of the opportunity to talk to a pretty girl. Flora's voluminous manual afforded him an excuse.

"I must be going to dinner," Lise said. Out of a sense of modesty, she did not take Jean's hand in the presence of his father. Tit-Blanc's face caused her to loathe this house when it was not illuminated with the light of Jean's spirit. She fled precipitately.

Tit-Blanc followed her with a hostile gaze as she disappeared behind the drapes. That was it, they had a contempt for the old drunkard; it was written down in the book there. Had she and his son been talking about him? With the book in hand, he came over to Jean and pointed to the word "scrofula." He vaguely understood what it meant and anger rose in him at those who went looking for causes, at scientists and the makers of books. His failure to grasp it all, completely, made him as impatient as would an alcoholic thirst. He proceeded to indicate those words that seemed to him mysterious.

"You're so well educated," he said bluntly. "What does 'premature employment' mean?"

Jean huddled back on the bed in an attitude of refusal. Tit-Blanc's eyes were bloodshot, his fists clenched. He was sure of the truth now.

"Tell me or I'll break your jaw."

"Go ahead and break it." Jean shut his eyes, waited for the blow, gladly. This, coming from his father, would be a pleasure to one floundering in the depths. Tit-Blanc turned pale, the tobacco juice from his pipe dribbling down over his long beard. "The sons-of-bitches, the sons-of-bitches." There was almost a note of entreaty in his voice. "Tell me, 'John,' it's not true, is it? What you read in books is always made up?"

"Sure, Papa, it's always made up." Jean was not being ironical. Tit-Blanc slowly left the room, turning his head a number of times to make sure of the look on his son's face.

Denis' worries disappeared more and more as the sun mounted toward the zenith. It was with a jaunty step that he returned to his own parish without the least suspicion of what had happened that morning. Jean was going to get well, would no longer be a rival. With a little cleverness, it would be easy to turn Jean's feeling for Lise into a jest and to make him believe it. Love now appeared to Denis under a novel aspect. On Sunday, he would go out bicycle riding with Lise. They would stretch out together for a long time on the green grass. There would not be a single mosquito to kill. But kisses and kisses. How they would laugh at the pangs of adolescence. He was happy over this new formula, adapted to his own strange temperament. The chief thing was not to look upon love any longer as a sentimental prelude to marriage, but rather as a splendid adventure broken off at the very peak of happiness by an ever-lasting separation. He would perhaps drop out of sight, in an-other city. They would never write. But these were dreams—

It was with an unfeigned interest that he listened to the Abbé Trinchu as that priest set forth the objectives of the newly formed St John the Baptist section at St Joseph's. He even let it be understood that he would consent to be the secretary. Then he ran into the conservatives' gang, victims of last night's attack in which he had taken a violent part, and greeted them in friendly fashion. With an even, rhythmic step he walked along and was about to enter his house when the door of the Colins' house opened and Lise appeared. He must surprise her by being especially charming.

"How do you do, young lady?"

The smile on his lips suddenly froze as Lise paused a second, her breath coming fast, her eyes indignant, then turned and fled. Dumbfounded, he came near calling after her, but the cry stuck in his throat as his feet did to the sidewalk. She had come out of Jean's, alone! What were they doing, trying to make a fool of him? They were a couple of petty individuals, meant for each other. The threat that his mother had made came to mind, and he burst into the house like a gust of wind. His eyes fell on the two volumes that had been laid out on the sideboard for him to see. As he stopped short, Flora drew herself up with dignity and began rattling the dishes noisily. She needed to steel herself for what was to come. She might regret her cruelty, but she would not admit the accusation of having been unjust. That was too shameful. Denis was very pale and Flora's regret was fast becoming a plea for forgiveness. If only she could wipe away that telltale pallor as she had wiped his face when he was small.

He weighed the volumes in his hand; he was thinking, thinking terribly hard. How did those books come to be there? It must be awful, what Lise was thinking of him. A distressed smile on his lips, he came over to his mother.

"I know it was you."

"They belonged to me," said Flora, in a dull voice. "She's a conceited little thing."

Denis set his jaws to keep his teeth from chattering. It was as if he had a chill.

"I loathe you!" he spat at her.

Casting a scornful eye at his brothers, who were overwhelmed by it all, he went out the door. It was truly an astonishing family, this one. How could he be the son of that woman, the brother of those ordinary young ones? The insistent rays of an oppressive sun took him by surprise. Like Jean's illness, they seemed to be bent upon inflicting a lasting burn. It seemed to Denis that he could see the trees moving on the Cape, yet not a breath of wind was stirring. The illusion that everything about him was swaying to the rhythm of his own tumultuous thoughts tended to calm him. He drew himself up, on his guard. Despair was taking him by assault. Could he afford to let himself go under for a day at least, abandon himself humbly and without shame—could he do this and still remain a man? Was it not cowardly to slip away and refuse to come to grips with sorrow?

The sufferings of others as he had observed them with a tinge of envy in the past seemed small to him now that he held grief in his arms. Lise would despise him, would despise Denis Boucher, who so often had had to make himself appear abominable to others in order to preserve his own conception of beauty.

He sat down on the curb. What was he to do? Lise would take him for a common thief, and this after all the sacrifices he had made in saving up for that present. He was tired of sobs before they came, for they would never void his bosom of the weight of his heart. Not a tear stood on his sunburned cheek. And then, there was his mother! Would he forget everything tomorrow as he had done on other occasions when she had hurt him? He had a desire to see strangers that he might not think of his wound nor behold the reflection of his distress upon their faces. He rose abruptly. What had Lise been telling Jean, who, looking out for his own interests, would be only too glad to console her?

Crossing the street, he went into the Colins' without knocking. Tit-Blanc was anxiously examining himself in a mirror, opening his mouth, rubbing his eyes. The Tit-Blanc of the firecracker had become an old man. The bantering Mulot, the great talker, the bully who had never quite grown up had disappeared, and in his stead was a white-haired drunkard whom his son accused of being responsible for his troubles. Denis said nothing to him but quickly parted the drapes. It made him impatient to see Jean with his eyes shut.

"Don't pretend you're sleeping, you hypocrite."

Jean looked him over, licked his lips. "Another one?" he said. "Listen. Hypocrisy is a game, and I don't play games any more. Say what you have to say and beat it."

Denis was out of countenance. The atmosphere of this room, the tone of voice in which his friend had spoken made his own little family quarrel seem ridiculous. Jean was not sharing anything with Lise. All the grandiloquent wrath that he had come here to vent upon the sick lad vanished at sight of that unaffectedly tragic face. Even in sorrow simplicity won the day. Denis dropped down where Lise had been sitting a short while ago. He shrugged his shoulders.

"I've come to tell you that you are petty, both of you, getting together like that while I am down."

"So you're suffering, eh?" Jean was half smiling, as if to calm him, as he tapped Denis' elbow with his emaciated fingers. He was the superior one at last. Suffering was something that he knew by heart, whereas Denis every minute had to be erecting a fresh rampart against despair. And such a little despair it was. What a ridiculous thing, his stealing the money to get those books! Why, all that Lise and Denis had to do was take each other by the arm and go running away like the wind, forgetful of everything in their flight. Jean smiled; to be accused of treachery confirmed for him the fact that others feared him still.

"Do you remember, Denis, how you used to boast that you knew how to handle suffering? Do you see now how presumptuous you were? Just because you found your pleasures mediocre, you thought that sorrow would be insipid, too. And now you are all upset. No, true suffering is that which carries us away, not that which we carry off."

"May the devil carry *you* off with those pathetic phrases of yours. Come tell me: just how far did you betray me? She must despise me a great deal if she could bring herself to come here—"

"Shut your mouth!" Jean screamed. "So you do love her! You do love her! Own up to it. But that is the thing that saves you because it makes you more simple. You thought love meant a loss on your part; for the young always like to make things seem as complicated as possible, and they hang onto troubles of that sort. I have been thinking of all this for a year now. And so no more threats. I feel strong now that I have nothing more to receive. I know all about that affair of yours and I don't think it's serious." He was thinking of his own rotting leg which could not be cured.

Denis seized the bedclothes in his fist. "She came to tell you about it, did she?"

"Yes, and she also came to have me console her."

Denis was struggling with himself, half ashamed. "I do not like to have those I respect believe me guilty of something I have not done. Tell me," and he assumed an indifferent pose, "does she think I did it?"

"You don't need to worry about that. We succeeded in convincing ourselves that you are not a thief. And how she does love you!"

Denis' face shone with a naïve joy. "I'm glad of that! You explained to her, didn't you, that it was out of the question? Apples and milk jars yes, but money never. Put it there, old man!" He held out his arms but did not come forward. He was calm once more, with comfort to bestow on all the earth. "You're a rascal, Jean. No use to deny that you are far from indifferent to her. Have you kissed her already?" He waited for the answer with an anxious heart. Jean gave a kind of sob, a sob of anger. He seemed to be trying to get out of the bed.

"That's enough of your comedy. You needn't thank me. I did it for my own sake, because I did not want to be petty. Of course she loves you. She never thought of kissing me; she can't see me, I'm sorry to say. If I told her the truth about you, it was not out of friendship but out of selfishness. It is only by keeping silent that I am charitable to you. You needn't shrug your shoulders; for I don't like that way you have of taking others under your wing like a great man, of being condescending toward me as if the fact that you are happy should be enough for me."

He was silent for a moment, then went on bitterly. He seemed to be speaking to the lampshade.

"Now that you don't fear me any more, you're happy. I am no longer your imaginary rival, a good lad you encourage to persevere for our own amusement. The fact that I happen to be in love does not matter, but it would matter if I were to die. Yes! With me gone, what would Lise mean to you? If only you were not in the way! You don't know how good I would be to her, how I would make any sacrifice for her sake."

He was almost sobbing as he ended, but, growing calm he buried his face in the rumpled pillow. Denis stood over him.

"Jean! it is you who are talking nonsense now. I'm a bastard, that's understood, but I like you very much." He had seized the sick lad's wrist, and his voice was cajoling as Lise's had been a while ago, when she wanted to be reassured. Jean was resisting feebly, like a small boy who refuses to be comforted.

"Everything's all right," he said. "You have nothing to worry about."

"Good!" replied Denis, "we'll begin over again. I'm going out right away and polish up your bicycle for you, and on Sunday we'll all three go for a picnic. Whatever you do, get well."

Jean smiled in a strange way. They were silent as Barloute came in with the compress soaked in kerosene and laid it on Jean's knee.

"Doctor's tricks," she grumbled, "when Madame Trousseau with her gift of healing was there all the time." She hurriedly left the room, for Denis intimidated her. The latter looked at his friend.

"Yes, the doctor was here." Jean appeared to be suffering at this sharp reminder of the catastrophe. "Denis, you don't know what has happened to me, do you?" He opened his mouth as if to speak further, then let go his breath. No, he would say nothing; he would not be an object of pity to others. That would mean no end of regrets and consolations and would prevent him from accepting his lot with the proper humility.

Denis was impatient with him once more. "What now, young leading man?"

"My worms are all dead, dried up. Go ask my father." He pointed to the door.

Denis took his departure without understanding what it was all about. He wandered aimlessly in the narrow little streets. The new belfry glistened amid the shanties. Then the drone of flies effaced everything else. This interview with Jean had made a strange impression on him, as if his friend, seemingly on the way to a cure, had lured him into a deathbed atmosphere. But Jean had drained off all his pain, leaving him empty, ready for joy. No, that was not so; for Lise had not forgiven him; she still believed he had been guilty of that ignoble deed. His mounting impatience choked him. Now that he was once more pounding the well-worn sidewalks among other individuals who were upright and active, now that he was again breathing in the all too familiar atmosphere of daily life, he began to burn with a renewed sense of humiliation. He would not go home to dinner.

Behind the window curtain, his mother watched him as he walked away. She beat the youngest one for having taken Denis' place at the table. That was the way it had been with Gaston. The first month after his death, no one had been permitted to sit in his chair.

Denis was in a terrible state of mind during the days that followed. He would not look at his mother, would kick the chairs around and bang the doors as noisily as he could. Anxious to bring him back to her, Flora was exceptionally attentive to him; she pressed his suit for him every day and washed his shirts more often than usual. In the evening, when he was the only one who had not yet come home, she would leave tarts and other dainties on the table as if to tease him pleasantly. What a good sign it would be if he were to begin munching the pastries once more, imitating the bites of the little ones! In his presence, Flora remarked that she was on the trail of the thief —and she used the feminine form: *voleuse*. Sometimes she would go on to speak of what good taste in clothes Lise had and with what an air of distinction she wore them. But Denis remained insensible to all her wiles. He hung out with the gang at Bédarovitchs' and accompanied the rowdies on their expeditions, smashing windows and jaws alike. At the table the only time he had anything to say was when he hinted that the girls of the "Palais" (the segregated district) were making a big fuss over him.

When a week had passed, all his impulsions to revolt had disappeared. He was now letting sorrow have its way with him. The gang at the Liberal Club was repugnant to him, and he would go all around the block in order to avoid passing Lise's house. Truly a soul in purgatory, the gossips remarked as they saw him go by. His melancholy had become a kind of somnolent routine. The only thing that aroused any enthusiasm in him was literature, the fever of creation. He regretted that in his novel he had said nothing of the injustices done to noble hearts through false accusations of theft.

It was one Thursday morning, about nine o'clock, that this state of mind suddenly came to an end. There was a commotion at the Colins'. Indifferent at first, he thought he would pay no attention to it, but he heard a rapid step behind him and Germaine seized his arm.

"Denis! Denis! Jean's knee is rotting away. It's flowing like a fountain. He's burning up with fever. The doctor says he will have to go to the hospital at once. Jean wants to know why you don't come to see him any more."

He stopped in confusion. He felt a mad desire to weep, to run and embrace Jean, to beg his forgiveness. This threw light on those mysterious words his friend had spoken last week, about real suffering. Entrenched behind his own distress, Jean had been offering consolation to petty beings. Denis did not stir, however. His voice was distant.

"I'll be in to see him this noon. I'm late for work."

Lifting her wrist, Germaine stood in front of him, pouting. "It's my birthday today. Not a very rosy one."

"Happy birthday." He was on his guard. Already he regretted the emotion he had shown. Germaine was taking advantage of the situation to get him to wish her a happy birthday. She was still holding up her wrist.

"Do you like my watch? Robert gave it to me. It's worth fifteen dollars." She was looking for a ray of sunlight to make it sparkle.

Was she trying to rub it in on him? "If it had been me," he said, "I'd have bought you a library."

Hesitantly Germaine held out the two-dollar bill. She could not bear seeing Lise suffer. And Robert had given her such a pretty watch. But Denis had not even noticed her gesture. He had caught sight of Lise's pale face at the window and had fled. Head high, he did not look back. What if he had known that she was smiling at him, tremulous with repentance and with the desire to have him come back? Ah! how could she have doubted him for an instant? And now she had lost him forever.

IX

It was a time of catastrophes. That morning, in addition to his self-conceit, Denis lost his job. He rushed out of the office like a whirlwind and went down the street with huge strides, waving his arms and making a little speech to himself on the subject of employers. But what kind of speech would he make to his mother, who was waiting so impatiently for that raise of a dollar a week which she expected him to receive? He must break that oppressive silence between them which he had almost come to enjoy. He forced himself to imagine in advance what her recriminations would be like. He translated them into words and sentences and braced himself against the coming storm in order that, when he came to confront her, he would have no fear left and would be able to be calm.

That would teach him to correct his boss's letters to such an extent that they were no longer recognizable by the one who had dictated them. Greatly annoyed, the manager had given Denis to understand that he, the boss, had passed the age when he could permit his copy to be rewritten. To this Boucher had brazenly replied that, no matter how much money one might have, one should not miss an opportunity to learn French, even from a humble stenographer. Moreover, for seven dollars a week he did not propose to betray his native tongue.

"Out with you, my young friend. We are not schoolboys here, working for medals."

Confident of his own strength, Denis had sneered as he heard these words; but now he was beginning to be tortured with doubts. Who would have any respect for him after this? A feeling of hopeless mediocrity came over him as his feet pounded the sidewalk. He would pay dearly for having entered the business world when his mind was that of a diligent schoolboy. The word "unemployed" threw him into a sweat. He was sorry for his mother, who would have to endure the knowing smiles of the jealous Mulotes. It was too much to think that someone would have to suffer out of shame for him. Deeply distressed, he went over in his mind the aptitudes he possessed that might be turned to commercial use. The strength that had given him all his confidence ever since he left school seemed to him a nebulous thing. All that was left him was a kind of modesty. When one is out of work, one suspects that his noble sentiments, his impulses to greatness, are but a form of spite that pride reserves for itself. He felt empty; all that he had ever done was work up enthusiasms. Stenography alone remained—stenography and his biceps. He thought of the Parliament Buildings for a moment. Gus Perrault, whom he had ridiculed, would play the part of the impotent protector. Nothing to be had there. A sign in a window attracted his attention: CHEMIST WANTED.

He was no longer merely distressed, he was ashamed. What did he know of chemistry? At school all they had done had been to study the lives of great men between periods of recreation. There was also the catechism, two phrases of which he remembered: mortal sin and venial sin. Higher education had always seemed to be something that appertained to serious-faced young men in evening clothes whose pictures one saw in the newspaper.

From that moment, something in him ceased dying: his honesty with himself. Colin was not the only one who had wasted his youth. It was in vain that Boucher struggled against that "something" from above that condemned him to nothingness. He had a vision of his past, and the meaning of it was becoming clear. The parish had betrayed him in a different way from what he had thought. Not through love but through a kind of segregation. He was the victim of the unfortunate somnolence of a class of people for whom education means a shoe or a hat. So long as the horizons the parish imposed had not been rent by the lightning flash, a youth like himself, possessed of a real superiority but rendered restless by ambition, had seen fit to discover his enemy in love, and had preferred to look upon that sentiment as coming from his flesh rather than from his heart. Later, when he found how disappointing love was, suffering had seemed to him a thing to be desired. He had approached it mockingly, and it had come to be a species of interesting occupation which he would abandon when it became too displeasing to his self-esteem.

The young ones of St Sauveur, deprived of a field of action which might have provided their country with a body of strong and capable young men, were obliged to content themselves with the semblance of moral torture, from want of anything better to do. Jean Colin alone knew the greatness that lay in sacrifice and a real enthusiasm. He had to pay for having come from a line of drunkards, but he did not sulk about it even in death. He was a hero who tyrannized over no one and kept his smile; and yet, might not such a life as this have better been given for an idea, for his country? For Jean, heroism was not an occasional but a permanent state of being.

There was an odour of potato chips in the air and Denis bought a bag of them. As he opened wide his mouth, he was carried away by a desire to pray. The God whom he had reserved for the day of downfall was bending over him, overwhelmingly kind. Denis thanked Him, nodding his head vigorously by way of acquiescence. By munching hard on his potato chips he was able to conceal his stammerings from the woodcutters who were entering the taverns. He felt suddenly light-hearted. Life was becoming beautiful. Humility and happiness could be attained at one and the same time. Jean was a brother whom he loved. He would get down on his knees and beg Colin's forgiveness. Lise! Lise! If he aimed at magnanimity, it was to torture her with regrets.

There was a new lightness in his step as he went down the street. The houses seemed to fall back to let him pass. What did it matter what Lise thought of him, now that he was going to give her to Jean? There was a clutch at his heart. How was he to explain to his mother that he had lost his job? It reminded him of his infancy, when he had trembled to face her because he had dirtied his pants.

"A couple of letters for you." The postman, who for Denis was in the same class with the gendarmes, presented him with two envelopes. Disconcerted, he weighed them in his hand. These first letters he had ever received held an infinite sweetness and a hope. He broke the seal of the heavier one and the life-saving medal of the Safety League, which Zépherin had promised him, lay glistening in his hand. He ripped the other envelope open. The words danced in front of his eyes but meant nothing to him:

Dear Sir:

We are happy to inform you that your novel, *Snow and Sun*, has been awarded the first prize in our contest. Herewith enclosed, please find our cheque for two hundred dollars . . .

How could he have believed for one moment that he was a mediocre being? The threat which had paralysed the whole of his youth had merely glided over his head. By a stroke of genius he had freed himself, had overcome what for others was an unsurmountable obstacle; he had crossed the bounds of the parish and made a name for himself in the country at large. Fame! Frantic with emotion, he stamped about, turned around and looked up at the trees, shook the doorknob.

He had to shout, to cry aloud. "Mama!"

The kitchen was empty. And Lise! She believed him a thief when he was in reality a great writer. Already he was being misunderstood. At that moment he caught sight of the doctor's car drawn up in front of Jean's house and remembered how frightened Germaine had been that morning and the act she had put on by way of showing off her watch. He went across the street.

In the presence of the sad spectacle that met his eyes, he realized how ridiculously unimportant that letter was which he wanted to flourish in the air with trembling hand. Jean lay there moaning, his neck drawn back while his head made a hollow in the mattress. Then that head was raised and he contemplated with admiration the knees of the others present; for to the sick lad nothing in the world was more charming than knee joints that bent gracefully. Something of the atmosphere of Gaston's last illness was revived for Flora as she busied herself with the patient, doing her best at the same time to console Barloute, even though she felt that since Jean was not dying this sorrow was as nothing compared to her own. Deep inside her, was she not attributing this affliction to the hand of God, who was punishing those who had "stolen" her shop?

Grandfather Pitou was parsimoniously chewing on a twist of tobacco given him by Chaton, who was prospering more than ever with his worms. They were paying dearly for having turned down the services of Madame Trousseau. It was she who had cast a spell on them. Then, too, the young fellows of today did not have the powers of resistance of the old-timers, who stuffed themselves not with the stories that you read in books but with good beer. The old man bent over and shook Tit-Blanc, who, crouched on the stool, his forehead bathed in sweat, was running his stubby hand through his dirty grey hair.

Shocked at finding Jean's knee wrapped in a kerosene rag instead of an alcoholic compress, the doctor began muttering about the ignorance of the Mulots as he hastily jotted down something on his pad. Germaine, who kept telling him the time every minute, followed him about wherever he went, overwhelming him with her zeal as a benevolent nurse. He was a good-looking young man, the doctor. Suddenly the physician looked up with a glow of interest and admiration in his eyes.

Lise had just lifted the drapes. Pale and anxious, she came over to Denis' side. Wasn't Jean getting any better, then? And was not she to blame for it all? Denis did not reassure her, did not even return her greeting. The doctor spoke to her, discreetly, and contrived to pass near her.

"It was nice of you to bring my patient those lovely flowers I saw here on the dresser the other day. I take it you are not one of those who hold that flowers give off a poison?" He was trying to strike up a conversation.

Lise, much embarrassed, assented to what he was saying, but Denis clenched his fists; he was bristling.

"Yes," he said, "my friend adores flowers. And you, too, Doctor? Are you a poet by any chance?" His tone was sarcastic.

"I'll bring you some others," Lise murmured to Jean from a distance. Her glance was imploring, filled with regret. The truth was that she had to look at someone intently in order to conceal her great emotion, her joy, at having near her the one she loved.

Abashed at having let his interest in Lise be seen, Denis avoided the doctor's astonished gaze and stared obstinately at the wall. The newspaper containing his and Jean's pictures had been put up above the invalid's head. A silence fell, and he fancied that everyone was watching him because of his newly acquired fame. He must suggest the possibility of a catastrophe to divert their curiosity.

His tone was a false one as he remarked: "Who wants to die here, anyway?"

With a shrug of his shoulders, the physician went over to Jean. "Well, then," he said, "it's understood, is it, that leg has to come off?"

"My God!" Horrified, Lise clung to Denis, who wiped an imaginary sweat from his forehead. What sort of nightmare was this? Jean eyed them closely, eager to hear them express their regret that they had not known.

"If you had read my book, Barloute," said Flora, in a satisfied voice, "you would have found it there. I didn't want to frighten you."

Jean continued to rock his head back and forth in the hollow of his pillow as he wondered at the curiosity of the spectators. He suddenly felt a need of absolute solitude in order that, without any witnesses, he might assure himself of the impotence of his limb before parting with it; he could even caress and coax it. That poor leg of his! How distant it made the love of Lise and Denis seem as they all but cowered there at the foot of the bed.

"With an artificial leg, you'll be able to get along very well," the doctor was saying encouragingly.

Barloute had left the room in tears, and she could now be heard calling out to her women friends that they were going to cut off her son's leg. From the outside, angry murmurs rose, directed against doctors in general. Bédarovitch, making his daily rounds, came up to the window and inquired if they could use a good second-hand bedstead. A real bargain.

"Wait until next week," Jean was imploring the doctor. "I want to have a few days more."

Breaking his silence, Tit-Blanc in a trembling voice asked how much an artificial leg would cost. Jean shut his eyes. He could see himself hunting worms again to pay for it. Dr Boutet hesitated, his eyes resting on Lise.

"Two hundred dollars. He'll be able to wear it after six months."

Jean gave a nervous laugh which no one understood. He could see himself losing that appendage on the street. Denis searched his friend's eyes, wishing to laugh with him. Tit-Blanc sighed. "We'll never be able to buy it," he said.

Denis did not think about what he did next. "The leg is yours, old man, I have the money." And he tossed the envelope on the bed. The gesture was a disinterested one on his part; he had no thought of parading the news of his success. "A little contest that I won. But the money is the important thing." Would they think that he had chosen this moment simply to attract attention? He meant to write at once to the company that sold such limbs.

Jean tried to rise to a sitting posture. "You've won? I'm so glad! You said something about the factories, didn't you!"

"I always knew you would write books," said Flora. "I read whole boxes of them while I was waiting for you to be born."

Lise had clasped her hands, radiant at first, then despairing. With a soul like his, was Denis to be doubted for a single instant? But now that he had fame and was convinced of his talent, he would take his revenge by being indifferent; his interest would be worldly young ladies.

Flora, meanwhile, was directing uneasy glances at all the others in the room, her eyes finally coming to rest upon her son. She was dumbfounded. Two hundred dollars! And here he was throwing it away in an unthinking act of generosity. She began talking volubly.

"I've a good idea. We'll organize a raffle and get together enough for that leg. It ought to go like hot cakes. You know I have the knack for that sort of thing. It worked with Gaston's hens." Going over to the window, she ordered the children to start preparing some lottery tickets. "And you, Denis, go see if the soup's boiling over."

Flora's nervous prattle was interrupted by a stifled sob. Germaine, not thinking what she was doing, was tearing up the newspaper that covered the commode.

"Don't cry, dearie," said Flora, "he's going to get well."

"It's not that. Here are your two dollars. I'm not a thief. I took the money from the cupboard while you were outside. Forgive me, Lise. Forgive me, Denis."

"They make a nice-looking couple, all right," put in old man Pitou.

"Jean would be still better," said Barloute, who came back just then. "They are the same height."

With an air of bewilderment, Flora pocketed the money.

"Do you want me to kiss you in front of all of them?" Lise asked of Denis, who was perspiring all over. Flora Boucher knit her brows, then started crying to hide her embarrassment. As a result of her tears, Lise and Denis would forgive her, too, as well as Germaine. Denis angrily broke away. The surprised look on the doctor's face as he witnessed this scene was too much to endure. Leaving the room for a minute, he went to get a drink. Tit-Blanc was at a loss to understand it all.

"What have you done, Germaine?" he wanted to know.

"Nothing!" said Lise, who was beside herself with joy. "It is a little misunderstanding that has been keeping my friends and me apart." She squeezed Germaine's arm and Flora's too, and they smiled back at her, absurdly, through their tears. Germaine leaned on the other girl's shoulder.

"I loved him, and I was too jealous."

Lise grew pale again. Denis had lied to her; his past was strewn with little fleeting love affairs. "Is he fickle, then?"

"Oh, no! It's not that. I hated you because you were the first one he ever looked at."

Lise kissed her. Jean raised his voice. It was serene rather than bitter. "There, you see how everything works itself out."

Lise was already at his side, smoothing his hair, straightening the covers on his bed. She was ashamed that she was so ecstatically happy when he was suffering so deeply. "You were right in saying that he could not be guilty of such a thing. I will tell him that you were the only one to stand up for him." As Jean made a tired gesture, she came close to his ear and murmured: "I am convinced the doctor is wrong. I am beginning a novena tomorrow morning, and the Blessed Virgin doesn't refuse me anything I ask of her, Jean dear."

He listened with a melancholy smile, not daring to tell her that he did not believe her. He could not wait for them all to leave. Their presence annoyed him; in this sorrow which was all his own, he felt that he was soaring above their heads. Just at this moment, for example, he would rather have seen them leap with joy than accuse him of having spoiled their pleasure. Lise held his hand, but there was no answering pressure. From behind the upraised drapes Denis had been observing them. He now came forward. He spoke in an altered tone of voice, hunting for words.

"I am glad," he said, "that you have declared your love at last. I beg your forgiveness, Jean, for all the trouble I have caused you." He was looking for something to twist in his fingers but found only large objects near at hand.

Lise was bewildered. She glanced at Jean questioningly. Overcome by it all, he shut his eyes. With some hesitation she then looked at Denis, ready to fall on his neck. This pleasant little joke must be his way of bestowing forgiveness.

"Kiss each other," Denis insisted coldly.

"But—" Lise smiled, half rising. And she added : "You know, Denis, I never believed it."

Jean opened his eyes. His breath was short. "Love," he said in a low voice, "love is not a gift but something you win. Go ahead and kiss and get out of here. You annoy me."

Denis was desperate. Jean, then, would not accept his sacrifice. "I'll dedicate my book to you."

"How nice of you," Lise put in.

They were silent. Germaine came in, beaming, with the lifesaving medal she had found in the letter box. She went through the motions of pinning it on her brother's chest, but he repelled her.

"I'm not a captain of the guard ! Take it away."

Lise turned pale at the allusion to her father. Old man Pitou picked up the medal to examine it as Dr Boutet came back, followed by Barloute, Flora, and Tit-Blanc. The decision had been made. Jean was to have the first available bed at the Public Hospital. The doctor gave Lise a prolonged glance as he took his departure, and she flushed beneath his gaze.

Left alone in the room, the three young people were ill at ease. Suddenly there was a loud burst of laughter and the Abbé

Bongrain with his broad shoulders stood there, parting the drapes.

Tossing his hat on the bed, he went over to the sick lad, holding out his hand. "My dear Jean Colin, and who gave you permission to be ill?"

Jean grasped his hand and a moment later began sobbing. "I'm in trouble, Father; say something to me, no matter what."

Feeling out of place, Lise and Denis slipped away. Haunted by what he had read in Madame Boucher's medical work, Tit-Blanc came up to inquire of his son, timidly, if his knee was giving him any pain.

"Get out!"

"Yes, Tit-Blanc, leave us alone, old man." And the abbé led him out of the room. It was then that the drunkard formed a mighty resolution.

When Flora sent the books back to Lise by one of the children, Lise did not even look at them. As they were leaving Jean's room, Denis had uttered a single sentence and then had run off as usual: "It is no use to love you, seeing that I will never be a hero."

The Abbé Bongrain was in a thoughtful mood as he left the sick-room. The invalid was accepting his affliction proudly. The idea that God might be punishing him did not appear to have entered his mind. The good priest was used to encountering incurable diseases among the Mulots, and those who suffered from them commonly ended in a state of Christian resignation. In the present instance, he was trying to find the causes that lay behind the patient's attitude, which was by no means a simple one. This pride in suffering, this silence and unwillingness to share one's sorrow with others, might they not become the greatest of sins: the sin of indifference toward a God who has a thirst for those that are heavily laden and who holds His arms open to them? He hesitated a number of times, about to turn back. No, he would first go to the church and pray.

Once he was quite alone, Jean sank back exhausted from the fight he had just waged with the Abbé Bongrain in order to protect the thing that belonged to him: his pain. He was conscious of a sort of buzzing in his head and the objects in the room appeared to be swaying in front of him. When would he be able to take his eyes off the waves and eddies formed by the bed coverings? He had a great desire to feel his dying member, but he did not stir. It was best to regard that leg as gone and think of it in the past tense. Upon the floor, the leather

266

tongue sticking out of his left shoe looked like a black flag. It sometimes happens that our mouths water at the thought of atrocities, and such was Jean's feverish condition at this moment that he took a sanguinary pleasure in picturing to himself scenes of cruelty.

For example, he saw himself stretched upon the operating table, under the knife. They were attaching his veins to one another and the blood was flowing abundantly. The surgeon, an attentive look on his face, was holding the amputated leg in his hand. It was swollen and black, and it bent with an ease it had not possessed when it belonged to Jean. Then they buried the member like a stillborn child. He could see it down there, under six feet of transparent earth; it was lying in an empty cracker box, or perhaps it was his worm box which he no longer used. They were all dead, too, those worms. He went on to imagine a protective rite which he would observe toward this truncated member. He would be very sympathetic to it, would even go visit it and say a few prayers for it on All Saints Day. His lips widened in a sarcastic smile. He might well say then that he had a friend in the great beyond and one foot in the grave. How unique he would be: angel, corpse, and living being at one and the same time, a form of superiority achieved through amputation. These thoughts with him were the first signs of delirium. His reason was foundering.

Minutely now he strove to look at his infirmity from the practical side. Paid for by Denis, his new leg would be a poem, since it would be purchased with money earned by writing. He would have to keep it oiled. It would be a leg that did not swell up. How wonderful! This metallic member would be resonant and he could tap on it with a hammer at the shop, when he did not have much to do. Lise's photograph would be hidden in the centre of it like a diamond. His pillow was a patient crab, drawing his head back into the hollow once more, and he struggled with it. His neck was made of metal, of molten metal, and there were sharp, darting pains in his temples and in his forehead, as if everything were about to burst. He saw himself married to Lise—she was taking off her metal leg for him. Now his brain was gone and his head was filled with a stump streaked with pinkish-coloured bits of flesh sewn together.

Of a sudden, he let out a loud scream: "Beer! Beer! Whisky! Children who work!"

Tit-Blanc, who had been on the watch for the last couple of hours, came running in, greatly alarmed.

Jean kept screaming, in a kind of rage: "Beer! Whisky!

Whisky to oil my artificial leg!" After that he began talking calmly enough. "The verb *huiler* takes—*er* in the infinitive. You don't believe it? Go ask Denis. No, he hasn't the time. He's kissing under the trees. Ha, ha!" He was devouring Tit-Blanc with reproachful eyes. "Save me! Save me, Denis! I'm drowning in a sea of microbes and whisky. I have a temperance medal to give you. But save me!"

Tit-Blanc was suffocating. He had had all he could stand. He struck his forehead with blows of his fist. His son, well educated as he was, could not be in his right mind. Returning to the kitchen, he hastily donned his jacket. He would have recourse to that supreme and marvellous act of faith that often had saved the most incurable cases at St Sauveur: the pilgrimage on foot to St Anne de Beaupré, without a halt and without any provisions other than hope. This was an expedient to which one resorted when all other means had failed.

He started off, running north in the direction of the shrine where the great Lady had done so much for others. Carried away by his fervour, he crossed the city at top speed, but his pace soon slackened, for he had stumbled over his shoelaces. He still had many miles to go.

The way seemed endless. Tit-Blanc was now dragging his feet and looking up at the sun, too tired to wipe away the sweat that stood on his face like oil and matted his hair. From village to village he found himself fighting off mirages as he thought of streams of good cold beer that might be flowing down his throat. (He was naïve enough to believe that it was through drinking beer that he had killed his son.)

As the bell in the cathedral rang out over the countryside, curiosity-seeking tourists were astonished to behold a haggard-faced man kneeling in the middle of the road as he muttered a prayer: "Good St Anne, dear St Anne, will you still cure him for me if I stop drinking?"

This childish exhibition of faith was sufficient to relieve him. His vow in itself was so heroic that it could not fail to cure one man at least. But vows are powerless to stay the pitiless march of events, and misfortunes are fruits which must fall from the tree of life whenever they are ripe.

Returning homeward along the banks of the St Lawrence, after his pilgrimage had been completed, Tit-Blanc watched the water flowing to the sea. There was a heavy odour of slime on the air. It took him all night to cover the distance back home. With swollen feet and so exhausted that he scarcely knew what he was doing, he finally entered the rue Colomb. Would he have the strength to make it? The Latruche sisters, who were pacing up and down the sidewalk as nuns do their balcony, gave him a sardonic look. The news of his pilgrimage had spread and they were indignant. They were being ignored.

"That may cost more than a leg before it's over," they grumbled, loud enough for him to hear. "To go encouraging foreigners like that!"

But what did their pettiness mean to him when he was blind with despair? He was deaf to hatred, his eyes were too misty to permit him to see reptiles. He suddenly had a feeling that his own legs were giving way beneath him. Was that the doctor's car in front of the door? His strength came back to him now, the strength for flight. Going up to the house, he stared at it as hard as he could, as if hoping to discover that he was wrong, that it was some other house, not his. Féda, terror-stricken, flung the door open and threw herself in his arms.

"My God, Tit-Blanc, where have you been? Jean has lost consciousness."

"I knew it." The man converted to the faith, the twilight pilgrim, acquiesced. Caressing the back of his wife's neck with an absurd gesture, he drew her into the kitchen. The doctor was there, washing his hands. Tit-Blanc looked at him, long and hard. The doctor had kept the catastrophe hidden from them, and this made him seem almost a hypocrite. Abruptly shutting off the faucet, he spoke.

"I may as well tell you." Like a culprit, avoiding their gaze, he told them what the true nature of Jean's illness was. It was the first time he had had to do anything like that, the initial drama of his professional life, and he came near stammering as he fumbled over medical terms.

"It is very serious, an organic disease. With a constitution such as his, you might have thought he would overcome the germ, but—well, the truth is, it has been communicated to his brain. Your son has had too much on his mind, and the tuberculosis of the knee has degenerated into an incurable meningitis. But you may rest assured, I will do everything I can to see that he suffers as little as possible."

Never before had Tit-Blanc understood fine words so well. It was only his ignorance that afforded him any gleam of hope whatever. Barloute was searching his eyes, eager for him to deny it. There they were, husband and wife, stupefied at hearing a truth which they hoped to combat by sheer obstinacy and refusal to understand. The doctor was trying to find words to make it clear to them.

"In one night," he was saying, "the disease made giant strides. I feared a complication of this sort. Did you notice that convulsive movement of his jaws yesterday, when the young lady was whispering in his ear? What astonishes me is the great speed with which it developed. But we will put up the best fight we can. Change the ice every hour. I'll be back this afternoon. Call me if anything happens before then. You may send for the priest, also."

"Then he's going to die!" Tit-Blanc exclaimed.

The veil had been rent and the terrible truth was there for them to see. Féda took her husband's jacket off him as she would have helped a child.

"But St Anne," he kept muttering, "St Anne seemed to be granting it."

Old Pitou, who had had some experience making coffins, was insisting: "He'll take a six-foot grave. Have to get an oak coffin."

Dr Boutet did not wait for the outburst that would follow this mood of dull despondency but left the house as if he were running away.

Like an automaton, Tit-Blanc went over toward the drapes. Would a skeleton be waiting for him there with its frightful grin? In the bedroom the only thing that broke the silence was a sound of heavy breathing. To Tit-Blanc's ears it was a gentle soothing sound, soft as a kiss, and he listened to it in a kind of transport.

From outside came Bédarovitch's everlasting cry, along with the rumbling of his cart over the pavement: "Ra-a-a-ags, ra-a-a-ags—"

Jean opened his eyes upon a troubled world. The word "rags" was swaying like a loosely hung veil over his thoughts. His pinkish face gleamed from its wreath of ice wrapped in a dish-cloth.

Tit-Blanc coughed and twirled his hat in his hand as if ashamed of his long beard and dishevelled hair. "You've a bit of colour this morning, my lad. Don't feel so bad, eh?" He broke off, alarmed by his son's fixed stare.

Putting an arm about her husband, Barloute helped him over to the bed. "Guess where your father's been for you. All the way to St Anne and back, on foot."

"Papa! Papa!" the dying boy rolled the words on his lips intensely, in a little ball of saliva. Tit-Blanc could only nod and hold back the tears. This shaggy fellow, this new father whom Jean had just discovered now took his son's cold hand and rubbed it, feeling each of the fingers in turn, then pressed it against his bearded face.

"Yes, that's what I did, all right. I was nearly crazy. All I want, you know, is for you to get well and not suffer any more. Today, I'm your father again, the way I was when you were first born. There's nothing to cry about, my lad, come— Listen, what was that?" It was a clucking sound in his own throat. Unbuttoning his shirt at the top, he went on. "The books tell you that I'm to blame. I did you harm and you have a right to hold it against me. But you must also remember the times when I bought you presents at Christmas, when I played horse with you and you made me run all over the kitchen and laughed at me because I was a little drunk. You see, I'm not holding that against you. Don't 'kick,' Jean dear. Let's forget everything."

He stopped short, delighted to have heard himself use that word "dear" for the first time in addressing his son. Jean appeared to smile. Tit-Blanc now spoke in a wheedling voice and a childish expression came over his brutish face. His stubby hands, too, were as playful as a child's.

"I made the hardest kind of vow to St Anne. I promised her I would stop drinking. See, like this, hard as I can take." And with his hairy fist he gave himself a stout blow in the chest, as if to drive in the emotion that he felt. He was transported by his faith. "When I looked at the image, let me tell you that her eyes moved just as yours do. And do you want to know something else? You're going to go to any school that you pick out." Enthusiastically he patted his son on the shoulder. It had taken a disaster to bring about this heroic concession, and Jean's happiness made Tit-Blanc forget the boy was going to die.

Jean was aware of his father's words despite the atrocious hammering in his head. Why did anyone speak of rancour, of bitterness? Those things had no place in his heart. The turmoil of feeling was over for him, now that he had routed his anxieties one by one. Why was it that, from his present point of observation, men seemed to him so changed, so lovable and childlike? As he watched Tit-Blanc, he regretted that he could not interrupt and offer him an automobile. It would be nice, too, if he could have sent flowers to his mother. All this by way of showing his gratitude to them for suffering on his account.

It was he now who took his father's hand and brought it up to his own downy face. "I could stand a shave," he said. "You're a good walker," he went on. "Was the sun very hot? The water in the river must have been bright and clear. Thanks, little Papa, thinks."

Tit-Blanc bowed his head despairingly, and the sobs in his throat made a purring sound. His son's eyes were glowing with a melancholy elation.

"School," said Jean, "is over for me. I am old, very old." Then, feigning enthusiasm: "When I am better, I will work; for I've come to realize that there is only one thing that matters, and that is to learn how to suffer. I'll start my worm business again, I'll have agents in all the parishes; we will fix the prices and Chaton will be one of our dealers. But leave me alone now! My head is bursting; I can't talk any more."

There was a rattle in his throat. Overcome with grief, Tit-Blanc dragged himself out of the room and collapsed. Barloute, deeply moved by her son's speech, was sobbing aloud.

After a while, however, they came to realize that they had accepted Jean's death from the start. With her hair freshly curled and wearing a new dress, Féda began setting the bedroom to rights, changing the curtains and throwing covers over the furniture. Razor in hand, old man Pitou was insisting that he ought to shave the down from Jean's face, but Tit-Blanc swore that no one but him should touch the lad from now on. Germaine, on her knees, was scrubbing the floor vigorously, pausing now and then to dry a tear. Féda lifted the invalid's head to change his pillow.

"You're not surprised, are you, Johnny boy?" The Abbé Bongrain is bringing the good Lord to pay you a little visit."

As he suddenly emerged from his torpor, an indescribable look came over Jean's face, of the sort that is to be seen once in a lifetime. How could he have been so stupid as not to have guessed it before? Those strange, almost magical states of mind through which he had been passing for the last two weeks— what did they indicate if not a feverish haste to bring to an end an existence that was already consummated and that could not wait to achieve a definitive close. Every young person who dies is already ripe for death when the time comes; the only thing he lacks is grey hairs. All this is due to the fact that there is such a thing as justice in this world. Jean was chewing over the word "die" with the same pleasure he had felt when he smoked his first cigarette.

"They are going to administer the Sacrament, are they?" He appeared to be chanting the words. "That's all right with me. Send for the relatives." By an unconscious impulse, he was joking, for he was neither sad nor happy. Everything was a show, and he was insensitive to it all. Visions whirled around him. He saw, in particular, cemetery crosses, thousands of cemeteries where one went splashing in the November mud. The souls of the departed, whole bands of them, danced about, sneering, entreating, but the cemetery-lovers did not understand; they only knelt and prayed. Then they all disappeared, and he, Jean Colin, was dead and everything was topsy-turvy. His grave was first luminous, then dark. It was the little wooden cross with his name on it, daubed on with pitch, that blackened everything. How despairing they are, those cemetery crosses, in comparison with the light that is given off by wayside crucifixes and the one atop the church. The former are planted *on* man, the latter in front of him. Salvation is a thing that is to come, and all that is to come is of the essence of light.

His heart burned with a sudden jealousy. Where were Denis and Lise? Were they praying somewhere by themselves? Were they ashamed to be seen in this hole of a room? They would undoubtedly hurry with their prayers, for they would be anxious to get back to the riverbank and realize those dreams that he had fashioned for them.

"Dear Papa, dear Mama—"

He saw them on their knees, at the foot of his grave; they had not even spread their handkerchiefs down to protect them from the dampness. The Langevins were there, also. They reminded him of the old apple-stealing days. And every one was very sad, not from thinking of those who were gone but at seeing so many people walking about in the cemetery who were as dead as the ones underground. Then the place was empty, the visitors had fled. Were they going to leave him there with the others? That was the final act of abandonment. So long as they were kneeling in front of him, a semblance of life had remained with him. It was all over now. Everything was finished. Death was swallowing him up forever. With a haggard look on his face, he gave a start, A fierce passion for life gripped him once more.

"Mama! I'd rather have them cut off both legs and let me go on living."

"Don't say that, my boy," put in Grandfather Pitou, who boasted that he had never wept at the death of any of his kin. "They tell me those stumps hurt so much in bad weather that you can't stand it."

"Germaine!" Jean called. She came up on tiptoe, from fear of extinguishing the little breath that remained in her brother's throat. "Be a good girl and run an errand for me. You will, won't you? I'll never again put my feet on your chair. Don't refuse me, just this once. Go for Lise as quick as you can." He was begging her, knowing her aversion to doing errands for others. He could not conceive that her attitude toward him might have changed. It seemed to him a marvellous thing that, without even saying yes, she ran out at once to do as he had asked.

Not long afterwards, the drapes were lifted again and Lise was left standing there alone beside his bed. He gave a kind of hiccup as he became aware of her presence. "This is nice of you."

Trembling, she drew up a chair. "I'm going to stay with you all day long," she said. "I expect you to be cured any minute now. This is the eighth day of my novena." She stopped, ready to cry, as she saw him shake his head. The pinkish hue of Jean's face made him look like a bashful lover in bounding health. Lise ran her hand through his hair.

"Many grey ones?" he inquired with an air of resignation.

"No, your hair has never been so beautiful. Just look at that wave you have." She smiled playfully, spreading about her something that was very like joy. To Jean she was a heavenly creature, all the more pure by reason of her simple dress, her unrouged face, and especially her enormous eyes. He, however, did not see her as clearly as she thought he did. To his eyes, she was surrounded by a dense mist and he could not free her from the nimbus that surrounded her head. He could better perceive the sounds that came from out of doors, the cries of children and bickering women, and, much nearer, the buzzing noise as of flies seeking to settle upon his hot forehead. The mosquito netting had been taken down, but to his hallucinated mind the neighbourhood gossips seemed nevertheless to be peering through it, trying to catch a glimpse of him. He could hear their remarks, and his only fear was that Lise would notice these intruders. He watched his breathing for a moment, saw that it was regular, and was happy; he would be able to keep Lise with him for a long time, imparting his love to her bit by bit.

"What a big person you are!" she whispered to him roguishly. "Without leaving your room you have brought Denis and me happiness. When you are well you will see what a nice life we are going to have, the three of us, with you, our best friend, watching over our love."

Jean's breath came with a hiss, his eyes had a wild look, he wanted to scream. There was no time to wait for Lise to guess the truth. Was he to go without her knowing that he died for love of her? The sounds in his throat now fused in a cry that was at once victorious and despairing.

"I am the one who loves you! Forgive me!"

Lise wrung her hands, spoke to him gently. She was sure he was delirious. "Why, yes, of course, our love is wholly spiritual."

He sat up in the bed, a terrifying figure. With the cry that came from him he sought to hold her, for her bright image against the black was blurring fast. He put out his arms as if to mould her to his desire. "I love you! I love you!" He fell back with a sob.

Kneeling beside him, Lise at last understood Denis' reticence on occasions, a reticence which was to be explained by loyalty to his friend. Everything was clear, and above all, the sacrifice that Jean had made. But only formal words of consolation came to her lips.

"You are going to get well, and then you will see things more sensibly. I shan't mean anything to you then. After you have gone through the ordeal you will be happy."

With an eye on his breathing, he hastened to give her those other scraps before he choked.

"There will be no more ordeals for me. I've had too many as it is. I am going away and shall have no more memories; that is why I am not ashamed. Please let me kiss your hands. It means nothing."

She held them out to him affectionately, as one would offer toys to a little child. "Anything you like."

From the kitchen they could hear the sobs of Barloute and Germaine mingled with the rattling of knives and forks.

Jean stroked her hands but did not kiss them. Instead, he stared at them intensely. "I don't see them. I don't see them." She took his hands and covered them with kisses. He smiled beatifically, with a sort of supernatural voluptuousness. He was giving himself over to a strange kind of drunkenness in which all illusion became reality, especially the illusion that his love was returned. Her lips brushing his hand became a passionate avowal of love on Lise's part, and then, for the first time in his life, he felt the desire to kiss her on the mouth. He was well recompensed for having waited so long, for having kept silent, for having let pass so many days of sun, so many days of rain, during which he had contemplated her profile, so many evenings when he had seen it fade in the distance. He thought of all this with a kind of childish excitement as he put his arm around Lise's neck. (She did not dare resist. Was this disease contagious?)

"Do you remember that day you hid me? How foolish we made the cops look? And the dirt on my nose?" He tried to laugh but only hiccuped, and went on to tell her how surprised he was at her attitude. "And you did not know all this time that I loved nobody else but you? Surely you must have guessed it. I should have told you before. I meant to do it the day I wanted to take you down to the riverbank. It's so nice to watch the little whitecaps on the water and point them out with your finger as you sit cheek to cheek. But I had to count the people at the wrestling match."

He shook his head as he recalled this disappointment, but he did not think of the kiss that Denis had given Lise on the ruins of the old church. In his delirium, obstacles were eliminated. Muttering incomprehensible words, he rolled his head over on Lise's arm, bent at the elbow. He wanted to tell her how much he had loved her, how he had waited for her as he forged his heart with suffering. He spoke with a joy that came from having unburdened himself and laid his love before her, freely and without shame. Raising himself up again, he pointed a finger at her.

"And that time your father threw the plums into the street and I ran after them, holding my knee. You didn't know about it then? It was a tree branch that did it. I did not think that one day that knee would swell up and burst. Lise!"

She forced him to lie down. He shut his eyes, which made Lise fear that she had killed him. When she saw his bosom heave once more, she was so happy that she threw her arms about him and kissed him on the lips. He was sleeping now. At least he had not had to steal that kiss. Tiptoeing out of the room, she ran home as fast as she could to dry her face, then hastened to the church.

Denis was waiting for her under the portico, there where she had seen Jean for the first time. He held out his arms to her tenderly, a teasing smile on his lips.

"We are being very silly. Everything is forgotten. Give me a kiss, you foolish little girl." The publicity that he was receiving in the newspapers had caused him to look down upon the years of mediocrity that lay behind him and upon his ridiculous scruples. Lise's flesh remained, and he would possess it now with the smile of the victor, without any twinge of conscience. And others after her.

At sight of her pale face, his manner froze. He was annoyed with himself but could do nothing about it. Overcome by emotion, she clung to him, breathing hard. "Let's go into the church at once and pray. Between the two of us we can save him."

He fell back, somewhat abashed. "I am not religious," he said. "I would only disturb you. What good are my prayers for a leg that has to come off?"

He was displeased that his amorous exaltation should be met with reddened eyes, features distorted by grief, and above all this exhibition of piety. He was angry with her for reminding him, at a moment when he felt that all the world was his, of those few minutes when he had prayed so desperately after losing his job. Now that happiness had come to him, he looked upon that impulse as a weakness on his part. This day of triumph that he was living now was not one for kneeling beside a young girl in tears as she prayed to God on behalf of another whom she might have loved.

"What of it?" he asked abruptly. "With an artificial leg he'll make out, won't he? It won't even show."

"But Denis, he's dying, and he loves me!"

He was dumbfounded. He watched Lise stupidly as she burst into sobs. Her statement that Jean loved her, her tears, the thought that he was losing his only friend, grieved him sorely. Jean had won after all. There was nothing for Denis to do but withdraw into a retreat of his own fashioning where he could nurse his pride. But Jean Colin, that lovable fellow, would be gone; he would never see him again. He was deeply distressed, forgetful of his jealousy. Was there no chance of saving Jean? He did not even wipe away the sweat that stood out in little drops on his temples. He shook his head.

"You go to church alone. Jean needs me. I belong to him now." His voice became reproachful. "He loved you so, why didn't you realize it? I blame you for my treachery toward him. You shall never have me now. But it is still Jean who pays. Good-bye, then; you will find men who will love you better than I."

Whirling around, he leaped the fence and came down on the sidewalk. Lise, the veins of her neck swollen from the pain she felt, was too overcome to put out her arms. How cruel he was, how ungrateful! He was going away, abandoning her to the

Gonzagues. Why was it he found her so dull all of a sudden? Because she wanted him to kneel at her side and pray to God?

Now that the thought of Jean's death had put an end to his amorous desires and had filled him with grief, Denis was ready to defend bitterly the friendship that had existed between them for so many years, and was inclined to look upon Lise, an intruder of the last few months, as being responsible for the meanness of which he himself had been guilty. He must accordingly see to it that Jean died more imbued with their friendship than with his love for her. When you came down to it, who was this Lise, anyway? He put it to himself like this:

Daughter of a Soyeuse, a flower of the parish. She had disturbed them for a while because they were men and love was the only adventure within their reach. The approach of death had shaken them, making heroism possible. Love as he and Jean had conceived it in the past was the lot of inactive heroes; but now that the time for action had come, he must participate in it with all his soul, must sweep away the past with his will power as Jean was doing with his death. As for Lise, she was merely one of the minor disturbances. Just because she was beautiful and differed from the others by reason of her silences and her reticence, they had chosen her to be their Golden Fleece; the bounds of the parish were too narrow for them to be aware of any other heights to scale. Things were different now, and true greatness appeared to him to be possible even within the parish, and so it was with a feeling of joy that he proceeded to rid himself of this chimera, of this mirage of spiritual nobility, while removing at the same time the thing that had acted as a check upon the ardent impulses of their youth.

Those adolescents who have not yet known love believe themselves to be all but godlike, animated as they are by a desire to make of their future a magnificent altar. Comes love, and the dim horizons of heroism take on precision and are incarnated in a woman, who reduces them to their simplest expression. For some while the young man endeavours to retrieve this lost horizon in eyes that for him are filled with dreams; later he seeks it in caresses, in a feminine body, in sensual pleasure. And then, of a sudden, he is aware that he has lost all pretensions to heroism; and in this illusory manner whole generations have foundered. That is why the human race remains so mediocre.

Denis, moreover, had some cause for believing that he had been saved from love for the time being. Because men of exceptional ability are likely to be at odds with society, and because he could see no social order that left room for genius, he who did not happen to be a genius but who still could not accept the existing order of things, found refuge in a stubborn struggle against it. By his erratic conduct, his false moves, he was merely deferring a payment that always has to be made in the end: through absorption by society. Is it not here that the drama of adolescence lies, an adolescence that manifests itself now by strange withdrawals into solitude and now by sudden impulses toward woman, who is society's essential element? That was why Denis did not turn back when Lise's low cry reached his ears. She would perhaps go on loving him, would not give up hope. Later, as he thought of her waiting for him, a feeling of sentimental weakness was slowly to take possession of him.

Was he losing control of his thoughts? Had he not found the secret of mastering life, since he was able to overcome any kind of suffering simply by charging it up to inspiration? His tall body cast a long shadow on the sidewalk as, standing with his back to a telephone pole, he scribbled a few words on his note pad in an effort to capture his emotion. He stopped shortly. He must show this masterpiece to Jean, astonish him one more time. Then once again, the thought that Jean was dying in that house was more than he could bear. Armed with his notebook he rushed inside.

The room lay wrapped in a heavy silence; the air itself seemed to be in pain from having been inhaled too often. Was that his friend there, with the emaciated countenance, the pinched nostrils, he who barely a month ago had gone forth to meet life so eagerly? He must wake him. As Jean opened his eyes in bewilderment, Denis forgot all his intellectual complexities and was carried away by the flood of affection that mounted within him. He was ready for any humiliation, any sacrifice; he was willing to be a perfectly simple person. Coming up to the bed, he tenderly stroked the dying lad's hands.

"Jean! Jean!" he stammered, "I have come to tell you that I am your friend for all eternity. You have shown yourself a man. All is over between Lise and me, and I have come back to you, old man. That's final. You have to admit, don't you, that we have been silly to let ourselves be taken in by that myth called love?"

"You've come back because I am going to die."

Denis bit his lips until the blood came, strove to hold back the tears. At last a little heroism had come within reach of his heart. He bent over his friend, grieved to see him cling to Lise

279

like this until the very end. As he went on speaking, his voice was bitter, not on account of the lie he was telling but because it might be the truth.

"You've seen through me again, old boy. You can say that I've been a hell of a friend to you even in death. But do you want to know something? Lise has just confessed to me that it is you she loves. That was why I wanted you to agree with me that love was a myth, for I've come to make myself believe that. And here you go, knocking everything down. Have I lost your friendship, then?"

Jean made no response. He was mumbling like an idiot. Denis Boucher loved to be heroic, loved the admiration of others, and these mumblings were not sufficient for him.

"Do you want to hear what I wrote about you?" he asked. He began reading from his note pad: "Lise looked at Jean, that wonderful Jean whom she had not known before for the reason that she had not known love. And now that the two of them were there, lying happily together in the long grass, drinking in the light of the stars, they realized that the most beautiful love of all is that which makes itself known at the end."

"Liar! Liar!" cried Jean, choking. His head rolled to one side and the purring sound continued.

Denis, lulled by his own words, had unconsciously hoped that Jean would tell him how well written it was. But that word "liar" had frozen him, recalling the terrible accusation which Gaston had made upon his deathbed. Burying his head in the covers of Jean's bed, he found to his dismay that he could not weep; he could not even plead remorse. With his long fingers he tore up the lines he had written.

Jean received the Sacrament at eight o'clock that evening. The two Langevins and Denis stood at the back of the room, while Lise, kneeling by the commode, prayed with a fervour that was meant for Denis' heart rather than for the ear of God. The Colin family also knelt around the bed, their arms upon the mattress. The flame of the candles, fanned by a light current of air, was reflected in their tears. Jean's glassy eyes were fastened upon those of Lise, for they were the only stars to accompany him in the night. As the Abbé Bongrain made the sign of the cross over his feet (after having nearly tripped over Barloute's skirt), Jean with an instinctive modesty drew up his feet— were his toes clean enough for Lise to see? As soon as the ceremony was over, everyone began whispering.

"I don't like litanies," said Jean. The remark had a hollow

ring. His entire body was writhing, for his agony was lasting like a mass that is too drawn out. He called for Denis, who at once sprang to his side. Tit-Blanc seemed very much taken aback that he had not been the one. Jean was hiccuping. "You're a good lad and I like you a lot. I didn't love her as much as all that, you know."

"Spoken like a lad of St Sauveur at last," declared Tit-Blanc, and Grandfather Pitou agreed enthusiastically.

Long hours went by. The waiting became intolerable, and they even came to wish that he would die.

The next morning Denis was awakened by his mother, who was shaking him to tell him that Jean had died in frightful agony.

"Toward the end, he said some fine things. Tit-Blanc is like a crazy man. It seems that Jean said to him: 'Papa, all this is the fault of love.'"

Denis was astonished to find this regarded as an ordinary event. He did not touch his breakfast but kept a cold look on his face, for his mother was watching him. As he left the house, he saw a hearse standing in front of the Colins'. Leaning on the old automobile tires that served them as hoops, young Mulots were waiting to see them bring the corpse out. Boucher had a feeling of anguish, almost of terror. A desire to go away for a week and not come back until after Jean had been buried took hold of him. But was that being faithful to Jean's memory? No, it was rather an unwillingness to face the relationship that henceforth was to be established between himself, overflowing with energy, and his friend, now still and ripe for the cemetery. If Jean, for all of that, could only take with him all pettiness, all meanness of spirit!

He let his gaze roam, down the street, up to the summit of the Cape, let it come to rest upon the street corners, the telephone poles against which they had leaned so many times. There was growing in him a simple, unaffected regret that was close to tears. Jean, then, was dead. No more would Denis hear him revolting against his lot or see his face lighting up at the prospect of happiness. Ah! to be able to go back, to take him to Lise, to have them make love on the banks of the river and in the bushy lanes, with all the ardour of their youth. Shrugging off the emotion that gripped him, he rudely pulled a tire from under an urchin who was leaning on it, causing the lad to take a tumble. The victim had picked up a pebble to throw at his tormentor but was restrained by two young monks who came up to shake hands with Denis and congratulate him on his literary success. They spoke of teaching, feeling out the ground to ascertain if he looked with favour on those laymen who conducted classes along with them at the school.

Suddenly, silence fell on the group outside the house. They were bringing out the body. There was a rapid step on the sidewalk. It was Monsieur le Curé. He let the undertaker's men pass and then went in and grasped Tit-Blanc's hand as the latter held out his arms toward his son. Father Folbèche was radiating good will.

"Tit-Blanc, my friend," he said, "I have great news for you. I congratulate you. Your son will be the first one to be buried from the new church."

With a pardonable pride, the priest went on to speak of the magnificent funeral that would be accorded Jean without any additional charge, by way of worthily inaugurating the newly finished edifice, the ebony catafalque and the sumptuous sacerdotal vestments. And so on and so forth. (It was felt at the parish house that they could not wait any longer, there being no funeral of any person of means in prospect such as would permit of a display of the splendid accessories.)

It was not until the next day that Denis made up his mind to go and view the remains of his friend, now on display in the Colins' home. His mother had been scolding him for his ingratitude, for she had already performed her duty. She had spent a whole night at the wake, discussing the points of similarity between Jean's last illness and that of Gaston.

"Hurry up. You'll see, he doesn't look the way your brother did at all.

She was interrupted by the postman. The letter was addressed to her son. With a suspicious glance, she handed it to him. He waited until he was outside before he broke the seal.

Denis, I understand your grief and the way you feel toward me. But remember that all the cruelty I may unconsciously have shown Jean was due to my love for you. Do not abandon me. I have been praying all night long. This morning, I am no longer weeping. Come back to me, my dear; I am ready to do anything to win your forgiveness. . . .

Crushing the letter in his hand, Denis made for the Colins' with a firm stride. A number of urchins were trying to crowd in and some housewives were coming out, remarking that the corpse did not smell in the least. Once inside the room, he chased away the children who were lingering there and then stood motionless by the bier. Lise emerged from the shadows and came up to him, red-eyed, imploring.

"You received my letter?"

He opened his hand, made sure he still had the sheet of paper. Crazed with anxiety, she followed his every move with her eyes, her head, her heart. Going over to the casket, he slipped an arm under the body and deposited the missive. His head was heavy with excitement; he felt as if he were strangling.

"Old man!" he cried, seizing a handful of Jean's hair, "you're leaving us. Just look at him. He doesn't say a word." With all the tenderness that was in him, he pressed the crossed hands of his dead friend.

"God but they're cold!" And he made for the door.

And Lise felt that she had lost Denis Boucher forever.

Flora was counting the cards of condolence that lay upon the coffin. She concealed her disappointment at the fact that there were more of them than there had been for Gaston. The gang at Bédarovitch's had taken up a collection and had sent a huge wreath with a card attached to it bearing the names of all the members of the club who had contributed.

Then came the funeral ceremony. It was a triumph in black and gold decorations. The Abbé Charton, who had manœuvred to have the requiem mass assigned to him, wore a chasuble which he spread out like a fan when he opened his arms. The sacristan, his leg healed now, ran about like a rabbit, adjusting the banners every minute. There was also much gossip on the part of those who were jealous. Here was Colin's son—Colin of the firecracker—getting a two-hundred-dollar service for thirty dollars. And above everything else, they took him out through the main entrance.

As the funeral procession got under way, the weather turned foggy. Tit-Blanc, victim of a premature old age, dragged himself along behind the hearse. A few uncles followed and then came Denis, who immediately after the burial was to begin studying with a private tutor. The Langevins were also there, and all the gang from Bédarovitch's. They passed Chaton, who was going along with his St Bernard dog hitched to a small cart. His business had increased to such an extent that he had to gather his worms during the day, digging for them in the earth. As they passed the foot of the Cape a police whistle sounded and the procession came to a halt and waited. Some urchins were scrambling down the slope pursued by police officers. The ranks of the mourners opened to let the fugitives pass and closed again before the pursuers could go through.

Then they started up the slope and Denis turned back for a look at the quarter. The shanties had the appearance of white-washed stakes upon a piece of land that no one would think of trying to cultivate. From those huddled dwellings there arose the odour of a mode of life tenaciously wedded to the past and resistant to all progress, obstinately refusing any kind of change for the reason that all change was brought about by outsiders. "Foreigners" had had their fingers burned trying to stir up the quarter and embellish it. Only the priests were listened to, and it was toward them that all eyes were turned.

This, moreover, was a poverty that asked for nothing. Viewed from midway up the Pente Douce, the grimy houses appeared to be laughing at beautiful things because beautiful things always turn to tears and melt away. Jean was dead.

Denis was not yet social-minded. He would work no revolution in all this. He felt, without any sense of humiliation, that he would like to set up in the grocery business in the quarter and create for himself there a superiority that would be protected by the insularity of the parish, its hostility to outside influences. Then, too, his writing would soon be bringing him in something. Already he was being called upon to write speeches for various occasions, for wedding anniversaries and the like. In that manner he would be able to shun those literary salons where interested and coquettish ladies monopolized young talents.

He growled as he stumbled suddenly. He had caught his foot in a crack in the cement pavement. There had been an old privy-dump there and the paving blocks had been pushed up. By way of punishing himself for his hopes, he imagined what it would be like to be in Jean's place. The wind was blowing now, the sun was bursting through the clouds and creeping over the fields, the thickets were bright. An enervating obsession laid hold of him : before autumn came, he must laugh and sing in those thickets with Lise.

From below came the sound of life. Enthusiastic preparations for a wedding party were under way. In the new church young Mulots would be settling down, after their twentieth year, to become steady workers, good family men, and excellent parishioners.

THE AUTHOR

ROGER LEMELIN was born in 1919 in Quebec City, the eldest of a family of ten. Leaving school at the age of fourteen, he worked in a number of capacities from market vendor to bricklayer, at the same time becoming a skilled athlete. From the age of ten he had nourished the dream of becoming a writer. This was achieved with the publication of *Au Pied de la Pente Douce* (*The Town Below*), written while working for a lumber company of which he later became proprietor. He is now a successful businessman and writer in Quebec City where he lives with his wife and five children.

Au Pied de la Pente Douce was published in 1944 and received the Quebec Government's Prix David and the French Academy's Grand Prix de la Langue Française. This was followed by *Les Plouffe* (*The Plouffe Family*) in 1948, *Fantaisies sur les Péchés Capitaux* (untranslated) in 1949, and *Pierre le Magnifique* (*In Quest of Splendour*) in 1952. He has also written series for television on *The Plouffe Family* and on *The Town Below*.

THE NEW CANADIAN LIBRARY